Jan Kjærstad (borr ⸱ge number of novels and short stories, ⸱ day as one of the country's leading writers. His most popular work, the trilogy *Forføreren* (*The Seducer*, 1993), *Erobreren* (*The Conqueror*, 1996) and *Oppdageren* (*The Discoverer*, 1999), won him the prestigious Nordic Council Literature Prize and has been translated into a string of languages, including English. Stories and story-telling, and the relationship between fiction and reality, are central preoccupations, and his works are often set in his native Oslo and address urgent contemporary issues, such as how to live authentically in an increasingly unstable world. Kjærstad is also a respected essayist and widely-read cultural critic.

Janet Garton is Emeritus Professor of European Literature at the University of East Anglia, Norwich. She has published books and articles about Nordic literature, including *Norwegian Women's Writing 1850-1990* (1993), *Elskede Amalie* (*Dearest Amalie*, 2002) and a biography of Amalie Skram, *Amalie. Et forfatterliv* (2011). She has also translated Bjørg Vik, Cecilie Løveid, Kirsten Thorup, Johan Borgen and Erik Fosnes Hansen.

Some other books from Norvik Press

Johan Borgen: *Little Lord* (Translated by Janet Garton)

Jens Bjørneboe: *Moment of Freedom* (Translated by Esther Greenleaf Mürer)
Jens Bjørneboe: *Powderhouse* (Translated by Esther Greenleaf Mürer)
Jens Bjørneboe: *The Silence* (Translated by Esther Greenleaf Mürer)

Vigdis Hjorth: *A House in Norway* (Translated by Charlotte Barslund)

Amalie Skram: *Betrayed* (Translated by Katherine Hanson and Judith Messick)
Amalie Skram: *Fru Inés* (Translated by Katherine Hanson and Judith Messick)
Amalie Skram: *Lucie* (Translated by Katherine Hanson and Judith Messick)

Anton Tammsaare: *The Misadventures of the New Satan* (Translated by Olga Shartze and Christopher Moseley)

Ilmar Taska: *Pobeda 1946: A Car Called Victory* (Translated by Christopher Moseley)

Kirsten Thorup: *The God of Chance* (Translated by Janet Garton)

Selma Lagerlöf: *Mårbacka* (Translated by Sarah Death)

Viivi Luik: *The Beauty of History* (Translated by Hildi Hawkins)

Dorrit Willumsen: *Bang: A Novel about the Danish Writer* (Translated by Marina Allemano)

For our complete back catalogue, please visit
www.norvikpress.com

Berge

by

Jan Kjærstad

Translated from the Norwegian
by Janet Garton

Norvik Press
2019

Original title: *Berge* © Jan Kjærstad.
First published by H. Aschehoug & Co. (W. Nygaard) AS, 2017.
Published in agreement with Oslo Literary Agency.

This translation © Janet Garton 2019.
The translator's moral right to be identified as the translator of the work
has been asserted.

Norvik Press Series B: English Translations of Scandinavian Literature,
no. 80.

A catalogue record for this book is available from the British Library.

ISBN: 978-1-909408-53-1

Norvik Press
Department of Scandinavian Studies
University College London
Gower Street
London WC1E 6BT
United Kingdom
Website: www.norvikpress.com
E-mail address: norvik.press@ucl.ac.uk

Managing editors: Elettra Carbone, Sarah Death, Janet Garton,
C. Claire Thomson.

Layout and cover design: Essi Viitanen.

This translation has been published with the financial support of NORLA.

INE WANG

Apparently it was a crime beyond all comprehension. A hiker had rung the papers. Several people had been killed in a cabin in the wilderness of Nordmarka, way off the beaten track. Slaughtered, according to the tip-off. In a bestial way. Amongst the dead were well-known people, it was said. Extremely well-known.

Terrorism. That's what flashes through my mind. *So it's our turn at last.*

I'm standing here with my mobile phone in my hand. Trembling. Is this to be my lucky day after all?

I'm shocked at the thought, I try to stop it, but it won't be stopped, I feel a kick, because I'm at a low point, not just in my life, but here too, stranded on an island. I've been feeling out of place for a long time, standing here dressed up and sweaty, watching young couples running around in the sand in just their underwear, I can see that the party's already getting wilder, I read the long text message again, just to make sure I haven't read it wrong, and let my mobile slip back into my bag, like a weapon into its holster, I think, as Marie waves and points, I have to come down and sit on the rug, she pulls funny faces, I smile and indicate that I'm fine just here, raise my glass, at the same time concealing a grimace of contempt, regretting that I could be so stupid as to accept this wedding invitation, on Hovedøya island in the Oslo fjord of all places, the bridal couple in white, the guests in white, even I'm in white as the invitation demanded; and they were in luck, the weather on this late August day made you long for a parasol, and everything was so unbearably romantic, with the wedding ceremony in the monastery ruins and everything, the word of God and birdsong and tears of joy, a cool female, presumably lesbian, vicar, lots of hot air, solemn, far-too-solemn words about love, the greatest of all and la-di-da, doggerel, doggerel, but just the tiniest bit moving. It was just as much a Celtic ritual, a dash of Tolkien, surrounded by tall leafy trees, the flock of people in white amidst all the shimmering green, poetry reading, kissing, unrestrained kissing, champagne in plastic glasses, masses of champagne, the vicar too drank the champagne greedily, and I was surrounded by shouted conversations which became even more meaningless as they all got mixed up together. 'Skål for the newly-weds,' I hollered, just to be a part of it, people began to stumble on the stone steps of the ruins, screaming with laughter, I should never have come, Marie was a much younger colleague from the paper, *murdered*, and she was pregnant as well, she had admitted, *in a bestial way*, I felt like an old-timer alongside Marie's contemporaries, to hell with them, lucky bastards, and everything was so resolutely informal and improvised and abandoned, we were hippies in 2008, forty years too late; of course there was not to be any stiff wedding lunch, it was a picnic, *many dead*, they'd brought rugs and baskets, occupied the meadow sloping down towards the northern beach, the one facing Lindøya island, and they spread it all out with shrimps, French bread, lemons, salad, wine from cooler bags, some people lit barbecues in the designated areas, so that an aroma of grilled meat, mixed with the smell of grilled lobster, soon lay over the rocks and the hill up towards the forest, and we had an orgy of food, we drank, we toasted, spontaneous speeches were made, one platitude after the other, of course people had brought guitars, there was singing, raucous singing, 'All you need is love', to hell with them, lucky bastards, all these shamelessly attractive young people with their lives ahead of them, *well-known people*; some danced, some smoked, and not just ordinary cigarettes, there was abandoned kissing, there was abandoned petting, several couples disappeared into the forest, giggling, soon they'll be skinny-dipping, I think as I watch, I recognise the mood, fifteen years ago I would have gone skinny-dipping myself, now I'm just depressed by all this happiness, genuine happiness, I admit grudgingly, whilst searching for an excuse to be able to sneak off home.

That's why I see the text from Ulrik as a life-line, a chance to get out of here. These killings. Many people murdered in the forest. I catch a whiff of something, a whiff of a heaven-sent opportunity. *Who would have thought that on one of the loveliest of late summer days ... In the city no-one knew that in the forest not far away ... Sooner or later it had to happen here too ...*

I can feel it. A current of air. Something is happening. Everything is changing.

I turn away, no-one takes any notice, I find the steep path up towards the westerly canon emplacement, the high point with a view towards Bygdøy, towards the Fram and Kon-Tiki museums, towards the town and the looming hill to the north. What has happened in the spruce forest behind it? *In a bestial way.*

The yells from the beach below get louder and louder. I catch a glimpse of Marie, whirling round and round like a Dervish. Shouldn't she be a bit more careful? My gloominess returns. Where did this melancholy come from? Is it the awareness that Heggholmen is just nearby – the island of Heggholmen, where I met Martin one tropical Midsummer Eve at the beginning of the nineties? I didn't feel at all out of place at that party, a bacchanal which was held in a large outbuilding decorated with leafy branches, just next to some summer cabins near the water. There we had garlands of flowers in our hair, paper lanterns in the rafters, parma ham and melon, a whole roast lamb, bowls of strawberries, barrels of wine, two acoustic guitars and everyone singing – when I think about it, it was not very different from the wedding celebrations I'm running away from right now. The difference was Martin. And that I was young, younger, in the middle of my journalism course, Martin had just finished and got a job on a paper, I was unsure, wondering whether I should drop out of studying and do something else, but Martin urged me to go through with it, said it was the world's most important profession, we were the fourth estate, for Christ's sake, he was glowing with eagerness, pushed a strawberry between my lips, I had nothing against creeping into the bushes, kissing, felt just as carefree, just as crazy, as the wedding guests I can see on the beach below me; there was something about Martin's eyes, a look that struck sparks, I didn't feel horny, just turned on when I looked into them, and later in the evening we were shown around an artist's place on the southern point of the island, and were given more wine, an exclusive wine, in a studio down by the water's edge, and we sat there drinking amongst extraordinary paintings and sculptures, and I was the finest work of art in the place, whispered Martin, and we swam, we swam naked, that first evening we met, we kissed, we did everything you do when you meet on a warm Midsummer Eve by the fjord and fall in love at once. I wasn't drunk, I was turned on.

I can feel it flare up. Long ago. Lost.

Slaughtered?

I ring the paper and get through to Jakob who is holding the fort this Saturday, he doesn't know much more, but there are blue lights, he says, top priority, he says, people are on their way there now. 'Where?' I ask. 'Blankvann, not too far from the Kobberhaug hostel,' he says. Bloody hell, could that be right? I'd gone skiing there on the way to the Kikut viewpoint together with Martin. Sodding Martin. 'According to what we've picked up from the police, the tip-off is right,' says Jakob. 'Someone found the bodies this afternoon.' 'How many?' I ask. 'Five,' he says. 'Perhaps more.'

My eyes follow a wedding guest as he strips off his shirt before helping himself to grilled lobster. I feel groggy, and it's not from the champagne, the wine or the smell of burnt meat. 'Terrorism?' I ask. 'Looks like it,' says Jakob. 'Five dead?' I repeat. 'Yes, at least, they say it's a hell of a mess,' he says.

'Who?' I ask. 'Don't know,' he says, and his voice is different from normal. 'I think it's something sensational,' he says. 'Something we've never seen before.'

Again a shudder goes through me, and not because I'm scared. For a long time I've had a feeling that nothing is happening. Or that the same thing is happening over and over again. Not just in my life, but in Norway. It's a mixed blessing for a journalist, living in a prosperous society where no-one gets passionate about anything, with such a damned limited range of events. But now. Something is happening. Something different. *On Sunday morning a peaceful country awoke to the news that ...*

Holmenkollen hill looks strangely dark in the fine weather. To the right of the masts is the tower of Tryvannstårnet – like a rocket no-one's ever managed to fire. And behind that. Seven or eight kilometres into the forest. At least five dead. Suddenly it looks as if the ridge of the hill is holding back a dark evil.

I can't stand any more, I must get home, I don't know whether it's because of the news, the agitation I feel, or whether it's because the guests on the beach have all stood up and are singing 'Love Is All Around' with glasses raised, accompanied by guitars, actually quite tunefully, actually not a little movingly, and I feel sad, melancholy, without quite understanding why I feel sad and melancholy. Martin, it's all to do with Martin. I send a text to the bride – the pregnant bride – who most likely won't glance at her mobile till the next day, before I leave the bastion and stroll past the monastery ruins and onwards down to the quay, where I stand waiting for the little ferry; it's just me and a few remaining bathers, no-one else from the wedding, they've booked a special boat so they can carry on partying in town. I try to keep my eyes on the ferry dock at Aker Brygge, but my glance is drawn irresistibly upwards until it rests again on the ridges of Holmenkollen and Vettakollen, blue-black in the near darkness, as if I'm hoping to catch a glimpse of something further in, *behind*. Bestial? Have they been shot, hanged, dismembered? As I board the ferry it seems the evening sky has an apocalyptic gleam.

Is this such a day? Is this one of those days which will give rise to a recurring question: where were you on 23 August 2008?

From the train window, from the incline above Mosseveien, I can see Hovedøya from a new perspective, and there's something about its outline which makes it into an alien island, an off-putting island, an island I've managed to escape from, but despite that it's no consolation, because I'm on my way out of town to a life which is no life, a life which is divided into just days and sleeping, life on the back burner. The train is practically empty, no-one is on the way home now, in this weather and so early in the evening, people are staying in town, partying, treating themselves to a taxi home, like I used to do. Someone has forgotten a paperback on the seat opposite, or left it behind on purpose, a novel, I can't be bothered to look at it, who needs novels these days; I pick up a newspaper instead, but it's thin, thin in both senses, there's nothing in it, the pages are full of print, but they could just as well have been blank. The fourth estate, my arse. I stare out of the window. *A grey reality suddenly stained red with blood … Norway wrenched out of its apathy … For five people summer came to a sudden end …*

The fjord disappears as the train swings inland towards Hauketo station. I ring Jakob at the paper again. Do they know any more? It's not many seconds before he says a name, and the name makes me sit bolt upright. Is it true? It's hard to hold my mobile steady at my ear. Jakob repeats the name, it's been confirmed, he says, I ask more, but everything else is drowned out by the knowledge that Arve Storefjeld is dead, killed – *slaughtered* – in his cabin by Blankvann lake in Nordmarka. I am shaken up and calm, both at the same time, I'm thinking, but I don't know what I'm thinking, I don't remember what I thought, and it's only out of habit that I get off at the right station, Vevelstad, and start to walk towards the town-house district to the west of the station, walking past tricycles and toys left behind in sandpits, garden tools leaning against the walls of sheds; I've started to hate this area, not because there's anything wrong with it objectively, it's a pleasant residential district, identical town houses with small gardens in front and behind and paths in between, I'm no snob either, I grew up in a massive block of flats in Etterstad, in many ways I'm an East End girl, but it's as if I've been abandoned out here, in Ski, in something which in recent years has felt more and more like a backwater, at least an existential backwater. It was supposed to be something temporary until Martin and I could afford better, move into a detached house, ideally nearer to town, Kolbotn perhaps, or Nordstrand, with children and all the rest of it, and after that perhaps a town house in the centre, no less. Then we split up. No children. Fortunately. Unfortunately. I stayed put. Always with a plan to move into town. I stayed put. I'm still here. Uncoupled. On a siding.

I walk homewards in the dark blue evening light. The politician Arve Storefjeld is dead. The government minister. *A steamroller has reached the end of the road.* I can't get it into my head, I'm struggling to breathe, I have to stop, then I walk slowly on.

Three weeks ago I delivered a manuscript to a publisher, a book about Arve Storefjeld. It's already been accepted.

Again I stand still, or my legs stop of their own accord, I can't believe it's true. That I can have been so ... *lucky.* The word pops up, I want to delete it, but it remains. Of course parts will have to be rewritten now. The foreword. And the book will need a new last chapter. *Arve Storefjeld's testament.* But what a ... stroke of luck. I can't help it, the words just float up. I'm standing staring at a trampoline. There are trampolines in every other garden. They look like ... I'll have to write about it some time. All those trampolines, they must symbolize something or other. Arve Storefjeld. Good God. What timing. Again I'm ashamed of my thoughts, but it's impossible not to think them. I mean, I'm sure I'm just as shocked as everyone else, just as full of sympathy, but if I'm honest, I can also feel an intoxicating quickening of my pulse as I realise the possibilities which have suddenly opened up. And at the same time impatience and curiosity: what now? What's going to happen? I realise that I'm standing shaking my head, as if I still can't believe it. What a coincidence.

A spark plug.

Everything will change. This autumn is mine.

It couldn't last … One day the idyll had to shatter … Delete that last bit. Cliché. I have to find new words.

Martin will be green with jealousy. No, don't think that. This is too big for such trifles, makes it sound as if we're going through a nasty divorce.

What luck I left the party early. I feel relatively sober. I ought to write something now, something long. Put down a marker. It's too late to get it into the Sunday papers. But on Monday. An overview. An analysis of Arve Storefjeld's importance. Storen, the big guy, as he was called. The Labour Party's most high-profile figure, called after Norway's third highest mountain, Storefjell. Bigger, more important for the party than the Prime Minister himself.

No journalist in the country knows more about Arve Storefjeld than I do.

I make my way through the kitchen, closing my eyes to the clothes lying thrown around, the plates and cups which haven't been put in the dishwasher. The dust. The stains on the floor. Bloody hell, I can't help thinking, what a miserable existence.The town-house district is like the abbey on Hovedøya, a secluded convent, where I live like a godless nun, observing my rituals, my monotony. It's news time, I switch on the radio by the microwave. Nothing about the killings, not one word; presumably it's too early, the news hasn't broken yet. I go over to the window on the first floor and stand there looking at the fronts of the houses across the path, a row which curves up the hill, seemingly endless, longer than the Great Wall of China. There's a sprinkler going on one lawn, someone must have forgotten to turn it off. The first year I lived here alone I consoled myself that I could be an observer, and I did write quite a few smart and amusing little articles, full of self-irony about life in the Mecca of the middle classes, from this mini-house idyll which was only different from Cardamom Town because it wasn't the robbers' house but a shopping centre, incidentally one of the country's largest, which was just nearby. I had also written droll columns in the paper, and later in the magazine, about my expeditions into the 'lion's den', into Ski centre's labyrinth of shops, about my shopping mania, a break from my self-disgust – they were of course spiced up with critical reflections about the transition from being a citizen to becoming a consumer – but the longer I lived here, the more colourless and pathetic the satire became. I wrote nothing about my dawning desperation, and the thought makes me remember that embarrassing incident the previous Saturday evening; it was hot and I was sleeping with the window open, and I was woken by a crash, it was my neighbour who had guests, and they were sitting round the grill in the garden, it was a merry gathering, there were coloured lights hanging from the trees. I felt depressed at the sight, I was also depressed at the sight of my own garden, or rather the dry scrap of lawn, because when we moved here I dreamt of making that little garden into a kind of meditative space, something Japanese, with a small artificial fountain in the midst of carefully chosen stones, some cherry trees and a bed of perennials which flowered at different times, and it had all come to nothing, so just the act of leaning out of my window and being reminded of my own garden made me feel dispirited, but despite that I managed to ask politely if they could be quieter, turn down that dreadful pop music, but they just laughed and suggested I should come out instead, join in the party, they didn't mean any harm, but I was already on the way downstairs, outside, in through the silly little gate in the fence, and without stopping to think about it, I tipped over the grill – a well-aimed kick – tipped it over with meat and embers and everything. Someone quickly appeared with a hose and put out the embers – of course I didn't even own a hose – and instead of getting cross they just carried on laughing, they asked if I practised kick-boxing, I was wearing oversize pyjamas, they complimented me on my brilliant kick, put out a chair for me and offered me a drink, I could see that there were parasols in it, but I was so angry, and at the same time so shamefaced, that I stormed back. I thought afterwards that I did it, kicked the grill over, because I wanted to break free, I wasn't a nun who had taken refuge here by choice, I, once a rebel, had been imprisoned by a sun-scorched lawn and a flowerless bed and the eternal grill smoke and lawnmower clatter of my neighbours.

All the important things in life lay behind me.

A few hours before leaving for the wedding I'd been sitting at my desk, in the little room I called my office, leafing through my electronic calendar. Empty. No entries. Proof of how lacking in initiative I was. Previously my calendar had been full of reminders, not just of lunches, dinners, friends, but also of work meetings, journeys, absorbing assignments: introducing debates, chairing them, lectures, women's conferences, hosting radio programmes. Fun things. It struck me – and the realisation was a heavy weight inside me: all the important things lay behind me. My moon landing, if I can use that phrase, happened long ago; I'd swept into the Norwegian newspaper world, into readers' living rooms, and was immediately praised for my 'youthful tone', a language which hadn't been heard before, I'd become trusted, gone on to write investigative journalism which shook the world to its foundations, the Norwegian world at least, and then moved on to portraits which were called innovative and were the topic of conversation at dinner parties; but then, before I was aware that I'd reached the summit, I discovered that I'd passed the summit.

An uneventful life.

In an uneventful country.

I raised my eyes from the empty spaces in my calendar and looked out of the window. On every other lawn the water sprinklers were running, sending peacock tails of spray up into the air. On a playground in the distance two children were competing to be the one who could swing highest. I don't know whether it had anything to do with the water spray in the air or the children on the swings, but at that moment it dawned on me that I would never be editor or play a leading role. And I wouldn't get a job in the Norwegian broadcasting corporation, which I had dreamt of for a long time. The problem was that my ideas had dried up. I thought about our editorial meetings, how crushed I felt when the youngsters' bad ideas were better than mine – for the simple reason that I had no ideas. I felt dizzy, even though I was only staring at a wall of town-house fronts, I knew I was in a gigantic negative spiral. All that remained was circles upon circles, down and down. Towards a retirement package. Towards death. Everything I wrote was repetitions, in the best cases variations on my finest reports – occasionally it might be better written, but it was always less cogently thought out. Take my most recent article in the magazine, about Harriet Fett, the wife of the famous art historian and director of historic monuments, that remarkable woman who suffered so much in the male-dominated cultural circles of the day. Interesting, perhaps. And with fine illustrations and an attractive layout. But absolutely trivial. Why was I standing here, in a town house in a completely colourless area, why was I not standing in a villa in Kolbotn or in a town house in Homansbyen? Why was it so long since I'd made any significant contribution?

All the important things in life. Behind me.

I stood there for a long time, half hypnotized by the water sprinklers and the kids swinging in unison, at the same time as I managed to think that I'd better pull myself together before I reached a dangerously catatonic state; I played with the thought of contacting my doctor, asking for antidepressants, or at least something to make me feel more cheerful. When I come to think about it, wasn't I standing there almost in tears? God help me, hadn't I had a lump of self-pity in my throat?

But now, only a few hours later, I'm standing at a different window in the same house, repeating to myself, as if I still can't quite believe it: Arve Storefjeld is dead. And not just dead – murdered. It was … it is Norway's Olof Palme moment. A red cross on the nation's timeline, of the sort people draw in textbooks. There would be an unbelievable uproar. *When great trees fall.* There would be a need for Ine Wang's competence. The scene was set for a once-in-a-lifetime comeback. A new moon landing. No, not a comeback, Ine Wang has never been away.

Until now the word has only existed in foreign language dictionaries … Terror is something which happens elsewhere … I shiver with horror. I feel jubilant.

I find the bottle of Jack Daniel's, the one I got from Rachel on my 39th birthday, 'One year of rebellion left', I take a dram, not too much, it's mostly for the taste, to feel the charge in my insides, recall the outsider feeling from a time when bourbon was an everyday event, and it works; I open a cupboard I haven't opened for many years and fish out an LP, I put it on the record player and move the pickup arm far enough in for the needle to hover over the blank space before the third track on the B-side, and I stand there staring down at the black disc going round and round, so that I am drawn into a whirlpool of memories, before I let the needle sink down onto 'Brass in Pocket' and turn up the volume, and as soon as the guitar riff, the bass, hits my ribcage, I start to dance, the natural thing to do, I dance with the bottle of Jack Daniel's in my hand and sing along to the tune, lyrics I have known by heart since I was twelve, lyrics which have never left me, which were the national anthem of my teenage years thanks to Chrissie Hynde and The Pretenders, because I too had brass in pocket, I was special, so special, I was bloody well going to conquer everything and everyone, I was gonna use my arms, I was gonna use my legs, I'm gonna use my, my, my *imagination,* I was gonna be an outstanding success, because I was special, for fuck's sake, I was just *so* special, I was Ine Wang from Etterstad Palace, no lousy boys were going to stand in my way, not now, not ever, I sing along, I sing at the top of my voice, and to be on the safe side I swallow another mouthful of bourbon, even if the taste also reminds me of many dreadful hungover mornings, and I avoid looking towards the windows and seeing a reflection which will make it clear that I'm dancing, that I'm playing at being a rebel in a white summer dress in an conventional living room in an conventional town house in an conventional neighbourhood, in a district inhabited by people with nothing else to while away the time than grilling as much meat and drinking as much wine from a box as possible in the shortest possible time, until they can once more deaden their restless feelings in the enormous Ski shopping mall; just this evening I don't wish to be reminded that even though I'm special, or at least believed I'm special, I've got no further than here.

*

The whiskey has made me hungry, I ate hardly anything on Hovedøya, and I get out the only things I eat when I'm at home, the ingredients for sandwiches, good bread for two thin slices with plenty of filling, and I spread butter and pastrami and mustard and a kind of small gherkins which burst between your teeth like fireworks, I make one of my speciality sandwiches and stand eating it off a small plate whilst looking in vain for news on TV; I go to my computer in the office and see that the online news has it as the first item, it tells me that at least five people have been found dead in a cabin in Nordmarka and the police are treating it as murder, but otherwise there is irritatingly little, it is clear that it's uncertain what has happened. No names. As if they want to be careful. Not to spread panic. But I know that Jakob's sources are reliable. It looks as if they've been executed, said Jakob. I go back to the TV in the living room, zap between programmes and stand watching a boring programme whilst I eat the rest of my sandwich. I keep zapping. Nothing but boring programmes. I switch off and can see my reflection in the shiny black screen.

Arve Storefjeld is dead. What a catastrophe. What a chance. What fantastic luck.

I was in my life's doldrums. Then this happens.

You think you choose your life, but when you turn round, you just see a long row of random events.

I've always been open to random events. I call them spark plugs. Small things which can make something stop, or something else start.

I had my first real boyfriend when I was seventeen, and we were soon necking so violently that our faces looked red and swollen. I longed to go further, but Christian hesitated. One weekend Mum and Dad and my little sister went off to our cabin by Lyseren lake, and I was left on my own in the flat in the majestic building which was nicknamed the Etterstad Palace. On Saturday evening Christian and I lay on the sofa kissing and touching each other for so long that I was at bursting point. I reckoned we were ready to push the boundaries further and suggested that we should lie down on the bed, but Christian didn't want to, and in the end he had to go home; he lived in Årvoll, I went out to his scooter with him, but it wouldn't start, it must be the spark plug, he said. In that case you might as well stay till the morning? I said, and he gave in, stayed the night, and that was how I lost my virginity, because of a spark plug, I thought later, and the next morning one of Christian's friends from Årvoll came over with a new spark plug, and Christian gave me the old one. I kept it and carried it everywhere with me, even after we broke up and I started studying journalism, sometimes I placed it in front of me when I was going to write. Look for the spark plug, I said to myself, and the slogan helped me find unexpected angles in many reports and portraits.

And now I had written a book about the tub-thumper and Labour party chieftain Arve Storefjeld, and in retrospect I realise I had been a little uncertain when I submitted it; it was my first book, I had wanted to try something new and daring, and force myself to move forward in a career which had stalled. It was too late to go abroad, launch myself into a war zone and travel around in a bullet-proof vest, become a new Lise Lindbæk, whose book *Burning Earth* Martin had read aloud in bed as I lay beside him, exhausted with screwing, when I was still at college; the publishers were also a bit doubtful, but that was probably mostly because of its format, and that annoyed me because it was the format I was most proud of, or the method I had used, because the book did not follow Storefjeld slavishly year by year throughout his life, but jumped here and there, as well as touching on many different themes, even though all of them were connected to Storen's life; I had even felt, in the course of my work, a breath of inspiration – almost a forgotten phenomenon – and now, with Storen's death, I suddenly realise that it is a good book, the publishers will see that it is a good book as well, it's perfect as it is, and it's a book that many, very many, will feel the urge to read right now. Perhaps it will even bring some consolation, I think. *We are not going to award a number of stars to this book, we just recommend it warmly: read it!*

The first thing my eyes meet on Sunday morning is the green wallpaper, with a pattern so surrealistically ugly that it has made every hangover feel worse over the years. We said we would change the wallpaper when we moved in, but it was never done, not when I was on my own either, and I consoled myself that it was fine to keep the tasteless wallpaper because I would be reminded every morning when I woke up that I had to get out of there.

Then I remember the previous day and I'm wide awake at once, not just awake, I can feel a new revved-up feeling, an impatience which has me standing in the kitchen only minutes later making coffee. It was only a day ago that I was at a standstill. Now I'm on the move, or to put it bluntly it's full steam ahead, I've written a book about Arve Storefjeld, 'the steamroller from Bjølsen', a book I had perhaps not expected great things of, but then Storen goes and dies in the most dramatic of circumstances. I can't suppress the thought: as if to order.

The morning paper has managed to get the news on the front page. They have also included the information that Arve Storefjeld, Minister for Transport, is among the dead. But inside the paper there is hardly anything. I check the online news. Nothing further there. Still not much is known. Or people don't want to talk. I can find short summaries of Storen's career, I find the first reactions, the Labour front bench talking of their consternation. What a loss it is for the party. Nothing about terrorism, nothing about the way he was killed. I return to the kitchen and the front page of the paper. A dark picture of the ridge to the north of Blankvann lake. 'What has happened?' is the headline.

Suddenly I feel doubtful. Perhaps I see the darkness of the picture as a warning. Should I really throw myself into this event and write a commentary? Could it damage my book? Or would it have a positive effect on the book, on reactions, on sales? Make me stand out as an incisive commentator? I *am* an incisive commentator, at least I used to be.

Not unexpectedly I get a phone call from my publishers already that morning, not from my editor, but from the head of publishing, he apologizes, he knew it was Sunday and blablabla, the whole incident is of course dreadful, a tragedy beyond all description and blablabla, but he just wanted to say, he feels the *need* to say, that he has read my manuscript, yes, of course, he says when he hears my surprise, even though this 'of course' doesn't make me any more convinced that he has read it, but he does say that because of the specially sad circumstances and blablabla, the urgent need for information about the victims and blablabla, the press will pull out all the stops so that the book is available as quickly as possible, which means in three weeks, four at the most, he adds, and nothing can disguise the fact that he is on fire; he praises my sharp pen, before he says, and this he also has from my editor, that I will of course need to adjust a few details, nothing to worry about, just trifles, plus revise the foreword and write a new final chapter, and I answer, in fact I interrupt him, I am Ine Wang, I'm filled with a new self-confidence, and I explain that I'm already working on it; I don't know why I say that, but I add, as if it's a sales pitch, a good blurb, that Arve Storefjeld – regardless of how you evaluate his political importance – will be worth more to the Labour Party dead than alive. After I've uttered this remark it is quiet on the other end of the line, for a long time, and then umm, yes, but perhaps you'd better not write that, says the publisher, you know, some people might be upset by it, you know, we have to show consideration, you understand what I mean, and I say yes, of course, it was just a thought which occurred to me, and even before we've finished talking I have it all in my head, whole passages, I am inspired, I am *turned on,* I am capable of scribbling down fifty pages in a day, in a couple of hours, my fingertips are prickling; before the morning is over I've already jotted down by hand ten pages of keywords, sentences, whole fragments which can be inserted directly into my manuscript, and perfectly formulated, right on target, which suddenly just pop out of my subconscious. I love it, and I've always loved it, writing, adding one word to the next, linking sentences to sentences, creating perceptive connections, approaching my material from a different angle than everyone else, and if I didn't know it before, I can now see clearly that my book on Arve Storefjeld is an ambitious and valuable project, because from the start I had wanted to write about real life, real Norwegian life, and Storen *is* real Norwegian life, that is to say he *was*, because now real Norwegian life was lying deep in the forest with no pulse, 'executed', as Jakob said.

As I put down my pen I register my excitement, it catches up with me like the waves from your own boat when you reduce speed, I'm sitting with my heart racing and enjoying the situation, enjoying the sight of the closely-written pages, with arrows to extra notes in the margin, I'm enjoying the feeling of having woken from my torpor, being full of energy.

But who were the others who were killed?

I've forgotten to eat, I make myself a thick sandwich, a classic club sandwich, apart from the fact that I make do with two slices rather than three, I add turkey, bacon, tomato, mayonnaise, lettuce, I eat it hungrily whilst I put the kettle on for a cup of tea. It has to be green tea today, I think. This is definitely a day for green tea. And for thick sandwiches with turkey and bacon.

For the whole of the rest of Sunday I sit in my town house in Ski writing my analysis, the overview I'm planning for the Monday paper, that is if I can have a good enough idea, *The Day Norwegian Naivety Collapsed* ... I leaf through my notes on Arve Storefjeld looking for something I can use, a motif, a thought which hasn't found its way into the book, I read through all those pages of bullet points, witty insights, quotes, little anecdotes I jotted down when I was talking to other people about Storen, about his time at Folk High School, Bjølsen, technical school, Sandaker, on military service – he served in Finnmark, which explained his love of Northern Norway and as a consequence his popularity in that part of the country: 'We need a better connection between the molly-coddled south and the heroic north!' During the oil crisis in the 70s, before his time as a member of parliament, Storen became famous overnight when during a live TV debate he threw off his heavy belt so that the studio echoed – the belt had a buckle which was so solid you might think he was the chairman of Iron and Steel: 'Now is not the time to talk to ordinary working people about tightening their belts, but about loosening them,' he shouted. 'We'll not bloody well carry the can for fluctuations in the grubby capitalist game.' Otherwise he normally dressed in old pilot jackets and battered skipper's hats, as if to remind voters about his grandfather from Østfold, a man who had been a marine pilot before he became a fisherman in later life. *A political pilot has hung up his jacket* ... I'm sitting at my desk, looking through my notes, reading about Storen's time as international Trades Union secretary, and his travels abroad, especially to South Africa before Nelson Mandela was released from prison. *Our international conscience has been silenced* ... I read about his wife Mosse, who worked for the Trades Union Organisation, later for the FaFo Research Foundation, and her all-too-early death; I have created a whole little archive on Storen and his family, organized my research notes and cuttings according to subject, and put them in separate plastic folders.

The book came about by chance. A spark plug.

A good year ago, in the summer of 2007, I was given the task of writing a focus piece on Arve Storefjeld. He had just launched a fusillade of unusually sharp political pronouncements, as if to underline the fact that local elections were imminent. We did the interview at Dovre, it was Storen himself who insisted we should meet there, and I remember that the magazine photographer and I set off by car at the crack of dawn, and I was looking forward to it on the way up, because I enjoyed portraying well-known people, the challenge of writing something new about a person everyone believed they knew everything about, and if I was to boast of anything, it would be that I was able to get people, even buttoned-up individuals, to say unexpected things about themselves, to find words for experiences they had not expressed before, and discover memories they had never referred to in public. You would be a good Catholic priest, Martin told me whilst we were still married, you get people to confess; several times I'd known interviewees thank me afterwards because now for the first time they could make out the arc of their lives, the story which underpinned everything; so I was looking forward to meeting Arve Storefjeld when we reached Dovre and turned off to the right, towards Grimsdalen, and not long after, with some difficulty, found the side road which led up to Storen's cabin, or property, because it was a whole group of small houses with turf roofs. It was a dramatic summer's day with a blue sky and heavy, slightly threatening clouds, brilliantly lit, and Storen himself was standing in the yard to wish us welcome to the settlement, and he was wearing his campaigning costume, as he called it, a white shirt with rolled-up sleeves and his baccy in his breast pocket – he was known for shedding his jacket at the first opportunity, as if to signal that he was ready to get his hands dirty, even in a white shirt; and I must admit there was something about those shirts, they were so white that you searched for words to intensify the adjective white, and as if he anticipated my comments Storen explained that he hung his shirts out to dry so that they were filled with sunshine. As he said that he stood there in his yard with feet wide apart and his thumbs hooked into the trouser belt which had become a nationwide symbol many years since.

The sun king, I wrote on my notepad, but I didn't use it.

On the grassy slope below we could see the bulk of the Old Man of Dovre, a black Chevrolet Blazer, which he had owned since he left the Highway Department in 1977, and which he sometimes drove around in to political events even after he had become Minister for Transport. He excused himself with the remark that it was important to make yourself visible, and a car with the rumble of a V8 engine and the kind of tyres which could get you through to the remotest corners of the land certainly attracted attention. When it's a matter of campaigning, then I'm a bit less environmentally conscious, he would say. Actually many people thought that applied at other times too. Storen would never say he hated trains, but if he could get his way it was roads, roads, roads all the way. If you're going to win votes in Western Norway, at the top of a fjord surrounded by high mountains, it's no good standing in the marketplace talking about utopian high-speed trains, he would say.

After a short guided tour we were back in the yard. 'Trygve Lie's cabin by Ruglsjøen lake, just north of Røros, must be the only one with a finer setting,' said Storen, opening his arms wide. He was a sight to behold as he stood there with his mane of tossed-back hair and eyes which became two slanting lines when he smiled – caricaturists have always loved Storen. 'Sometimes I wonder whether I should change my name from one mountain to another, from Storefjeld to Raudberget,' he said jokingly as he posed for the photographer in front of the main cabin with the mountain in question in the background. This will be great, I kept thinking. Arve Storefjeld on Dovre. His monumental self-assurance and the Dovre mountains went together. 'I've always been red, I was bloody well born red,' he laughed with a voice which was hoarse from many decades of smoking, if it wasn't just rusty from agitating and countless speeches and unstoppable discussion and raw laughter. Storen always underlined the importance of party organization; he was a popular lecturer and had probably visited every single local party association in the country, with or without his Chevrolet Blazer.

The bedrock. I rejected it even before I had written it down.

We sat down by the wall of the cabin and I quickly established a good rapport with him, whilst warning myself at the same time not to fall for his kingly charm and become uncritical. He asked about my parents, and when I told him that my mother worked for the Royal Mail and my father was an employee of the Oslo Tram Company, and that I had grown up in Etterstad Palace itself, I was accepted. 'Not bad for a journalist,' he said. 'I'm special,' I said. I'm *so* special, I sang to myself, and with that we were off, he answered all my questions willingly and at length, and I got a barrage of ripe swearwords into the bargain. On the day we were there he was concerned about the decline in numbers qualifying in a skilled trade. 'You can't fucking well get a more respectable qualification than as a tradesman!' he shouted across the yard. He would have preferred to conduct the interview whilst we were walking in the mountains, but since we had to return the same day there wasn't time, so he told us instead how he would normally take visitors, especially political opponents, to a place just north of Dovre village, where they parked and he then marched them up the old King's Road, a pilgrim route, and exhausted them by walking quickly up the steep Brattbakken. 'It's bloody strenuous, you know,' he said, laughing, as if it gave him pleasure to torment other people; 'I've softened up many bloody impudent rivals by taking them on that trip,' he said, 'and talking symbolically about how hard the old days were. But they forgive everything when we get to Allmannarøysa cairn and the view north to Snøhetta mountain unfolds in front of us. We ought to have taken a picture there, for Christ's sake,' he said, turning to the photographer, 'that's my favourite spot in the whole of Norway. On top of Brattbakken, with Snøhetta in front of you. The Eidsvoll lads were fucking well right when they talked about standing united till Dovre falls,' he said. 'Nothing can fall here.'

But in the forest things can fall, I think, as I sit there in my town house remembering my visit to the settlement under Raudberget.

The interview had given me lots of valuable information, about Storen's extended family, about his time in the Highway Department, about things that had formed him, but what really made a stir, what everyone remembered, was a detail which was revealed after the meal – he served us meat and potato fry-up, campaigning food – when Storen wanted a whisky. He offered us one too, but we were planning to share the driving on the arduous journey home. He got out a Glenmorangie – a gift, he emphasised – and I noticed that his glass was a washed-out preserves jar, and as a corner of the label was still attached, I could see it had been peanut butter. When he saw my glance, he began to explain about Mills, that Norwegian trademark, and Grünerløkka, and that he was proud of it, he always bought cod roe and Italian salad and peanut butter from Mills, and I used that detail as a leitmotif – a seasoned politician who swilled fine malt whisky from an old peanut butter jar in the same way as a child drinks milk – that opened up a great deal about his background and who he was now. I liked that scene. To be honest, I would have liked to sit there and drink together with him.

Afterwards I was contacted by a publisher. No-one had written a book about Arve Storefjeld, and that was strange, because he was a figure everyone had an opinion about. I said yes at once, also because it was a chance to do something new, to shake off my stagnation, my *ennui*, and even if the book no doubt had a few imperfections, I was satisfied with its form, the fact that I was bold enough to let the story consist of a series of relatively short passages, separated by blank lines, and often with considerable leaps in subject matter, because I wasn't only writing about his time on the committee for public transport or as a minister, I inserted short descriptions of Lom and Røros, where his mother's mother and father respectively originated, and of Kråkerøy, where his father's family had their roots, I wrote about the Christiania Steel Company where his father had worked and the food shop in Sagene where his mother was an assistant, about Bjølsen, the part of town where Storen grew up, and about Voldsløkka where he threw the discus; I wrote short, almost essayistic, chapters about the Oslo Highways Department, Storen's workplace for the first ten years of his working life, I wrote about the whole road system in Oslo, which Storen knew better than any taxi driver, and about asphalt, that material he had such a close relationship with – 'The only thing I love more than the smell of newly made waffles is the smell of newly laid asphalt' – I made a short foray into his two favourite authors, Tor Jonsson and Johan Falkberget, and much more; of course I included passages about Dovre, about kings' roads and pilgrim routes, it was a compendium of a book about a compendium of a person.

A little piece of Norway. I didn't use that either. Of course not.

We met several times during this period, and I included some conversations where I let him talk freely, not least about politics, and where I allowed his whole cavalry of hobby horses to influence my presentation, with some fairly strained metaphors from fishing and piloting and steelworks, but the tone was affectionate, not least because deep down I envied him, especially his bustling and lively home in Maridalsveien, in one of the refurbished old workers' quarters down by Akerselva river, the seemingly warm relationship between father and two grown-up children, the exchange of views, the joking, the openness, the hospitality; I thought that also because I myself was childless, lived alone and longed to live in the centre of Oslo, have an old house on Maridalsveien, and fill it with light and warmth. Children.

And now he is dead. I'm horrified. And the horror is real. I feel that I know him. Knew him.

Something has fallen. And fallen heavily. *On Saturday you could feel a tremor passing through the Dovre mountains.* Could I write that? It was true, mentally at least.

Now my year's toil was paying off. I was in front of all the others by a head.

I look out of the window, straight across at another town house, I've got the points for my commentary in my head, I begin to write, write quickly, touch-typing, I want to see if my material hangs together. At home I still write on an iMac G3, in one of those colours which caused such a sensation when the marvel was launched: neon lime-green, a colour which always makes me think of my childhood's jelly puddings, and I don't know whether it's nostalgia, but writing on this machine gives me a special pleasure, it may have something to do with the innovative design, an almost egg-shaped computer in transparent plastic, unless it's more to do with a tactile sensation, the stimulating feeling from the soft give of the keys; yes, this will be good, it will be more than good, I ring the paper, get through to the news chief, Foyn, he's at work because of the terror attack at Blankvann, here it's all hands to the pumps, he says, more fired up than I can remember hearing him, I get the impression of an elderly general who is out in the field again at last. I'm a journalist on the magazine, but I also write in the paper now and then, and I tell him that I'll soon have an article ready, a mixture of reflection and political commentary, I explain the content and the angle, I say that I want it printed tomorrow, Monday, and Foyn gives me the green light, a lime-green light. 'Great, Ine,' he says, 'I was just going to ring you, I know you've got a book on Storefjeld on the stocks.' Foyn and I have a good relationship, we sometimes sit side by side on the cycling machines in the gym and chat. I ask for the latest update. He says that the other victims have been identified, but the police don't want to release the names yet.

'Oh, who are they?' I ask, and my fingertips are tingling, I don't know whether it's nervousness or as a result of my typing. 'The daughter,' says Foyn. 'You mean Gry, Gry Storefjeld,' I say, and I have to swallow. 'The one everyone thinks will become' – I correct myself – 'would become Prime Minister.' 'Yes, her,' says Foyn. Pause. *The day Norway lost its innocence.* 'Who else?' I ask. 'Storen's partner,' says Foyn. 'Sofie Nagel,' I say, I affirm. 'And Jules Lefebvre, Gry Storefjeld's boyfriend,' says Foyn. 'The Frenchman,' I mutter to myself. Pause. I can hear that Foyn is struggling, and that must mean the circumstances really are extreme. 'And a little girl, Lefebvre's daughter,' he says. 'It's sickening,' he says. 'Nine years old,' he says. 'Killed. It's just sickening.'

We finish our conversation. It takes me several minutes to absorb it. The dimensions of the crime. I put my hand on my heart as if to slow my heart rate. Doubt surfaces once more: should I leave this ghastly subject alone? Should I choose instead to stay in familiar territory, in my town-house existence, my protected convent? Imagine if this messed everything up, just made things worse? I haven't finished thinking the thought before my fingers start to itch. *Terror has inflicted an irreparable loss on the country ... It is the best who die ...*

I need air, I throw on a fleece and go out, taking the path down to a pond nearby. To be honest I had been wondering for a long time whether I should stop working as a journalist.

Ever since my first glory days, when I wrote about David Bowie, about his changing phases and roles, his sudden shifts of musical style and costume, I had thought that it might be possible to pass through several incarnations in the course of a life; already back then I could see that my career as a music reporter would be short, that I would change my field frequently, go from culture to news to investigative journalism to features to ... Perhaps I should get some more qualifications, I think now, on my way down to the pond, *The peaceful waters of Blankvann have become the lake of the dead,* perhaps I should become a teacher, I think, open a café, anything. There's also something about the way things are going in my profession which disturbs me, the fact that newspapers, especially the tabloids, are more and more writing for the scandal seekers, I'm sick and tired of the endless search for items that can cause a sensation, as if the aim is to fuel people's ability to get indignant, except that this indignation doesn't lead to anything, you just want to inflame people's brains for a few seconds – you're not much better than a drug dealer, some kind of Dr Feelgood – and the same thing with the other extreme, stories of success, the one more absurd than the next, not to mention how desperate the newspapers were to stuff consumers with gossip – basically it all boiled down to providing material for entertainment, for distraction – and now you had to add the new social media, as they were called, and I have asked myself several times whether we journalists won't soon be superfluous, or at least lose our power, the fourth estate will soon include everyone, any Tom, Dick or Harry writing comments and blogging, or posting on the newest platforms, Twitter and Facebook – Martin was enthusiastic about them all. But I've decided to fight anyway, to fight for what I consider serious journalism, which is a guarantee of quality, the professional view, the ability to recognise spark plugs, and that's exactly why I search for exceptional ideas for essays, for unexpected portraits, and now: for points for an article which can throw light on the terror at Blankvann from a surprising and original angle.

I think about this as I sit down on a bench by the pond. If I didn't know that it sounded too pompous, I would say it was a calling. The first time I felt it was when I got a permanent position on a paper in Akersgata and arrived at the offices. I had done it. I had gained access to the columns of a national newspaper. It was like standing on holy ground. I would educate the public. Give them information which *mattered*.

I stare out across the pond. My thoughts shift to the lake in Nordmarka and the horrific killings. Should I not be thinking the same thing now? That the newspaper, the public, the *nation*, needs a voice which can speak wisely about this shattering event. Assuage the grief. Call for unity. I have a responsibility, I say to myself as I throw small pebbles into the water and watch the rings spreading. Few people possess as much material as I do; thanks to my work on the book I also know a good deal about Arve Storefjeld's partner and his daughter Gry. I walk quickly home to my town house and up to my little office and sit down at the lime-green Mac. My task is an honourable one. I must write, and I write in a way that makes my whole body crackle, the lavish firework display I watched on TV, alone on the sofa, at the opening of the Summer Olympics in Beijing earlier in the month has moved into my head, I don't know where it comes from, but I also feel a touch of radicalism, even aggressiveness, a desire to act as a critical corrective, which I lost long ago, it's as if I have rediscovered the drive from the early days in Akersgata. I'll show them, I think, I feel inventive, I sing quietly, there's nobody else here, no one like me.

I don't eat anything other than a couple of sandwiches, the fridge is full of ingredients, a whole little emergency food store, enough to make sandwiches for a battalion, and all because of my constant raids, expeditions to distract myself, to the enticing Ski hypermarket, where I glide along the counters and shelves with a huge trolley – as if in a gondola past the palaces of the Grand Canal, I once wrote in a humorous sketch – and squirrel away everything I need, ham and pâté of various kinds, shrimps in brine and good cheeses. Emmental! Mustards and pickles. I don't know where this sandwich habit comes from, just that it dates back a long way. Martin was irritated by it, he always wanted to make ambitious dinners, often with several courses, leafing through cookbooks; perhaps it's a protest against the female role, this eternal focus on food, food, food, a protest against all the new food magazines and blogs, this ceaseless hysteria around nutrition, I wanted to keep it simple, good quality, but simple, I wanted to use my time on other things, I want to write perceptively about Storen, I want to write perceptively about this diabolic event at Blankvann, I can already see that it will be a collective trauma. *Terror has come to Norway, my little country.*

I finish the article and submit it in good time before the deadline. In between I have been following the news online and on TV. Everything is still desperately unclear, only Arve Storefjeld's name is mentioned, and the police don't want to say any more than the absolute minimum. Nevertheless the affair seems to grow larger and larger. On the evening news the Prime Minister makes a short statement, saying that it is a day of sorrow. He looks indescribably sad. I am almost frightened by the solemnity of his behaviour. Behind him stands a Norwegian flag, as if to signal that this is not just an attack on people.

*

On Monday morning I make a detour to Oppegård station to buy newspapers in the shopping centre, and on the train to town, whilst I have to look out of the window now and then because my surroundings seem to have changed character, I can confirm that my article stands out from everything else which has been printed about the Blankvann incident. My commentary is more political, gives a broader perspective, has a sharper focus; it's not just about Arve Storefjeld, but about what we have lost and how we just can't make certain assumptions any more, that we quite simply have to reckon with a 'before' and an 'after' in Norwegian history. It's a long time since I got any response to what I write, but now, even while I'm still on the train, an unusual number of messages appear on my phone. You're bloody well setting the agenda, I think.

On my walk from Jernbanetorget it's as if my steps are lighter, I have the same feeling I had when I changed from winter boots to spring trainers as a child, I feel a buzz, and I have the impression that others must feel the same, because there's something about the way people are walking, the way they're looking around, a new alertness, and when I come into reception in Akersgata it's like being in a pressure cooker, I've never experienced such a rush as there is around this incident, everything is *speeded up,* it's as if I'm suddenly living in a country where something of decisive importance is happening; I sit down at my place, and in the next few hours, in front of my screen, on the phone, it's as if I'm filled with supernatural powers, I have super-hearing, super-vision, and in the midst of it all I decide to move house, to move at last, as soon as this affair is over, even though I hope the affair will last a long time, that the state I'm in, the energy, the adrenalin surge, will last a long time. But the incident is a signal, I must get out, out of the quagmire, out of the belief that everything is behind me. During the course of the day, at some point or other, I also see in my mind's eye a flash of a newspaper page – it must be many years ago that I saw it – a picture of Gry Storefjeld, and she's not alone, she has her arm round a young man, Nicolai Berge. 'Young Labour's new dream team' was the headline.

Then I forget about it.

The magazine normally has its planning meetings mid-week, but we've moved this one forward, a kind of state of emergency has been declared at the paper. We've just heard that the police have now released the names of the others.

The whole editorial team gathers in the meeting room to throw ideas around. 'Blankvann, our Pearl Harbour,' shouts someone, but is silenced by Martin. 'It's not that,' he says, 'don't get carried away, folks.' I almost have to admire Martin's calm authority as he chairs the excited session – for a few seconds I even manage to forget that he is my ex. When we split up I moved newspapers, I thought it was best for both of us. But then, a few years later, he suddenly followed me, unfortunately with a watertight alibi: he'd been offered the job of editor of the magazine I worked for. I bit my tongue and stayed on. I refused to move yet again.

A magazine has a fairly long lead time, and it's not easy to make a sudden U-turn. Nevertheless we decide at the meeting to create a new lead story for the issue due in one and a half weeks, a report which will reflect reactions, the mood on the street as it were, and I'm the one who suggests the title: 'A Quiet Mobilization'; photographers and journalists are allocated, I'm going to work together with Ulrik, and with Cappelen, the photographer we just call Capa, we haven't got many days before the deadline, but we'll have to do it.

I go back to my desk. An open-plan office has some advantages, but I made sure that I got set up with earbuds and headphones early on, not just in order to be able to concentrate better, but also to signal that I didn't want to be disturbed. *Noli me tangere.*

I go online at the same time as I spread out the newspapers around me. The whole time there are two questions which are pressing for an answer. Why? Who's behind it? Everything is bewilderingly fragmented, and many people are also repeating an upsetting rumour: the victims are said to have been decapitated. I can suddenly picture Arve Storefjeld lying there. *A white shirt stained red with blood.* For some reason the image leads me on to a famous photo of him – I had even used it in my book – from the year he was elected to the Storting for the first time. The picture was taken at the settlement below Raudberget, and Storen was standing outside the sauna one cold winter's day, wearing nothing but tight-fitting black boxer shorts with a Dovre label. It was quite something to see – Storen standing there bare-legged and bare-chested, the mountains glistening with snow behind him and frosty breath coming out of his mouth. It was a picture which rather than bringing to mind that old photo of Prime Minister Per Borten in underpants and a hat, made people think of the picture of the skater Eric Heiden in underpants at Savalen in Hedmark, and the caption explained that Storen was happy to advertise Dovre in both senses of the word – and he did later express his vociferous disapproval when Dovre's underwear production was moved out of the country to Lithuania. Presumably this iconic picture had attracted just as many female voters as the Chevrolet had won male voters in sparsely-populated districts.

By skimming through all the reports, all the pictures, all the maps – not least the updates after the rest of the names were revealed – I can piece together a fairly clear picture of the chain of events. According to the latest statement from his son Ståle Storefjeld, it was his father who had taken the initiative for that fateful trip to Nordmarka, they ought to use the place more, he said, his partner Sofie Nagel had only been there once previously. Storen rang Gry and asked her to come along, we must keep the footpaths open, he is supposed to have said. Arve and Sofie got into Storen's Chevrolet Blazer on Friday afternoon and drove into Nordmarka from Sørkedalen, they parked by Myrås and walked the last short stretch up to Valen, as the cabin was called. Gry drove up later that day together with her boyfriend, the French film director Jules Lefebvre. And the latter's daughter, Sylvie, nine years old, went along too because her mother couldn't have her that weekend after all, as they had arranged, she had something urgent to do – and this is a detail which does not escape attention, in online comments there is a great deal of scorn directed at this mother who could have saved her daughter if she'd been a bit less egocentric. Lefebvre and little Sylvie had slept in the annexe, it seemed as if they wanted to make the child feel welcome, and let her and her father share a room. The three others were sleeping in the main cabin, Arve Storefjeld and Sofie Nagel in one bedroom, Gry in the other.

Decapitated? The little girl as well?

It was Torben Lerche, a party colleague – and, as it transpired from a tactless parenthesis in one of the many reports: the chairman of Friends of the Hip Flask – who found them around four o'clock on Saturday, after he had 'on a whim' taken the metro up to Frognerseter and walked over to Blankvann to see if there was anyone at Valen, 'to share a cup of coffee and some waffles'. The police were alerted at once, and after that all hell broke loose, first with a patrol group which informed the central police station, then with police technicians and tacticians, followed by the media wolf-pack, a few on Saturday, and then the whole horde on Sunday; there were in general such comings and goings on the forest roads, including the one up from Hammeren, and a lack of respect for regulations of which the people at Blankvann farmstead had never seen the like.

'A barbaric attack on our civilization', read the headline in one paper. It was as if they regarded Storefjeld's cabin by Blankvann as a Roman outpost, on the frontier to the dark forests in the north.

Not even all those who lived in Oslo had known about Blankvann, but now the whole country knows where it is. A map with arrows was printed next to the news for the first few days, and especially for older Norwegians, all those who could remember that the 50-kilometre Holmenkollen ski race used to pass by Blankvann, it was sad news to hear about this place in connection with brutal killings. For many it must have seemed almost like a murder in a church.

The papers are full of photographs. I notice especially the ones taken from the southern end of Blankvann lake. How *evil* the steep hill at the north end looks, as if the devil himself has left an impression there. The pictures convey a creepy grey-blue atmosphere. Capa had been on the spot, and as we left the planning meeting he told us that an unpleasant odour hung over the whole plateau, almost as if it was scorched. Several others have said the same.

Before we go into town to look for material for the magazine, I meet Ulrik in one of the quiet rooms. Ulrik likes the quiet rooms, he has three boys aged nine, six and three. I get on well with Ulrik. He's from Horten, and started his career in the local paper, *Gjengangeren*. We have a common interest too: reggae. Ulrik maintains that his passion for reggae derives from Haile Selassie's state visit to Norway in 1954. When the Ethiopian emperor Ras Tafari Makonnen visited the navy harbour in Horten, Ulrik's grandfather got to meet him, and that had of course become a family legend. "'I and I" was ready for Zion from the moment I was born,' Ulrik used to joke. As if that was not enough, Robert Nesta Marley played at the Horten festival when Ulrik was ten. Incidentally, Ulrik thinks that The Clash, one of my favourite bands, know nothing about reggae. We argue about that a lot.

On a whiteboard there are sentences and names from a different story, and along the edges are yellow post-it stickers with mysterious keywords. 'Anything new from the investigation?' I ask. 'Worryingly little,' says Ulrik. 'Nothing about samurai swords or any of the other things people are speculating about?' 'Not a peep,' says Ulrik. 'The police have asked the public to give them information, they want to contact people who were out walking in the Blankvann area that Saturday or the day before.'

We discuss the approach for the magazine. I make suggestions about places we can visit. Ulrik says yes or no, he's a good sparring partner. 'Should we make a trip to Grønland or Tøyen?' I ask. The question remains hanging in the air. 'We have no idea of the nationality of the perpetrators, whether they are Norwegian or foreign,' Ulrik says after a while. I look at him. 'You mean: whether Muslims are behind it?' Ulrik nods, we both know this is an incendiary question. 'Didn't Storefjeld recently make some crass criticism of Muslims,' I said. 'Not of Muslims, are you mad,' said Ulrik.

'Of *Islamism*' – Ulrik looks at something he has noted on his notepad – '"this frightful mixture of religion and political ideology, a devil's brew". That could have provoked some of the most thin-skinned and extremist Muslim groups. As well as that he's made provocative statements about Iran on several occasions, recently as well.' 'Fuck,' I say. 'Fuck,' says Ulrik.

In the lift we meet Foyn, the news editor, on his way to the canteen. Foyn is wearing a T-shirt with the words Lifeguard Bondi Beach on it. He lets us know that something else has been leaked from the investigation. The terrorists used knives. The five victims weren't just killed, they were slaughtered – the tip-off used the right word. All were lying in their beds, presumably they were killed while they were asleep. During the night or early in the morning on Saturday. 'It's already circulating on the web,' says Foyn. Ulrik looks at me as if he's disappointed that it's not swords after all.

We reach our floor. Foyn holds us back to say that someone has started a wild theory that the terrorists might have killed the wrong people, that the target was a different one. That it was like the Lillehammer attack in 1973, when Israeli agents from Mossad killed the wrong person. I shake my head. 'Unlikely,' I say. 'Utter nonsense,' I say. Foyn has more theories, and won't let us go. If you asked him, the whole affair might just as well have something to do with Jules Lefebvre, he is supposed to have made an outspoken anti-Muslim film a few years back, with scenes which could be interpreted as mockery of the Prophet.

'Yaya have mercy,' mumbles Ulrik, making a note on his pad. 'This is a right tangle,' he says. 'I picked it up on the net,' Foyn says by way of excuse as he goes to the canteen to join the queue at the hot food counter. 'People aren't saying it out loud, but many think it was a bad thing that this Frenchman came to our country,' he says over his shoulder.

'Bloody internet,' says Ulrik, 'we haven't a chance in this race.' 'Don't complain,' I say, 'this story is big enough for everyone. We have to use our advantages. Write well, write thoroughly, write differently. Do you think Foyn's been on Bondi Beach in Sydney?' 'Hardly,' says Ulrik. 'And he'd never go swimming anywhere where there are larger fish than sprats.'

The following days all run into one. Out in the streets we experience something like a country in mourning. People are *grieving*. The whole country is affected by the incident; five dead people is perhaps not so many, but in Norway it is, there's also something about the method of killing, a knife, a dagger, which makes people shudder, and among the dead are people nearly everyone has a connection with, significant people, popular people, it is an incident which casts a shadow over everything. We, Norwegians, are not prepared for such things to happen, I think. We see it happening abroad, but we don't have enough imagination to see that it can happen here too. Even if only a few people have been killed, it is a whole nation's *consciousness* which has been hit. I discover that several of the large foreign papers are writing about the killings. Norway, otherwise invisible and uninteresting, is suddenly on the map.

The days are hot, and after lunch we often have downpours of tropical intensity. When I leave the office, the streets are soaked and it smells as if the town has been moved to a different place. The lime trees by the government offices are shining an other-worldly green. I am full of energy. The gleaming asphalt somehow has a stimulating effect. Small spontaneous memorials are held. Together with Ulrik and Capa I am present at one of them. On Youngstorget. Many have red roses with them, like people normally give out during election campaigns. Someone stands with a microphone and sings, a well-known troubadour from the Labour movement. People are crying, they are clinging to one another. There are speeches, people talk about the incident as a turning-point. The whole time I feel an upsetting mixture of emotions. I am deeply moved, just as affected by the memorial as everyone around me, but at the same time I'm on a job, I'm going to write about it, and it's easy to write about, because the scenes are perfect, as if heaven-sent. What material! This story has *everything*. Bestial killings, unknown terrorists, a spooky location for the crime, the forest beloved of all Oslo dwellers – nearly all the newspapers have used 'The Heart of Darkness' in one of their headlines – even a cabin which was used by the resistance during the war, and in addition one of the most written-about families in Norway, connected to the Labour Party into the bargain, the party which is the backbone of our state. It's almost too good to be true – I correct my thoughts at once: too awful to be true. 'Absolute evil,' it says in a wartime font on the front page of a paper – as if there are degrees of evil. 'Norway will never be the same again.'

The atmosphere in the editorial offices in Akersgata is so agitated that I take refuge several times in my secret thinking place, a place where I usually write by hand. I cross the street and walk up to the path between the two still pools of water in front of the government offices – a building which has always reminded me slightly of the United Nations headquarters in Manhattan – where I go in and sit down on the little group of chairs by the windows facing Grubbegata, around the corner from the lifts. First I pass through the barrier, entry check, they know I'm from Akersgata, they know me, see me sitting here often, doing little interviews here.

I get out my journalist's notebook and put it on my lap. It always puts me in a special mood sitting here by the wall of rough concrete with sandblasted art by Inger Sitter and Carl Nesjar. Right outside is the square called after Einar Gerhardsen; it occurs to me that I am at the core of Norway's modern history, I can almost feel the weight of it. I like working here because, paradoxically enough, it is strangely quiet in the lobby, as if it contains a kind of infectious concentration, and because, when I have seventeen floors of ministers and civil servants above me, I feel that I'm sitting in a centre, a control centre, at the same time that it gives me the feeling of something safe; it says a lot about Norway, about what a peaceful spot it is, that anyone at all can wander into this citadel of power. Whilst I think and make notes I can keep an eye on who comes in and enquires at reception, and who comes out of the lift. I've had some of my best tips from politicians who recognise me and stop by for a brief chat.

I sit jotting, look down at my pad, and see that I have written 11.9. And then I've written 11.3 and 7.7 – the last two dates referring to the terror attacks in Madrid and London. I write 23.8. Then I scribble it out. Not that. That's too dramatic. It would be wrong to link anything in Norway to those tragic dates. This will remain exceptional. Yes, it's a momentous incident. But not a knockout punch, after all.

According to the latest theories the killings are a plot against the Labour Party. So the terror action was deliberately targeted as an assault on our national system of values. I think: *It's an attack on the Norwegian model,* our improbably successful political system, our distribution of wealth, our enviable welfare, our ... *happiness.* The Labour party is closely bound up with social democracy and a tradition which is anathema to many Muslims, with its emancipation of women and sexual equality. 'Our twin towers have fallen,' declared one headline, which I suspect will appear a little exaggerated in retrospect, but in these days it expresses what many feel. Arve and Gry Storefjeld are the old and the new Labour Party, and it really is as if someone has attempted to topple two of the central pillars of the house of Norway. Both outside Storen's house in Maridalsveien and outside the flats in Westye Egebergs gate, where Gry lived, people have left flowers, many flowers. I have been there to interview neighbours and others, together with Ulrik and Capa.

It occurs to me that I was not far off the mark after all when in my conversation with my publisher I said that Arve Storefjeld would be more important for the party dead than alive. Storen – and Gry – have not just been killed, they have suffered martyrdom.

A high-ranking individual from the Department of Justice makes a detour over to me and asks if we have any fresh leads. I shake my head. 'Terrible, absolutely terrible,' he says and disappears into the lift. From my seat I can see the wall where Hannah Ryggen's blue tapestry 'We Live on a Star' is hanging. Occasionally I go over and look at it, just to adjust my short-sighted perspective. But not today. I'm thinking. I'm trying to fit the pieces together.

It has emerged that the dead Frenchman was a member of Parti Socialiste, the sister party to our Labour Party, and this, together with the knowledge that Sofie Nagel, Storen's partner, was also a central figure in the party machine in Youngstorget, fuels the speculation that the attack is directed against the social democratic philosophy, or if you like the house of Norway, as if it was known that even a relatively small bomb in the foundations would shake the whole social edifice. Only one thing is puzzling, and doesn't fit in: little Sylvie, and few things upset me more than that one of the victims is a nine-year-old girl. That is unbearable. A sylph. And she played the violin. Even worse. She is said to have been a gifted musician. Unbearable. The thought of her lying in bed asleep, and then someone comes along and puts her to death, sticks a knife in her. How can a human being be capable of something like that? I can't find any better explanation than the words of the headline: absolute evil.

There's something else as well. My own yearning for children. Martin and I tried in vain. Consulted experts, in vain. No-one could help. In the end we just accepted it. Our fate to be childless. But I yearned. Every time I see one of the many pictures of little Sylvie printed in the papers I get a lump in my throat. It is unbearable. That lovely little girl. She should have played Paganini's Cantabile in D Major so that it brought tears to people's eyes.

A blessing on every bomb which struck a Gothic building, if only a child was spared! Yes, says a voice inside me. Nordahl Grieg was right.

We get the new leading section for the magazine ready in time. Everyone is pleased, only Martin looks doubtful. But he keeps the title 'A Quiet Mobilization', and nods to me without saying anything.

The next few days are quiet, but in the same way as my fellow countrymen I am caught up in the horrifying incident; I try to remain sober, keep it at a distance, but I am caught up, my whole sensory system is affected, I talk to people differently, in a lower voice. Despite the limited extent of the terror, it is a watershed in our history; it is as if a new sensibility has awoken in the population, I can see it in social interactions, in people's eyes. Isn't there also some fear mixed in with it? Many are feeling afraid. As if the security we have practically taken for granted for so long has been pulverized. From the train window I discover that the Norwegian flag is flying from many flagpoles. *Precisely at this moment we know what freedom is.* Nordahl Grieg has taken on a new relevance.

Even though nothing has been leaked from the forensic examinations, the post-mortems, rumours begin to circulate about the kind of knife used, it is said to be a specialised one. This strengthens the suspicion that professional assassins were involved, it's quite a feat to manage to put five people to death without any of them getting out of bed, it must have happened quickly and silently. Ice-cold, premeditated. Several newspapers speculate, print pictures of a number of potential knives, and suddenly, like everyone else, I know the difference between an SOG combat knife and a butterfly knife.

The significance of the crime slowly becomes clearer. Five people are killed on a weekend cabin trip. It's not just an attack on a political system, it's an attack on the folk soul of Norway, on the hub of Norwegians' existence. Forest trips. Cabin life. *Hygge. The target was chosen to spread as much fear as possible,* I wrote in a new article. That is the aim of terror: to create fear. Calculated, heartless violence.

I work on finishing the book about Storen, making the necessary adjustments. When the time comes I go to the funerals, the one in Trefoldighets Church for Arve Storefjeld, the one for Gry in Gamle Aker Church, the one for Sofie Nagel in the chapel at Vestre Cemetery, the one for little Sylvie in Grefsen Church – Lefebvre was buried in France. I don't know whether it is planned or by chance, but they are on different days, so that anyone who wants to can attend them all. And it's not just me who attends, the whole press turns up, there's an unprecedented media presence, streams of celebrities, especially in Trefoldighets Church, but also in Gamle Aker Church where there's simply not enough room for everyone; I struggle with forbidden thoughts, because it's like at a première, I can't help thinking that, and everyone competes to assume the most convincing expression of grief, it's like an entrance test for drama school, 'act grief' – there are cameras everywhere too – but actually there's no need to act, everyone *is* shocked, not least at the thought of the little girl, the whole church is filled with sniffing, with hankies constantly pressed to eyes. It is … it is … impossible to describe, a shiver, the scratch of a knifeblade down your spine, and I am surprised at myself, I haven't been in a church for a decade apart from a couple of weddings and a baptism, I never go to funerals, I detest funerals, but now I can't get enough of sitting on hard church pews saying goodbye to people, even people I hardly know, these individuals who have been put to death in such a shockingly brutal fashion in a cabin deep in the forest. I sing those psalms I haven't heard for a long time, some I haven't heard since my childhood. 'When other helpers fail and comforts flee / Help of the helpless, oh, abide with me.' Especially this 'help of the helpless' brings me to my knees mentally; I sing as loudly as I have ever done, and even so I can hardly hear my own voice in the swell, and I cry; the sight of the coffins, the nave decorated with flowers, the chords of the organ which make walls and floor shake, the ritual, the whole ceremony is unbearable, the chiming of the bells from the tower sinks into my body in a deep and meaningful way.

I cry. Storen was known for crying; once a spiteful critic had said that his only talent was his ability to cry. Storen always had a tear in the corner of his eye as he sang workers' songs, or when in a speech he uttered some particularly unctuous words, he could resemble Dickens crying over his own text as he read aloud from his novels; a radical left-wing newspaper commented a little sourly that it seemed that Storen's ability to cry had infected a whole nation, but not even that sarcastic remark could prevent the tears flowing, I cry and cry, I can't cry enough, no-one can cry enough, and everywhere we are reminded of the same values, the Prime Minister too, more steadfast than ever, mentions them in his moving speech at Arve Storefjeld's funeral, and it makes no difference if they are the Labour Party's traditional values, suddenly the whole country is social-democratic: community, unity, solidarity. The Prime Minister's final words, as he faced Storen's coffin, provoked a hushed collective sob: 'You were Norway, when Norway was best.'

I included that sentence in the book.

There are also a couple of special arrangements with singers; one of them is an open-air concert in Eidsvolls plass, from a stage erected in Studenterlunden. It takes place in the evening and the whole of Spikersuppa is chock-full of people, because it's not just a matter of five murdered individuals, not even if some of them are famous, even idolised, it's an attack on Norway, and people want to show that they're not afraid, that they're standing together, *each sister and each brother*, and several of the country's most well-known performers sing their most emotional songs in memory of the dead, and it's a bit cold and people stand close together, and many take out their lighters or light up their mobile phones and hold them up, the whole area between the Storting and the theatre is a human sea full of phosphorescence. Of course it is moving, especially when a popular ballad singer goes on stage and performs one of his most folksy songs which now, in this mournful context, takes on a new, almost religious tone, with the result that afterwards it becomes even more beloved, played over and over again on the radio, from now on always accompanied by tears because so many, at the sound of this song, think about that black Saturday, the five dead, meaninglessly wiped out, and we cry even more, it's as if we find a release for pent-up feelings, as if the incident is a welcome opportunity and an excuse to let it all hang out, a kind of therapy. It's on one of these days, by the radio in the kitchen in my town house, that I realise that I'm not just crying for the dead, and especially the little girl, but that I am crying just as much for myself, for all that is sad, all that is lost, all I can't put into words, the dreadful thought that all the important things in life might lie behind me; it is liberating to be able to sit there on a bench in a church, stand there in Spikersuppa, close to other people, sit alone at my kitchen table listening to a simple song, and let the tears flow.

The media have rarely seen better days; the news broadcasts have even more viewers, the print runs of newspapers reach record heights, people log in to online newspapers as never before. Proprietors and editors adopt sorrowful expressions, whilst in secret they are thanking the powers that be for a story that is so exceptional that the public can't get enough of it. I would like to suppress my own thoughts, but at the same time I must be honest: that's the way things are.

And in the midst of all this I am a whirlwind, my body is simply bubbling with adrenalin and dopamin and serotonin, and in the course of a few days I get a new final chapter written for the book about Arve Storefjeld, plus a gem of a Foreword, I sit writing in my study at home with a sandwich on a plate beside me, something simple, egg, tomato, mayonnaise and chives; I also insert several new sections, or 'fragments', as I call them, sections of a third of a page with a blank line before and after – I write more about Valen in particular, the cabin by Blankvann which was originally built by Storen's father and which has been used ever since by Labour Party people for 'confidential' conversations, as well as giving shelter to resistance fighters during the war. It was one of the few cabins in Nordmarka which was owned by a private individual and not by the Løvenskiold family, and I feel that it must have played a role in the history of the party. The cabin was a kind of secret enclave. It must have echoed round the walls when they sang that line from the Internationale in Norwegian 'Så samles vi på valen' – 'Let's unite on the field of battle' – at Valen. And now, in almost prophetic fashion, Storen has fallen there.

I also put in more about Mosse, Arve Storefjeld's wife, who died when Gry was young; I include more about her research into working life at Fafo, because several interesting facts have emerged about her in connection with recent events – the words just come to me, ready formed, I sit at my green iMac and can suddenly channel a new linguistic vitality, the sentences well up from an underground spring which until now has been hidden from me; I go to the hairdresser's, get my hair cut shorter and coloured darker, as if I want to prepare to be in the media spotlight, want to look as good as possible, but also because I feel different, less grey, less middle-aged, less apathetic – less left behind. Several people remark that I look good, they ask if I'm in love – no, I think, it's just a Norwegian tragedy which has brought the colour to my cheeks – and to crown it all I feel more rebellious, I think about getting out my old red leather jacket, the Chrissie Hynde jacket, but I stop myself, I mustn't exaggerate; nevertheless I spend more time on make-up, use my black eye-liner liberally, I make my mind up that I'm going to the Øya festival next year, to hell with it, I think, even if I'll be forty by then, and one day I give a pretty cheeky answer to a remark by the chief editor himself, something I would never have dared to do a couple of weeks earlier; he looks at me in surprise, then smiles and gives me the thumbs-up, I can do whatever I like, go with the flow, I'm a valuable resource for the paper, I am indispensable, I'm on fire, I'm special, so special, I was one of the living dead, I've got my life back, I'm gonna use my, my, my imagination.

After having written a new in-depth article about Storen's career, where in long passages I used the racy and subjective language of new journalism, and after being on TV, in several programmes in fact – 'We will be hearing comments from Ine Wang, who is about to publish a new book about Arve Storefjeld' – I can feel a rush of intoxication, a wish for it to last; I think about the folk tale of the magic flounder, which is all about never being satisfied no matter how well things are going, but I suppress the thought quickly, because I want more, more attention, I want to feel more of the kick I get in my insides, this glow of wellbeing, and that's when I have a brilliant idea, which to be honest must have been in the back of my mind for a long time – ever since that flash of memory, the image of a newspaper with the headline 'Young Labour's New Dream Team' – because suddenly it just pops up as an obvious thought: Berge.

I must mull it over. Let it mature.

On the train home in the evening, which is later with every day that passes, I read the property adverts in the morning paper. I'm looking for something in Kampen, or why not the steep hills above Ekeberg, with a view over something completely different than the wall of a town house.

I'm sitting with Ulrik in the canteen. Ulrik always eats bread with mackerel in tomato sauce, it's one of his peculiarities, or rather the peculiarity is that he doesn't bother about the fact that it makes his breath smell. Stabburet's mackerel in tomato sauce is Norwegian garlic, he says when I tease him. He for his part laughs at me, always using two slices of bread with the filling between them. The sandwich lass, he calls me. At least I don't just eat lettuce like the others, I say, pointing to the queue of slim female journalists at a counter which is spilling over with greenery. We talk about the story. The police are still not giving out much information. According to Ulrik that's because they're not getting anywhere. Everyone understands that there were few or no traces, that the terrorists must have been remarkably well-trained. It seems as if the investigators are just waiting for a group to announce that they are behind the crime. For some document or other to appear on the net. Every day on the evening news the ramrod-straight police spokesperson, the female head of the Violent and Sexual Crime division of Oslo Police, stands by the steps of the police headquarters, looking sad, and talking in metaphors, saying that they are still looking for the black box which can provide an explanation of what happened in the forest. My sources can't contribute much either, but I have one good contact, and he can confirm what Ulrik said: there were neither fingerprints nor footprints left by the terrorists at the scene, they simply had no significant leads at all. The police had searched in vain for tyre prints on the two possible roads nearby. Neither did they have any tips about suspicious cars. One person who had spent the night at a student cabin not far away reckoned that she had heard the sound of a helicopter early in the morning. Impossible, I think. A helicopter! Can that be right?

Ulrik is the only person I know with rasta hair, short dreadlocks. I suspect it is more a camouflage than a reflection of his musical tastes – it gives him access to many unorthodox milieus. Ulrik is a capable journalist, with some of the qualities of a hacker, and now he tells me calmly about an important detail which the police have still not made public: the criminals had not used their knives in random fashion. 'Oh really?' I say. Ulrik pauses before he answers: 'All the victims were found in their beds with their throats cut.'

I am shaken. Perhaps it's not strange that there were rumours about beheading to begin with. I look at the bits of mackerel and tomato on Ulrik's plate. I feel like spitting out the food I have in my mouth. I can visualise it. Try to visualise it. It's impossible to understand. That in this idyll, this peaceful place deep inside Nordmarka, a cabin surrounded by wild flowers, people have been slaughtered like animals. In Ulrik's eyes this strengthens the theory about an attack on the Labour Party. 'The symbolism is obvious,' he says. 'Someone wants to throttle the party.'

The information makes my heart beat more quickly. I have to get up to fetch more water, as if I suddenly have problems with my own throat.

Why were they put to death in there? I stand with my glass in my hand, looking at Ulrik's woven locks as I listen to him speculating. Might it be connected to the fact that Valen was for a long time a kind of secret in the party, a place where central decisions had been made for several decades? Ulrik holds out his hands, gives up. 'Do you vote Labour?' I ask. 'No, I don't,' says Ulrik, 'I vote far left of Labour. "Get up, stand up." Do you want another sandwich? Have you tried mackerel in tomato between goat's cheese and salami?'

Then the news breaks. I don't pick it up at first, I'm late that morning and have to run for the train. On the way into town I sit and doze, but just before the central station, as I look out and think that the smooth façade of Oslo Plaza resembles a gigantic knife blade pointing at the sky, my mobile vibrates. It's a text from Ulrik: a terrorist organization called 'Norway for Muslims' has declared it is behind the attack. In the central station I see fewer people than normal from an immigrant background. Perhaps they don't dare come out after they've heard the news, I think. Perhaps they're ringing one another: stay indoors! Now there'll be trouble! The news dominates all the media for the whole day. The net overflows with hateful comments. Several dark blue politicians demand immediate closure of the borders. Then it is revealed that a group of lads from the West End are behind it, that it's a joke, a bet about how far you can get the public to believe something so far-fetched. They should thank their lucky stars that they're not lynched by indignant people. 'What is wrong with the youth of today?' can be heard from all sides, not least in letters to the papers from older citizens over the next few days.

There are in fact few indications to support the idea that the terrorists are Muslims. We need to keep an open mind, explains the police spokesperson after the blunder. That pale blue blouse really suits her, I think, and her mascara is perfectly applied. I watch it on TV that evening, at home in my living room, holding a cup of green tea in my hands. As if to take her at her word, another TV channel puts forward a theory about Russians. They dig out something I have touched on in my book, which is just about to go to press. The background is that Storen did his military service in 1968. He was at the Elvenes border station on that June day when Soviet tanks were driven up to the Norwegian border. It was a response to an extensive NATO exercise in Troms. People believed there was a danger of war and an incipient global conflict. Arve Storefjeld never forgot it, perhaps because he had literally stared down the barrel of a Soviet tank gun. And not many weeks later the armoured tanks rolled into Czechoslovakia. I'll never trust those bloody Russians, was one of Storen's most well-known slogans. In his eyes the Cold War was not over. Russia will never be more than a nest of bandits, he is supposed to have said during an official dinner, after a couple of glasses too many. I thought about the girl who had heard a helicopter. Could it really have been the Russians who put paid to him? But then why not poison him with polonium? I didn't go much for that theory. What's next? I think, putting my teacup down. Nothing seems impossible.

During this confused time I often seek out the lobby of the government offices; I sit there in deep concentration with my pad, making notes, searching for spark plugs. The calm reception area has become a refuge, an air-raid shelter, where I try to write, to gather threads, to draw up a kind of chart which hopefully can give me an overview. Now that some time has passed since the incident, criticism has begun to be heard: people want someone to blame. Could the killings have been prevented? Some claim that the police had been warned of threats in advance. The police deny this. People don't give up. It leaks out that the scene was contaminated before the forensic technicians arrived to preserve the evidence, the newspapers overflow with complaints about the incompetence and lack of vigilance of the police. And since everyone assumes it was terrorists, an attack on Norway – where was Special Branch? Why did they not pick up the danger signals? Why wasn't the plot detected? In general: shouldn't key politicians be better protected?

Yes, and why is this place not better protected, I think, as I nod to one of the state secretaries from the Prime Minister's office, a man I once flirted with at a boring reception in City Hall.

On the other hand: who could predict something like this, I think, and discover that I have been doodling instead of noting points. Is that not the core of the matter? Our inability to predict. It has become a chorus, an excuse, at the same time an expression of impotence: who could have foreseen that a crime like that was possible on Norwegian territory? And in the forest? It is beyond our imagination, said a well-known cultural representative on one of the many TV programmes.

So cold-blooded, so efficient, so totally without warning. Again and again in the columns, in the commentaries.

The population is waiting for answers, as if that would be some form of comfort: who is behind the crime?

I'm sitting in the government building with my eyes resting on Hannah Ryggen's tapestry 'We Live on a Star'. I try to look at the Blankvann incident from a distance, to discover a new opening. I can't find one. All I have on my notepad is an embroidery of ink. Suddenly I feel afraid. The affair is beginning to be exhausted, and the amazing euphoria is diminishing; I'm like a drug addict, I want to find something to keep my energy going, I search for something unusual, something to write about that no-one else has thought of. A surprising angle, I think, a shift of perspective, I think, the far side of the moon, I think.

Then I have it: Berge. I've been thinking about it for a long time, not been sure, suddenly I am sure.

I look around, one of the receptionists sends me a smile, as if to signal that she recognises me; perhaps she's just seen me on TV. I write it on my pad in capital letters: BERGE. I study the name. The word. I am aware of a slight resistance. The fear of crossing a border. Once more: should I let it drop?

One of the few things I dislike about my daily life at the magazine is that I have to enter Martin's glass office in order to get the green light – Martin, once my lover, now my ex, and to crown it all: my boss. I curse this working arrangement, and when I come back from the government offices I have to sit in a quiet room for several minutes to collect myself before I enter the enclosure where Martin is sitting. Almost without looking up he tells me that he was not happy with the report in the magazine about the wider repercussions of the Blankvann incident, it was too flat, he says, too sentimental, but without sending a shiver down any spines; he said nothing about this at the post-production meeting, but now he drones on as if he thinks it's entirely my fault, and finishes with a salvo that the whole effort had no punch. That last word makes me want to remind him that he once sang in my ear 'Every Little Thing She Does Is Magic', but I bite my tongue, and I don't argue either, instead I present my idea. 'I want to do something about Nicolai Berge,' I say. Martin says no abruptly. 'A bad idea,' he says. 'You haven't even heard what the idea is,' I say. 'Well, tell me then,' he says impatiently. I explain. Nicolai Berge was Gry Storefjeld's boyfriend for four years, they lived together. I want to do a portrait of him in the magazine. Pause. Martin looks at me. I can't understand how I could once have been *turned on* by that look. I'm nervous about what's coming, and at the same time it irritates me to have to stand there like a schoolgirl in front of a man who once lay on my breast like a contented child. To make it worse Martin now affects the kind of goatee beard which reminds me of Magne Furuholmen of AHA and other trendy men, and which he is constantly stroking with his index finger. 'I doubt whether you could manage it,' he says then. 'It's a tricky assignment.'

That last remark was unnecessary. He's sitting and I'm standing, several pairs of eyes are following us through the glass walls. Are they hoping for a scene? 'How about doing an interview with little Sylvie's mother?' says Martin. On his desk is a picture of Sylvie performing at a concert; the sight of it makes me go weak at the knees, adorable Sylvie in a black velvet dress and with a face absorbed by the music. 'She won't do it,' I say. 'And anyway too much has been written about little Sylvie.' Martin looks at me sharply. 'Surely enough has been written about Gry Storefjeld too,' he says. 'Because that's what you're after, isn't it?'

He's right as far as it goes, of course. Page after page has been written about Gry Storefjeld, the young woman you could say was killed on the threshold of a brilliant future in politics, a clear candidate for Secretary of State if Labour won the election in 2009, or at least an undersecretary, and many regarded her as a future Prime Minister. 'Gry is the new Gro,' people said when she arrived on the scene, young and sexy and quick-witted, just like the former Prime Minister Gro Harlem Brundtland. I remember that Martin – it must have been at the end of our relationship – thought people made too much of her. He doesn't dare to repeat that statement now. 'What about if I find the "other" story,' I said. 'It may be that Nicolai Berge can tell us things about Gry that no-one has heard before.' I'm not sure, I just throw it out, I've heard rumours about how depressed he was after the break-up four years ago. Martin plucks at his artistic goatee and shakes his head. For me it's an idea which ought to catch on at once. 'I want to do an extended interview,' I said, 'he must be affected by it, he shared Gry Storefjeld's bed for four years.' There's always a chance – and this I just think to myself – that he'll be able to tell us something about how it was in Young Labour and the Labour Party, which both were a part of. People can't seem to get enough of information which can tell us more about the dead, not least Gry Storefjeld.

'I'm not convinced, it might just as easily be a complete mistake,' he says, pretending to clear a desk which is impossibly cluttered. I can see a packet of crispbread and a tube of cream cheese. I feel a flicker of my old tenderness for him, he hasn't time to eat in the canteen, he sits here in his glass cage snacking on a crispbread. Nevertheless: to my ears his tone sounds condescending. Instead of giving reasons for his scepticism he begins to ask how things are with me, as if he knows that I'm struggling, or has heard someone say that I'm struggling, that I'm not too good. He has married again, lives in Nordstrand, in a villa, has had a child as well. This last fact niggles at me, makes me think that the fault lies, lay, with me. I would like to have had a child. More than anything I want a child. To give birth. Rachel told me that it felt as if gravity was suspended. That she had never felt so alive. I smiled when she said that, but I cried on the train going home.

'Are you seeing anyone at present?' he asks. 'Maybe,' I say. Too quickly, he knows I'm lying.

His refusal makes me feel a stirring of hatred. How could it turn out like this? How can I suddenly regard a man whose tongue I loved to feel between my legs as my biggest opponent? And at the same time I cannot deny that my relationship with Martin changed my life, he helped me to become a better journalist, made me sparkle, he encouraged me to write some of the articles I now regard as my finest. Can you hate someone who has practically saved you?

'But think about it,' I say. 'What a headline!' I say. Martin is not so stupid, of course he understands. To get a picture of Gry Storefjeld through Nicolai Berge's eyes would be an incredible scoop.

'Is that what we need now?' he says. 'Another portrait?'

I'm standing inside Martin's glass office. He is talking loudly. People can hear us through the walls. I think about the expression 'bull in a china shop'. What if I broke something?

'I'm not talking about an ordinary portrait,' I say. 'You'll get a *once-in-a-lifetime* portrait. Just think of reading an interview with Prince Charles the week after Diana's death,' I say. 'You're exaggerating,' he says, 'you've always exaggerated.' But he has to smile, I can see he can't find any more arguments against it.

The whole situation, me presenting a good idea to a sceptical man, reminds me of something I have experienced before, and I have to dig down in my memory to find it: the Beat boys. Music's patriarchy. A bearing which proclaims, without saying it out loud, that girls have no idea. An attitude which is funny when you're nine, but depressing when you're nineteen. How ambitious I was during that time. And ruthless. I remember the savage music reviews I wrote in *Beat*, fierce criticisms with just one aim: to make people take note of my name. My musical taste. My skill as a writer. Because I could write, I could write the pants off them all; I had been an outsider as a child, as a teenager, the others took up sports, dancing, scouting, I sat in my room in Etterstad and listened to music, read English and American music magazines. But then I discovered writing, wrote a diary, wrote with fearless honesty, wrote about music, wrote with fearless honesty about that too, openly subjectively, I collected words, aggressive words, I grew my fringe as long as Chrissie Hynde's, I drew lots of black round my eyes, dressed in black from top to toe like a Blitz supporter, including the obligatory Doc Martens, and moved from Etterstad to the centre; I was single-minded, I was unstoppable, I found the places where the Beat boys hung out, like Los Amigos, the editorial 'canteen', where I ordered tex-mex food and found a place beside them, worked out the jargon, asked if I could write; OK, show us something, they said, and I slammed some reviews of records they certainly hadn't heard of on the table, and they liked it, they were actually a bit impressed, printed them in the magazine, but I wanted to write more, OK, they said, do an interview, they said, show us what you can do, they said; we drank beer at Sardine's, I'll bloody well show them, I thought, I'll do an interview they've never imagined possible. I went to London, because I had picked out a concert in the English magazines, and I got hold of a ticket to the Dominion Theatre; there were several artists on the programme, but I was sitting there to hear David Bowie with a new band, it was July 1988, and Bowie was between stations, perhaps at the lowest point of his career, both the latest album and the latest tour had bombed, and afterwards I stood waiting outside the performers' entrance, and there was actually no-one else waiting, I was nineteen and boldness incarnate, and when Bowie came out I held up a placard: 'I'll write the best interview ever!' Of course it was the purest luck, but he came over to me with a grin which showed his sharp incisors, and I wasn't star-struck, I was just firing on all cylinders, and he said 'You'll have to prove it', and the next morning we met at a little café, or rather a pub, in Charlotte Street, and I did the best interview that anyone has done with David Bowie, in Norway at least, and I smacked it down on the table in front of the Beat boys, and now they were really impressed, because the interview made no mention of 'Life on Mars' or Ziggy Stardust, but outlined Bowie's progressive thoughts about just being a band member and playing in a group called Tin Machine, and with that I was one of the few girls who gained entrance to this pretty sectarian male environment.

I'm standing in Martin's cubby-hole. I want to grab his shoulders and shake him, say fucking hell, wake up, but I manage to stop myself. 'Don't you remember how people talked when their relationship became public?' I say. 'Gry Storefjeld and Nicolai Berge, two children of the two powerful Labour dynasties? It was as if Crown Prince Haakon Magnus had got together with Crown Princess Victoria of fucking Sweden! It's a gigantic story!'

'OK, go with it then,' he says, looking down and not wanting to meet my eyes. And as I'm on the way out: 'Be careful'. Perhaps I should have turned back and asked what he meant, but I don't, instead I smile at all the faces outside which can't hide their disappointment that the expected scene didn't materialise, that nothing at all was hurled against the glass wall. Fuck you, I think. Just wait, you stupid losers.

I'm a quick worker, and already the same day I manage to get hold of Nicolai Berge on the phone. He seems surprised at my request and says no to start with. Firmly. Damn, I think, but I know you must never give up, so I explain the idea behind the portrait, appeal to him, say it would interest our readers greatly – I almost come right out with it: it would satisfy a desperate need. He asks for time to think.

The thought occurs to me in a flash: look at anybody's life. There are perhaps twenty days over the course of it which are dramatic or decisive. I was living through some of those days now.

I'm sitting at my desk with my earphones on, and I've already noted a few keywords about Berge, 29 years old, things I know, and the most intriguing thing about him is not that he studied the history of religion but that he made his debut as an author whilst he was still at university, straight after he and Gry Storefjeld broke up. Unfortunately – or unfortunately for the interview, I think – his two short-story collections have been received with a solid dose of scepticism. In my own paper an old hand dismissed the latest one in few words. When I look online I find that another reviewer makes fun of a novella in which a small place in Siberia is slowly transformed into a place on a different planet, whilst a third mocks a story called 'The Great Macaw', in which a scarlet macaw which has been captured in the jungle opens its beak and reveals that it is Pablo Picasso, and proceeds to *prove* it. 'When fantasy runs riot' is the headline. I had leafed through the first collection, *Incomprehensible Stories*, but there was nothing in what I read which caught my attention, perhaps partly because the first one I read seemed so divorced from reality. When I did more research I discovered that the second collection had been rejected by the Norwegian Cultural Council, which supports almost all published fiction. Berge had applied to join the Norwegian Society of Authors, but been refused. Most people seemed to agree that Nicolai Berge should never have tried to become a writer.

I feel tired, and go over to the coffee machine. Ulrik comes past. Thanks to a source in the police he now knows more about the method of killing. 'It was definitely not amateurs who were demonstrating their skill with knives,' says Ulrik, looking meaningfully at me. 'The strike didn't come from in front, aimed at the throat, like you see in films,' Ulrik explains. 'The knife was probably held as you would hold a ski stick, which is something only professionals do, with the blade facing away from you, and the knife was stuck in from the side of the neck, thrust in and pulled backwards towards the ear and the back of the neck.' Ulrik is demonstrating how it happened, acting out a pantomime next to the coffee machine; 'You can get much greater force with the knife by using this method,' he goes on, 'and presumably he held his left hand over the victim's mouth in order to stifle any sounds and stop blood coming out that way too.' As Ulrik tries to show what he means and his arms wave about in front of me, I see that he has a stamp on the back of his hand from some club or concert; we're the same age, I think, and he has three children, but he still has time to go out, he never sits at home sulking about the misery of existence. Ulrik's eagerness is almost comical, several others have been attracted by the performance and gather at the coffee machine, and Ulrik has to repeat everything again; he likes talking about technical precision, how you hold the knife, how you thrust, as if he's revelling in the bloody details. The art of liquidating another person. But this of course strengthens the theory that the killers have military training. 'We can't rule out that they might actually be elite soldiers,' says Ulrik. 'It's not certain they killed from hatred or evil,' he says, and pauses as if he knows he's about to say something controversial: 'They are soldiers, they're at war, the mission was to destroy the enemy.'

So genuine terrorists, I think. I look at the cup in my hand, suddenly the liquid looks reddish-brown. And it doesn't smell of coffee any more.

Before people can protest, Ulrik tells us that another piece of information has been leaked: on Saturday an early-morning hiker had observed a man with a black beard walking stealthily through the forest just below Blankvann hill. When the man realised he'd been seen, he stared back at the hiker with what the man described as a 'fanatic' look, before he sprang onwards through the fir trees, away from the path. The man appeared well-trained, moved silently and with great suppleness. 'I'm not prejudiced, but he looked like a Muslim, a jihadist,' the hiker apparently said.

'Bloody hell,' said someone. 'Better get your Koran out,' said another.

I go back to my desk and jot down what Ulrik said, though I don't know why, I'll never forget it. I underline 'military training', just to have something to do, but my thoughts wander back to Nicolai Berge and Gry Storefjeld again. There was something piquant about their relationship, because even if you can't talk about a turf war in the Labour Party, there had always been two distinct wings, one which favoured the trades union movement and one which emphasized ideas and visions. Arve Storefjeld represented the first, and Olaf Berge, political scientist and academic, the second. Many people thought that Olaf Berge had no business being in the Labour Party, even though he had grown up in Groruddalen, where his father worked in an ironworks. Olaf always said that his father reminded him of Kjell Aukrust's fictional inventor Reodor Felgen, because he was unusually inventive; he designed a new kind of door handle and window catch which he patented, and in time he founded his own factory in Groruddalen. He became a wealthy man and moved his family to Bygdøy allé. Together with his younger brother and sister Olaf played tennis and went sailing, but whilst they disappeared unprotesting into the middle classes, Olaf remained true to the family's working-class roots and became involved in politics from an early age. Maj Runesen, Nicolai's mother, came from Odda and belonged to the aristocracy of the Labour movement, with a heroic hiss of smelting furnaces and the nobility of labour.

When Gry and Nicolai became a couple you could hardly talk about a Romeo and Juliet story, but it stirred enough curiosity to be discussed in the media, and as far as I remember some people wrote that they were 'the future of the Labour Party', a sign that the old conflicts had vanished into the mists of time.

I ring Nicolai Berge again. He says OK, he'll do it. I feel elated. Do I? Yes, I feel elated. We agree a time and place.

I don't see Ulrik for a few days. Then he's back, and gets me to go out with him to the smoking terrace, even though I don't smoke. He lights a cigarette with the Zippo lighter he got after he saw one for the first time on the original cover of the Marley album *Catch a Fire*. I can see how he enjoys the first pull, at the same time as he complains that fewer and fewer people use the terrace. 'People are such sissies nowadays,' he says, before we pass on to an exchange of the latest news about the Blankvann incident, like most people in the offices. For the first time Ulrik airs a theory that perhaps terrorists weren't behind it. 'There have been several whispers about this,' he says. 'What if it's all to do with sex? Jealousy of the most bloody and Othello-inspired type?' I don't know whether it's because of what he's saying, but I feel the desire to begin smoking again, and I'm on the point of begging a cigarette; I've rediscovered my inner rebel, I think, and at the same time I wonder whether I've thrown out my Doc Martens or not. 'Storen had some dark secrets,' says Ulrik, 'and there are lots of rumours that Lefebvre left behind a complicated love life in France, including a particularly nasty divorce, and a wife with several ambitious brothers.'

I have to laugh. 'Honestly, Ulrik,' I say, 'are you sure there's no ganja in that cigarette?' I laugh, but I'm listening, I take note of everything he says, I pay attention as I've never done before, as if I'm a Sherlock Holmes and believe that I alone can solve the case, see the bagatelle which no-one else has seen, a clue, something or other which can reveal the identity of the perpetrators. On the train on the way home too I play with various theories. The newspaper headlines have almost reached mythological pitch. People are greedy for any new bits of information, regardless of how small they are, and the papers know that. Now and then they spend several days and tens of pages on embroidering a single detail, as if it's the key to everything. Just take this Scottish handkerchief. The crime scene investigators had found a handkerchief with an unusual pattern just by the cabin. There was a picture of it in the paper. A checked pattern of green and black, but also with some thin blue stripes. It resembled a tartan. Suddenly every Tom, Dick and Harry knew everything about kilts and tartans and clans in Scotland. The strange thing was that this pattern was not one of the almost 6000 known tartans. What was the link? Was the handkerchief a symbol of a fight for independence?

I read everything I can get my hands on, follow every last snippet on the case on TV, sit on the sofa at home in my town house with a tuna sandwich or a sandwich of roast beef and horseradish sauce, watching the news, watching the TV debates which pick up on the Blankvann killings, watch interviews with terror experts, and in Storen's case, documentaries made up of clips from old newsreels – fortunately I don't see anything which makes me need to revise the content of my book. Several hikers took pictures in Nordmarka on the same Saturday as the murders took place, and these now find their way into the papers. The evening news even shows a video, in fact they show it over and over again, of the police arriving at the scene in the afternoon, with weapons and everything; the video lasts perhaps half a minute and is taken with a mobile camera by a man on his way to Kobberhaug hostel. It's poor quality, with shaky images, but people want to see it again and again, the video gives them the illusion of being close to the crime, almost like that famous Zapruder film of the shooting of Kennedy; you shiver and imagine that the killings happened just minutes before this was filmed, even though you know that the terrorists attacked in the morning. I try to resist, but I too sit there as if it's the first film of life on Mars, I too want to watch this video again and again. Afterwards I go to my little office where I sit at my machine and let my fingers dance over the yielding, inspiring keys which give me the impression that my fingers are rebounding. I write more or less just to be writing something, I'm preparing for my meeting with Nicolai Berge, I have the feeling that this meeting might give me some stories, not least about Gry Storefjeld, which will make readers sit up and take notice. I'm having a ball right now, I'm a journalist, on the front line, carrying out reconnaissance, I'm supplying the product everyone is hungry for: reality, or fragments of reality, and every tiny detail is received as precious knowledge, precisely because it can lead to a greater understanding of the whole, can quite simply lead the reader to the truth.

It's cold and drizzling when I meet Nicolai Berge on a day in the middle of September, he's the one who suggested the place, I don't know why, it's a small restaurant on Olaf Ryes plass in Grünerløkka, and the light in there is soft and restful due to the red awnings shading the tables which are still standing outside, perhaps that's why he prefers this place, or because there's no music, it's easy to talk, there are few cafés in Oslo where it's possible to have a conversation, it's as if the owners believe that guests want to listen to music rather than talk; anyway, I like the fact that it's a perfectly ordinary restaurant, not one of those trendy places where my girl-friends send the wine back or complain about dishes they had no notion of ten years ago. Otherwise this is a neighbourhood which puts me in a slightly melancholy mood, it reminds me of a time when I was invincible, when I conquered new frontiers every day, it was here I lived with Martin in the years when everything was possible, the years when Grunerløkka was transformed into a Greenwich Village, when young entrepreneurs were opening shops and clubs and restaurants everywhere, and you could buy genuine Hawaiian shirts before you tucked in to Mexican food. Martin and I owned Løkka, owned Oslo, we spent more time in bars and cafés and restaurants than we did at home, it was a time when we were Sartre & Beauvoir, high-flying, critical, we listened to jazz because Martin maintained that it could teach us the art of beginning an article, striking a note which captured the attention immediately, just as the best jazz musicians did, announcing the melody and the chords before beginning to improvise and lifting a hackneyed old tune up into the stratosphere; we're going to be journalism's Bill Evans and John Coltrane, said Martin, and if we weren't going out to talk over mojitos and vodka shots, we stayed home and screwed, it was as if it was all talking and screwing, tequila and cunnilingus, and working of course, even if it didn't feel like working; in the middle of the night we could sit there naked, each typing on a different machine, reading aloud to each other what we had written, we competed with each other for ideas and formulations, we were on a roll, I was starting my last year at college and Martin was working on one of the city's smaller newspapers. Spark plugs everywhere. Sparks flew.

I've arrived too early, I want to register the atmosphere of the place, just as I learned to when I was studying, and I make notes about the view of the fountain in the middle of the park – it could be inserted after one of Berge's (hopefully) pithy comments – something about the sounds from the kitchen, the smells, but I'm on edge too, without really knowing why I'm on edge; I want to see him as he enters, see whether it can tell me something, reveal something about him, give me a clue. I suggested that we should meet on the hill above Fredensborgveien, by the octagonal square in Westye Egebergs gate, where he had lived together with Gry Storefjeld, screwed Gry Storefjeld, I thought; he told me over the phone that Gry went to the honorary corner in Vår Frelsers cemetery every Sunday to lay a flower on the graves of the feminist pioneers Aasta Hansteen and Gina Krog. 'Is that true,' I said, 'that's just the sort of thing I wanted to know'; I was already jotting down key words, *instead of going to church*, I suggested that we should do that, use that as a background, that would work so well, I said, perhaps take along a rose and lay it on Hansteen's or Krog's grave, *the roses have been replaced by roses on her own grave,* but he refused, he refused adamantly, it was enough that we were going to talk in Grünerløkka where they often went – like Martin and I, I thought, when all the important things in life lay ahead of me. I tried to dismiss my own thoughts, but at the same time it was impossible not to let these strong memories intrude; the whole area reeked of ambitious plans and giddy love, cocktails with strange names, spray from the fountain, Martin's sinewy body beside mine in bed.

Am I nervous? I am nervous. I have to laugh at myself. I have interviewed David Bowie, one of the world's greatest artists, and now I'm sitting here nervous about meeting a superannuated young politician, a failed author.

I have to wait a long time, I shiver a little and regret not having worn a thicker jacket, I drink a glass of Chardonnay whilst constantly checking the door; photographers always take too long nowadays, they fancy themselves as more important than the journalists, everything will be good so long as the pictures are good. I've asked Capa to take some photos of Nicolai Berge by the open-air café Blå – Blue – down by the river, I'm toying with the idea of calling the portrait 'Blue Days'; so no doubt that's why he's late, perhaps he'll be tired after posing. Fuck, I think. And then: relax. I glance over at the door constantly, I want to study him as he comes in, those often irresolute seconds as you look around, searching for the person you're going to meet, especially if the other is unknown, as I am to him – unless he's looked at the picture on my byline. I think about my byline picture, whether it's good or not, whether I should perhaps have a new and smarter one taken, since I'm now on an upward trajectory, and at the same time I think that I have actually seen him once before, because quite by chance I popped into a bookshop the autumn he published his second short-story collection, and I remember that I was surprised at what he looked like in reality; I'd only seen some pictures of him in the paper, ones that were taken when he was active as a young politician in Young Labour. I was really about to leave, but my curiosity was aroused, so I stood at a distance and watched him; it was a day in December and he was sitting between two lighted candles and several piles of books, ready to sign them. It was possibly the only bookshop he'd been invited to sign his books in – a kind of consolation prize – and there was no queue, no queue at all, in the course of the fairly long period while I was in the bookshop not a single person came over to him to get a book signed; I even remember that I went closer and stood behind one of the bookshelves so that I could get a closer look at him, first and foremost because he was the son of Olaf Berge, and I felt almost sorry for him, sitting there twiddling a fountain pen between his fingers, I could imagine how painful it must be, sitting there like some sort of exhibit between two candles with piles of unsold books, holding an unused fountain pen, whilst people hurried past with bestsellers in their baskets, taking no notice of him. I remembered something he had said in an interview, it must have been in connection with his first book – it was the only interview I could remember having seen – and he said something comically grandiloquent about wishing to influence his readers on a fundamental level, something along those lines, and if I remember correctly he even added something about shifting the deeper levels of consciousness by using the literary text as a bulldozer, and I'd smiled at that, perhaps not laughed, but smiled. I'm thinking all this as he finally enters the restaurant on Olaf Ryes plass and looks around – slightly awkwardly – before he strides over to me with his mouth curved into a small smile, as if our meeting, or the idea behind our meeting, amuses him a little, despite the sombre circumstances which led to my request. The first thing I notice is his unusual suit, a grey suit with matching waistcoat – straight out of a film from the 1950s, I think. His dark hair is damp and shining. Without looking down I note 'classic three-piece suit' on my pad.

It's only when he gets close I see his earbuds, he pulls them out, Nicolai, he says, his handshake and glance reveal nothing. There's a contradiction between his sober clothes and how he smells. It's a surprising smell – not eau de cologne, but ... bonfires. Yes, bonfires. That's what I think. A man in a suit who smells of bonfires. Unless it's a new fragrance for men which plays on precisely such an image.

'What are you listening to?' I ask, pointing to the earbuds which he stuffs into his inside pocket.

'Shostakovich,' he says. 'Shostakovich?' I say, though it doesn't sound like a question. He just nods, as if it's quite normal for a young man to go round with Shostakovich in his ears.

His expression now is more melancholy – I think 'becomingly melancholy'. Not so strange, perhaps, after everything that's happened. *He never stopped loving her ... He's playing funeral music ... He's attempting to soothe his sorrow with classical melodies ...*

The first minutes are given over to chatting, warming up, I've placed my little recorder on the table, and it strikes me that he is extremely polite, *gallant*, I think, and to a certain extent that matches his somewhat anachronistic, or at least atypical costume; he orders a beer and a hamburger with bacon, the hamburger well done, he adds, smiles at me, I choose an omelette, knowing from experience that I can eat it with just a fork in my left hand whilst I make notes, and one of the first things I note is that he has a remarkable voice, a strikingly pleasant voice, I find myself listening more to the sound of his voice than to what he's saying. But I quickly register the fact that he's stumbling over his words, he has trouble expressing what he means, he often has to stop and start again, and in the middle of one of his answers he gets out a fountain pen from the inside pocket of his jacket, as if it will help him express himself better; it must be the same fountain pen I saw him with on that December day several years ago, and he starts to scrawl something on the tablecloth, which is paper – that could be why he likes this place, I think, because it gives him the chance to use the cloth as a notepad – 'splinter, a moral compass' I think it says, but I'm not at all sure, and the fountain pen looks old, I ask him about it, but he ignores the question and scribbles more, then he looks up and smiles. *Bashful*, I note, looking at the scrawl which is illegible to anyone else. I search for a different word but don't find one.

He holds my glance briefly before he looks out. He seems not just shy, but shut-in. I start to feel doubtful; perhaps the idea was worse than I thought. Hoped. I'll have to rely on my ability to get people to open up, at the same time as I'm searching for a telling detail. The waiter brings the drinks, a beer for him, I order another glass of wine, ask if they have a Soave, this is exceptional, I don't normally drink more than one glass when I'm interviewing.

'Why do you listen to Shostakovich?' I ask.

'Because of a short story,' he says, 'or something that might become a short story.' He looks at me as if he's uncertain whether I'm interested. 'I had an idea,' he says, 'when I discovered that Shostakovich got a splinter of metal in his brain because a grenade exploded right next to him during the Second World War. Shostakovich claimed that he could hear tunes if he just tipped his head to one side. The splinter provoked activity in the cortex's hearing centre.' Berge looks searchingly at me again, as if he still doesn't know whether this is worth telling me about. 'Go on,' I say. 'It may be it's not even true,' he says, 'but this information, or this myth, stimulated my imagination. I imagined a story about a young man who has an accident' – again Berge sends me a searching glance – 'an accident which introduces a foreign body into his body, so that this thing, it might be a piece of crystal, becomes a kind of compass, a third eye, which helps him in difficult situations. Something like that.' Berge smiles, as if to excuse himself.

I ask a stock question and half listen to his answer as I note down a couple of keywords, I think that I can perhaps use this idea of a splinter, *Gry got into my brain, she will always be a part of me*; I keep asking as I take a look in the front of my notebook, I've done a bit of research, in the normal way, not the exhaustive research I used to do back at the beginning when I threw myself into the life of a journalist, hungry and irrepressibly eager, when we still lived in Grünerløkka and there was no such thing as night, when all the hours of the day were potential working hours, especially if the material was important; like when, with Martin's help, I uncovered the incredible negligence in the construction industry, it was a piece of investigative journalism which has now become an object of study in colleges. Why don't I ferret out such things any more, I think as I half listen to what Berge is saying. Why was I sitting here interviewing an unknown author, a man most people would regard as a fiasco? Or could this too, if I was lucky, be seen as investigative journalism of the highest quality?

I had rung some of Berge's friends, or rather it soon became apparent that he didn't have many friends. And no best friend. That was unusual, I made a note of that. And the friends gave me answers and descriptions of him which were completely contradictory. I couldn't find much about him in the cuttings and online archives either, just a bit from the last few years in connection with his two books, a small number of reviews, and a few older articles from his time in Young Labour; I discovered there had been a heated quarrel in connection with an election in Oslo Young Labour – a couple of his friends mentioned that too as a sensitive issue. To me it didn't seem particularly dramatic, more like something quite normal in that wasps' nest; I couldn't understand why anyone would want to be part of the leadership of a youth party, full of intrigues and battles about positions and future power. I had noted the following about Berge's life: childhood in Romsås, youth in the city, Bygdøy allé, Nissen secondary school, a mother who had been a clerk in what was now called the Department of Health and Social Care and who died in an accident, a father who had been a central figure in the Labour Party all his life, and then all that about the grandfather as an entrepreneur, which led to both Berge's father and Berge himself being well off, a fact which was continually used against them. But I concentrated most on his time in Young Labour, that was what I was most interested in, his relationship with Gry.

Our food arrives. Omelette with mozzarella and serrano ham for me, hamburger with salad and roast potato wedges for Berge. 'Perfectly grilled,' he murmurs after the first bite, and begins to cut his burger and bread into small pieces, then puts his knife down and just uses a fork, the way you see Americans do, and I speculate as to whether it is in solidarity with me, since I am only using a fork for my omelette and salad, or whether it is because the knife reminds him of the killings; in any case, I promise myself not to write anything about the way he eats, I hate portraits with descriptions of cutlery, a cliché, I won't even mention what he's eating.

I wade straight in and ask him about Gry, about their relationship – some things he's already talked about on the phone – he's aware that this is the point of the interview, or at least the angle I'm interested in, he understands that there would never have been a portrait if he hadn't been the boyfriend of Gry Storefjeld, *Prime Minister in waiting,* for many years. Despite that I tread carefully. Could he say a little about how they met?

He hesitates, looks out of the window, over to the trees in the park with the fountain in the middle, as if he's far away. The woman sitting with her back to me exudes a perfume which is far too strong. I think this is not going to work after all, but then he straightens up and tells me that they met at secondary school, at Nissen. 'I was studying general subjects and she was specialising in drama,' he says, 'I fell in love when I saw her perform some monologues she chose herself, speeches from Brecht's *Mother Courage,* that was what they did in the second year, and I knew immediately that we were on the same wavelength – can you play the guitar?' I have to shake my head, wonder whether I should tell him about my background as a rock journalist, perhaps that would give me some cred, make him more friendly. 'You know, sometimes you can tune a guitar untraditionally,' he says, 'quite ... Well anyway, she was tuned the same way I was. Differently. But we didn't get together until the year after we left school.' As he says that, his eyes glisten, I jot down a keyword without looking at my pad, a code word for the look in his eyes, my recorder rarely fails, but I daren't take any chances, it could be a good comment, *eyes brimming with tears,* but at the same time I know I won't use it, it's too cheap.

'She was interested in English literature even then,' he goes on. 'She often read aloud from Donne and Tennyson, Shelley and Wordsworth. And especially Coleridge. No doubt you know that she wrote about Coleridge as a student,' he says. 'Because of the language she bought herself the compact two-volume edition of the Oxford English Dictionary, thick books in a case, you had to use the magnifying glass that came with them to be able to read the words – this was just before they launched the on-line version of the work. I fell even more in love with her when I watched her sitting on the floor with the magnifying glass over the pages, as if she was studying insects.' He laughs. I laugh too, so that he isn't ashamed of laughing about a person who's died.

This is good, I think. No-one has mentioned this, *she will never read Coleridge again,* I must have a look at Coleridge, see if I can find a moving quotation from a poem.

'Once she climbed up the steps to that little platform in the Theatre Café,' he says, ' – you know, where the musicians sit – and declaimed Tennyson's "Summer Night" in beautiful English, she got a standing ovation.' Berge smiles, as if at the memory, but I can see that there is something doubtful about his smile. 'You know, she always insisted on paying the bill,' he says, 'or at least her part of it, when we went out to eat, even though I was better off, she said it was a feminist principle, she got frightfully irritated when waiters automatically gave me the bill, she had a rare self-confidence, that was another reason why I fell for her, there are all too few girls with self-confidence.'

He's right about that. I think about my own friends, about how uncertain they are, even the ones with good degrees, how depressingly easily they can be manipulated by their menfolk. For once I have no definite strategy; I want to see where the conversation, my questions, can lead us, although the aim is to reveal something which no-one up to now has uncovered about the dead, lauded young politician, who has already acquired a heroic aura. *Things you never knew about Gry Storefjeld.*

'Is it true that you got together on Utøya, at a Young Labour camp?' I want to know. I ask in a calm voice, but inside I feel agitated. Sitting here opposite Nicolai Berge I have a strong feeling of getting up close to the tragedy, the horror. I look down at the omelette on my plate, thinking I should take another bite, but I can't bring myself to do so. 'That's right,' he says. 'In the fateful year 2000,' he says. I glance at the recorder and put down my fork, but he says no more about it and I don't ask either, several friends have told me that particular story, it was quite a sensation, a buzz of approval passed through the party.

'Being with Gry Storefjeld was perhaps not always … was perhaps not simply a walk in the park?' I ask cautiously, feeling I should divert the conversation to a different track. At the same time I'm uncertain. What is it I'm after? The question forces itself upon me. Would I like to reveal something negative about Gry? Was that what would make it a scoop? Hadn't I perhaps been surprised, or rather irritated, at how often she appeared in the papers, despite the fact that none of her achievements, either academically or politically, was particularly remarkable; she was only interesting as a member of a dynasty. Just as Martin had said. At the same time I would hate it if Martin turned out to be right.

Berge holds his hand round his beer glass, but doesn't lift it, as if he just wants to cool his fingers. 'No, it could … It wasn't always easy being together with Gry,' he says, begins a new sentence, but doesn't get anywhere, stops. 'I see,' I say, signalling that I am all ears. 'She could be a bit mean,' he says, then breaks off, as if he doesn't want to say anything negative after all. 'Once we had to take a break in a game of chess because I had to go out,' he says. 'I was in a far stronger position. When I got back she had glued all the pieces to the board. "Now you can't move," she said. "Checkmate." She was the sort who refused to lose.' He smiles crookedly. 'And it was an expensive set, a present from my father, bought in Istanbul.'

An unconventional game … a final move … lost his queen … the relationship had got stuck … He gets on with his food; the same thing happens every time in an interview, the other person's food gets cold, people talk, concentrate on making a good impression, and forget the plate in front of them. I lift my glass, as if to remind him to drink some beer as well. I can't quite get it to add up, that this seemingly modest and awkward man was together with Gry Storefjeld, who, if she wasn't promiscuous, nevertheless behaved in a, what should I say, liberated fashion. I heard a rumour early on – it was probably something one of the Beat boys told me when we met up at a garden party – that Gry Storefjeld had screwed Liam Gallagher at Roskilde; Oasis had played in the tent called Green Stage and had attracted an enormous crowd. Nevertheless Gry had been noticed, according to the story; Gry Storefjeld, only seventeen, was the kind of girl who stood out in a crowd, and the story goes that she was invited to an after-party. I didn't know whether to believe it. Who in their right mind would want to go to bed with Liam Gallagher? But what if it was true? In that case it must have been … not momentous, but … How would you react to something like that when you were in the sixth form? I'd always thought that Gry seemed somehow burned out, I thought that the very first time I saw her in the news. As if she had no more to live for, had lost her drive.

I don't want to confront Berge with that rumour. Bad timing. He's also started scrawling on the tablecloth again.

I become fascinated by the gold of the nib, it looks like an ornament dripping ink, and without me having to ask he tells me that it's his grandfather's pen, a Parker, and shows me the clip on the cap. 'Look, it's shaped like an arrow,' he says. 'Grandfather wrote with his eyes half-closed, as if he was a Zen master and wanted to fire the arrow into the text. Whilst he listened to Charlie Parker. The music recorded in the Savoy and Dial studios.' Berge sketches musical notes on the cloth, looks at me and laughs. 'I don't know whether Grandfather bought the pen because he liked Charlie Parker or the other way round,' he says. I think about Martin and his interest in jazz, Martin would have appreciated that anecdote. 'A propos this pen, Grandfather also told a story,' says Berge, 'he told us about Joseph Gillott, who in the nineteenth century invented a slight improvement in the nib of a steel pen and made a fortune from it, he collected art as well, and bought several of Turner's paintings. It doesn't take very much, Grandfather always said,' says Berge. 'A small adjustment to something already known – and hey presto, you have a new invention. I was glad when I got the fountain pen,' he says, 'I always look at the nib when I'm writing, so that I remember that. Just a little variation, a fine stream of ink, and the course of history is changed.' Suddenly Berge is lively, he's almost eloquent, and as he talks he keeps on scribbling, or drawing an ornament, perhaps it helps him to express himself better, I think, and at the same time it's as if my assignment slips into the background; I realise I'm enjoying the situation, sitting with a glass of wine on Olaf Ryes plass, opposite Nicolai Berge, who suddenly seems more engaged as he fills the white tablecloth with blue writing, drawings, I don't know what it is, *tracks,* I think, tracks I would like to follow.

I wonder whether I should ask a couple of questions about his books, but I'm afraid that my lack of knowledge about his literary career – if two books can be called a career – would become apparent, together with my awareness that they have been labelled trash. Besides, Berge has lost that enthusiasm I caught a glimpse of; he seems somewhat dejected again, I don't know whether it's caused by grief, that I have awoken something he's trying to forget – or whether it's caused by the fact that his stories haven't found a readership. In any case, he doesn't give the impression of being as self-obsessed as other authors and artists I have met. For a moment I catch myself feeling sorry for him.

Suddenly it's raining so hard outside that the raindrops are ricocheting off the asphalt. A member of staff has lit a small wood fire in a fireplace in the corner of the café, it creates an even cosier atmosphere. I like this place, I think I must come back here, bring a friend, perhaps Rachel, tell her about Nicolai Berge, because there's something about Nicolai Berge, something I can't put my finger on. The longer I sit here opposite him, the more it strikes me how attractive he is. Not just because of his unusual and really rather stylish outfit, but because of his face, his body language. His voice. Something is happening. At first I don't know what it is. Then I feel something. A faint tingling. I write something on my pad as if to prevent it, *someone's lighting a fire*, I write, but that just strengthens the feeling, there's no denying it: my body has begun to tingle.

'Would you like dessert?' I ask. He asks for coffee. I order coffee as well.

He's brought three photos from his past which I can use in the portrait. On the phone I asked him tentatively whether he also had any pictures where he and Gry are together. He shows me one where they're standing with their arms round each other, not too intimate, from a Mayday procession. 'You haven't got anything from the cabin at Blankvann?' I ask straight out, knowing that I'm pushing things too far. He doesn't take offence. 'I'm afraid I never saw that cabin,' he says.

We get our coffee, two espressos. He stirs a sugar lump into his. I take a chance and ask how things ended between them. He says, without stopping to think, that it was completely undramatic, Gry called it a quarter-life crisis, she had just become twenty-five, she felt they had grown apart. That doesn't sound very convincing, I think. 'After four years?'

I ask. 'Can you grow apart so quickly?' He pauses before he answers, then begins a sentence three times without getting anywhere. 'I suppose you can, at least in that phase of your life,' he finally manages, glancing at me and smiling, but he looks sad, as if he doesn't believe it himself. 'She said that our relationship wasn't sustainable.' He tries to laugh, but can't. *Gry is the new Gro,* I think, remembering the headline. Someone drops a casserole on the floor in the kitchen, first swearing, then laughter. I don't know whether it's because of the crash, but for a moment Berge seems to drop his mask inadvertently, and at once I get the feeling that he also *hates* Gry Storefjeld. But I'm not certain as to whether I am interpreting his expression correctly – and in any case it wouldn't do for the magazine. We have drunk our espressos in the same way, in three mouthfuls, almost in synchrony. I am on the point of asking him whether he has ever thought of revenge, or has felt like hurting her. I bite my tongue. 'She was ambitious,' he says, as if to explain the breakup in a better way. 'In a political sense,' he says. 'And she was tougher than me.' He says something about the leadership election in Oslo Young Labour. His distaste for propaganda. Again a pause. He looks down into his empty cup. 'It was also the fact that I had started to write,' he says. 'She didn't like that.' He picks up his fountain pen and carries on drawing on the cloth, adds arrows and circles round some of the words, the blue ink glistens before it soaks into the fibres and dries. It makes me want to buy myself a fountain pen. *Blue days, blue ink.*

I have enough now, really. He has given me several small glimpses of Gry, things I can link together to make a moving account. *Their happiness was not sustainable.* I ask a further couple of questions, at random. None of them leads anywhere. 'What was your relationship to Gry's father like?' I ask then. Berge straightens up. 'Good,' he says, and as he screws the cap on his fountain pen he describes Arve Storefjeld warmly, far too 'correctly', I think, he stumbles over his words, singing his praises, even recounts a couple of amusing anecdotes about Storen, whilst his whole expression betrays the fact that he's not being honest, that it's possible he even cherishes a deep aversion to the man; there's something behind this, I think, something bigger, perhaps it's connected to those conflicts in Young Labour. It's as if I have had a bite from a completely different fish than the one I had imagined I would reel in.

I dismiss it, I have no use for that.

It's got darker outside, and it's as if Olaf Ryes plass looks even more attractive in the lights from all the shops and cafés and restaurants. The word *continental* occurs to me. I feel like staying here, I would like to order another glass of wine, I don't want to take the train home to my town house, to the paths between the sandpits and the swings, and as an excuse for staying for a few more minutes, sitting here near an open fire, I ask him about his writing, about why he writes short stories rather than novels, and he immediately becomes eager, more eager than at any of my other questions, and he doesn't stumble over his words so much; he could understand my asking, he says, his publishers also suggested that he should write a novel, a grandly-conceived work, a modern epic; he laughs and says he didn't want to do that, he wanted to stick to the short story, the truth was to be found in fragments, in the gaps, no-one should write at length these days, he says, no-one has time to read a four-hundred-page novel, at least not with the necessary thoroughness – no, you had to be able to say it in ten pages.

What a pity, then, I think, that no-one wanted to read his short stories either.

On the other hand I approve of what he's saying, especially about fragments and gaps. A long, coherent narrative is always a lie.

His face resumes its melancholy expression. I feel like consoling him, saying something comforting. Being caring. Is that how I feel? That is how I feel. It strikes me how unusual this interview situation is, how little it resembles for example my meeting with Arve Storefjeld at Dovre, an interview which would earn brownie points, and be important for my career. This could be the same, but it's more personal, more approaching something … something inflammatory.

I regret not having bought one of his books, so that he could finally get to sign a book. It could have been great, a personal greeting, written with an old Parker fountain pen.

I don't have any questions left on my pad, but we carry on talking nevertheless, talking more like two people who have met by chance in a bar, I think, yes, in a bar, the expression strikes me, actually I feel like asking him to come with me, cheering him up, doing a pub crawl round the bars in the district, all those lively new bars full of young people, drinking cocktails with strange names, just like Martin and I did in the golden age of our love; I'm a bit tipsy as well, I allowed myself a glass more than usual, because I'm nervous, I'm still nervous, and even though I'm carrying on trying to be professional, to keep a cool head, something is happening, and I don't know when the adjustment – to use Berge's word, or rather Berge's grandfather's – occurred, but I'm in the process of losing my balance, something is happening in my pelvic region, it's responding with a thrill I haven't felt in a very long time. He's sitting there opposite me in a grey three-piece suit. A grey young man, I think. Who's on fire nevertheless. *A Zen master*. There's a contradiction here. Something exciting. Something *dangerous,* I think, without knowing why it might be dangerous. *To shoot the arrow into the bull's-eye.* If we were alone now, somewhere else, I would take his clothes off; the thought just hits me so that I almost jump. But it's true, that's what I'm thinking, looking into that open, handsome, shy face and not wanting to go home, I can feel a half-forgotten warmth between my legs, a faint flame, I haven't had sex for … I daren't even think how long ago it is. But now. I'm sitting here registering a, what's the word, an intensity which over the years I have forgotten existed. A fever. It's burning. This material is burning. I'm burning. And the fact that I'm burning makes me ashamed, and the fact that I'm ashamed, because the circumstances of our meeting are so tragic, makes me burn even more. It doesn't get any better when we start to talk about music, since he reveals that he's listened to David Bowie a lot – and not because of the shifting identities, but because of the music – and that was in a period when few others of his age were listening to Bowie, and he cannot possibly know that I once interviewed Bowie. 'I've spent some time with the *Heathen* album recently,' he says, and I just have to pretend that I know what he's talking about, since I haven't heard this relatively recent album, I who once sat opposite David Bowie in a place which is actually not unlike where Nicolai Berge and I are sitting now. *I'll write the best interview ever!*

It's as if the person opposite me is letting me glimpse a different side. There's something … yes, precisely something *heathen* about him, something off the beaten track. I become curious, I become even more fascinated.

Something is happening.

It's still raining, I don't want to go out in the bad weather, I want to sit here and talk, sit here the whole evening, with the smell of the fire, forget the interview, just talk about whatever occurs to us, feed this flame I can feel, this flame I had almost forgotten existed. I remember that we have some set questions in every portrait, so I ask them, it becomes a bit flippant. Favourite book? He fools around at first, but eventually answers *Our Man in Havana,* Graham Greene. Did he mean that? Yes, he meant it, it was something about the protagonist being able to make intelligent people believe that the drawings in a manual for vacuum cleaners had something to do with secret rockets, he said, our ability to invent stories was phenomenal. Suddenly we're laughing a lot. I don't know why, but I'm thinking at the same time about all the crazy theories which were flying around about the Blankvann incident – weren't they too a proof of our unique capacity to make up stories? 'What about you?' he says. 'What's your favourite book?'

Suddenly I'm embarrassed, I don't read, I've never read. '*Bleak House* by Dickens,' I say, on an impulse.

He looks oddly at me, looks very oddly at me, he makes a move as if to take hold of my fingers, but stops at the last moment.

'What's the most important advice you've been given?' he goes on. I raise my hands in the air, we mustn't swap roles, I say. It's ages since I've had such a good time.

For a moment I'm on the point of doing it, suggesting that we should carry on, go to a bar. Order a Screwdriver. No, too risqué. Better a classic White Lady. I could try to get him drunk, see if his mask dissolved then, or whether I was already seeing his true face. Was he really so straightforward? Or so enigmatic? It was as if I could see success behind a façade of failure.

But what if it was me who got drunk under the table?

Would I mind being drunk under the table?

I dismiss the thought. Be professional, be careful, I admonish myself, and mentally slap my cheeks with my hands to make myself wake up. I ask for the bill, pack things away, put my notepad and recorder in my bag.

He tears off a large piece of the cloth, the bit he's been writing and drawing on, then folds it up neatly and sticks it in his jacket pocket.

I'm tempted to ask if I can have it. For some reason I would like to keep that piece of paper. I could have framed it, perhaps hung it up in my little office. Words with circles round them, arrows. Rockets.

It has got dark. We stop outside. The rain, the sound on the awnings, makes me think of that time I was sixteen years old and sitting in a moored sailboat on the south coast together with a boy, listening to the drops on the canvas, the same excitement; the journalist in me is once more in retreat, I want to stand here and keep talking, listening to the rain, letting my thoughts wander, enjoying the effects of the wine on my body, to hell with the interview, I just want to keep talking to him. Go further. Yes, go further, in both senses of the word. In my mind's eye I see a spark plug.

We say goodbye, he shakes my hand, almost solemnly, thanks me for the meal, it was ... he hesitates, enlivening, he says, the rain diminishes to a drizzle, and even though the streets and trees are wet, even though autumn is coming, Olaf Ryes plass reminds me of somewhere which could have been much further south in Europe, Málaga, for example, there's something about the darkness and the gleaming lights from the pavement cafés around the square, the sound of the fountain; I walk towards the tram stop, I'm in a special mood, I've been close to something important, something real and true, a man in grief, a man who is deeply unhappy about the fate of a former lover, I know that I've got the material for a good portrait. *Four years which changed my life ... Arve Storefjeld taught me a great deal ...*

I planned to leaf through my notes and add to them from memory on the train going home – I got out the red felt-tip pen which indicates where there are amplifying remarks – but I just sit staring out of the window where the rain is making diagonal stripes whilst the countryside and stations glide past outside; I only just remember to get off at Vevelstad, I'm in a mood I've never known before, no, *never,* I have never felt so alive, so, what's the word, *with it,* I am in the midst of events which preoccupy a whole country, and I'm one of those who influences what people think, what they feel, and now I can make a further contribution, I think as I walk past the front of the town houses, past sandpits with abandoned toys and gardens where the trampolines look like empty circus rings, and I almost have to smile when I remember the low point I had reached on Hovedøya, at the wedding.

The thought makes me stop at a point where I can see a little grove between two rows of houses. It is difficult to deny the fact that the Blankvann killings have saved me.

Once home, I realise that my stomach is rumbling, I haven't eaten anything other than an omelette, or half an omelette, since breakfast. I make myself a sandwich with smoked salmon and dill, I take a slice of lemon and cut off the circle of peel before I divide the flesh into small pieces which I scatter over it, together with capers. I sit on the sofa with the sandwich and a large glass of water, without switching on the TV. I write a few sentences on the pad which is always ready on the living-room table. I pour myself a small glass of Jack Daniel's, as if to remind myself of a time when I believed I was a Joan of Arc. Special. That I had a calling. Could achieve great things. I scribble down several good sentences before tiredness overwhelms me.

Something is happening. All the important things in life are not behind me.

I'm at the publishers. People know who I am. Even down in reception the tone is warmly welcoming, as if someone has sent out an alert: roll out the red carpet, a potential golden goose is approaching! I sit in a meeting room together with the editor and three people from sales and marketing. There's a cheerful atmosphere, coffee cups on the table, we talk about the launch, which has been postponed until the first week of October in order to ensure maximum coverage. If all goes as planned, my magazine portrait of Nicolai Berge will be printed at more or less the same time as my book about Arve Storefjeld appears. *The Road Builder* – my working title was *My Way*, that was something I thought of because I was present as a journalist at the celebrations for Storen's fiftieth birthday in 1999 in the Trades Union Centre, where he sang an ear-piercingly false but charming 'My Way', with a Norwegian text written by former colleagues from the Oslo Highways Department, as the department was called at the time. The marketing director tells us that interest is already at its peak, pre-launch sales to the book chains are amazing, it's all going like clockwork. She doesn't need to say that, I know that I'll be flavour of the month, I'll be Norway's Journalist, people will woo me from all sides, I'll be invited onto every last talk-show, I will – well, I will have my own portrait written. I laugh at the thought, start half-speculating about what to say and what not to say, what I shall wear.

And in the midst of all the cheerfulness, the pleasure at the bright prospects for my book, we are of course serious, we shake our heads at regular intervals as if we're shocked, or rather we *are* truly shocked, we can't forget the terror which surrounds our meeting like a dark, albeit golden, frame.

We talk about where we should have the launch. I suggest that we hire the restaurant Fyret for a morning. It has just the right amount of folksiness, appropriate for Arve Storefjeld, and it's on Youngstorget, surrounded by the buildings where Storen made his mark. And then there's the name, Fyret, The Lighthouse, which chimes perfectly with the host of more or less appropriate metaphors which Storen drew on from his grandfather's activities as a pilot and fisherman. Everyone is enthusiastic. We laugh, even though we know that we shouldn't laugh, we use the word terrible at regular intervals, but we laugh; it's like at a wake after a funeral, where you almost have a bad conscience because the mood is so merry. The publishers are extremely happy with everything, even with the book's form, which they had reservations about at the start, because I have stuck with the form of my biography, the leaps in content, that's the way everyone with any respect for reality is writing now, at least in other countries, I'm still trying to keep up with developments, I want my writing to be true, not like in a novel – whilst we were married, Martin gave me Dickens' *Bleak House,* he believed that as journalists we could learn a lot from it, and I had it on my bedside table for over a year, but I fell asleep every time I tried to read some – no, not like a novel, that shamefully over-valued humbug with its fabricated and wildly improbable coincidences, I want to portray reality as it is, fragmentary, scattered in pieces of widely differing kinds; I want to show the complexity of a human destiny, its many contradictory angles, without the reader giving up. And I want to draw a different picture of Arve Storefjeld than as a clown, an impression I myself had contributed to with my portrait of him at Dovre. In my book I have also included some of his darker sides, for example his temperament, his tendency to smash the furniture when he didn't get his way, a quirk which was in sharp contrast to the politician who was known for his lunches with waffles: 'To untangle a knot you often need no more than a waffle heart.' At the same time I hope the book presents a refreshing picture of Norwegian politics and Norwegian society reflected through an activist who specialised in hitting the nail on the head, a politician who managed the feat of balancing between populism and defending the core values of social democracy, one who could appeal to 'the lads on the shop floor' as well as the stay-at-home wives who still wore their furs with pride. While working on it I had slowly started to admire him. By representing the roots, or you might say the best of the workers' movement, Arve Storefjeld had been of inestimable importance to the party.

And now he was dead. Worth even more. An election winner even as ash in an urn.

On the way out I get pats on the back and friendly nods from everyone I meet. Near the main door I pass the plexiglass shelves with the novels the publishers are bringing out this autumn and from which they no doubt expect a great deal. The sight makes me snort. Back in my childhood I was vaccinated against 'good stories'. People harped on about Father having 'a gift', that he was an inspired storyteller. I don't remember when it happened, I just remember that at a certain point in time I began to hate the moment when Father said: let me tell a story. At family get-togethers, in the car, at receptions in the Tram Company, sitting on my bed in the evening. I can illustrate that by telling a story, he would say. I winced, but I could see how much other people in the company enjoyed it, how they settled back in their chairs as if the lights were going to go out and the curtain rise on a stellar performance. It didn't take long for me to get bored, since his stories were too simple, they resembled fairy tales. It must have been during these years that I made myself a promise: I was going to tell true stories, taken from the world as it was, difficult stories, without a moral. And over time I discovered that few things gave me a better opportunity to follow this programme than descriptions of people who had gone astray. From that angle Nicolai Berge was a good choice. Or rather he was perfect. Good as a human being, a failure as a person.

On the way up to the paper I stop at Oslo Courthouse, that white cube on C.J. Hambros plass. I think about the drama that will unfold there if the police one day manage to arrest one or more of the men behind the Blankvann terror. Like everyone else I hope, I expect, that the investigation will yield results. Not only for the sake of the bereaved. The whole nation has need of some sort of therapy. It will be a long séance, a unique piece of theatre, a golden opportunity to feed the public with report after report. *The difficult reckoning.* In my thoughts I can already glimpse an original angle, the whole opening section of what could be a brilliant prologue.

I must concentrate on the Berge interview, and I barricade myself in at my desk at the paper. I would like to give the portrait an unconventional form, but Martin doesn't like experiments in the magazine, so I have to give in and follow the template. I put on my earphones and I work on *the voice,* my speciality, I drop the canteen, I've got a tube of cheese and crispbread out of the cupboard – I'm starting to resemble Martin, the workaholic – I read through my first draft and correct it, I go through my notes; normally I have too much, now I can see that I have too little, I can't get into the flow, I, the portrait master, known for being able to capture a person in three sentences, I'm stuck, I don't know what's missing, unless it's a focus, a centreboard to balance the whole – a spark plug. The sum total is basically nothing more than the superficial fact that Nicolai Berge had been together with Gry Storefjeld, together with a string of little anecdotes about her – possibly amusing, but not compelling. I put my earplugs in instead of the earphones and listen to the whole recording again. No aha-moments. Silent keys.

Fuck. I think Berge must have infected me, I've begun to fumble for words just as he does.

I'm not satisfied, I don't think Martin will be satisfied either, and I want Martin to be satisfied, want him to swallow his scepticism, to congratulate me, to … Fuck. What if he demands a major rewrite? Or says it's not good enough? Bloody hell. It's as if Berge is avoiding all my practised attempts at a description, despite the fact that I've been sitting opposite him, had the man at my disposal for several hours; I leaf desperately through my notes, listen to parts of the recording again, he remains … he remains something my words don't have the power to grasp.

I get up and walk around a bit, but avoid the coffee machine. I'd like to hear the latest about the Blankvann killings – I did pick up the experts' warning that the terrorists can strike again at any time, in an equally unexpected place – but I want to be alone; I move to the newsroom where I stand on the stairs watching the bustle. I catch sight of Foyn, the boss, in the midst of it, wearing a T-shirt with a sketch of a typewriter, and underneath: FCC Cambodia. FCC stands for Foreign Correspondents' Club; it looks cool, but as far as I know Foyn has never been in Phnom Penh where the club has its headquarters. I remain on the stairs with the Berge problem buzzing in my head. If you want to compose a portrait of a person you can actually write about anything at all – nothing is strictly speaking irrelevant. The art is to pick out those seemingly random details which give the illusion that you are portraying *that* person and no other. For example Foyn's T-shirts – they tell the whole story of a globetrotter who has hardly been further than his own front door. To make it simpler, and especially if time is short, I often employ what I call my 'prismatic' method. All people consist of different layers, just as light, to put it simply, consists of seven colours. Therefore I try to include elements from each layer, each colour, in the individual I'm writing about, with the result that the readers imagine they have met a uniquely complex person. But with Berge it was different. He appeared to be a simple, transparent man, he seemed to consist of only a few colours – and in that fact lay the challenge. He was hiding something. He had peculiarities which he took care not to talk about or reveal.

I stop in the part of the offices where we hang the finished pages for the next issue of the magazine side by side, 'the mirror on the wall', we call it. There's a portrait of a musician – for the hundredth time, I think, and it is, not surprisingly, the musician I heard in Spikersuppa, the artist behind the popular old ballad which has now become even more popular, if that is possible, because of the terrorism. I stand in front of the wall of pages with their attractive layout, remembering my first successful portrait. It was around the time I had decided to put my phase as investigative or current affairs journalist behind me, decided that the magazine was going to be my domain from now on. Features. A playground with extensive artistic freedom. One day, quite by chance, I saw the philosopher Arne Næss in the street, and I immediately decided I wanted to write about him. During those years he wasn't often in the papers; it was a long time since the ascent of Tirich Mir, it was a long time since the protests at Mardøla and Alta. I'd always been curious about him, a man who had influenced several generations of students. I went over to him and asked politely. He said yes, and I believe he was pleased that I, a relatively young journalist and a woman into the bargain, wanted to interview him. A couple of days later we met at the Bristol Hotel, in the Library Bar. I had done some research, but our conversation dragged to begin with. Then came an unexpected spark of inspiration as he was answering a rather general question about his childhood, and he told me how he used to sit under the piano listening to his brother, especially when he was playing the Moonlight Sonata. Arne Næss almost became a pianist himself, he even went to Vienna in order to play for one of the most renowned teachers there, and as if to round off the story Næss said spontaneously, as he did on occasion:

'Sit down underneath this grand piano and you'll hear how fantastic the Moonlight Sonata sounds from that angle.' The house pianist was having a break, so Arne Næss sat down on the piano stool whilst I cast off all inhibitions and slid as far as I could under the grand piano, until I was almost lying on my back. The other guests watched us curiously, including a famous author who seemed to be in the middle of an interview about a new book. Arne Næss began to play the first movement – and it really did sound fantastic, it was as if I had never heard that well-worn classic before. 'That's what we have to do in life as well,' he said afterwards, 'search for surprising positions.' With that I had a great opening image, and in the course of the conversation Arne Næss presented many of the viewpoints he would go on to formulate in the book which came out the following year, *Life's Philosophy*, and which sold amazingly well for such a book. I called my portrait 'Examen Philosophicum by Moonlight.'

Perhaps it's a place I lack, I thought. A place with props which might reveal something. Perhaps I ought to ask if I could meet Berge in his flat in Nordberg.

I meet Rachel at Oslo central station. She too comments that I look good. That my new haircut suits me. My dark lipstick. Had I won the lottery? Hugs, laughter. Rachel works at the newspaper *Aftenposten*, in the old Central Post Office building just nearby; we usually meet here and have a simple meal together. Today I'm on my way home, and she has a late shift. We sit in a restaurant on the first floor over the departure hall. Now and then it's good to eat a normal dinner, pasta all'arrabbiata with chicken, and drink a glass of wine, although any sense of rabidity and Rome itself are very far away. We sit over our dessert, pecan pie, and even if the food is not fantastic I like this place, I like the view over the throng in the hall below us and out to the platforms on the other side of the large windows, the trains which come and go. Rachel often says that she envies me, says it must be good to live alone, to be able to do exciting things all the time. I'm not sure whether she means it. We've been friends since Beat days. She had an English mother and we shared an interest in British rock. Now Rachel has become more respectable, dresses respectably too, in suits and dresses with jackets. Handbags which cost a month's wages. Rich husband, very rich husband, son of some property mogul or other.

I tell her about Nicolai Berge, about the portrait I'm working on. 'Oh yes, poor thing,' is Rachel's immediate reaction. I look at her questioningly. 'Think of being the son of Maj Runesen and Olaf Berge,' says Rachel. 'The only child. Think of the expectations – and then not living up to any of them.'

I feel like protesting, but I remain silent. It irritates me that she talks about Berge like that. Again it's as if I feel a need to protect him. Without paying any attention to my irritation, or rather no doubt without even noticing it, Rachel begins to talk about the Blankvann incident, and we sit there for a long time talking about terrorism, exchanging information, and it strikes me, as it has struck me on several occasions recently, that it's a marvellous topic of conversation, an inexhaustible fount of material, of threads that can be followed in all directions. At last we have something to talk about, speculate about, tut-tut about – it's a goldmine. And how great it is to sit here on high, eating delicious cakes, drinking wine or sparkling water with a hint of lemon, discussing terrible things … I feel like a child on her grandfather's lap as he tells stories of trolls – it's thrilling but safe.

Rachel disrupts the picture, she picks up a bit of cake on her fork and points out how vulnerable society has become, points at all the trains, all the passengers. 'We're not safe anywhere,' she says, and she mentions the terror attack on the station in Madrid four years ago, almost two hundred people killed. 'Relax, it won't happen here,' I say. Rachel looks at me. 'Have you forgotten already,' she says, almost angry. 'Think about the bomb which exploded here in the early 1980s, when we still had left-luggage lockers, one person killed and many injured. It happens here too,' says Rachel emphatically, pointing her fork at me. 'We think these killings at Blankvann are the first time.' I have to agree. Rachel is right. We forget. It happens here too. 'We're just as vulnerable as all the others,' says Rachel. I nod again, and look out at the trains. It's a long way from Madrid to Oslo. To such an act of terrorism. It will never happen, I think. Not here. Not in Norway. Despite everything. A bomb in a left-luggage locker. That perhaps. But not anything big. Not bigger than the dreadful killings at Blankvann. 'This too will be forgotten in a few years,' I say. 'It's difficult to believe it now, but it will be forgotten.' 'That's a pity,' says Rachel, 'because then we'll close our eyes to the fact that it can happen again.' 'Good Lord, Rachel, stop talking nonsense,' I say. 'Believe me, it will never happen again. Nothing as shocking and barbaric as this. In the worst case scenario this sort of thing happens every twenty-five years in any one country. In Norway at least. A political attack of this nature. You need a double macchiato. To wake up.' I wave at the waiter.

We both sit watching the trains coming and going, or the people thronging the hall below us. I think that we've finished with Blankvann for today, and I begin to search for something else to talk about, good films perhaps, but of course we're not finished with Blankvann, because it transpires that Rachel – and this surprises me – has begun to doubt the terrorist idea. 'We have to keep all possibilities open,' she says, sounding like the police spokesperson. 'Perhaps we're all looking in the wrong place.'

I'm glad when the coffee arrives, I feel light-headed. I'm about to ask if she has heard Bowie's *Heathen* when Rachel admits she has her own hypothesis: she believes that the perpetrator might be a misfit, a loser. Perhaps even a man who is mentally ill.

'What if it's a woman?' I say.

'I refuse to imagine that it can be a woman,' says Rachel. 'Just try to rewind to the beginning,' she says. I pretend to turn a dial on my temple and make her laugh. 'What if there was just one killer,' she goes on, 'and that he has stayed under the radar, or lived completely anonymously – how could you pick up the danger in advance? It's every investigator's nightmare. "The solo terrorist.'"

'The lone wolf,' I murmur.

We eat the last crumbs of the pecan pie. 'Exactly,' Rachel replies. It's as if the words spur her on to think of something related, because she starts to tell me about another matter which is worrying her, to explain that she's been wanting for a long time to write about these extreme right-wing networks which are spreading on the internet – inspired by gangs of lads who play violent digital games all day long and post hate messages the rest of the time. Rachel looks at me. I can only shrug, I know very little about this. 'I put forward the idea at a meeting,' says Rachel, 'I suggested that we should write a series of articles about the phenomenon. I got no response, no-one takes it seriously. Or rather, the editor-in-chief asked me to write something. I don't know whether I can bear to. These forums are also brimming over with hateful comments on feminism. And on the Labour Party. They're dangerous thoughts,' says Rachel. 'And we're sitting here eating cakes and talking about it as if it's entertainment.'

It *is* entertainment, I think, but I daren't say it out loud.

Then I remember that Sofie Nagel wrote a comment piece about something similar this spring, without it leading to any debate. She too – an activist for equal rights – pointed out the large amount of misogynist material on the net. The problem is that too many men feel inadequate in modern society, she wrote. It provides fertile ground for a bitterness, a build-up of energy, which can have destructive consequences. I describe the piece to Rachel, I remember it well. She nods. 'That's exactly what I'm talking about,' she says. 'The murderer may be an angry man, someone who feels *excluded*, misunderstood by everyone.' Rachel looks at me. I can see a trace of fear in her eyes.

'All this hatred,' she says. 'What if Sofie Nagel was the target, not Arve Storefjeld. And the reason was hatred.'

On the train home I try to look through a book about evil, but I can't concentrate, I just sit looking out of the window, looking over at Hovedøya and thinking of everything that's happened since I stood in the monastery ruins a few weeks ago, toasting the newly-weds. Perhaps it's not so strange that a new discussion about evil has flared up, about what evil is. I play with the idea of writing an article, or even compiling a longer theme issue for the magazine where I, or we, take up the theme of *evil*. We could ask for contributions from philosophers and theologians; because if what happened in that forest was not purely and simply evil, what could you call evil? I get out my pad and write 'idealistic evil?', then sit pondering about it. Before we've got to Holmlia I put my pad away. I think about Arne Næss, now 96 years old, I think about the Moonlight Sonata, and I drift off. I don't wake up until we're at Ski, I've travelled too far, but I decide that I might just as well do some shopping at the shopping centre, amongst other things I've run out of the fruit jelly I use in my peanut butter sandwiches.

I must finish this portrait. I sit in the lobby of the government offices with my earbuds in, checking through the recording of Berge – partly just to hear his voice – and I notice again that there's something hidden behind it. As if he's only giving me half the truth, I think. Damn. I'll have to throw in the towel and ask for another meeting – I still need more information about Gry Storefjeld as a young politician. That's nothing to get worked up about. On the contrary. For several of my best portraits I've met the person several times.

I feel a kind of vibration in my body, a fired-up appetite for work at the thought of another conversation with Berge, of getting close to Gry and the Blankvann incident again. For a moment I feel ashamed of my sense of well-being, of the fact that I'm using this tragedy to my advantage. Then I push the thought away. I can't be blamed for the terrorists setting things in motion; Gry is dead, and by writing about Berge I can be part of honouring her memory. My task is to write incisively, to provide surprising insights. I have to recover the self-confidence I had in my Beat days. Fuck it all. I still have brass in pocket, I'm so special, I'm gonna use my arms, gonna use my legs, gonna use everything I have of imagination. Gonna make you, make you, make you notice. I'll bloody show you.

The Prime Minister comes out of the lift, sees me and wanders over, I don't know whether it's because of my expression, my rock face – perhaps I was unconsciously swaying along to the Pretenders' hymn in my head – he asks if I'm waiting for anyone, I half nod, he says he's read my articles, they've been good, especially the one about Arve Storefjeld's significance; he stands there in front of me – so solid, I think, so impressive, so *irreproachable* – he raises a hand, as if he's giving me his blessing, before he disappears in the direction of Akersgata with his entourage. I notice the teak frames in the windows, think again what a magnificent building I have my secret thinking and writing corner in. I must apply to be able to use this place always, I think. Who knows, one day there may be a blue plaque on the wall decorated by Inger Sitter and Carl Nesjar: Ine Wang worked here.

I carry on making notes, I must ask Nicolai Berge more about Young Labour and the Labour Party. That's relevant to the story as well. More and more people are interpreting the killings in the forest as an attempt to 'strangle social democracy' – it was Norwegians' core values which were under attack, freedom, the ability to move around freely.

As soon as I'm amongst the mirror pools in the avenue of limes outside I get out my mobile to ask Berge for a new meeting. It dawns on me that I have a double motive: I do have further questions, but I am also plagued by an inexplicable restlessness, I might almost say a longing. Will I be able to conceal it? Am I mixing work with something more personal? It is not so unmanageable that I won't be able to control it. I'm willing to take that risk.

One of the policemen who has been stationed close to the government offices recently follows me with his eyes. I phone, Berge says yes, without hesitation this time. He asks me up to Nordberg. Just as I hoped.

Rachel's comment about internet groups makes me remember Berge's blog. I've been thinking for a long time that I ought to take a look at it, but it's only now that I switch on my pale green iMac at home and visit the blog where Nicolai Berge has been posting for many years. Pens, it's called. Was that a hint at something French – *penser, pensées*? The layout is unfussy, elegant, and at the same time a little old-fashioned. The focus is on the writing, and he has chosen a font which makes it easy to read. A counter reveals that not many people have read it. Before I met Berge the first time Ulrik told me that several people were critical of Berge's writing; especially Young Labour were indignant that he blogged about problems in the Labour Party instead of taking it up at internal meetings.

I read it quickly, skim it, let post after post glide up the screen like a long, long curtain, without discerning any overriding intention, but I can see straight away that his opinions are provocative. 'Is it not the case that the Labour Party building on Youngstorget bears some resemblance to the Potala Palace in Lhasa?' he wrote at one point. 'It is perfectly possible to regard the Labour Party as a form of Lamaism. With a Dalai Lama quarrelling with a Panchen Lama. Leader against leader, faction against faction.' And in another place: 'Norway has had its own Margaret Thatcher, a front for New Liberalism. She's called Gro Harlem Brundtland.'

As far as I can make out many of the blog posts are close to being offensive, but there are few who have written in the comments field. As if hardly anyone thinks it's worth starting a discussion. But just before I sign off, I do find a long commentary which describes one of Berge's posts as bordering on fascism. I switch off my machine and sit staring at the town house opposite. I am confused. Nothing of this accords with the impression I got of the person I met on Olaf Ryes plass.

My preparations for the meeting with Berge are interrupted by an excursion, a walk in the woods with Ulrik. There's a breath of autumn in the air the day we enter Nordmarka. We're driving in Ulrik's car, a run-down Passat with child seats in the back and unbelievably messy. Ulrik is playing Bob Marley at top volume. He wants to write something about the crime scene and has asked me to come along. 'I don't want to walk up to that place alone,' he says. I hesitate at first, but then I say yes, I think perhaps I can use it somehow. Whilst our heads sway to the beat of *Rastaman Vibration* we drive up the forest road towards the Blankvann clearing; I think Ulrik has deliberately chosen an album without 'I Shot the Sheriff' in order to spare us associations to the bloody occasion for our day trip. I'm glad as well that we have permission to drive, I've never liked hiking in the forest. During recent weeks there have also been fewer people in these parts, according to a notice in a paper. It seems that people are consciously avoiding the area around Blankvann.

We park. I'm a little hoarse after having sung along to several of Marley's tunes. It's a fine day, still fairly warm, and we sit down on the open slope above the Blankvann clearing and look at the lake while we eat the picnic I've brought. I'm the one who suggests that we take a rest before we walk the last stretch; I think Ulrik too is dreading the sight of Valen, Storefjeld's cabin, and it may be that we won't feel much like eating afterwards. Ulrik is impressed by my sandwiches, praises them, says that I ought to start serving them in the canteen at work, especially the one with mozzarella and tomato and basil, with a little pepper. Quite simple, quite unbeatable. We don't say very much, we study the grassy slope, the hills, the glittering surface of the water, and try to absorb the fact that such an idyllic place can have been visited by such a violent deed.

Ulrik starts whistling, and for a while I don't realise that it's one of the popular troubadour's ballads, one of the simple songs which has become even more popular these days, and as if there's a connection my thoughts move to one of the many 'words of wisdom' created by youngsters which has spread after 23 August and has been embraced and quoted in the media as if it was one of Solomon's proverbs: 'They came with hatred, we answered with love'. Of course, that's utter nonsense when you stop to think about it. The truth is that people would have flayed those terrorists alive if they got the chance.

We are reluctant to get up, both of us, but in the end we have to pack up and walk up the hill. Ulrik has covered his short rasta locks with one of those head coverings he otherwise doesn't use any longer, a crocheted cap in colours which make me think of a Kvikk Lunsj wrapper. I think he's doing it as a kind of protection. Soon we come to a section where the trees are close together, surprisingly close. Suddenly it's a little dark. Between the branches spiders' webs give off an unnatural silver light. There are four other cabins in the area, and we wander round for a while before we find the path to the right one, to Valen. There's no trace of any smell here now, anything 'scorched' as Capa said; instead it smells fresh, it smells of autumn. As if nature has already forgotten the evil. My fantasy is working overtime, I think about those overgrown temples you can find in the jungle, temples where people were once sacrificed.

Almost automatically we look around us, as if for clues, for objects which might have escaped the notice of the police. I remember that mysterious Scottish handkerchief. Soon the whole of nature will be a tartan of green and yellow and red.

As we catch sight of the cabin, just before we come out into the clearing on the ridge of the hill, it's as if something happens. The whole colour spectrum changes, and the trees on both sides seem to form an avenue leading to one of the outhouses. If I step outside the avenue something bad will happen to me, I think, without knowing why I'm thinking that. I remember that the crime scene investigators found something mystical in a gully full of nettles, a round, olive-green object. At first they were afraid it might be a small land-mine, and a specialist team was called in. But it turned out to be a tin box containing military field rations. No-one could explain how it had finished up there. It must be pretty old, since the armed forces didn't use that kind of combat rations any more. But could it mean that Norwegian soldiers were involved in the killings? Some people pointed out that the order for new fighter jets, with a price tag of around ten billion kroner, was to be decided later this autumn, and Arve Storefjeld had been outspoken in his support of the Swedish Gripen planes – and according to some people that was because half of his mother's family came from Røros; our historic links to Sweden had always been one of Storen's favourite topics. Might supporters of the American fighter planes, which were competing for the contract, be behind the attack?

I wouldn't be surprised if I stumbled over a spark plug.

All of a sudden there are no insects, no birds, no sounds. I can feel pressure in my ears as if I've dived down too far. I'm nervous, I tell myself there's nothing to be nervous about. There aren't any bloody bodies lying here any more, there's been a fingertip search of the whole area.

What if someone was standing hidden, watching us?

The area around the cabin is still roped off. I feel an impulse to crawl under the tapes, but I don't. We're more than close enough. Ulrik is clearly uneasy. He's got out his Zippo lighter and flicked back the cap. He's rolling the spark wheel as if he feels like burning the whole place down. I look towards the cabin, towards the annexe. The cabin has fine wooden carving on the doorframe. I wonder who did it – was it Storen's father, who worked at the steel works? That's a detail I've not included in the book, I wonder whether I should follow it up.

I remember another detail. Something about the information Ståle Storefjeld, Gry's brother, had given the police.

His sister always wore the same necklace round her neck, he told them, a chain with a golden heart and a silver anchor, with a small diamond in each. He didn't know where she had got it, whether it was a gift or something she had bought herself, but it was the only jewellery she used. Ståle had popped in to see her in Westye Egebergs gate a week before the cabin trip, and that evening she was wearing it round her neck as usual, he remembered that clearly. But when her brother saw her body, he noticed at once that the necklace had gone. Had the terrorists taken it? But if they had, why had they bothered with that, of all things? According to the police nothing else had been stolen from the bodies or from the cabin.

We stand there for a while. Everything is quiet. Or perhaps we can't hear the sounds. We examine the walls, the grass in the yard, the vegetation around it, we stand there reverently, silently, as if we're in a museum. The barrier tapes look out of place in these surroundings, swaying gently whenever there's a breath of wind. Ulrik takes some pictures with his mobile. I don't know what for. As a souvenir perhaps. I am holding my pad, but I don't make any notes. I just stand there. Trying to imagine a figure, or several figures, coming out of the forest in the early morning, or during the night, gliding into the cabin and into the annexe. The knives. Steel being thrust into the side of the neck, pressed downwards towards the base of the bed, pitiless, professional. Perhaps it took only a few seconds before they were out of the buildings again and disappeared into the trees without a trace.

Can anything be worse than such a monstrous act? It is, it was, a devouring by the jaws of wild animals out of the dark forests. Who could stand over a child, perhaps even as the child opened its eyes, and stick a knife into its throat? The thought is unbearable, it leaves a stabbing pain in my body. It is no comfort that evil on this scale is so rare in a country like ours.

Without saying a word, we turn together and begin to walk back. 'Fuck,' says Ulrik when we reach the main track.

'Fuck.' He's walking behind me. Suddenly I can't hear his footsteps any more. I feel afraid, turn round. He has gone in between the trees and is standing throwing up over a tuft of blueberry plants. The colours in his cap seem to gleam – red, yellow, green. I can't get back to the car fast enough, it's as if the whole landscape is cursed.

The day I'm to visit Berge I'm in a strange mood. I'm looking forward to meeting him, but at the same time I'm nervous. On the metro I play with possibilities: *The prince who abdicated … What was it that went so wrong … After Gry's death I'm considering returning to politics …*

It's the afternoon, he couldn't manage earlier, but he promised to make us a late lunch. He lives in one of the high blocks at the top of Nordberg. On the way up it seems to me that I'm on a journey, a journey that is much further than that short distance would imply. The idea comes back to me as I move in between the tall blocks. It might be because I'm just near Sognsvann lake, on the edge of Nordmarka. Do I have the impression that I'm on my way into the forest? I don't think so. But as I cross the threshold and enter the hall, I get the feeling that I'm doing something risky, without being able to put my finger on what's causing this feeling.

Do I suspect that it is all more complicated than I want to believe?

Berge is dressed in the same slightly old-fashioned style; it's true he has discarded his jacket and tie, but he's still wearing a waistcoat, an elegant waistcoat, over his shirt. All he needs is a watch chain, I think. On the way into the living room he shows me his study, in which the most noticeable thing is the long desk in front of the window. In an old tea caddy with the picture of an elephant there are at least twenty black pencils, all of a make I don't know, all with the points facing upwards, all so sharp that I think he must have a special pencil sharpener. I note that he has not just one but three large screens linked to the computer, placed side by side like a triptych. He must have been working when

I rang, because all the screens are lit up – and all are full of documents, of writing. I have to laugh, and I ask whether he really needs three screens – in order to write short stories, I'm thinking – and he answers that they date from the time he was writing a paper in religious history on religious structures in computer games. 'For some years I played a great deal,' he says. 'Far too much,' he adds, laughing. 'I nearly got repetitive strain injury. Since then they've just stayed there, but I like to fill the screens with writing, to see chunks of text in relation to one another, actually in space, as it were. Have you ever looked at the Jewish Talmud?' he asks. I have to shake my head, and for a moment I'm embarrassed at my lack of knowledge of the Jewish Talmud. 'It's a little bit like that,' he says, waving his hand at all the windows of text. 'It's a special method,' I say, and I notice that the desk is covered with slips of tracing paper, which are full of writing as well. I raise my glance to the window. How I would like to live like this. It is impossible not to think of my own town house, where I can just see into other town houses. Here the whole of Oslo is spread out beneath us. Perhaps like a Talmud of districts, I think. Due to the screens I get the impression of standing in a command centre, or in the control tower of an airport.

I know that his mother is dead, but it's now that he tells me this was his mother's flat, that his parents divorced whilst Berge was at secondary school and his mother moved here. Berge took over the flat when his mother died in a traffic accident, just after he began his studies. He never lived with Gry Storefjeld in the city, or rather, he only stayed there for a few days at a time. 'And she stayed here?' I ask. 'Yes, of course, she often stayed the night here,' he says.

The information gives me a kick. I'm on the right track. This can breathe life into the portrait. I can see the two of them in here, over by the window, or perhaps in front of the three screens, eagerly involved in a game. *They had the whole world at their feet.*

Otherwise the little flat doesn't hold any surprises. I can't make out any traces of his mother in the living room, any pictures or objects. Through one door I catch a glimpse of a tidy kitchen. From the ceiling hangs a three-tier basket full of fruit and vegetables. Fresh colours. On a bench there are tins and bottles of olive oil and balsamic vinegar. I would like to have seen his room when he was a boy, all that a boy's room reveals; I wonder whether it still exists, in his father's flat on Bygdøy allé.

There is quiet music coming from two old loudspeakers. At first I don't recognise it, at least it's not Charlie Parker as I half expected, but then I can hear that it's Frank Sinatra, even if the songs are unfamiliar. I discover a record player, and then an LP cover down near the floor, *In the Wee Small Hours,* I try to memorize it, feel that I'm a kind of detective, knowing that everything can be important, everything can be a clue, everything can lead to a gilt-edged story about Gry Storefjeld.

I sit down on a light-coloured sofa, and even before I switch on my recorder I ask a few questions about his parents, I ask him to tell me about his childhood, and he surprises me by telling me a lot about his childhood, about the time in Romsås and in town, and whilst he talks I sit looking out, taking in the same panorama as from his study. It strikes me how strange this is. Only a month ago I was sitting in a town house with no view, feeling depressed, the incarnation of *tristesse,* and now I'm here, with an attractive man and a view stretching practically as far as Denmark. Shortly my book on Arve Storefjeld will appear. I imagine the critical acclaim. What will Martin say, will he perhaps regret the fact that we separated? I mustn't think like that. Or is it that simple? Are all my efforts motivated by the desire to impress one person: Martin? Do I still love him? I dismiss the thought. I discover that I've written a lot on my pad, somehow or other I have managed to follow Berge's stories from his younger days.

He serves freshly-baked croissants with poppy seed, tells me that he occasionally bakes, mostly bread. I can't help myself, I have to ask if he learnt it from Gry. 'She never baked,' he says. 'She couldn't bake, she couldn't cook at all.' He says it as if it's an accusation. I note it as an interesting detail. But how much does it say about Gry? I think of myself, I never cook either. I just make sandwiches.

He brings in the teapot and more food, puts it on the table, salami with fennel, pâté, a couple of cheeses, jam. The tea service is of porcelain. Elegant. Must have been his mother's, I think. It occurs to me that there is something slightly feminine about Berge, he seems delicate, or not very robust.

I scribble down a couple of keywords on my pad, thinking that this is real fieldwork, I'm a researcher. I ask if he can say a little more about their relationship, whether there any events he remembers particularly well.

He gets up and turns off the low background music, looking apologetically at me. Again he hesitates, in the way he did when we were on Olaf Ryes plass. 'We went to Dovre several times, to the cabin under Raudberget,' he says next, and I nod and make a note, even though I can hear at once that it's nothing I can use. I change the subject and move on to something I have planned to ask, about the time in Young Labour, politics, you were both members of the same Young Labour group, I say, St. Hanshaugen. Yes, he joined when he returned from military service, he tells me, the year before he and Gry got together. 'You did military service?' I ask, astonished, I don't know why, but I would have guessed he was a conscientious objector or had been excused like so many other well-placed youngsters, perhaps by pleading some obscure defect or other. 'I served in the army,' he says, not without a certain pride. 'Inner Troms. I believe that Norway's defence capability should be strengthened,' he says, as if to pre-empt me, 'I met a lot of opposition in Young Labour because of my position on defence matters, there are still many who dislike our membership of NATO.' He is fired up, and in his voice I can suddenly hear an aggression I've not heard before.

I return to him and Gry in Young Labour. He's not so comfortable with this, twists on his chair, searching for words, but he does answer my questions. Yes, Gry was less critical of the main party than he was. 'You lost an election?' I drop the remark in lightly. 'Yes, I lost an election,' he says. 'I felt bitter, at least I did back then.' He smiles, while his fingers play over the buttons in his waistcoat as if they were the buttons of an accordion. He talks about his shyness, about how he struggles to express himself orally – he looks as me as if he knows that I'm going to remark on his deficiencies as a speaker in my portrait – and he tells me about an ignominious TV debate where he almost caused a scandal, about his disillusionment afterwards, followed by him nailing a poster with theses against the Labour Party to the door on Youngstorget, and being excluded. All this I know, but I make notes for the sake of appearances. And then finally he gets to what I've been hoping he'll touch on, Gry as a politician. 'She was a much better debater than I was,' he says, 'she had an exceptional talent.' I ask if he believes Gry could have become Prime Minister. 'Why should she have been limited to Norway?' says Berge. 'For all I know, Gry could have become General Secretary of the United Nations.' That sounds so great that my mouth almost starts to water. *Perhaps the greatest political talent Norway has seen was snatched away at Blankvann.*

I mention his blog. Pens. Why did he start it? He stumbles over his words again, expresses himself so clumsily that I feel sorry for him. 'I suppose it's because … I'm hoping to reach the few people who are concerned about the future of social democracy,' he says. I try to press him a bit further, and suggest that many of his recent posts are very critical of the Labour Party. He answers that it was in the Labour Party's own interest to encounter some opposition – he looks up, as if he's worried that the word opposition might be misunderstood at a time when the party is hard pressed – he meant, to sharpen its arguments by meeting other views, so that they could work out a better ideological foundation than they had now. He pauses, perhaps fearful that he's gone too far, he insists I take another croissant, says I ought to try a little fig jam together with the cheese. 'The Labour Party today is not far from being a conservative party,' he says as he pours me more tea. 'It's only a veneer of socialism which prevents it from being any old liberal party, with market and growth as the two central pillars.'

'Is that the main theme of your blog?' I want to know.

He thinks about it for a long time, as if he's weighing up whether it's worth the effort of answering. Then he says: 'I've written several times about the Norwegian people's increasing and indefinable dissatisfaction. Because it is a paradox: our discontent with the way things are is growing in proportion to our increased standard of living. It ought to be our goal to reduce the discontent and open up perspectives, so that we can see that there's no reason to be so indignant and dissatisfied as many of us are.' He puts his hand to his left breast as if he's forgotten that he's not wearing a jacket, with no fountain pen to get hold of, gold split nib and blue ink. 'I think the Labour Party has let people down,' he goes on. 'By raising our expectations even more they are contributing to the discontent. And that's despite the fact that we already live in paradise.' Berge has warmed to his theme, his sentences flow better, at the same time as he uses his hands to underline some of his opinions. I can't help smiling, I like to see him like that, it appears to be a contradiction, a man in conservative clothes putting forward radical ideas. I like it, I like the glow on his face. 'May I offer you a glass of Armagnac?' he asks. 'Mother was fond of a little glass of Armagnac, and I'm trying to keep the tradition going.'

I think that I ought to say no. I say yes.

I discover a photograph without a frame, leaning against the books on a little shelf behind him. It's a picture of Gry and Nicolai with their arms around each other. It's too far away for me to be able to see the details, but it looks to me as if it's been taken on the grass outside Valen, the Storefjeld family's place in Nordmarka – I've just been there and I think I recognise the entrance behind them. Last time we met Berge claimed that he'd never been there. Of course the picture *might* have been taken outside the main cabin at Dovre, I can't remember any longer what that looked like. I refrain from asking, it could be awkward.

'Did Gry smoke hash?' I ask. It's the right moment to confront him with this.

His thoughts are elsewhere. We have both sipped our Armagnac, I'm sitting enjoying the afterglow. I repeat the question, checking at the same time that the recorder is working.

'No, Gry never smoked hash,' he says.

'I've heard rumours about it.'

'They're not true,' he says.

I'm surprised. I know that no-one has written about this, but my source was a reliable one. 'They're supposed to have found a little hash in the cabin at Blankvann,' I say.

'No doubt it belonged to that Frenchman,' Berge says. 'A prick. A dopehead. It was a misfortune that he settled in Norway. Excuse me. You shouldn't speak ill of the dead. I'm just trying to say that he was a dubious character. Gry was far too good for him.' *Even after her death he defends her.* No, scrub that.

'Didn't she have any dubious sides at all?' I can hear that my question has a challenging ring, but something or other has provoked me. I remember too what he told me about the chess game.

'She was sceptical about my short stories,' he says. Laughs it off. 'Have you read any of my books?' I shake my head, I'm afraid not, I say. He doesn't seem upset about it, just waves his hand at the table to indicate that I should help myself. 'Try the blueberry jam as well,' he says.

I'm about to ask a question about money, he can't earn a living as an author – I almost said a failed author. But then I remember about the grandfather, the entrepreneur, and that Berge doesn't have to worry about money. 'Did Gry criticize you because you were, what would you call it ... comfortably off?' I ask instead.

'We never talked about money,' he says. 'But the fact that my family had money was of course used against us. By almost everyone. Somehow people couldn't imagine that you can be a kind of aristocrat and nevertheless vote Labour. Look at Olof Palme, he came from a bourgeois family and grew up in a fashionable quarter of Stockholm, but he became a social democrat anyway.'

Apropos money, there was something else that surprised me when we went into his study. It was almost empty, made a kind of minimalist impression. No pictures of Gry on the walls. No letter racks, ring binders, filing cabinets, books, piles of paper. Only a glass tortoise on top of some cuttings, lying on the corner of the desk. But on the windowsill there were four empty vodka bottles of different brands – I recognised the labels on a couple – with a white lily in each. I couldn't remember on the spot whether the lily was a symbol of love or death, or perhaps both. The question popped up at once: did he drink? Did he sit here drowning his sorrows? When I turned round, my eyes met something equally mysterious: in one corner there stood a large old-fashioned safe, four-square, the sort that could have been a prop in a film about the Olsen gang. The sight made me laugh. I pointed. 'Crammed with something worth more than gold bars,' he said. 'Good stories.' He smiled. 'You keep your manuscripts in that?' I asked. 'Backup,' he said. 'An external hard drive. And printouts. I've got twenty finished manuscripts inside that steel box. Dangerous things. Explosive!' I was uncertain whether he was being serious or joking. 'You're only twenty-nine,' I said. 'I work hard,' he said. 'It's all I do. I sit here writing. Day and night.'

Thinking about his study, I have a sudden idea. I grab my notepad and write 'NB! The safe – love letters?' I could ask him? I don't ask. I look out of the window. It's good to sit on the light-coloured sofa. Good to be in this room. A room for social intercourse. Sexual intercourse. Freudian thought associations.

'May I offer you another glass of Armagnac?' he says. I think about it, I know I should refuse. 'OK, perhaps a small glass,' I say. There's something in the air. Intensity? Electricity? I can't remember the last time I felt so … present. Is it because I have a feeling of being close to Gry Storefjeld, a dead person, a murdered person?

'Do you have any theory about what might have happened at Blankvann?' I ask, then regret it at once; it was too abrupt a question, it could sound brutal.

He doesn't react, just looks at the old LP cover, Frank Sinatra standing in the street smoking, evening, blue light. *Blue days, blue music.* 'I'm not so sure that they were victims of … fanaticism,' he says. 'Like the papers say. Perhaps the fact is rather that we, the whole nation, have been victims of a lack of imagination.'

A cryptic statement. Droll. I hide my confusion by sipping my Armagnac. It burns my throat, burns in a good way. I pick up on the word 'imagination', one of *my* words. One of the 'Brass in Pocket' words. A battle cry. I try to get him to say more. What could the motive be?

'I believe it's inexplicable,' he says, studying his glass. 'The question as to why those five people were killed has no answer.'

'You can't mean that,' I burst out. 'No-one could live with that.'

'I know,' he said. 'Nevertheless. What if this whole incident is without meaning,' he says. 'That the reasons are so banal that they're incomprehensible.'

His voice has taken on a different timbre. He understands that he's saying something unbelievable, but he chooses to say it anyway. I want to ask, but can't formulate the question. He points at the teapot. I hold up my hand to say I've had enough.

'Sometimes even cruel and shocking things are the result of chance,' he says, talking out into the room without looking at me. 'In our eagerness to find a compelling reason we're blind to that.'

There's something about the way he says it. He seems convinced. All this confuses me. I think: *he's mad with grief.* He's not making sense. I want to write something, but it just becomes a line, I can't find the words. I sit silently, for a long time. Berge says nothing either. He looks at the Sinatra cover, I think he wants to put the music on again, to change the mood, but he doesn't do it.

I ask about his reaction when he and Gry broke up, but I don't listen when he answers, or tries to answer; it's as if the interview, the project, is fading more and more into the background. He points at my glass. I want to shake my head. I nod. 'Just a few drops,' I say. He's put the bottle away, gets it out again.

There's a different light outside the windows, it will soon be evening. Two things have grown steadily stronger during the time I've been in the flat. Curiosity. Who is he? It's not just that he's less simple than I first thought, it's also as if I can now sense a strength in him, a strength he doesn't wish to use. He's a Jedi in hiding, I think, remembering how preoccupied I was with that universe in my childhood. I notice that Gry Storefjeld is being pushed into the background, even though it is Gry I want to cast light on, and Berge was just a pretext. And the other thing: attraction. It may be that he's a loser, but I feel, what's the word, a warmth towards him, sympathy, and of the kind, the dangerous kind, I think, which makes me want to go to bed with him, to show him that he is worth something, that he mustn't give up; although that's what I suspect he feels like doing – I'm not sure why – perhaps even like committing suicide. Surrendering to meaninglessness. I want to save him. But there's something else, I think, almost breathless inside, because behind this idea of a sympathy fuck, or whatever you would like to call it, behind this seemingly noble motive, there lies genuine lust, trembling, a desire I've forgotten I can feel; it's impossible to ignore it, my desire is so strong that I have difficulty stopping myself from touching him as he stands close to me to refill my glass. He is a fascinating man.

Different. *Unpredictable.* And I have registered his glances. He's interested too, he looks at me when he thinks I don't notice, and in a way I recognise from other men's looks in similar situations – although it's a long time since I've been in a similar situation. Far too long since. Suddenly I am tempted to throw caution to the winds. I'm sitting with my glass between my fingers, feeling the warmth spreading though my body, weighing the pros and cons; I can see all the things which weigh heavily against it, but despite that I'm willing, I can't rationalize it away, I'm willing to take a great risk.

On the other hand: I've got what I need now, I know that I've got enough material to create a good portrait, and indirectly to give a new picture of Gry Storefjeld; not just that, I've got a *damned* good interview which will impress people, but despite that I'm sitting here tempted to throw it all overboard, gamble it away, I have more of a desire to kiss him, try to kiss him, than I have to see my formulations in the magazine, *the attack on Gry Storefjeld was an attack on the future of the Labour Party,* to be rewarded with praise; it's a new situation for me, and I can't print the interview if I get into his bed, that would be to break the journalist's code spectacularly, I'll be in the stocks for life if I do something like that, publish the interview and it later emerges that I've slept with him. No, I would have to drop the portrait, and actually I'm less and less interested in finishing it, suddenly Gry Storefjeld is completely irrelevant; it's as if the glasses of Armagnac have lit a fuse, I don't want to feel people patting me on the back, *Blue days, white lilies,* I want to feel his hands on my hips, I want to hear his attractive voice whispering words in my ear, I want to run my fingers through his hair, I want to see this clean-cut, open face floating in the air over my naked body, make his gaze dissolve in ecstasy, nothing else seems to matter right now, I'm longing, I want him close. The only thing which annoys me is that Martin will be right, that is if I don't finish the portrait, because if I say I'm binning it I'll be admitting at the same time that I've failed, and if there's anything I hate it's failing.

I get up, thank him for his time, thank him for the food, praise the bread, the Armagnac, feel my legs wanting to go towards him, but I steel myself and carry the cups and plates out to the kitchen before I find my jacket in the hall; I did actually wear the red leather jacket, the Chrissie Hynde jacket, and I resist the temptation to give him a hug as he opens the door for me, I stand there and can't leave, my legs refuse to move, he's holding the door open for me, but I stand there impotent, ten seconds, twenty seconds, the threshold is an insuperable barrier, I want to say something, want to kiss him, but instead I manage to mumble a goodbye, something or other about sending quotes for him to check, and then I drag myself out into the corridor and press the lift button.

Down in the street I'm relieved. I take several deep breaths. The fresh autumn air cools me down. But then comes the chance event, the bagatelle which changes everything, which puts a stop to something or sets it going: I have forgotten my notepad. And I have not forgotten it deliberately. Normally I never forget anything, not in the whole of my professional life has anything like this happened.

I go back. Just before I get to the block of flats I stop. Something in me says no. I don't need the prompts I noted down, I have it all in my head and on my recorder. I turn and walk back down towards the underground, but I change my mind after a few metres, do an about-turn and hurry back towards the flats; I'm wearing my Chrissie Hynde jacket, why be so damned bourgeois, career-fixated, I'm a rebel, to hell with the portrait, to hell with the magazine, to hell with Martin, I take the lift up and knock on his door.

Something is happening. Everything is turning round.

He opens. The music is playing again. Loudly now. He's clearing up, has the basket of croissants in one hand. Frank Sinatra is singing 'Mood Indigo', I recognise the song. He seems genuinely surprised. But pleased. 'Hungry for more?' he says, holding out the basket.

It happens. It had to happen. *Catch a Fire*. We fall towards each other. Kiss. I'm so eager that I pull a button off his waistcoat. As if in a dance we drift into the bedroom, and again it strikes me that he smells of something different than his clothes would lead you to expect; we are naked and I curl round him in the bed, lie there breathing in his skin, and I realise what it smells of: he smells of ... forest. 'You smell good,' he says, as if we're on the same wavelength, and his mouth and nose are over my whole body.

It is different from anything else I have experienced, it's like making love to a ... Again the words escape me. Perhaps ... some kind of energy charge. Something happens to my consciousness. I expand, and so does everything in me – I can't find any other way of putting it. I try not to cling to him too tightly, try not to show how desperately I have been longing for such an embrace, but the truth is that I don't know what I'm doing, I just let it happen, and it is wonderful to have an attractive younger man make love to me so intensely, wonderful to feel that it's good for him too, that he values my body, and when I come, when the pressure, the vibrations, begin deep inside and spread further and further, it's so strong that I disappear, I'm absent, wiped out, I don't know how long for, I come round as he stiffens above me and closes his eyes, and later I shall remember that he unconsciously bared his teeth and that I noticed how pointed the two canines in his upper jaw were, that they made me think for a second of David Bowie, but at that precise moment I'm not thinking of anything, I just let my body receive the after-shocks of ecstasy, an ecstasy which, whatever comes later, is worth everything. Even several minutes later I regret nothing.

I go out to the toilet, and on the way I have to laugh at myself, just think, I was so horny that I tore a button off his waistcoat, I ought to find it and take it home with me, keep it as a souvenir; I shake my head, talk about taking Arne Næss's advice seriously, I think, changing positions, finding a surprising angle, sliding under the piano, I laugh quietly, and whilst I'm sitting there on the loo smiling at myself, my eyes take in the room. I went to the toilet once during the interview, but I tried to be as quick as possible and resist the temptation to pry into Berge's most private areas. Now I notice that there's a necklace hanging on a hook, almost hidden in the corner behind the cupboard next to the mirror. I wipe myself and wash my hands, then go over to the hook on the wall. I look at the necklace. My heart thumps. Another spark plug. A dangerous spark plug. It's a gold chain with two pendants: a heart and an anchor. Each with a small diamond.

There can be no mistake, it's Gry Storefjeld's necklace, the one her brother talked about, the necklace she always wore.

Everything falls into place. The picture I saw in the living room too, the photo of Gry and Nicolai. It was taken outside the cabin at Blankvann. He knew the way there. First of all I am angry, then frightened. I begin to tremble. I'm supposed to be a star journalist, how could I make such a fundamental mistake about someone? Despite his eccentric appearance, I had believed that I was interviewing a friendly and modest man, even a slightly weak and pitiable man. But he did it. I've let myself be charmed by a mass murderer. I'm the guest of … I'm terrified, I can see in my mind's eye how at that very moment he's sitting in his bedroom knowing that I've seen through him, or he's already on his way into the kitchen to find a suitable knife. I take hold of my throat, my head swims, I begin to sing as if to show that I haven't discovered anything suspicious in the bathroom, that on the contrary I feel better than ever, I sing 'Brass in Pocket', or rather I hum 'Brass in Pocket' or 'Positive Vibration' or 'Mood Indigo'; I don't know what I'm humming, I just hum, I wonder whether I should run naked out into the stairway, just run, get away, but he doesn't know that I know, I think, or I hope, and when I go into the bedroom he's still lying in bed smiling, as if he actually believes I'm in a great mood, or he's smiling because my humming sounds dreadful, presumably it sounds more like gurgling. I begin to get dressed, try to conceal my trembling, my terror, I nearly fall over as I push one leg into my trousers, I point at my watch, he nods, as if he understands that I have to run for something, the metro, a taxi, my life; I get my bra on, struggle with the buttons on my blouse, he pulls on underpants and trousers and sees me to the door, we kiss, he waves. In the lift I still think he'll be running down the stairs at top speed so that he can be waiting at the bottom. With a knife.

No-one. I run to the station and just catch the metro on its way from Sognsvann.

The following day in the newspaper offices. Behind me I have an almost sleepless night. The first thing I do is to go in to Martin and tell him that the portrait hasn't come to anything. I formulate it in vague terms, tell him I couldn't make anything of it, it was a dead end. Martin doesn't crow about it, instead he seems rather relieved. 'OK,' he says. 'OK.' He laughs and nudges me. 'Don't tell me I didn't warn you. The guy is too ordinary. Uninteresting.'

I don't know whether that's a comfort. Martin hadn't picked up on what Berge's capable of either. When, or if, Berge is arrested, I can just act surprised, shocked, tell Martin that I had a nasty feeling when I was interviewing him that he was hiding something. That I had even been frightened of him.

If he's arrested. Because I'm facing a bigger problem than an abandoned portrait. I have to tell the police about my suspicions. Or my certainty. At the same time I have to conceal that the tip came from me, from someone who's interviewed him. Will it be revealed anyway that I jumped into bed with him? *She made love to a mass murderer.* Unlikely. Why should he talk about it? If I'm honest, I don't believe he'll talk about it.

But *if* he talked about it?

Oh God, oh God, oh God.

I can't face going to the canteen, can't face talking to people, not even to Ulrik. I walk up to the reflecting pools by the government offices and sit on a bench under the lime trees. I've brought a sandwich I made at home in order to distract myself, chicken, pesto and sundried tomatoes,

I didn't feel creative enough for anything else, but it always tastes good. Now I can't manage to eat more than a couple of mouthfuls.

I'm tempted to wait for things to happen, to rely on the fact that the police already have Berge in their sights and will soon arrest him. No-one can blame me. I'm not guilty of anything at all. I've only gone to bed with him, I think.

Oh God, oh God, oh God.

Nothing happens. The days pass. I work on a couple of minor jobs, I can't concentrate, hardly notice the words I'm writing; I sleep badly, put it off, I'm in two minds. Then I'm diverted. *The Road Builder*, my book about Arve Storefjeld, comes out, and the interest is gratifying; I have to run from one interview to the next, I'm on TV again, I'm in all the media, I'm not myself, but the publishers are beaming with satisfaction, standing in the background applauding, and perhaps there's something about the microphones, the limelight, all the eager questions, which distracts me, makes me repress some of the worry; but it doesn't take long for my memory to recover and the worry to dig its claws into me once more, because I know that I'm finished if it comes out that I've been to bed with a cold-blooded killer. A monster.

Of course it will never come out. He won't say anything. I just know it.

Is he sitting watching me, listening to what I'm saying, when I'm on TV?

I must report it.

But what if I'm wrong? What if it *is* terrorists? Or some other explanation?

I'm not wrong. I must inform on him. Tell the police about the necklace.

I know a watertight way of doing it.

I walk over to a phone box, one of the few that still exist, at the crossroads of Rådhusgata and Rosenkrantz' gate. I ring up.

A few days later Nicolai Berge is arrested. The news is like a virus. The whole country is infected. People talk of nothing else. Berge is on everyone's lips.

I stay at home. Martin rings, asks if I can write anything. After all, I have met Berge. I just say no. Martin doesn't even try to persuade me. He understands. That's the best thing about Martin. I don't need to say anything. He understands that I'm throwing in the towel. First I've given up on the portrait. And now comes this revelation. He understands. He thinks he understands.

The days pass. I'm back at work. Sitting at my desk with my earbuds in. I work on various things, but stay away from the Berge case. The rest of Norway is preoccupied with the Berge case. Just recently Foyn grabbed hold of me and asked if I couldn't write an opinion piece. 'No-one has the same flair as you,' he said, standing there in a T-shirt with no writing on, no picture, just pure black à la Steve Jobs. I held up my hands, as if to signal that for once I had nothing to say. He dismissed it with a laugh. 'Bring me something when you've found an Ine Wang angle,' he said.

The weeks pass. One morning I realise that I'm pregnant. I've been longing for a child. I can't have this child. I can't give birth to the child of a murderer. A terrorist. And if I go ahead anyway, won't the risk be too great that it will be deformed? A monster? Of all things I start to think about the film *Rosemary's Baby*.

Is this a punishment, I think. Am I being punished because I've exploited these dreadful events to my own advantage?

That same evening I'm standing by my living room window, looking out at the fronts of the town houses curving up the hillside. My neighbour is putting a tarpaulin over his enormous barbecue grill, a proper little crematorium, and stowing it away beside the house. The strings of coloured lightbulbs are still hanging between the trees; I don't know whether he's forgotten them or whether you can light them during the winter as well.

I'll have to think about it. For a couple of days. To make sure. What if I were to have the baby? It would be perfect for a child to grow up here. Plenty of playgrounds and crèches nearby. A safe, protected environment. Actually this residential district is not so bad. I've been appreciating it more in recent days. The quiet surroundings. The well-kept gardens. A neighbourhood with pedestrian walkways. What if I stayed here, and got a cat called Ziggy? Why not have this baby? Experience the suspension of gravity that Rachel talked about? I could get a job at Østlandets Blad, the local paper in Ski. There was a politician who had a baby a few years ago and refused to say who the father was. She got away with it. What about Martin, would he put two and two together? Hardly. He didn't have enough imagination. And he was too wrapped up in his own affairs. For all I knew he might approve of me having a child, say that it was fine.

What about Berge? He couldn't know whether I had slept with other men around the same time.

But nonetheless.

I know what I must do. I have no choice.

On my way through the streets in town I see that my biography of Arve Storefjeld is being displayed in the windows of all the book stores I pass. It's selling so well that the publishers are sending me delighted messages of congratulation every other day. At home in my kitchen there are generous bouquets of flowers. I look at the cover and see my own name in shiny letters, but I have an unpleasant taste in my mouth.

It is not over. There will be a trial. Berge will be in the dock. I'm already dreading these coming weeks.

PETER MALM

I

Everything was perfect. Nothing was worrying me. I was sitting enjoying the few seconds before my drink arrived on the table and the impatient feeling in my throat, whilst silently praising Providence for decreeing that I should live in a country that I regarded, half in joke and half in earnest, as a model colony, a hidden corner of the world where we were able to live such an enviably comfortable and unruffled life. It was Saturday evening and I was sitting in Limelight, that distinguished bar inside the lobby of the Grand Hotel, just next door to Oslo New Theatre – hence the name, even though you could no longer stroll directly from the theatre foyer into the bar, as you could in the old days. The curious thing, but also the thing I liked best about the place, was that here I was as far *removed* from the limelight as was conceivable; there were always surprisingly few people in the bar, even on a Saturday, which I interpreted as a sign that the population of Oslo had abandoned all notions of quality and elegance, and would rather entertain themselves in noisy venues with gaudy interiors where to cap it all they were served by boorish waiters with no professional competence. I have often asked myself: can anything be compared to a bartender who really knows his craft, right down to his fingertips?

Edgar had just placed a Vodka Martini in front of me, on one of those soft coasters which soak up the dew from the glass. I shan't say anything here about Vodka Martinis, about the relationship between the vodka and the martini, far too much has been written about Vodka Martinis; suffice it to say that there are few things in life which can compare to taking the first sip of a masterfully prepared Vodka Martini. That means of course that the glass must be cold beforehand, the vodka must be cold beforehand and that the cocktail – naturally! – is not shaken, just stirred; that incomprehensible shaking is a sin for which Ian Fleming must take the blame, it is simply not a viable alternative. And Edgar knows it.

Edgar, yes, a genuine Anglo-Saxon name. Edgar confided in me once, after we had got to know one another, that his mother, who was interested in the theatre, had named him after the most reputable figure in Shakespeare's *King Lear*. And it suited him. Or rather, in my eyes Edgar was just as much the prototype of a butler, and made me think of Mr Stevens in Kazuo Ishiguro's brilliant novel *The Remains of the Day*. Edgar belongs to that dying breed of men who are invisible if you wish to be alone, but who stand ready within earshot if you need anything or are in the mood for a brief exchange of views, not least if this exchange is the precise reason why you have made your way into Limelight's cool interior on a warm Saturday evening in August, whilst other people fight for a place in the throng at the pavement cafés and restaurants, preferably with a view of a sunset which makes your eyes water (there's something about Norwegians and sun which borders on the pathological). I believe Edgar has the ability to read faces, that he can see when a guest requires an ear, and this evening I simply had to give vent to my – I won't call it frustration, but the slight irritation which had affected me since the day before when I had passed sentence in a criminal case. It was a case of a sexual assault, a brutal back-street rape, and in my opinion the sentence was too lenient; I would have extended it by a year, but I couldn't persuade my fellow judges (two well-meaning souls who didn't understand the aggravating circumstances). I gave no sign of it, but the judgement troubled me, and it continued to do so this Saturday. As regards the law there was no problem about the length of sentence, but was it just? I'm not saying that I don't support the humane tendencies in our criminal law. But nevertheless. Were we failing the victim?

That poor woman would struggle with the consequences of that terrible crime for the rest of her life. It must be permissible to express my misgivings over a Vodka Martini, which by the way was as perfect as ever, and when is a Vodka Martini perfect – well, when it's like drinking the Northern Lights.

I now disclosed my misgivings to Edgar, my sliver of bad conscience (without in any way transgressing the boundaries of my duty of confidentiality), and Edgar nodded seriously, as if he knew that simply by complaining I was able to loosen the knots that had tightened inside me; Edgar was no longer a bartender, he was transformed into a confessor, and in that role he seldom answered my questions, he merely supplied grunts and throat-clearings, and occasionally a brief laugh, as if to encourage me to continue – as he did on that Saturday when I kept going for a good while with my reservations and restrained jeremiads, and I was not required to raise my voice, because another feature of Limelight, my refuge, is the absence of that dreadful muzak which is often such a plague. I have never understood how people can talk when someone is mangling musical hits just behind their backs.

Edgar is something of a mystery, and to be honest I prefer him to remain a mystery. An omnipotent butler with no history. I value his poker face, the fact that he so seldom lets me suspect what he is thinking. It was a rare occasion when he raised his voice, as he did if he thought I had ordered the wrong drink, or a drink which did not suit me, especially if he felt it was too *vulgar* – it might be something I ordered because I'd read about it or wanted to try something new – and then he said with a disarming glint in his eye: 'Objection, Your Honour!' I always had to laugh at that. I answered: 'Sustained.' Edgar understood this noble art better than I. As a judge I have learnt to listen to experts seriously.

It was Edgar who, having cleared his throat as if to signal that he was taking the liberty of interrupting, asked me in a low voice whether I had heard the news that something particularly ghastly was said to have happened in a cabin in

Nordmarka. I shook my head (I had listened to neither radio nor TV before setting out on my expedition to Limelight). And I pushed the idea away immediately; I didn't want to allow the haze of vodka and vermouth, with a dash of olive, to be ruined by yet another story of people's incomparable talent for doing one another harm. 'I'll just have another one of those,' I said to Edgar, as if that was an answer to his question. This was my time off, and I'd spent enough time this week hearing about crimes in the District Court. Today I just wanted to sit here watching Edgar conjuring with bottles and shakers behind the counter in that eye-catching bar designed by a well-known Norwegian architect, and which with its slimline form and its mirrors on the back wall, with its shelves and sliding doors and teak counter edging, was a special exotic room within a room, a domain in which Edgar reigned supreme, and it did not take long before he arrived with a new tray and placed a new Vodka Martini in front of me. I looked at it for a long time, the cone-shaped glass and the clear liquid, it was in all its simplicity a work of art. By the time I was halfway through my drink I had forgotten Edgar's disturbing announcement. Only the word 'Nordmarka' remained drifting somewhere in my subconscious, like the olive at the bottom of the glass.

I never said goodbye when I left Edgar, I said 'See you soon', and it often happened that I was longing to return even before I emerged into the street and was standing under the hotel's splendid copper baldachin. But normally one of the fringe benefits of a visit to Limelight was my pleasure in the walk home, because I always saw the capital in a different light, or as if through a flattering veil, after a few centilitres of Edgar's elixirs.

On this particular warm late-summer evening the experience was if anything enhanced by the fact that I was wearing my lightweight linen suit – a miracle of airy comfort – and by the feeling that my panama hat and light walking stick set off the effect perfectly. I didn't need to

cast a glance at my reflection in a shop window in order
to confirm that I cut a fine figure (I have also retained my
abundant silver mane, and chosen a kind of rimless glasses
with thin gold mounts). Actually I looked like a judge; I could
have auditioned for the role of judge in a film. It happened
quite frequently that people, especially women of a certain
age, turned round as I passed with a smile I interpreted as
approval – as if there were too few people of my cast in the
city. 'You've always been a well-groomed gentleman, Peter,'
said one of the ladies in the courthouse recently, although it
was with a tinge of irony.

What do I do on my promenades through the streets? I
look. That's enough. I watch people, the small incidents which
take place, I observe everyone and everything I pass, and that
is enough. It's a pleasure in itself. It sets me thinking. I don't
demand any more.

I crossed Karl Johans gate and walked – I prefer to think
of myself with the French expression as a *flâneur* – across
Eidsvolls plass, where I stopped for a few seconds to register
the sight of the Storting between the two stone lions, or to
show my respect for the assembly which makes the laws
according to which I mete out justice to the country's citizens
to the best of my ability.

I had already managed to repress Edgar's tentative
remark, that sentence which contained the word 'ghastly',
and which, without my being able to explain it, had made
me hear an ominous bell tolling, even though I had no idea
what the threat was. I didn't want to be drawn into anything
either. That morning I had sat over my coffee cup leafing
through the paper, feeling glad that I lived in a country, or
a colony, where nothing of great significance happened.
After the headlines about seismic upheavals abroad, wars
and catastrophes, there followed the usual reports about
the small scandals and undramatic offences of our own little
kingdom. That was how I wanted it; I don't like disturbance,
I am a man who cherishes the small daily routines. I had
also – finally, I might say – got started on a project, a book

about justice, which I have been thinking about for many years. It was this activity, so dear to my heart, which kept me busy in my free time; in fact I had even been sitting at home earlier that day sketching out a kind of structure, and now I stood still with my nose pointing towards the Storting, towards the rotunda and meeting chamber which protruded like a friendly face, thinking about a thorny issue which had been bothering me for a long time. For what was the truth of the matter? The fact was that power always triumphed over justice. Was it for example possible to think that an American general or president might be brought before the International Criminal Court in the Hague as a war criminal? Of course not. And there were plenty of examples where courts did not uphold the rule of law if they were exposed to a certain amount of pressure; independent courts were unfortunately not always so independent, especially not in a country with a repressive regime. In such cases you could observe judges constantly putting themselves at the service of authoritarian leaders. If I were to be so bold as to set out a vision – although I would be careful about calling it a vision – it would be of a society, a world, where justice would matter more than power.

I strolled onwards towards Wessels plass, and fell into an enjoyable rhythm which enabled me to swing the thin walking stick which for the whole of my adult life has been a much more treasured possession than, let us say, the ski poles which the population otherwise esteems so incredibly highly. Of course I won't pretend that my great desire to write this book, to get it published, was not closely connected to Dobermann, or more accurately Judge Odd Bergmann, the leader of Oslo District Court. (He was called Dobermann behind his back because of his narrow face and irascible temperament, although some people would put a positive spin on it and say that he was merely a jealous defender of the court's reputation.) Now and then I had to visit his office, in which the most atypical piece of furniture was a Roman military commander's chair, and during these visits he always made sure to sit, as it were by chance, in the commander's chair, as if to underline the power dynamic, or the importance of what he was saying, and on the rare occasions that he smiled it seemed false, as if he was baring his teeth. I always thought that Dobermann saw through me, that he knew my deficiency and doubted my judicial competence. It was not least because of this that I wanted to write this book, I wanted to show him that he was mistaken. That I did have a certain pondus. To some extent at least.

I stopped by the Freemasons' Lodge and turned round. It often amused me to search out unusual perspectives, which showed Oslo from a surprising side, as it were made the familiar alien, and here, seen from the corner just next to the old café Halvorsens Conditori, the town assumed a cosmopolitan air. I say that well knowing that Oslo lacks any really ancient architecture, and that the few historic buildings we have are of limited interest; nevertheless, there was something about the outline of Studenterlunden's tall lime trees against the noble façade of Karl Johans gate behind, framed by the ornamentation and baroque exterior of the Freemasons' Lodge and the pale bricks of the Storting, which would give me the feeling of a certain historic aura and made me proud of the town, so proud that I thought – and there is no greater compliment – that it could be regarded as an exemplary colonial capital in a worldwide empire.

But on this precise Saturday I could not feel my accustomed pleasure at this vision – or to be more honest, this illusion – possibly because, without being able to put my finger on the reason, I suspected that a breach of normality was rapidly approaching. And I did not wish for any breach of normality, I wanted everything to be as it was now, with the days passing like pearls on a string, full of everyday activities in an overlooked province no-one took any notice of and which therefore could continue to be an unexciting backwater (in which from certain corners in the capital one might appreciate a far from sensational architecture). It was not many minutes ago that I had seen that all was good, as it says in the old Bible translation; I had been sitting with a Vodka Martini in my Eden, I had been in an elevated mood, despite the memory of an overly lenient sentence; but then my spirits had fallen, thanks to a couple of words which had crept into my mind and whose poisonous contents were only now beginning to affect me. And it was not the word 'ghastly' which almost made me stumble, but simply the word 'Nordmarka'.

I pondered this as I pulled myself together and tried to walk in a carefree manner along Nedre Vollgate, at the same time as I could not help glancing down towards Andvord as I reached the corner of Tollbugata. I don't know whether it was due to my uneasy frame of mind, but I disapproved of the location of the shop, which I took as a confirmation that something was out of joint. Previously Andvord's premises had been located between Stortorvet and Karl Johans gate, next door to the fragrant old chemist's shop Svaneapoteket, and it was there I used to buy my thick, creamy writing paper, together with the elegant envelopes with burgundy-coloured linings. My coloured felt-tip pens too, thin as tattooing needles, I had found on those well-stocked shelves. Now that honourable business was exiled here, almost to a back street, to a corner of town where few people passed. Of course I had nothing against the town evolving, but some things should remain unchanged. Like access to a handful of classic bars. Public baths with mahogany changing rooms, marble sculptures and decorative tiles. And top-quality stationery shops where you could go in and hold a sheet of paper up to the light in order to admire the sight of a well-designed watermark. That was the minimum hallmark of civilisation. Even in a colony.

At the end of Nedre Vollgate I caught sight of a white-clad figure walking up the slope along the green below Akershus Fortress. As far as I could make out it was the journalist Ine Wang. Even though I have limited enthusiasm for her tabloid paper, whose content seems to be shrinking along with the format, I did occasionally buy it on a Saturday because of the weekend supplement she now wrote for. I remembered one of her cutting-edge reports – or rather, it was a whole series which had appeared in the paper – in the mid-90s, about criminal activity in the construction industry; it was a really laudable piece of investigative journalism (and as far as I remember she won some prize or other for it too). It goes without saying that I have always applauded people who uncover injustices in society. In recent years she had also published a number of interviews which were worth reading; she had even portrayed Judge Odd Bergmann on one occasion when he was in the news, and I have to admit, much against my inclination, that the portrait was unusually thought-provoking, most of all because she revealed sides of that rather buttoned-up personage which none of us at the courts had seen a glimpse of – such as, for example, that he had been practising advanced yoga for 30 years.

I felt like stopping her and mentioning that, exchanging some friendly words with such a talented journalist (on the other hand I'm not the type to accost strangers in the street), but she hurried past, crossed Christiania Torv and entered Øvre Slottsgate. She was dressed up, as if she was going to a party or perhaps celebrating someone's birthday at a restaurant.

Before I walked on I turned my head to the right, as if my senses had picked up a distant scream. Or perhaps more a vibration. My eyes were drawn irresistibly towards Holmenkollen ridge. Nordmarka. Again the word popped into my consciousness. The picture of a dark, threatening forest.

It was beginning to get dark, and I set course for home, once more thrown off balance. I passed between the old Town Hall and the Garrison Hospital, Christiania's oldest preserved building (although it's not much to boast about), before I turned right at the crossroads with Kongens gate. I have always preferred this route, which in a way takes me back through history, and when I finally reached Bankplassen, my body felt calm again.

As always, I stood still for a few seconds, enjoying the sensation. This was *my* square. At the opposite side stood the new and almost camouflaged Norges Bank – so appropriate (and that's not meant ironically) for a country which would prefer to hide its newly-acquired and almost indecent riches – and on the right the old bank stood four-square, today the Museum of Contemporary Art. I looked across to the fountain between the two areas of grass with silver maples and registered the refreshing sound of water, before I looked back to the yellow awnings over the tables outside Engebret Café down by the corner of Kirkegata. I know it's an exaggeration, but for me this square represented something just as rare as Piazza Navona in Rome. It was a pearl, a precious idyll, and perhaps because it lay in Kvadraturen, the oldest part of downtown Oslo, it always gave me a longed-for feeling of stability, of something inviolate, and I wanted it to remain like that; I regarded myself as a judicial version of Archimedes, I wanted to be left in peace, I didn't like anyone trying to disturb my circles.

I let myself in to the building next door to Engebret Café and went upstairs to the top floor. I rarely used the lift; I enjoyed walking up slowly and admiring the unusual decoration on the staircase. No-one knows that there are private rooms up here, behind the yellow new baroque façade. The apartment is a secret.

Sunday is my favourite day, and it's also the only day when I make a bit of an effort with breakfast. I always make the same thing: eggs, bacon and toast, and it's important that the toast is so golden that it gives me the impression of eating gold. I tried one toaster after another, until finally I found a shiny marvel without too many buttons which provides the required quality, and which has the effect that my first mouthful of that crisp golden slice takes me back to my *annus mirabilis* in London. I must add that the way the slices pop up out of the toaster is also important, even the sound and how high they jump contributes a peculiar aesthetic element, a mixture of the kinetic and the musical. Toast is my madeleine, if I may use a literary expression. To cover all eventualities I also put a jar of English marmalade on the table; it has a slightly bitter aftertaste, a special piquancy. If all else fails, that does the trick.

It is perhaps on Sundays like this that I feel an even deeper gratitude than normal for this apartment on Bankplassen, and of course in addition for a view which unfortunately – or fortunately – very few people have seen: from the Ekeberg ridge to Bygdøy, with Kolsås behind it, not to mention the splendid old buildings in the foreground, with Akershus Fortress which draws the eye just in front of the fjord. I enjoy the privilege of being able to walk around my rooms naked, because there are no neighbours here; the apartment is 'not overlooked', as property adverts say. That is a term I embrace. I would like my whole life to be like that: not overlooked.

Unfortunately this Sunday did not turn out like other Sundays. I had put on my dressing gown. My bacon and fried eggs were immaculate, the coffee tasted wonderful, and my golden toast popped up out of the toaster with a kind of Pavlovian sound which made my mouth start to water. I had just tossed the morning paper on the table without looking at it. Normally I leaf through the paper whilst eating breakfast; I only do it to divert myself since there is rarely anything of any significance there – apart from the foreign news – but I must admit that it amuses me to read for example about completely trivial cultural events which are blown up over several pages by journalists without the slightest perspective or any idea of the context. (Quite often I think that I'm reading local church news, edifying notices about what is happening in our little diocese.) I was expecting some of the same bagatelles this morning, but found myself suddenly staring down at a banner headline on the front page which confirmed Edgar's hint that something dreadful was said to have happened in the forest. Almost half the paper was taken up with the news of Arve Storefjeld's death – or rather the fact that he was not just dead, he had been killed, along with four others.

Did a tremor pass through the building? Or was it just an earthquake in my own body which deceived me?

My first reaction was disbelief. Or was it more like irritation? Something in me wanted to deny that it was true. A terror attack, wrote the papers. I had to read the word several times, and if it was the case that the terrorists' foremost aim was to spread fear, then they had without doubt succeeded, for those bandits had not only killed five people, they had undermined the Norwegian idyll. *My* idyll. My Gold Coast. A morning devoted to lazy, unthinking contentment. I sat there with my coffee cup half-raised and noticed that my hand was shaking slightly. As I saw it, nothing was more precious than Norway's paradisiacal state, the fact that this country was almost untouched by major acts of violence. That was the most valuable thing we had. More valuable than Jotunheimen and Lofoten. Before the Second World War we had been spared conflict on Norwegian territory for 126 years. A staggering fact. And in the time after the war too we had on the whole managed brilliantly. I mean managed to keep our distance. We had been able to live in seclusion, to arrange matters so enviably well that we had avoided being drawn in. Into the muck, the barbarity of violence.

I tried to eat, but the food had acquired an unpleasant taste. I couldn't even summon up any pleasure at the bacon's crispness.

To be honest I wasn't a fan of Arve Storefjeld, 'The Orator from Bjølsen'. Despite my consternation I could not quite quell my antipathy. I had a mental image of him standing with his feet planted wide apart in his black T-shirt at Dovre, tossing out clichés, embarrassingly simple statements which were ridiculously over-interpreted, even presented as pearls of wisdom by a slavish press. For me, Storen, as he was called, had always been a phrasemonger, of the same ilk as my grandfather.

My father's father was a preacher, or he was a preacher when he wasn't at work at a small printer's. Grandfather was not just a hard man (I don't think Grandmother had a very good time), he was also the reason why I became sceptical about all religion from an early age. He passed his last years in a care home, but he lived long enough to be around when I started studying law, and as I sat on a chair beside his bed he held forth about the Book of Judges in The Old Testament, patted my arm and said that the judges there were the leaders of the people. 'You will be a judge,' he said in a prophetic voice, 'and lead the Norwegians out of their unbelief.' 'I don't think I'm aiming quite that high, Grandfather,' I said as diplomatically as I could, whilst at that moment it dawned on me for the first time that the gap between theology and law could be disturbingly small, that the Ten Commandments and the Constitution were in a way related.

Every time I heard Arve Storefjeld talk, booming out political phrases straight from the kindergarten, I thought about Grandfather, whom I saw now and then in my youth addressing a pietist congregation, and who to my surprise always said exactly the same thing, without anyone reacting to it. In addition, Storen behaved like a string puppet on the podium, with a repertoire of theatrical gestures which soon became familiar, especially the way he stood and aimed the words at us, or every important word, and for Storen every word was important, the words were footballs which he tried to head at his listeners. You could see how he got carried away by his own oratory, just like a preacher, to the extent that he might as well have been speaking in tongues, because much of what he said was just as incomprehensible as if he had, when you examined it more closely. But one thing you had to give him: no-one could enthuse a gathering as he could. Arve Storefjeld was popular, he was perhaps even what you might call 'beloved'.

But who were the four others? The names had still not been announced. There wasn't much on all those pages of newspaper, it was mostly pictures. So far little was known, but the main thing was that one fact: Storen was dead. The paper reported shocked reactions from leading members of the Labour Party. As I speared a large piece of bacon and egg on my fork, I registered my own consternation, but at the same time I realised that I was less upset than I ought to be. I must admit that somewhere deep inside me was the thought that they, the Labour Party, deserved it. I had always had problems swallowing their self-glorification – the fact that they claimed all the credit for rebuilding the country and creating a welfare state, and suppressed the fact that it was a joint political effort. I pushed the last piece of toast across my plate in order to pick up the last of the egg and bacon fat and thought that I must never say that aloud. For God's sake, I thought, you must keep quiet about this just as you've kept quiet about everything else.

On Sundays, if the weather permits, I risk an excursion outside the periphery of the circle I normally stay within. I embark on what I call my little stroll on the beach, and walk along the fjord all the way to Frognerkilen, where I tip my hat to Oscarshall before I turn back; but as a rule, and it was what I did this day too (perhaps because I was more shaken than I cared to admit), I content myself with strolling down the hill towards City Hall and along the quay by Akershus Fortress out to Vippetangen, before I turn into Kongens gate on the eastern side of the fortress.

It took me a long time to get ready, I think I needed a few hours extra in order to digest the significance of the headlines and decide that the incident would not be allowed to spoil an otherwise beautiful Sunday, and by the time I was standing in the square outside my entrance, letting the melody of the fountain cheer me up, I had almost managed to repress the whole affair. Unfortunately my anxieties returned as soon as I reached Christiania Torv. I was again reminded of how quickly things can change. It took no more than a glance at the display in Damm's secondhand bookstore for me to remember that it too had been ousted from its original location, the handsome premises in Øvre Slottsgate, where old sailing ships sailed beneath the roof over antique globes which stood on a sea of oriental carpets. A dried-up watering-hole. It would probably not be long before the bookstore had to move from here as well. That went without saying. Market liberalism demanded new victims constantly, and there was no-one who stood up for cultural monuments of this kind in a province with no respect for tradition and culture.

Presumably it was the sight of the books – combined with the frightening news about the incident in Nordmarka – which made me think once more that I ought to take a couple of months' sabbatical and go elsewhere, so that I could lay the foundations of my work about justice, or rather injustice. That it was on this Sunday stroll that the thought struck me could also be connected to the fact that I had treated myself to an early dinner at Solsiden Restaurant, on the quay beneath the fortress (splendid view of the fjord and a refreshing breeze through the open window, but too much of a racket for my tastes), for as I sat there with my crayfish *au gratin*, it occurred to me that it could do wonders for the progress of my work. For a rash moment I considered the possibility of a sojourn in the former Gold Coast in West Africa, but I knew that my courage would fail me. It would be better to travel to a Swiss mountain village, or a lake in Northern Italy – the latter especially seemed to me to be an appropriate place, since Italy also had a solid tradition of judicial history. Would that not be able to spur me on to a kind of literary feat? Days which began with an espresso on the terrace, croissants and orange juice, looking out at Riva boats (those shining mahogany marvels) on the water? I dismissed the idea, I could just as easily work here, and no doubt I would work *better* here. In this peaceful colony. At least this *previously* peaceful colony.

As I walked onwards along the quayside by Akershus, and stood on Vippetangen facing out towards Hovedøya, I thought some more about my book, or what was going to be a book – perhaps it would be a wasp sting in the broad backside of the administration. Even back when I was a student, it had startled me to discover that a law was not necessarily just. You obey a law because it has authority. Because it's been passed. No more to be said. No justice without power. From the perspective of legal history it had shocked me too to discover how *relative* the laws were! Just think about the leap from the idea that everyone in the old days believed in the Divine Right of Kings, to the present day where we believe that the people should govern, and think how unequally people were ranked in the Code of Hammurabi, whilst the American Declaration of Independence maintained that all were born equal. Yesterday it was obvious that you chopped the heads off murderers, today they had individual cells with a TV and a desk. Yesterday four legs were good, today it was two, to borrow from George Orwell. No laws were objective. Justice wasn't objective either. Justice was an artificial product of habits. Ideas about justice were as timeless as ladies' fashions. And yet everyone, everywhere on the planet, believed that precisely their understanding of justice was the only sensible one. That's why there was one question I never ceased speculating about: was it possible to create a set of laws which were universal or obvious or straightforward for everyone ('we hold these truths to be self-evident')? Presumably not. Unfortunately not (although the idea of natural justice does have its supporters). All this I wanted to write about. It would be my life's work, and at the same time a continuation of the modest fruit of my year in London: *An Eye for an Eye*.

Even Dobermann would have to take his hat off to it.

Yes, I had to rely on what was my strength: my inherent sense of justice, my inner compass, if I may be allowed to use that hackneyed phrase.

I stood there on Vippetangen, and perhaps I even rocked to and fro on my toes a little at the thought of the day I would go in to the office of Judge Odd Bergmann and give him my book, with a little dedication.

In the evening I had managed, to a certain extent at least, to push the news about Arve Storefjeld's sad fate into the background. I mixed a cocktail – I think I may make so bold as to say that over the years, naturally with the good help of Edgar's friendly advice (including with reference to the most essential equipment) I am not far from being able to prepare a decent cocktail – and got everything ready for an evening of celebration in front of the DVD player. That is my regular activity on Sunday evenings. Cocktails and TV series, *nota bene* British TV series. This warm late-summer evening I decided it would be appropriate to make a Long Island Iced Tea, and at the back of my mind I had something Edgar once said to me in his quiet way: mixing a good cocktail is advanced chemistry. You combine different liquids to act as catalysts for one another. It is a matter of stimulating reactions in unknown layers of consciousness.

My apartment is simply furnished. Tastefully, I believe, but simply. Ample-sized rooms with little furniture. Large surfaces, floors, walls, left empty. Sometimes I wish I could be there all the time, and never go out.

In the room I use as a study (the largest room, of course) there stands an old grand piano. Not all that large, but a grand piano – bestowing its grandeur on the room. (There is a deep groove in the frame, but I have not wanted to do anything about that.) In the smaller room next to it, which is also my library, I have two rather more special pieces of furniture: a Wegner chair and a divan. The Wegner chair is the sort which is called a Wing Chair, and it was a present. Like many pieces of designer furniture, it is practically impossible to sit in, but with the help of cushions I have made it extremely comfortable. It's here I sit when I'm reading or when I'm watching British TV series, and by that I mean documentary series, not dramas. Right now I was in the middle of a series I've seen four times previously, but which I never get tired of watching: *Civilisation,* in which Sir Kenneth Clark, the man who was Director of the magnificent museum The National Gallery in London when the series was made at the end of the 1960s, guided us through the cultural history of the Western World, in a way which made me wish I had been born British. At the same time I sipped my Long Island Iced Tea and thought about Edgar's pronouncement that a cocktail too ought to have a civilising effect. You were a Mr Hyde, and became a Dr Jekyll.

I enjoy these evenings more than I can say. Most other people are content to watch series like *The Sopranos* and *The Wire* (and intellectuals write profound analyses of them, as if to justify wasting their lives), if they're not watching crazy soaps, whilst I sit here holding a stimulating Long Island Iced Tea, watching *Civilisation.* It's true that everyone is looking for distraction, but I claim the right to choose my distraction myself, so here I sit in Wegner's wing chair, listening to Sir Kenneth Clark's sonorous English as he on this particular evening piloted me through the history of culture from the fall of the Roman Empire to Charlemagne, or more accurately his octagonal chapel in Aachen. If it did not sound so pompous, I would say that through these TV pictures I was *transported.* Few things can surpass the thrill I feel as I sit here holding my cocktail, in my secret apartment in a modest and unregarded colony, and pass the evening following Sir Kenneth Clark as he pops up in his tweed jacket in the most unexpected places in Europe, on the Hebrides, in Ravenna, always with a thought-provoking comment on his lips. What enrichment! A well-composed cocktail and Sir Kenneth Clark.

Yes, I have a weakness for British things, I admit that. I buy my suits on Savile Row. My shoes, my dressing gown, everything. There is a reason why my colleagues jokingly call me Lord Malm. And I won't pretend that I don't have a soft spot for the old British Empire. People talk about Ancient Greece, about the Roman Empire, but for me the British Empire is the pinnacle of civilisation thus far in the short history of mankind – because in the larger perspective the time it encompasses is frighteningly short. It is especially the British Empire's ability to build infrastructure and its efforts to lift people to a higher cultural level which I find myself constantly admiring – and obviously not its fixation with hierarchy and an almost feudal ranking of people, nor its demonstrations of power, which unfortunately at times could find violent expression. Now and then it seems to me that Norway is the modern equivalent of the Gold Coast in West Africa, that is to say as the British colony The Gold Coast took form in the first half of the twentieth century, when the level of prosperity was increasing significantly and they were building roads, railways and industry, schools and hospitals, telegraph lines and water mains, banks and post offices, and not least the institutions which guarantee a parliamentary democracy – before, that is, colonisation was replaced by independence movements (which brought more freedom on paper than in reality) and decline. I would never say it out loud, but it happens that I see myself as an administrator of the British school, in a country which at any time can be hurled into the abyss by the forces of chaos.

Yes, I have a peculiar philosophy, I am completely aware of that, and that's why I keep it to myself; these are theories which are not allowed outside the radius of my wing chair, if I can put it like that. But I have never felt myself to be a Norwegian, a supporter of the nation state with its narrow borders, I have always felt myself to be the citizen of an empire, and that Norway, however much we try to deceive ourselves, is a colony – not in the sense that we belong to another country, but in the sense that we are a part of an empire which embraces the whole planet and which consists of a nameless and supranational and faceless liberal capitalism and a network of communications which has no borders, in which not least the entertainment industry has free rein. The aim ought to be to exploit this to give everyone a new, healthy cosmopolitan consciousness and identity, accompanied by a unique chance to create a world-wide system of *justice*. The hope is that this first truly global imperium will be able to civilise us, to an even greater extent than the British one, that it might lay the foundations for a further development of democracy and welfare for all mankind.

The moment I think such thoughts I dismiss them; after all I am not Sir Kenneth Clark. But now, thanks to these sinister killings, which once more surfaced in my consciousness, I remained sitting there and let my speculation continue. I was afraid that Norway, like a well-ordered and peaceful province on the edge of this new global empire of civilisation, might be threatened by a regime of terror, that this attack might make a protective shield crack, that the country's character as a carefree Eden could simply be destroyed, in the same way for example as the British colony of Uganda, which was so rich in resources, was transformed into the evil nightmare which was signified by the name Idi Amin. I even went so far as to think about a novel I once read, or rather I just thought about the title: *Waiting for the Barbarians*.

I managed to push that thought away. I always manage to push it away. This was not my concern. Late in the evening, as I took up my position in front of the large arched window in my study and looked down upon the peaceful Bankplassen, where the water was cascading in the fountain even though there were no people in the vicinity, I thought as so often before that I had chosen to dedicate my life to aesthetic contemplation (almost in the spirit of Schopenhauer). Nothing must be allowed to ruin that. I had retired from the world, even though it looked as if I was in the midst of the world, taking part in it.

Monday was a strange day. My work in court did not throw up any surprises or particular challenges, but the so-called Blankvann incident was everywhere, on the front page of the papers, on screens, in corridor conversations, in the staff canteen. There is a general state of shock. There is a feeling of terror. The point is made that we conduct exercises where we defend railway stations and airports and other important hubs, and then this happens – a fatal attack in the depths of the thickest forest. In my lunch break I also read Ine Wang's commentary on Arve Storefjeld, about his importance in Norwegian politics, and I must confess that I was astonished; in my eyes, the homage was exaggerated, and I couldn't get it to tally with the critical journalist who had unearthed irregularities in the construction industry and revealed greedy business deals involving golden handshakes.

Now the names of the other victims were announced, and I felt a stab of pain when I discovered that Gry Storefjeld was one of them. In my mind she stood for something completely different than her father, she resembled a – what shall I call it – a tormented soul, and I found that appealing. It may be that my positive attitude to her had been sparked by a snippet of information in an extensive interview a few years back (she'd already been interviewed several times by then), that she had written a thesis on the poet Samuel Taylor Coleridge. I thought it was possible that she had the same affinity for 'the British angle' as I did. On the other hand I had been taken aback by a photo she must have given the paper herself – to all appearances taken early in the morning – which showed Gry at something that looked like a rock festival or a political camp. In the picture she was wearing shorts and rubber boots and a tight T-shirt (with no bra under it) which let you make out the contours of breasts which for many men, especially those who had read Plato, must have seemed to be the original template for breasts. 'Morning-Gry' was the caption – Gry being conveniently another word for dawn. It would not surprise me if that picture had been torn out of the paper by a host of young men, and that these men in their dreams made a solemn vow that at some point in the future they would demand that Gry Storefjeld should become president.

On several occasions I saw that the tabloid papers in particular referred to her as 'Young Norway'.

And now Young Norway was dead.

It incensed me that someone had killed Gry Storefjeld. It incensed me much more than the fact that her father had been done to death. I was sincerely sorry that Gry Storefjeld, the Coleridge expert, was dead.

After the court sitting I remained in my office in the courthouse, pondering as to why these five people had been gathered in a cabin in Nordmarka. Would it be possible to chart the chance events which had brought them there? Of all things I started to think about a novel I had read as a young man, Thornton Wilder's *The Bridge of San Luis Rey*, in which a monk attempts to find meaning in the fact that a rope bridge over a chasm in Peru breaks and five people are hurled into the abyss. Why were precisely those five people in that place at exactly that time?

My deliberations had been triggered by one particular factor. I had recognised another name, and it was undoubtedly this name which had caused the strongest emotion. Now I understood why the word Nordmarka had struck me so forcefully. One of the victims of the terror was Sofie Nagel. I had met Sofie Nagel once. Deep in the forest. In Nordmarka.

Thanks to the word Nordmarka I felt a strong desire to seek out nature, and nature in my small universe means only one thing: Slottsparken, the park by the Royal Palace. As soon as I had finished at the office I took my panama hat and stick and made my way to the park via the shady avenue of trees which leads to it from Wergelandsveien. This is a promenade I often take after work, at least in the summer months. I have a particular fondness for those lovely grounds on the hill over the town, no doubt because it is a so-called English park, and most of all I am in love with the Queen's Park, Dronningparken. To my mind 18 May is a greater day for rejoicing than our national day of 17 May, for that is when they open the gates to this most restorative of the town's green lungs. I need no more nature than this. Now and then, on extra hot summer days, as I sit by the pavilion with a newspaper, I imagine that Dronningparken is for me what Shimla was for the Englishmen who lived in New Delhi in colonial times, a place to take refuge when the heat became overpowering.

As I strolled around in the park that day – I have found a special route which allows me to see the grounds to their best advantage – and as I stopped frequently in order to admire the great variety of different trees, my thoughts returned for obvious reasons to a remarkable incident in Nordmarka.

I have never had a rosy view of life, I admit that, and indeed several times in my younger years I considered suicide (I was reading a lot of Camus at this time, and as is known Camus wrote that there is only one really serious philosophical problem: to decide whether life is worth living or not). Immediately after my degree – I had just got a job in a government department – I drifted into a particularly depressive period, and one morning I sat down in my small apartment and wrote a letter to my mother and father (they were still alive then) on one of the creamy sheets of paper I had bought in Andvord's stationery shop. I left the letter clearly visible on the kitchen table. Then I got out a small backpack, but I didn't pack anything other than a bottle of water (I think I saw the backpack as a form of camouflage), together with a bottle of pills which I put in the side pocket. I was quite determined to end my life in the forest. Later it has occurred to me how strange this plan was. I never walked in the forest otherwise (possibly a reaction to the fact that while growing up I was so often pressured into going along on a hike), but for reasons which were beyond my understanding, I had got it into my head that I needed to walk deep into the forest. I took the tram up to Frognerseteren and walked northwards on paths and forest tracks in what people call Nordmarka. It was a Monday and there was no-one to be seen, and I think I chose a Monday specifically because I didn't want to meet anyone. I walked for a long time. There was just me and fir trees and loggers' tracks and trails which led over hills and between lakes. I passed some buildings which I later found out must have been the farm Slakteren, and carried on northwards until I met a stream from which I filled my bottle, before I left the path and climbed up towards a high point. It must have been just south of Blankvann ridge, but I couldn't see the settlement from where I was. I stopped, as if a voice had said: here. You can do it here. I had reached a small clearing; there were even a few square metres of grass in between the mounds of heather. Here no-one will find me, I thought, perhaps I will never be found. The thought did not disturb me. I sat down in the grass; it was dry, soft and comfortable.

I lay back. I saw an ant, several ants. There was life everywhere, I thought, but now it would have to manage without me. I twisted round to reach my backpack, and just as my hand was on its way to the side pocket, some twigs snapped and a figure entered the clearing. There was a fluttering of white. An angel, I thought. Several seconds passed before I saw that it was a woman of my own age. I was puzzled, because she was remarkably unsuitably dressed for hiking; she was wearing a light, pale anorak over a white summer dress. It was true it was hot, but you don't wander through the forest in a dress. It was a fine dress too, not just white, I could see that now, but with an intricate pale blue pattern which made me think of the word arabesque – or perhaps that occurred to me because she seemed to *glide* into the clearing, moving like a dancer. To cap it all she had a garland of flowers in her hand; she must have found the wild flowers in the meadows down by the water. It made me think of Ophelia. To start with she seemed frightened, as if she, just like me, had never imagined she would meet anyone here, in the midst of the forest, on a hill away from the path.

I was thinking about this experience, perhaps the most cataclysmic event of my life, as I arrived at my regular bench by the pavilion in Dronningparken, in my Shimla; and as I was sitting there on that little rise, my glance resting on the pond with its fountain, it was as if it all came back more strongly than ever before, those minutes when I lay in the grass in a clearing, high on a slope by Blankvann in Nordmarka.

She had sat down beside me. I registered again the contrast between her light dress and the worn grey anorak. As if she was two separate people. She was called Marie, she told me. Marie Knutsen. Below us we could make out a lake, and she explained that there were some houses just north of this, a popular place, she said there was a marked ski track running past it in the winter. I told her I was not familiar with the forest, that I never walked round here. She laughed at that. It was a fine warm day. We lay on our backs in the grass. We talked about everything and nothing. She pointed at the clouds, and when she said something about cumulus it reminded me of a short story by Johan Borgen. Wasn't it even called 'In the Grass'? I smiled at the memory, and said something amusing about a thick cumulus cloud right overhead; I wanted to do nothing other than to lie here and listen to her voice whilst the fair-weather clouds scudded over the sky like white Rorschach tests.

Then she rolled over onto her side and kissed me. 'Don't do it,' she said. Nothing more. Just that: 'Don't do it.' As if she knew. Then she kissed me again.

Those kisses. The clearing expanded around us, the light changed, the grass seemed greener. And I lost all sense of time. The kisses lasted forever. Even today I can close my eyes and remember how her lips felt as they touched my lips; at any moment I can recall the softness, the moisture, the flame which seared through me.

It had to be one of the most mysterious events of my life. I was about to put lethal pills between my lips, and instead they were touched by kisses.

Saved by an inexplicable coincidence.

And she? Was there a trace of gratitude in her kisses? Suddenly she pressed herself against my body, threw her arms tight around me. I got the impression that *she was clinging onto life*. 'This was a lucky chance,' she said in a low voice. She must mean the fact that we had met. Yes, I thought, that's how you find another person, perhaps the person you're going to spend your life with: a lucky chance.

I was hungry. I hadn't brought any sandwiches. My picnic was a jar of pills. I had not thought any further than this point. By this point I wouldn't exist any more.

She took an apple out of the pocket of her anorak. She halved it with a small penknife, and gave me half. Later it occurred to me that that moment was reminiscent of one of mankind's oldest scenes. Except that it was the opposite: she un-tempted me.

She kissed me again. Her kisses had a new taste.

She pulled a water bottle out of her other pocket and offered it to me. I wriggled over to my backpack and found my own. She nodded. In agreement, I thought. We drank. We drank water and laughed. I drank water without any pills in my mouth.

Marie. She wanted to give me the garland. 'Leave it here,' I said, as if I wanted to honour the place where we had sat. We walked back together. It struck me that perhaps she also had a bottle of pills in her pocket. A bottle of water and dangerous pills. Now we were walking together through a warm and fragrant forest, along a wide trail, then on tracks through the forest, an avenue of fir trees and meadow flowers; we wandered homewards each with our unopened bottle of pills hidden in a pocket, I thought. We laughed a lot. As if we knew that we had somehow switched off each other's thoughts of suicide, rescued each other. Or: she had rescued me in order to rescue herself.

At Frognerseteren I bought her dinner. We were both hungry. We ate a great deal, I can't remember ever having eaten so much, it tasted divine, I thought that it tasted as good as if I had been saved after a shipwreck. She told me she had dreamed of becoming an actress and that she had been a member of an amateur theatre group for some time. I told her about the Young Lawyers' Reading Group. We finished with coffee and the place's famous apple pie. We sat there, slightly sunburnt and with pine needles in our socks, and closed our eyes, and I thought that this was definitely a better end to the day than I had anticipated as I wandered at random into the forest that morning. 'I'll never forget this meeting,' she said as we parted later at Nationaltheatret station. She told me she lived in the old part of town, near Harald Hardrådes plass, and was going to take a tram. I rented a small flat in Vika at that time. 'Thank you, Marie,' I said.

She disappeared. An arabesque, I thought. A complicated person.

Back home I read the letter lying on the kitchen table. It was as if it had been written by someone else.

It wasn't until the next day, when I was sitting at my desk in the department, that I realised my blunder. I thought about those kisses which had changed everything. Why had I not asked for a phone number, an address? I was in no doubt. We were two of a kind. She was my other half, the one Plato writes about in his *Symposium*. I went over to the old town after work, I trawled the area, looked round Harald Hardrådes plass, asked everyone I met if they knew a Marie Knutsen, sat in one of the cafés which were there at that time. I was almost on the point of standing up in the café and shouting: 'Has anyone seen Ophelia?' I never found her.

On two Mondays in a row I rang the department to say I was ill before I walked into Nordmarka, towards Kobberhaug hostel, eager and purposeful. With a backpack, with a large packet of sandwiches and a thermos full of coffee. An apple and a penknife. I walked to Blankvann and climbed up to the clearing on the ridge on the south-east side, I wanted to see whether she would perhaps appear in the same place, driven by the same thought as me. The same longing as me.

No-one.

A faded garland of flowers.

After that I stayed away from the forest. With the years Nordmarka became as unlikely a destination as the Amazon. But I believe it might have been because of this encounter that I always cut through Dronningparken, as if I hoped that one day I would experience another miraculous coincidence, and see Marie come walking up the grass slope towards the pavilion.

Then, perhaps ten years later, she appeared in a photo. I knew her again at once, even though her hair was different. It was a picture taken in one of the Labour Party offices on Youngstorget. I understood that she had a position there. And she was not called Marie. She was called Sofie. Sofie Nagel. Why had she lied? Because she was ashamed of having a bottle of pills in her pocket? Or did she give me the wrong name because she wanted no more than a kiss? That was enough. Nothing must be allowed to ruin it. Something inexplicable that had happened in the forest. Actually she had not lied. Later I discovered that she was called Sofie Marie, and that her maiden name was Knutsen, but she had married a Nagel in the meantime; she was divorced, but had kept the surname Nagel.

I thought many times that I ought to look her up and ask about it.

I had dismissed the thought. Now it was too late.

But how could she, who could kiss like that, become Arve Storefjeld's partner? Is it possible to comprehend the mysteries of existence, this impenetrable spider's web of coincidences which lets you meet a woman near a lake, and which several decades later lets this same woman be murdered on the other side of the same lake?

And why did I not find another woman who could kiss like that? I don't know. It's a mystery, and I shall let it remain a mystery. It's true that I had a couple of relationships with women, brief relationships. After that I lived alone. For me, and for a few other people, one can perhaps say that freedom (or should I say solitude?) is a greater good than love.

I got up from the bench by the pavilion and left Dronningparken. On a foolish impulse I went into the Theatercafé, but I regretted it the moment I was shown to a table in the room which must have the worst acoustics in Oslo. I was surrounded by noise instead of a low hum of voices. Of course I ought to have left the place at once, but out of pure politeness I remained sitting and ate one of the smallest dishes. I was a judge, people were nodding to me, I didn't want to create a stir. Fortunately the ringing in my ears wore off on the way home, and it was a solace to be able to sit down in my study over the blessedly quiet Bankplassen and enjoy the view of the familiar buildings opposite, all that architectural *pondus* which surrounded me and also implanted in me – or at least had done up to now – a feeling of being safe and protected.

It may be that my apartment was somewhat sparsely and randomly furnished, but I had got a carpenter to make my writing desk. It is T-shaped and placed in such a way that the bar of the T runs along the large bow window, whilst the stalk projects at right angles into the room. That means that I can work on four generous surfaces, and I have acquired an office chair on wheels in which I can steer rapidly around the whole T. It is a splendid writing desk, and it is also – in contrast to the rest of the dwelling – extravagantly untidy, with heaps of notes, magazines, old newspapers, and piles of books full of colourful bookmarks which indicate possible quotations for what is going to be my life's work. In one corner by the door to the hall stands the piano, in the other is an imposing open fireplace, and it is a festive occasion in the winter when I light the fire and then sail around this huge writing desk on my chair, as I search and leaf through books and make notes, without knowing where or how I'm going to use what I'm noting (and on evenings like this it's not so important to know where or how I'm going to use what I'm noting).

In the middle of the desk stands a treasure I have inherited from Mother, an old Sætre biscuit tin. I found it when I was clearing out the house. Mother used the metal box as a sewing basket. Inside there were reels of cotton and pieces of material, darning wool, needles and buttons – all those things from a time when people mended clothes, when we weren't yet rich, spoilt consumers who threw out any garment with a hole in it. In one of Mother's cupboards I found something else I hung on to. Several blocks of music manuscript paper. Mother was a piano teacher. The piano belonged to her, although I used to play it too. Now I cut the music paper in half and use each half as a memo slip on which I write bullet points, ideas, quotes from sources, things I think will be useful in my work about the precariousness of justice. I call it 'notes' for my magnum opus. I write with thin felt-tip pens, preferably size 0.3. I also write on the staves themselves; sometimes it amuses me to write sentences or words on different lines, as if I'm composing, writing a melody or a chord. I write these fragments with different pens, I have a system, and each theme has its own colour. I can remember my first year at school, when we wrote vowels in red and consonants in blue. What joy. These memo slips fit nicely into the Sætre tin, and when I put the lid on with the picture of a cockerel on it, it reminds me of my first ABC, the most important book in my life, the foundation of all my education, all the ideas which will now hopefully enable me to write an ABC of Justice. I think that one day I shall sew all these loose pages together into a seamless whole – or on the other hand it might be better to present it as a series of slips from which the reader can deduce the hidden links between thoughts which seemingly have nothing in common with one another. When I look at the cockerel on the lid I think not just of my first ABC, but of the fact that it's necessary to start from the beginning again. And at less modest moments, that this will be the cockcrow which will awaken the whole nation.

Nevertheless, during these days I did not experience the same feeling of joy in my work as previously. I had a persistent feeling that the killings at Blankvann were threatening my daily routine, my coveted skating around a T-shaped writing desk filled with sources of potential gold-dust (a small contribution to the civilising of mankind). I felt a steadily increasing resentment of these unscrupulous terrorists. The crime did not immediately appear to be catastrophic, despite the shock wave it sent through the population, but the phenomenon could be the start of something monstrous, like that famous iceberg which you would think would make just a scratch on the floating

paradise of the Titanic – a seeming bagatelle which struck
something colossal, something unsinkable, and made it sink.

On Wednesday evening I met my friend Lev at Limelight.
I have always envied Englishmen their clubs. I would like to
have been a member of an English club, a place where I could
pop in at any time and be met by distinguished hosts, get a
drink, a bite to eat, conduct a civilised conversation with other
members, regardless of how superficial our acquaintance was,
or sit on my own in a good armchair and read a newspaper
of the same quality as the English ones, in which even the
obituaries and the sports pages were miniature works of
art. For that reason I had decided that Limelight, this long,
narrow bar which was almost concealed behind reception
at the Grand Hotel, would be my English club, and when
you consider the dark Chesterfield interior, and not least the
ever-correct Edgar, as close to a butler as you can imagine, it
made sense; only afternoon tea was missing. We could have
been a stone's throw from Trafalgar Square, I often thought.
The name Limelight also makes me imagine that I've arrived
here from a kind of theatre, Oslo Courthouse, and perhaps
that's not so far from the truth, since large parts of my daily
life are passed witnessing the performance of tragedies (and
if I dare say so, also of comedies), and listening to a chorus of
speeches for the prosecution and the defence. In Limelight I
can shake off all of this, at the same time as I find an outlet
for any minimal need for conversation I might have. I can't
wish for more: a stimulating room in a renowned hotel on the
city's main street. A place in the midst of all the bustle, and yet
screened from the world. That was enough.

So I can't understand why I would start to talk about the
Blankvann incident, because I wanted to forget it as quickly
as possible. The killings were a threat not just to *my* carefree
life, but to the whole nation's carefree life, our position as a
retired and shamelessly favoured colony, an idyll untouched
by the world's misery.

Nevertheless I couldn't stop myself. 'It's dreadful about the other victims,' I said to Lev after we had settled ourselves in two comfortable chairs not too far away from the counter and Edgar's vigilant glance. It could of course also be that the place, Limelight, made me think especially of Sofie Nagel, the amateur actress. 'But I can't say that I was broken-hearted when I heard the news of Arve Storefjeld's passing.' Lev looked at me, visibly surprised at the fact that I, the circumspect Peter Malm, was talking so unguardedly. 'I can remember the years when he steamrollered into Norwegian politics,' said Lev, 'that was at the time when they just called him Arvingen, the inheritor – no-one is so keen on puns as journalists.' Lev laughed, or rather he whinnied; Lev, called after Tolstoy and with a face (something about the nose and eyebrows) which funnily enough can remind you of pictures of the Russian author. 'That was before people, including the brighter ones in the Labour Party, realised that he was an empty barrel,' Lev went on. 'But despite that they dared to make him a minister,' I said. 'There's no danger in that so long as you have good civil servants,' said Lev. I agreed with that, I knew all about it from my time in a government department.

It's always sad to meet old friends and see their decline, the gap between the student you once knew and the bowed figure before you. Not so with Lev Hambro. True, he was noticeably older, we are both 55, but he had kept his clear eyes, the spring in his step, his lively presence. Perhaps it was connected with the fact that he was a teacher. In a primary school.

'What would you like?' I asked. Lev glanced at the gleaming battery of bottles on the shelves behind the counter, as if they were prizes you could win in a lottery. 'I'll go for an Old Fashioned,' he said. 'I feel a bit like that this evening.'

One glance at Edgar was enough. He was already performing his artistry behind his architectural pearl of a bar.

'I've always wondered how such a glaringly shallow person as Storen could be so successful,' said Lev, and hopefully he didn't notice that I flinched, because he could just as well have said the same thing about me. 'Do you remember the magazine portrait that girl ... what's her name ... Ine Wang did about Storen last summer ... from Dovre?' said Lev. 'God help us if she didn't present him as a politician with the qualities of a statesman!' Lev looked skywards. 'Ine Wang is normally a good journalist,' I interjected; 'she must have been charmed, like so many others.' Lev moved up a gear: 'He was supposed to have charisma, but he had no more charisma than a snowplough. Utter rubbish!' Lev had large ears, and they were similar to an elephant's in that they stood out more when he got worked up. 'She could at least have weeded out all that prattle about "Einar and I", that mantra which seems to make all the party members wet their pants. As far as I know Storefjeld met Einar Gerhardsen once or twice, and they say that the old Father of the Nation was embarrassed when Storefjeld began to go on about their common background in the Highways Department. Yet Storen always got warm applause from the audience for every little reference to it: "We are now standing at an important *fork in the road*." He even said it with the same break in his voice as Gerhardsen.'

I laughed. I tried to stop myself, but I laughed. It was wonderful to laugh at all this, it was wonderful to sit here in Limelight, hidden away in the middle of town, it was wonderful to see Edgar gliding over with his circular tray and placing two glasses in front of us, each on its soft cocktail mat. I picked mine up and held it in the air in front of me, like a jeweller studying a precious stone. The colour is part of the enjoyment. I nodded at Lev, and we put the glasses to our lips with a synchronous movement. 'Aah,' said Lev quietly. 'Aah,' I said, just as quietly. Our enjoyment too was synchronous.

I sent Edgar a grateful glance. In Shakespeare's play Edgar finishes up as king.

If I was to say only one thing about Lev, it would be that he always wears an unusual garment which he calls 'my portable memory'. It's an old photographer's vest made by Banana Republic (he told me that he once bought five such gilets, so that he still has a couple of unused ones in his wardrobe), a kind of sleeveless khaki safari jacket with masses of pockets of different sizes, on the inside as well, and even on the back. The vest made him into a walking chest of drawers, I thought. Over the years I'd seen him pull the most amazing things out of his pockets; just for starters I can remember a Pez dispenser with a Mickey Mouse head on top, a nail clipper, a medal (genuine?), a colourful Swatch watch from the 80s, a jade dragon, a music box, packs of cards, wind-up toys, and the folded flag of Nepal – 'the only non-rectangular flag in the world!'. Lev explained that his pupils loved it, for them the vest was like a discovery from fairy tales, or the jug of the widow from Sarepta. I've always felt a special warmth towards Lev. It's as if I want to save him. I don't know what from.

It's possible I had a bad conscience, because suddenly I wanted to say something more positive about Arve Storefjeld. 'He could be an able parliamentarian, he often got people to agree,' I said. 'Yes, by deliberately misleading them,' said Lev; he was clearly not in the mood to dole out praise. 'At least he was colourful,' I tried. 'And randy,' said Lev. 'A womanizer. Even while his wife was alive.' I wanted to stop him, but on the other hand I wanted to hear the rest, because Lev had a friend, an insider in the Labour Party. 'Everyone knew about it,' said Lev. 'My Deep Throat says it was Valen where he fucked all his lovers; he drove them into the forest and fucked them till they could hardly walk.' I laughed; I didn't want to, but it was impossible not to laugh. 'I think you're exaggerating a bit,' I said. It wasn't surprising that Lev kept losing his job, I thought. 'It's God's honest truth,' said Lev. 'There are supposed to have been young girls amongst them, Young Labour lasses. They were rivals, they criticised Storen's policies. "I fuck them until they agree," he boasted once when he was drunk. There must have been a few who wouldn't mind seeing him dead.' Lev was quiet for a few seconds. 'But why kill the others then?' he added. 'Only heartless terrorists could have killed that little girl.'

The thought of that innocent child made us stop talking and focus on our glasses. I would have liked to talk about the four others. Gry, Young Norway. Lefebvre, the Frenchman. Little Sylvie, poor kid. And of course Sofie Nagel. But I couldn't do it. Lev was right. It was obvious that Storen was the target, the others must have been collateral damage.

Lev Hambro was the perfect man to meet, so long as it was just once a week. I would really prefer not to be exposed to his torrent of speech more than once a fortnight. Lev. A talent. In contrast to me. I had met him towards the end of my studies; he used to eat in the Aula basement even though he studied Norwegian and history up at the Blindern campus. He was always reading a novel he had borrowed at the Deichman Library. At that time there was a paper ticket in a pocket stuck in the back of every book, and the date stamps on the ticket showed you whether the book was popular or not. Lev always examined these tickets before he made his mind up, and only chose books which few people had borrowed. 'I want to be an outsider,' he said, 'I don't want to read what everyone else is reading.' After passing his exams brilliantly he got a post at the university. Then things went wrong on the career ladder because he was too honest. Or too clever. He got a job at a further education college. Here too he was squeezed out; he was too outspoken. Instead he became a teacher at a secondary school. Greatly loved. But not by the headmaster. So he finished up in a primary school, at Tonsenhagen, where he was teaching now. It must be like having Einstein as a teacher in your first year, I thought. Or was it not Wittgenstein who became a primary school teacher after finishing *Tractatus*? Whatever: his career had gone the opposite way from what Lev deserved. The most informed person I know, and he's standing in front of the blackboard at a primary school, I thought. If there's anything that shows how unjust life is, it's that Lev, the talented Lev, is a badly paid teacher, and that I, with my vastly inferior gifts, am a highly salaried judge. Lev never said what he thought about that.

I was considering whether I should mention a novel by Thomas Bernhard which I had just finished reading, but Lev would not leave the topic of Arve Storefjeld. 'And what can you say about those waffle lunches of his,' he said. 'Oh yes, the so-called waffle diplomacy,' I murmured. '"It's important to have a place for informal chats."' Lev mimicked Storen's voice. '"Coffee is the putty of Norwegian society."' I wanted to shut him up, but Lev was good at mimicking. 'The voters lapped it up,' he went on, 'they loved the image, a minister who was like them, who invited all and sundry round to his home on Maridalsveien, foreign politicians as well, and told them about his father who worked at Christiania Steel Company and all the factories which once lay along the river outside his window. Edgar, two more Old Fashioned!' I laughed; I didn't want to laugh, but I laughed. I turned round, concerned that we were attracting too much attention, but we were almost alone in the room. Lev crossed one leg over the other. He still wore some old Adidas trainers, which incidentally had had a renaissance, and now garnered envious glances from youngsters. Lev, 55 years old, was suddenly in fashion again.

We sat in silence for a long time. We looked alternately at the theatre pictures which decorated the walls and at Edgar, busy behind the teak fittings of the counter. Soon we each had a sparkling new glass in front of us.

'Well anyway, he's dead now,' I said finally, perhaps as a corrective to Lev. 'Yes, he's dead now,' said Lev, lifting his glass as if to toast his memory. 'Not even an idiot like Storen deserved such a fate, even though he was fond of calling his opponents idiots.'

'He was good at cutting ribbons,' I said.

'He loved marching over a new bridge with a brass band behind him,' said Lev.

'They ought to have a brass band in the church and forget the organ,' I said.

Lev was searching for something in one of his larger pockets. A timetable and an Australian ten-dollar bill fell onto the table.

'Have you been in Australia?' I asked, genuinely surprised. 'I went to Tasmania last year,' said Lev. 'Tasmania?' I said. 'In order to watch a big trotting race in Launceston,' said Lev, as if that explained everything.

Lev was interested in trotting races. It would have been better if he had been less interested in trotting races.

Later that same evening, after the effects of the Old Fashioned had worn off, I stood for a long time by the window in my study, looking at the Museum of Contemporary Art just opposite. It was rare that I was tempted to visit exhibitions there (too much kitsch for my tastes), but now and again I would feel like going in through the bronze doors in order to admire the unusually fine Jugend style of the old bank building, especially the light fittings and the use of metal in the décor.

I stood at the window looking at the façade, which was now lit up so that the rough-hewn granite was even more clearly visible, apart from the fact that the top was shrouded in darkness and I could only just make out the two large figures on either side of the heraldic lion. It was a good building to have as a neighbour, to rest your eyes on, especially this evening – and not simply because I was slightly dizzy after all that talk at Limelight, but because I felt shamefaced. I should not have brought up the subject of Blankvann, I just wanted to forget it, I wanted to return to the quiet of everyday life, I wanted to enjoy my freedom, including the fact that I lived here completely alone. Apart from my flat there are only offices in the building. It was a stroke of luck which gave me the chance to buy this apartment when the building changed hands many years ago – and I am eternally grateful to the new owner. I never invite anyone home. People would just begin to wonder. I don't want anybody to discover my hidden paradise. Only Lev knows about it.

I spend a lot of time on my own. Sometimes I think that I only have two friends – if I count Sir Kenneth Clark as one. My 'friends' otherwise belong in the category of head waiters, bartenders, shop assistants, barbers, receptionists. That is enough. There is a reason for that. It's not just my apartment which is a secret, I nurse an even greater secret: I am devoid of talent. Relatively, at least. I am lacking in talent compared with those who might be called talented. My consolation is that there are few who are talented. Extremely few. But despite my unremarkable abilities I dare maintain that I am a good judge. What makes a good judge? I understood that early on: common sense. Elementary understanding of people. It's not so much a matter of mastering the legal niceties as of the ability to listen, the ability to understand, the ability to demonstrate a certain tolerance. That I find easy (and I wouldn't call that a talent, it is a skill many people have). Often I can despise people at the same time as I feel pity for them. I think like the god Indra's daughter in Strindberg's *A Dream Play*: human beings are to be pitied.

Did I say understand? It's not just a matter of understanding, but of understanding that there is much which cannot be understood.

I was tempted to round off the evening by watching an episode of *Civilisation*, for example the one which ends with Sir Kenneth Clark mildly criticising the exaggeration and vanity of the Baroque at the same time as he walks through the prodigiously long Gallery of Maps in the Vatican museum; but instead I stayed by the large window in my study, as if that too was a screen, looking out, looking over to Akershus Fortress which lay there like a chain of gold in the floodlights, and as I stood there I thought again how fortunate I was to live there, in the centre, amongst three banks, two old and one new, and with the Stock Exchange a couple of blocks away. As if I was in the middle of a force field. Or was reminded that I was a citizen of one of the smallest colonies of the neo-capitalist empire.

I grew up in Kjelsås, practically on the edge of the forest, in a detached house which lay on the slope up towards Grefsenkollen, with a wide view over the basin in which Oslo lies. Mother and Father always wanted me to go with them on walking trips into the country, especially in the autumn when it was vital to pick as many berries and mushrooms as possible; they still remembered the food shortages during the war. But I hated the forest, I wanted to go down into town; I often stood by the living-room window dreaming about living in the centre, and it wasn't just because I liked the town streets more than the forest or the transparent milieu at Kjelsås, it was also because I understood that it was easier to hide in the heart of town than on the edge, even in the forest. Only in the midst of many people can you become invisible.

That is perhaps my only original thought: I understood early on what an advantage it was to be able to be invisible. To be left in peace.

Despite that I did not suspect that I was on the trail of my life's most successful strategy, the one which would eventually lead me here. To Bankplassen, the perfect hiding place.

I retreated into the room and ran my hand over the piano. Even though I don't play any longer, I sometimes get it tuned. On rare occasions I can lift up the lid and let my fingers run over the keys, the black ones of ebony and the white ones coated with ivory – both materials outlawed today – as if to let my thoughts return to my youth. Father was station manager at Kjelsås station (he moved to Grefsen when Kjelsås became an unmanned station) and lived in the pleasant house designed by Paul Due. Mother was a piano teacher. Both wanted me to be a pianist; I was good, people said, very good, but I knew that I wasn't good, I was only 'good' compared to the bad ones, I was good because I practised conscientiously. From my piano stool I could look out over the city centre, and it was not the University Aula down there and a debut concert I was dreaming of, even though everyone, including the teacher I studied with in later years, one of Oslo's best, was urging me towards this goal, but a life as a student of law, one of many students, in the buildings around the concert hall. One day whilst I was sitting in the house practising I was overcome by a tremendous rage, a need to protest, I don't know what you'd call it. I can't explain it, I have never understood what came over me. First of all I found a pair of pincers in the shed and tried to cut through the cords inside the piano, but I couldn't manage it, it may have been that the pincers were too blunt, so I fetched a saw and began to saw through the piano case. I don't know how it would have ended if Father hadn't come home by chance and stopped me – but not before I had made a deep groove. I didn't need to say anything about wanting to stop, not to Mother either. Later on I realised that it must have been the thought of being a solo pianist, sitting alone on a large stage in full view of everyone, which was distasteful to me. To pretend to be a master when you're not a master. I never played the piano again. But *listen* to music a lot; if nothing else, all that playing made me a good listener – something I have found useful as a judge.

The piano was not a 'road not taken'. I have never regretted it. In contrast to my parents – and several teachers – I recognised that my talent was sorely limited. That's why it gives me an extra pleasure to listen to the best pianists, to hear them playing a Beethoven sonata and remember how I played it myself, quite possibly without mistakes, but stiffly, to hear the difference and appreciate the quality. It's not so easy with judges, to hear and see the difference between good ones and poor ones; you can be stern or lenient, but as a judge you have your laws and paragraphs to refer to, precedence, judgements from the High Court, proof, cases made by lawyers, there's not much you can do wrong.

I often think how astonishing it is that I am a judge. That I dared to take such a risk. But when the opportunity arose, I couldn't resist the temptation to apply. My degree was good enough, and all my other formal qualifications were in order. Even though I half expected that someone, some alert and clever person, would come forward and upset the applecart, the process went through smoothly (fortunately Dobermann was not in charge of Oslo Courthouse at this point), and I must confess it was a festive occasion to be appointed a judge by the King in the Council of State. But in all the years since then I have tried to make myself as invisible as possible, so that people don't discover that I lack the capacity or the abilities I imagine that a judge ought to possess (it is possible that I set the bar high, but I think the bar *should* be set high for a judge). And if things – so far, at least – have gone well, it is simply and solely because I live in Norway, where quality is only superficially tested. It is easy to hide one's defects in a country which is characterised by the lethargy and the monumental indolence which always mark out a population living in abundance. I talk as little as possible, I write sensible judgements (in which the evaluation of the evidence is so thorough that it is not easy to appeal), and I treat everyone with respect.

It suits me admirably to be a judge. Without boasting, I must say that I have made the best of my unprepossessing potential, and I have made some choices which have had a particularly positive outcome. In the same way as I live invisibly in the middle of town, I have concealed myself in a high position. My camouflage is to be a judge. Most people who don't want to be noticed try to hide themselves in an undistinguished job, perhaps deep in some bureaucracy. I chose a different, and I might say a bolder strategy. I disappeared into a high position. I have placed myself in full view so that no-one will see me.

These were not normal days. I carried out my duties at Oslo Courthouse, I exchanged a few words with Dobermann, listened politely to his deep voice and cultivated, formal Norwegian (which disguised the fact that he seldom said anything of interest), and otherwise followed my normal routines and maintained my retired existence; but the whole time I was conscious of a kind of unease, and the cause was of course this horribly brazen terror attack. It was as if a sort of parallel dark world had emerged from the shadows, a reality which threatened to leak into my own painstakingly fenced-off reality.

To tell the truth I was afraid. For the terrorists' assault had not only been aimed at a target in the forest, I considered it to be just as much an assault on the country's greatest asset: our undramatic history, our invisibility in the global news picture. Even people in the US and China, people with advanced qualifications, had no idea where Norway was, much less what its inhabitants did. The advantage of this unique anonymity was that for decade after decade we had been allowed to live in peace, far from the world's curious glance. But now I noted that foreign papers too were writing about the Blankvann incident, or at least devoting a few column inches to it. I was so unhappy about this that the discovery made my heart pound for a few seconds. It was as if my own anonymity was threatened. I feared that what had struck Norway might also strike me.

I think it must have been this unpleasant feeling, this fear, which one afternoon made me stop on Universitetsplassen. I had finished work early and was on my way up towards Dronningparken, but now I changed my mind and directed my steps instead towards a favourite refuge, the Law Library in the west wing. On the way in I always glance up at the frieze above the main entrance where you see Athene giving life to the human being Prometheus has created; and although I will never be a Prometheus I can occasionally feel like that, as if I am being brought to life, when I climb the steps to the building called Domus Bibliotheca. Normally I go in here in order to look through books, searching for points and references for my book, my *work in progress,* or because I want to satisfy my thirst for knowledge, but today it was enough to find a place by the window overlooking

Karl Johans gate. I just wanted to sit there. Breathe calmly in and out. Watch the students. Be amongst the students. Out on the square it had appeared to me that that might be of some help. That it might steady me. Rekindle the spark of life. I hoped that just by being here I might be able to get back on the track of something I had lost.

On this particular day I sat there thinking about my stay in England after my studies, or rather after I had left my job in the department. My meeting with Sofie Nagel in Nordmarka was so decisive that it had changed my attitude to life, and before I started work at one of the large law firms I spent a year in London. A year which was not just a year, but an epoch, half a lifetime. During my law studies I had taken the history of jurisprudence as an optional subject, but since that only scratched the surface (it was Roman law which took up most of the course), I felt like going further with my investigations and finding out more about how laws changed over time and how they varied from one part of the world to another. In the Middle East, in the millennia before Christ, they spoke of an eye for an eye and a tooth for a tooth, and in Dante's *Inferno* we could read how the tortures of hell reflected the sin (if you had been a glutton, you had to vomit up food and then eat your own vomit again, for all eternity). I found all that stimulating. For how should we ensure justice, ensure that law-breakers were punished fairly, in a modern society? The result of my wrestling with this material was the little book *An Eye for an Eye*. It did not make any great waves, but it was read enough to secure me a certain reputation in the judiciary.

But London impressed me just as much as my studies did. It's true that I did spend short periods in Cambridge (Henry Maine!) and Oxford, and not least in Edinburgh – because the historical tradition was stronger there – but my base was London. Oh, what a city! Everything from the inexhaustible opportunities for enlightenment in the British Museum to the practically endless selection of tea and Turkish Delight at Fortnum & Mason. I lived just by Tavistock Square, that is in

Bloomsbury, with a short walk both to University College and to the London School of Economics and Political Science, and it was in the library at the latter place that I met Miss Huxley. She worked there. Her name was Ann, but in my thoughts I always call her Miss Huxley, because that was what a friendly man told me when I asked him a question: 'Ask Miss Huxley'. He pointed at a slender, charming woman by the desk, and as I addressed her, something incomprehensible happened between us. Despite the fact that I am not religious, I cannot do other than fall back on the wisdom of Proverbs: 'There are things which are too wonderful for me and which I know not, and among these is the way of a man with a maid.'

The year in London, when I undertook my special studies in legal history, was an *annus mirabilis* in more than one way. Not only did I write *An Eye for an Eye,* I was also mounted (in my thoughts I always use that workaday word) by Miss Huxley two evenings a week, regularly, on a small sofa in her office straight after closing time (a few times also during opening hours); she preferred to be on top, and she rode me until I panted. She didn't just like riding, she was a riding master, and I didn't wish for anything more than to lie there looking up at her swaying breasts (actually they were often covered by a blouse, since we hadn't the patience to take all our clothes off) and feel her rising and sinking down over me. I thought that with time it would become habitual, but it never did, every single one of those evenings aroused a desperate, almost explosive passion in us, as if we both believed the world would end the next day and this was our last chance to make love, on every one of those evenings we both gave all we had to give of desire. It is strange to remember it all; Miss Huxley rode me so emphatically and long-lastingly that I thought afterwards that I would never be able to complain, that I had had enough loving for the rest of my life; in a way I believe that I used up everything I owned of lust during these months, everything I had in stock, including my future stock. I would never be able to become a lonely, sex-starved man, because Miss Huxley satisfied the erotic longings of a lifetime in about a year, by means of around a hundred passionate couplings. (When I was about to leave for home she told me that she was engaged to a man who worked in Singapore, and who had only been home a couple of times during the course of the year – I remembered that she had been away from work for two short periods. She said that, I believe, to demonstrate that I didn't need to have a bad conscience about leaving London now, or to assure me that it had been an equal affair, or non-affair; neither of us had misused the other.) I must admit that sometimes, as I sit in the reading room at Domus Bibliotheca staring at the shelves of books, I can have a vision of little Miss Huxley rising and falling above me, and of how she regularly propelled me to a pleasure which bordered on madness, and at the same time gave me enough loving for a whole life. I am eternally grateful to her.

In a way I am also glad I can avoid being exposed to the complications and dangers of love. In court I see more than enough of what perverted love can lead to. It is not coincidental that the partner is behind one in three murders in Norway.

I thought my train of thought had finished, and that it would slip into one of those unconscious vacuums which follow on from a long speculation, but then it all turned upside down and emerged in an unexpected realisation: the hundred couplings with Miss Huxley had lasted a few seconds. Marie's kiss, or rather Sofie's kiss, in a clearing in the forest lasted an eternity. (Now and then I think of that clearing in the forest as the true Queen's Park.)

Poor Sofie.

I shuddered as I sat there in the library. The terrorist affair had unsettled me. Even my memories made me think of it.

I left the Faculty of Law – for once without a feeling of restored youthfulness – and since I had lost all desire for a walk in Dronningparken, I strolled slowly back down Karl Johans gate. I tried to recover my balance, I wanted to enjoy the last days of late summer; I raised my hat to an elderly lady, but she didn't smile. Even my walking stick refused to obey me, and the usual elegant movement (which I had believed was instinctual) would not materialize. On the corner opposite the music pavilion I suddenly felt a deep longing for the Chesterfield interior of Limelight and Edgar's gentle attentions. Hopefully he would be able to salve my worries with one of his rarer cocktails.

As I paraded down the main street, I registered that the atmosphere of the town was different from before, and at the same time I thought that it mirrored the mood of the country as a whole. People were grieving. I know it sounds over the top, but it reminded me of that cold week in January in the early 1990s when King Olav died. I kept walking, but nevertheless I felt surprised, because even though the country had been shaken by the horrible incident, I had taken it as a matter of course that the first reactions would ebb away and people would make an effort to return as quickly as possible to their carefree daily routine. But when I looked round, it seemed as if people wanted to *dwell* on their grief, even to *prolong* it. There was something about the faces. It was almost as if people valued the fact that something was happening, that they were revelling a bit in all the fuss. If I didn't know better I would believe that they saw this crime as some kind of tonic. Couldn't they see how dangerous this was? Because of all the hullabaloo our peaceful little patch was attracting attention, and that could lead to further disruptions to the enviable state of existence which ought to characterize, and which for many decades had characterized, life in our colony, our modern version of the Gold Coast, in which the capital's main drag, named for King Karl Johan, might just as well have borne the name of that other Oslo street, Sorgenfrigate – Carefree Avenue.

I was walking along unhurriedly, but I had to stop, I felt breathless. The incident in the forest had thrown the nation into a state of shock. Was the horror and the disbelief due to the fact that so *little* happened in this country? I must admit that people's behaviour astonished me. This – what should I call it – this *overkill* of feelings. I noticed that a remarkable number of people, in my work context as well, people I regarded as hard-nosed, seemed to love being in a state of grief. As if there was a pent-up need. It was as if they were on the point of wearing black armbands. I almost had a bad conscience for wearing my light linen suit. It was evident that all the other upsetting events in the world, the enormous and meaningless catastrophes, the thousands of deaths every day, were too far away. We can't, we won't let them affect us. With the Blankvann incident it had become possible to grieve here as well, even though only – 'only' – five people had died in the brutal attack. Mind you, I would not have dared to publish such a statement, I would be hounded out of the country. It was clear that people wanted to experience their cherished and consoling grief in peace.

I noted the fact that there were spontaneous memorials here and there. The obituaries, those glossy and prettified versions of a life, were many and long and humourless, positive orgies of lying prattle. Sofie Nagel was the only one whose life was assessed calmly, and I appreciated the information that she had been a great success in revue shows at festive gatherings. I could imagine how she might have presented a parody of Storen to the rapturous applause of the room. Perhaps that was why he had fallen for her. The thought was painful.

That white summer dress with the light blue pattern. An arabesque.

Then came the funerals, which were extensively covered in all the media. It struck me that in the midst of all the sorrow, in the weeping faces you saw on the TV, there was also a hint of ecstasy. And Arve Storefjeld was elevated into something he was not. It seemed as if the top brass in the Labour Party wanted to make him into a mystical character. The eulogies were out of all proportion. After all, we had brilliant politicians who wandered around the corridors of the Storting for a lifetime, without anyone producing more than an obligatory phrase when they died. I reacted like a child: it's not fair, I said to myself one morning over the newspaper, as I struggled to open a jar of marmalade which normally causes me no problems.

I was even more irritated by Gry's older brother, Ståle Storefjeld, an ignoramus who had previously made no impression at all in any walk of life, but who now spoke at his father's and sister's funerals and suddenly acquired a new aura, a respect which he in no way deserved; his speeches were actually full of banal and meaningless phrases (you could see that clearly when you read them on paper), but despite this he was quoted and revered as a fount of wisdom and consolation in all the media.

And what can you say about the Prime Minister? Arve Storefjeld was one of the Prime Minister's toughest opponents. Storen and his court, known for their perfidious chicanery and the kind of dirty tricks which are referred to popularly as pissing into the well, were a faction which the Prime Minister no doubt would have liked to see disappear without trace on an excursion into the seed vault on Svalbard. And what happens? The Prime Minister strides up to the lectern in the Church of the Holy Trinity and stands still for a long time, searching for words. And before the words come, it is clear that a tear has fallen. People are close to fainting. Statesmanship of the highest order, some say. The Prime Minister's popularity reaches a record high. He can do what he wants, next year's election is already won.

I tried to shake off my irritation as I wandered down Karl Johans gate, at the same time as I valiantly, but to no effect, raised my panama hat when I passed any lady who might possibly appreciate a polite gesture. But not even the fact that I was on one of my favourite stretches in the capital, particularly on warm days, beneath the lime trees by the pools and the fountain in Spikersuppa – and for me this easily trumps Unter den Linden in Berlin – could chase away my dejected thoughts. I really needed a drink now, a kind of fountain of cocktails. I believe that Edgar took the hint at once as I immediately afterwards entered the heavenly quiet of Limelight, where only two businessmen, who were presumably staying at the Grand Hotel, were sitting at one of the other tables.

However, my desire to experiment had disappeared. 'Give me a Manhattan,' I said, or practically whispered, 'or no, I'll have a Bloody Mary, I think that's the only thing which will help. I feel as if I've got a hangover.' Edgar nodded imperceptibly and retreated to his laboratory.

I always carry a half-sheet of my notepaper, folded up, in the inside pocket of my jacket. I had had an idea as I was sitting in Domus Bibliotheca, but it was only now that I took out the paper and wrote a couple of sentences between the staves. It was a thought based on something I remembered, a passage from Johs. Andenæs' book about the trials of collaborators after the Second World War and the German occupation; the thought just came out of nowhere, as they so often do, and it's vital to scribble them down before they disappear.

The book I was intending to write would be much more concrete than *An Eye for an Eye*, which bordered on the history of ideas and anthropology. My working title was *A Life for a Life* (specifically not *A Tooth for a Tooth*), and even though the plan was to write about the lack of objectivity in the practice of justice, I was going to use the Norwegian post-war trials as a starting point. Discuss whether they were just or not. The judgements, I mean. The idea was an old one. I must have had it whilst I was growing up, at the time when everyone thought I was going to be a pianist. And as I sat there, still agitated, in a soft armchair in Limelight, holding a half sheet of paper with my notes on, I found myself again thinking back to that time, and to one of the most crucial experiences of my life.

Four houses down from us there lived a man who had been convicted of treason. He had been a member of the Norwegian Nazi party, Nasjonal Samling, and even my otherwise so mild and tolerant parents despised him heartily.

I saw Herr Haug walking with his head bowed through the streets of Kjelsås as if every metre was a step of a lifelong penance. Even we kids glared sternly at him, and shouted Quisling and traitor and Nazi-Haug and Gestapo bastard after him when he was far enough away; we even shouted Judas, but it didn't stop us ringing at his door when we had raffle tickets or badges to sell, because he always bought some, and always several, he never refused us.

When I was a little older I found out more about him. Once I even stood in his living room with a book of tickets in my hand. Herr Haug owned a large wall clock, and when the clock struck the hour, rumour had it that a figure in Nazi uniform came out of the trapdoor and sang 'Deutschland, Deutschland über Alles'; but when I was standing in the room I discovered that it was a normal Swiss cuckoo clock, and the song was 'O mein Papa'. There were also persistent reports that Herr Haug had a swastika tattooed on his arm. It turned out to be a normal cross, ornamental, perhaps Celtic. That gave rise to my first suspicions about our tendency to misjudge our fellow men.

Edgar arrived with my drink. It is rare for me to drink a Bloody Mary, because for me it's practically a small meal, and all too often it reminds me of ketchup. Edgar's version is naturally a different matter; Edgar knows how to achieve the perfect balance between Worcestershire and Tabasco sauce, lemon, pepper and salt. I have tried it several times myself, but my drinks lack Edgar's refinement, his ability to combine the ingredients into a thing of beauty. I nodded appreciatively at Edgar – King Edgar – who was standing in his little teak palace watching me, as if eager to see my reaction. When I'm sitting with a Bloody Mary it often inspires me to search for metaphors, and on this particular day, of all things, I was reminded of the Norse god Balder, who died when he was hit by an arrow of mistletoe. It must have been the stick of celery planted in a sea of red which nudged me into that strange fancy; but perhaps it said just as much about the unusual, I might almost say morbid, frame of mind I was in.

'Anything new about Blankvann, Edgar? Have they finally got their hands on any of those barbarians?'

Edgar shook his head and lowered his glance, as if he regretted having to disappoint me.

In my experience Herr Haug always behaved with integrity. He had a garden – which we called Berghof – in which he allowed children to steal apples, and it seemed as if he tended the trees with the greatest care so that there would be many apples when we came scrumping in the autumn. We always believed that we were taking our lives in our hands, pinching apples from Nazi-Haug, and that he might come running at any moment and shoot at us with a Luger; but no doubt the truth of it was that he was standing behind his curtains enjoying it all. He came from a farm, and for some years he'd been at sea, and then later became caretaker of the Seamen's Church in London. When he came home he joined Nasjonal Samling because his girl-friend made it a condition – *him*, despite the fact that he was to all intents and purposes an anglophile (another proof of what irrational love can make people do). To top it all, this woman broke off their engagement during the second year of the occupation. Herr Haug had helped many people during the war – since he came from a farm, he often procured food for those with fewer resources – but that membership which he had been idiot enough to let himself be talked into, and which, even more idiotically, he did not annul as other people did when the wind changed, destroyed everything for him. After the war there was no mercy. Herr Haug was condemned and punished with a considerable fine and ten years' loss of voting rights, but the worst thing was of course that he became the object of a collective hatred which lasted for decades. At the same time I was aware that several people in Kjelsås had earned considerable sums working for the Germans, without being punished for that. Even when I was a child I couldn't understand the logic of it. When it comes to 'providing assistance to the enemy', surely you would have to say that working on German military bases was of greater importance than a passive membership of NS? I began to suspect that the post-war trials of collaborators might have been somewhat arbitrary. As far as I could see there was no kinder and more morally upright person than Herr Haug in the whole of Kjelsås, and I came to know a large number of them. I'm using the word 'kind' deliberately, because I believe it is our ability to show kindness which allows us to see beyond our own egoistic nature. I thought – again in the way a child often thinks: it's not fair. Was it actually *revenge* people were after? Not punishment, but revenge? I am oversimplifying matters, but I believe that this whole experience was a contributory factor to me dreaming (even whilst I was sitting on my piano stool) about studying law. I wanted to save my country, perhaps purge my country, to make amends for this blot on our legal history; I wanted to make Norway more civilised.

When my father became aware of my reaction to the treatment of Herr Haug, he said: 'You're too soft-hearted. You belong to the Silk Front.'

If there is anything I despise more than anything else, it's a *crowd*. Individuals who stop thinking when they are part of a crowd. Like they did when they condemned Herr Haug.

I was of course stripped of this indignation or naïve idealism, sense of justice or whatever you want to call it, early on in my legal studies, and I understood more nuances of the treatment of the so-called traitors; I did not altogether stop believing in fairness, but I lowered the bar, and decided that the goal must be to create *more* fairness. And when it came to my book, I knew that it would hardly be a global sensation. Nevertheless it would give me deep satisfaction to get it written. A kind of testament. To know that you have left behind a minuscule impression.

I was once given something by Herr Haug, something he had found in a market in England. It was a pocket compass from colonial times, and Herr Haug told me that it had also been used by soldiers in the First World War; according to the seller, this compass had belonged to a soldier who took part in the battle of Gallipoli. It was reminiscent of a German pocket watch, the case was of brass and slightly dented, as if it had been used frequently in the field; and when I opened the lid, the needle wavered to and fro, as if it could only find North, or something approximating to North, after considerable exertions. That might actually have been due to an air bubble. That compass became a symbol for me; it seemed to me that the instrument which was supposed to help us work our way towards 'justice' was extremely fragile. I carried it on me at all times.

The memory made me impatient. I paid, said goodbye to Edgar, and hurried off home. I could feel the kick from an extravagant Bloody Mary in my insides. I was imagining how I would soon be sitting at my sumptuous writing desk and placing pieces of paper, covered in annotations in different colours, in a half circle around me. I had the structure of a whole chapter in my head.

Out in town, on my way to Bankplassen, I could feel again the lightness which means so much to me. Soon the Blankvann incident will be solved, I thought. Soon this whole unhappy hullabaloo will be forgotten. Soon everything will return to normal.

II

My delusion did not last long. Several weeks passed, and there was no doubt: the still unsolved killings in Nordmarka were in the process of destroying the mental equilibrium which I had carefully built up over many years. Despite that, I made a valiant attempt to carry on with the same routine for my weekday breakfasts, which involved toasting two slices and spreading them with something sweet – perhaps a little grapefruit marmalade or a couple of teaspoons of rhubarb jam with ginger – at the same time as listening to the BBC World Service on my Sony radio, which at the time I had bought it was a completely new invention, a compact marvel, no larger than a pocket book. I knew that most people would check the internet for news, but I preferred my old radio which was tuned to the BBC via an aerial, and which gave me information about the most important things which had happened in the world, at the same time as I avoided the petty local news from the colony, including all the gossip. The morning paper was something I normally just leafed through quickly as I swallowed my last mouthful of coffee. But during these weeks I didn't even switch on the radio to listen to the BBC World Service, my precious rituals were ruined every day by headlines about the Blankvann affair which were impossible to shut out, and by one report after the other inside the paper, even though it was normally simply repetitions of what was already known. To me it seemed that both the security forces and the police were completely perplexed. If it was terrorists, they would certainly have left the country long ago.

This one-sided focus on the terrorism in the forest meant that I gradually began to feel a slight irritation, an irritation which could not be soothed even by the sound of my golden toast popping cheerfully up from the shiny toaster. There was something about all the *noise* created by this incident. Of course I could see that it was a significant event – a goldmine, to be frank – but it seemed as if the media were dragging it out and refusing to let it go; they were like drooling hyenas feasting on a plentiful corpse (I was ashamed of thinking that, but I did think it). Time after time you saw the same maps, with rings around the cabin and the annexe, portraits of the victims, and pictures from their lives. And everyone, absolutely everyone, was talking about it. People were not just grieving, they also wanted to talk. And that was all they wanted to talk about. Week after week. At the start it was perhaps a breath of fresh air – something different, something of a change – at the kitchen table in the morning. A shiver which made my hand tremble slightly as it grasped my coffee cup. But now I was tired of reading about it, and seeing the tabloids shrieking in the stands on my way to the courthouse. Was it possible to get tired of reading about something so horrible? Yes it was, mostly because it was so introverted and lacking in perspective (from my imaginary standpoint as the inhabitant of a small colony it was not difficult to see that). The media presented the killings as if they were of global significance, on a world-historic scale. I began to feel a rage building inside me, a rage which I obviously did not reveal to anyone else, least of all to anyone at the courthouse; just the thought of Dobermann's astonished face was enough to make me behave as normal, or rather, I made every attempt to express the same shock as everyone else. And sorrow. But internally I was outraged. For a fortnight, three weeks, everyone forgot that there was a world outside, a world where things happened which put our much-hyped barbarity completely in the shade. Our 'tragedy' was, when all was said and done, a bagatelle. How would we react if something far more serious happened, like the terrorism in Beslan a few years back? Over three hundred killed, most of them children?

I thought – it would never occur to me to say it out loud – that it was all getting too much now. The pornography of grief. Of course it was dreadful, it was incomprehensible. But at the same time, shouldn't we be questioning ourselves? It was practically unreal to be living in Norway, where so many years passed between each catastrophe of the kind we were now struggling with. Should we not be able to see it in relative terms as well? That in some other countries, Mexico, Brazil, Nigeria, five murdered people would be almost an everyday occurrence? Even a murdered top politician. Just think of being a journalist in Iraq. What words could you use when 8 or 28 or 88 people were killed by a suicide bomber every other week? That's all very well, no doubt some would say, but this is Norway. Was it necessary to be the world's most spoilt and over-protected people, to live in a place where nothing dramatic happened, in order for it to strike so deeply, and create such an apocalyptic mood? (For God's sake, I thought again, you must never say this aloud, not to a living soul, not even to Lev.)

After the terror at Blankvann had dominated the entire media for a good month, I began to register a strange weariness. One evening, when I switched on the TV and saw that it was once more the leading story, I noticed a faint feeling of indifference. At the same time it struck me that this was entertainment. Of course it is true that many people felt and showed empathy and genuine compassion, but on a deeper level the events had been transformed into a diversion. It wasn't just me, the majority of the population settled down in front of their TVs every evening in order to see and hear the latest about this dreadful business. 'Bring the coffee pot, Karen, the news is starting! The biscuits are on the counter. Hurry up! They've discovered a new lead in the Blankvann affair!'

Another thing which annoyed me was the disparity in the attention given to the different victims. I know that Storen was a well-known figure, and his daughter as well for that matter. But what about Sofie Nagel? Why was there not more about her? Perhaps it was precisely Sofie Nagel who was the key to understanding the motives of the perpetrators? And what about that Frenchman, the film director – not to mention Sylvie, the little girl? What if she was a clairvoyant, had a dangerous gift, and someone wanted to eliminate her?

And why were people suddenly so nervous, especially in Oslo, in the city itself? After all, Blankvann was a long way out in the wilderness. The crime might have disturbed the idyll, but what if these barbarians had blown up the Storting? Or the Labour Party headquarters on Youngstorget? Then they would have had a reason to be afraid. But something like that was unthinkable, of course it would never happen.

Let's be done with it, I thought. That's enough now.

Nevertheless I have to admit one thing: when I first read the information that the killings had been carried out with a knife, it unsettled me. For some reason it even spoilt the memory of Sofie Nagel's pen-knife, the one she halved her apple with. I noticed that the word 'evil' was a constant in the reports. In one article it was claimed that the killings were 'satanic'. All of this piqued my interest almost involuntarily, as a judge as well, and I sat at my writing desk for several evenings, noting down my own thoughts – I even decided to miss a concert with a couple of Haydn's more lively string quartets at the old Masonic lodge, Gamle Logen. Was there such a thing as purely evil people? Sometimes I thought about the perpetrators, about what would happen if they were caught. What was a just punishment for someone who had slit the throats of five people? Including a child. A child! The moment I had thought that I pushed it away, I didn't want to think about it.

But another thought followed on inescapably from that: pity the judge who had to preside over such a case.

For a few seconds I sat there with an ice-cold chill spreading through my body.

*

As if to distance myself from all this, I concentrated on everyday matters – the calm normality I valued so highly. I toasted my bread in the mornings and carried out my work in the District Court punctiliously, I strolled in Dronningparken and tried to observe the town's inhabitants with unprejudiced eyes. It had grown cooler, and I had to change into a heavier suit and put away my panama hat (I didn't wear a hat normally, except for an eye-wateringly expensive astrakhan one – what we called an ambassador's hat – if it was cold in the winter). In the evenings I sat at my writing desk, or in Wegner's wing chair with a cocktail, listening to music or watching a programme where Sir Kenneth Clark talked confidently about civilisation, taking me to Blenheim Castle or showing me Thomas Jefferson's amazing Monticello, the residence which he designed himself, inspired by Palladio.

Despite this my feeling of unease persisted. I don't know why, but it was as if this national agitation, all this hoo-ha, was a threat to me personally. The terror attack did not just destroy my illusion of living in a protected enclave, a model colony which for many decades had been able to provide its citizens with the most favourable living conditions in the world (because we were able to conform so loyally, without putting our heads above the parapet, to the economic and technological systems of the global empire) – it was also as if I sensed that I myself, in my own humble capacity, risked being drawn into events. One day something happened which I interpreted as an omen. I met Dobermann in the corridor, Judge Odd Bergmann, the courthouse's zealous guardian. We have never liked each other, even though we used to have long conversations in the Aula basement in our student days. He even attended a couple of meetings of the Young Lawyers' Reading Club (though I might add that he did not demonstrate any marked understanding of the potential of fiction for penetrating the deeper strata of the human condition). Later we lost touch, and it was not until he became a judge that we met again. I suspected that he had his eye on the position of Chief Justice, that he had wet dreams about being the fourth most powerful person in the kingdom. Over the years I had become aware that he had a grudge against me, and that he was sceptical about my knowledge, even about my fitness to be a judge.

On this occasion he stopped me and said that he had heard rumours about a book? A wolfish smile. Yes, I said, there was going to be a book. He smiled again, and it looked to me like a mocking smile, as if he believed that I was bluffing, that a talentless man like me would never be able to produce another book, at least not an interesting one. No doubt in his opinion *An Eye for an Eye* was just a flash in the pan. As we talked, or rather weighed up how long it was polite to stand there without having anything more to say, I noticed his fondness for cufflinks and ostentatious rings. In addition he was known for choosing socks of a colour that was supposed to be a bit bold, but wasn't really bold at all. Dobermann, another mystery. I remembered Ine Wang's portrait of him in the magazine – and not just the information that he practised yoga, but also that he had a dog; not a greyhound, which would have been my guess, but a Pomeranian. I tried to visualise it, Dobermann going for a walk with that little dog. What was its name? I thought up an excuse, and nodded in the direction of my office. 'Of course,' he said. 'Always lots to do, Peter.' The same suspicious glance. As if he couldn't believe that I had made it this far, into his courthouse.

I can't explain why, but it was as if the meeting with Dobermann had strengthened the disquiet I felt at the thought of the Blankvann incident. Was I in danger of being unmasked? Exposed as incompetent? When I had closed the door to my own office I was overcome for a few seconds by a dizziness so acute that I almost lost my balance. There ought not to be any reason for it, but it was as if my whole well-adjusted existence was about to capsize.

By making a huge mental effort I managed to concentrate on something else; it helped too that I had to finish off my preparations for a couple of civil cases which were in the offing. That was what I wanted. I wanted to work in peace and quiet at the courthouse, I wanted to collect my thoughts about the negotiations I presided over in court, I wanted to write wise, well-formulated judgements in my office. I wanted nothing to do with these disturbances; I wanted above all to have my evenings to myself, to be able to sit in my reclusive apartment with a drink in my right hand whilst I listened to piano pieces, preferably late Beethoven (the Diabelli variations!), I wanted to be alone, to roll my office chair around my T-shaped writing desk and note down small insights on half-sheets of manuscript paper (the old Irish laws from the fifth century!), I wanted to lean back between the cushions in my wing chair whilst I watched *Civilisation* and saw the inimitable Sir Kenneth Clark popping up in Florence and Urbino and explaining about the early Renaissance and the belief that man was the measure of all things. And before I went to bed I wanted to stand at my large window above the empty Bankplassen and look up at the floodlit Akershus Fortress placed there to protect me. Guarding an apartment, a life, which was not overlooked.

We were nearing the end of September. I had invited Lev along to Statholdergaarden; I do that on occasion, since I am well off, live on my own and often eat out, and if I don't eat at Engebret Café just next door, I prefer Statholdergaarden, a couple of stone's throws away. I like also to give Lev a bit of a treat, since teachers' salaries are a disgrace. The only problem is that Lev, unfortunately, would just as happily eat at Egon's or the Mona Lisa, or at Burger King; the point of his life is to talk, not to eat. As long as he was able to express his opinions he could happily live on bread and goat's cheese. And a splash of whisky. When he came up to my place, he was wearing his usual photographer's vest over a fleece and a creased shirt – it was as if he wanted people, or his pupils, to believe that he was really a fly-fisher or a hunter. The *Trotting and Racing News* was always sticking out of the largest pocket; I assume that's what he reads on the bus to and from town. Lev lives in a small flat in Tonsenhagen, not far from the school where he teaches. And not far from Bjerke trotting track, I might add. I have never dared to inspect his residence. According to Lev the only object worth remarking on is a shelf where he exhibits his collection of nearly eighty miniature bottles of different kinds of whisky. 'I regard it as my altarpiece,' he said.

Otherwise I know little about Lev's past. Once he showed me a battered photo of a young, long-haired man with a Rickenbacker guitar. 'Who's that?' I asked. 'Me,' said Lev, 'I played in a band called Revolver.' In his wallet (an old-fashioned type, a positive filing cabinet) I once saw quite by chance the picture of a stunning beauty in a bikini. 'My ex,' said Lev before I asked. 'We were married for five years.'

'Listen, Lev,' I said, as tactfully as I could. 'We're not going into the bush today, so just for once you could dress up a little, so that it's more in keeping with the place we're going to. Slip off your trainers and try these on. We take the same shoe size. They're from Church's on Regent Street. Freshly polished.' He sniffed. I ignored it. 'Here you are, try this white shirt, and you can borrow a black jacket. Size 52?' He nodded, took the clothes and vanished into the bathroom. I actually believe he washed under his arms as well; at any rate he came out in a white shirt and jacket and with wet hair combed back, and was unrecognisable. 'Mr Hambro, I presume?' I said. 'Ready for an evening on the town? Let's go somewhere where they serve something other than popcorn and bacon crisps.'

Lev is an eager filmgoer. But I gather from what he has said that he has now been refused entry to several Oslo cinemas because more than once he has flown into a rage and snatched tubs of popcorn and jumbo bags of bacon crisps and thrown them into the aisle, berating the owners of the snacks for not being there to watch the film but to stuff themselves, like Romans in the declining days of empire.

What a hair-raising lack of *savoir faire*! That was what he was trying to convey to the schoolchildren: *savoir faire*. Despite the way he dresses, in my eyes he is the Oslo school system's Sir Kenneth Clark. He battles tirelessly to suppress his pupils' tendency to distraction, to transfer their attention to learning. To create calm, curiosity, pleasure at being encouraged to make an effort. And what pupil would not delight in a teacher who suddenly pulled out a fossil shell from a pocket in his photo vest and launched into a story about Darwin and his discovery of fossil shells high up in the Andes in Chile?

Out on Bankplassen, where the jets of water in the fountain were still shooting optimistically into the air, Lev told me that he had gone to one of the screenings at the Film House which the National Film Institute had arranged in memory of Jules Lefebvre, Gry Storefjeld's lover. Lefebvre had met his Norwegian ex-wife, little Sylvie's mother, at a festival abroad. She was a film director too. That was how he came to Norway, where he managed to milk both the state and various organisations for vast sums of money by setting up an extremely doubtful collaboration between Norwegian and French films; he had even managed to secure for himself a half-time position at the film school in Lillehammer, where he, that terrible director, lectured Norwegian greenhorns about how to make films. 'A dreadful man,' said Lev. 'The incarnation of French arrogance. His mother was a career diplomat as well, apparently hated in Arabian circles. Perhaps someone ought to search for motives for the killings there, and take a look at the French Connection. The despicable Lefebvre family.'

The Film House had devoted a whole week to Lefebvre's films. On a masochistic impulse Lev went to see the one that people said was Lefebvre's masterpiece. And even if he managed for once to avoid the crunching and the stink of popcorn and bacon crisps, it was according to Lev nothing less than torture to watch the film: 'So excruciatingly embarrassing that it made me ache all over.' Lefebvre made films in the tradition of Eric Rohmer, but so badly that it was insulting. Before that he had been responsible for a series of more or less pornographic films, all with a veneer of seriousness which made the cultural elite overlook the tastelessness of some scenes. During the showing of the 'masterpiece' Lev had to bite his lip to stop himself from groaning in the darkness, whilst the others sighed, entranced, as if the director's tragic death gave the film a quality it did not possess. 'To put it politely,' said Lev, 'Lefebvre's death was no loss to art.'

As I walked into Kirkegata, Lev had disappeared. I turned round and discovered that he had stopped to talk to a prostitute, and I caught him passing her a bill, as if she was a beggar. 'How much did you give her?' I asked cautiously when he caught up with me. 'A thousand kroner,' he said. 'You're mad,' I said. 'She needs it more than I do,' he replied. 'I won a bit at the trotting races last week.'

Sometimes I wonder whether there is any point at all in inviting Mr Hambro out to dinner.

However, all my reservations disappeared as Statholder-gaarden's well-known façade appeared before us in Rådhus-gata, and we stood a few seconds later in the entrance. I always enjoy that moment, and try to make time go more slowly as I enter these premises, with their aura of history and gastronomic nobility. So it was now. I opened the door for Lev and we stepped into that yellow room. Immediately one of the staff was there, as if I was a long-awaited guest. 'Herr Malm,' she said. 'Always a pleasure to see you.' A friendly smile at Lev, as if the very fact that he was in my company was sufficient guarantee of class. She led us through the salon with its warm red colours and into the sky-blue room which is referred to as the Cleopatra room, and installed us at one of the window tables. 'Excellent,' I said, and intimated with just a nod that we would of course, without any more ado, be eating the day's five-course meal with the recommended wines. I asked for a glass of champagne, whereas Lev insisted on a whisky, an Ardbeg, and although I found that slightly eccentric, I approved of the choice – even Edgar would have nodded approvingly – and in actual fact it surprised me that Lev knew the name of that distinguished malt whisky, unless it came from one of his miniature bottles, which had their uses after all. When he didn't call it his altarpiece, he maintained that it was his 'wine cellar', and that he'd been collecting it for almost 40 years.

I indicated the room with a wave of my hand, as if to call Lev's attention to it and get him to appreciate the rare stucco work in the ceiling, the tasteful Oriental carpet on the floor, the orchids on the windowsill; but he had already launched into a lecture about the rise and fall of social democracy. I got the impression that these were thoughts which had occurred to him after reading about Arve Storefjeld and a theory that the aim of the killings was to damage the Labour Party.

As I sipped my champagne and listened to Lev's analysis, it struck me that he always expressed himself incisively. Of course it was extremely subjective, but behind the provocative statements there were stimulating perspectives. He really ought to have been teaching at university, not sitting in a classroom with boisterous eleven-year-olds. His talent is so great that it has imploded, I thought.

Lev, who drank the single malt as if it was an espresso, in three gulps, found it diverting to take part in social debate in his own special way. He wrote readers' letters, he composed an endless stream of opinion pieces for the papers and participated in debates on social media, posting messages in chat rooms. He often wrote under a pseudonym. Varied his style. Like Søren Kierkegaard, he claimed. He enjoyed it. Best wishes, a boy (8). Best wishes, Fru Hammer (retired). He could write long pieces about serious matters, for example about the dubious ethics of some of the oil fund's investments, but he was just as happy writing about bagatelles – furious letters about the dog poo which could be seen everywhere, especially in spring, or about the unreliability of the Oslo tram service. Best wishes, Colonel Bull. I amused myself from time to time guessing which expressions of opinion he had written in my morning paper, but I have never dared to turn on my computer in order to see how he expresses himself in web debates and chat rooms. I have a suspicion that it would give me considerable pause for thought.

Our waitress, a young woman who was actually slightly reminiscent of Gry Storefjeld, with her abundant hair pinned up and her clear eyes, placed the evening's first course in front of us: marinated salmon with leek ash and mango, a little coriander and ... a velouté sauce made from mussel stock (I had to ask her to repeat that last part). 'I hope you enjoy it,' I said to Lev, completely redundantly, because he just shovelled the food in as if he was in some canteen, whilst he carried on preaching about how the Labour Party had sold its soul to market liberalism. That may be true, I thought, but hadn't we all gladly sold our souls to it? I said nothing, it would only get him more worked up.

For some reason – as he glared suspiciously at the leek ash – he started up about Arve Storefjeld's wife Mosse, and all the hypocrisy which had emerged in the tributes after her death, as if it was a perfect family. 'When I hear about that home on Maridalsveien, it reminds me of the plays of O'Neill or Lars Norén,' said Lev. Lev's outburst was fuelled by information which once more came from his friend, who was an insider in the Labour Party. Storen's wife had died when Gry and Ståle were teenagers, and Storen always mentioned her in later interviews and made much of her. Mosse was a well-known figure in party circles as well. 'Died suddenly,' it said in the notices of her death. 'I wonder,' said Lev. 'In actual fact she was deeply unhappy.' 'You mean she was suffering from depression?' I said. 'I don't think there's a medical diagnosis for what was wrong with Mosse Storefjeld,' said Lev, with a grimace. 'I think she quite simply suffered from sexual neglect. Plus the lack of an equal partnership in her own home – a paradox for someone who was working on equal rights in the Trades Union Organisation and Fafo. Don't you remember her embittered expression on the few photos the newspapers carried of her?' Lev drank some wine as if it was water. 'She was in Modum psychiatric clinic for a period.

Truth to tell, she was a wreck.' Lev searched for something in his pockets, forgetting that he had borrowed a jacket from me. 'By the end she was taking such strong medication that she was on sick leave,' he said. 'Rumour has it that she killed herself, a pill overdose, but my theory is that she died because her life was miserable.'

I'm sure he didn't notice, but it made me start when he mentioned pills and an overdose.

'All of this was suppressed, in order to preserve the Storefjeld myth,' said Lev. 'The perfect marriage.' Lev looked down into his empty wine glass. 'Officially she died of heart failure, they claimed she had a weak heart.'

I was so engrossed in Lev's speculations that I hardly registered our waitress's friendly explanations of the next course, I just heard something about 'petit pois and crisps' and something about 'Gotland truffle'. I should have liked to ask about that truffle. Really? From Sweden? And at the same time I realised that Lev had changed the subject and was suddenly talking about the Chernobyl accident, and how this was the main reason for the collapse of the Soviet Union; I had no idea how or why he had started on this, but Lev never tired of talking, and it was good to talk under the chandeliers in Statsholdergaarden's Cleopatra room, blissfully free of muzak and with plenty of space between the tables.

'Skål, Mr Hambro,' I said.

'The next time they show Tarkovsky's film *Stalker* at the Arts Cinema, I'll take you along,' said Lev.

We were served the evening's main course: sirloin of calf with calf sweetbreads. After one mouthful I was ready to pronounce it excellent (as far as I could gather, there was also a little kale and radish, with thyme stock). A Vignamaggio Chianti Classico 1999. What more could anyone wish for? Even Lev paused in his monologue for a few minutes, and I even caught him closing his eyes in relish; suddenly he mopped his lips with his serviette in a remarkably elegant gesture. As if he came from an upper-class home and had been brought up by a strict governess.

Then he was back in the saddle. Litanies about nations sleeping on their hoarded wealth. About how public relations people and media strategists wormed their way into parties, with the result that politicians thought they were in the PR industry. I could only get a word in now and then. Then Lev steered the topic onto the current turbulence in the financial world. 'It had to come,' he said. 'Greed has its limits.' Lev worked himself up even more, spoke even louder, launched into an account of the banks' tricks, lending people money they couldn't afford to borrow, and how the present-day economy was built on a capitalism founded on debt. 'Why do we put up with it?' asked Lev, putting his glass down with a bang. 'As long as all goes well, a few people cream off the profits. When the bottom falls out of it, the collective has to foot the bill!' I motioned to him to quieten down a bit; several of the guests had turned towards us – and some of them might well be financiers. Lev lowered his voice, and it is possible I missed something, because suddenly he had linked this too, the state of the economy, to the decline of politics. Because what was politics, Lev asked rhetorically. Politics was the art of foresight. Thinking beyond the here and now. Visualising possible consequences. It was precisely the politicians' lack of imagination which made it possible for the banks to drive the whole economy into the ditch. 'A lack of imagination is the root of all bad politics,' said Lev.

There were little dishes to cleanse the palette, there was more wine, there was Lev's cascade of ideas about the finance world's criminal behaviour, and afterwards I remembered little about it, but at the end he began to talk about shares, that it was now that you ought to buy shares. 'You should buy,' he said. 'You've got a bit of money. Buy Statoil and Norsk Hydro and Yara and Telenor. But wait a little with Den norske Bank, they have quite a bit further to fall, wait until after the New Year.'

'Don't talk now,' I said to Lev. 'I just have to be alone with this dessert for a few seconds.' The first mouthful had transported me to heaven. I forgot everything about the bank crisis and shares, I forgot everything about Storen and Gry and Sofie. Even about little Sylvie, the whole tragedy. Did I have a bad conscience? I did not have a bad conscience. I was in a state of perfect balance. I had to call our waitress over and get her to explain it again. It turned out to be raspberries from Holland on a passionfruit curd (at least I think that's what she said) ... coconut sorbet and flakes of white chocolate ... what else, oh yes, pineapple and mint. I thought about making a note of it on the notepaper I had in my inside pocket, but instead I lifted my glass filled with a noble Tokay wine and said: 'This is a meal which could accompany one of Sir Kenneth Clark's programmes.'

'Clark – is that the one in *Superman*?' said Lev.

And despite the Statholdergaarden dessert, did my thoughts not for a few seconds revisit that scene from several decades ago, that unsophisticated but unforgettable apple pie at Frognerseteren?

It was as if that dinner at Statholdergaarden got me back on my feet, and helped me to return to my usual routines. The days which followed were characterised by simple breakfasts, toast with lemon marmalade or rose petal jelly, uncomplicated cases in court and recreational walks through the town and into Dronningparken (they would be closing it soon, and in my eyes this was the weightiest argument against the monarchy; I considered it an incomprehensible crime against the population of Oslo that this park, right in the centre, should be locked for eight months of the year). I was well on the way to regaining my calm. Thank God the media had begun to focus on other matters than the terror attack in Nordmarka, even though the unanswered question about the perpetrators was clearly an open sore. In the mornings I returned to my old Sony radio and the BBC World Service, and in the evenings I could sit undisturbed in my out-of-the-way apartment with a cocktail in my right hand whilst I watched *Civilisation*; my existence was as I wished it to be, and more often than before I could sit down at my desk to study the sheaf of notes I kept in the Sætre tin ('All things have I seen in the days of my vanity: there is a just man that perisheth in his righteousness, and there is a wicked man that prolongeth his life in his wickedness.' *Ecclesiastes* 7:15). I was not far from making out the shape of a unifying thought in *A Life for a Life*, a book in which the post-war trials would be just a starting-point, or a central hub, for further thoughts and more speculative associations (I wanted to allow myself the freedom to speculate, to a certain extent at least). I felt a new driving energy, I might say I felt *indomitable*.

In the intervals I even managed to read a novel which, strangely enough, I had never read before, Albert Camus' *The Fall*, in which a lawyer makes a kind of confession. Yes, I was on course again. My time was my own again, and everything was blessedly quiet.

On the days when I came home late I stopped on Bankplassen and looked up at my apartment. It had become darker in the evenings, and I could see a warm light in the window right at the top (I always left the light on in my study). Once again I had to register my good fortune. No-one would believe that there was anyone living there. They would just think that someone had forgotten to switch off a light in an office.

Despite my renewed enthusiasm for my work it seemed that this restless autumn was refusing to leave me in peace. Suddenly the Blankvann affair took a sensational turn – and for once that cliché was appropriate. A man was arrested and charged with the killings. And a hundred white elephants would not have been able to prevent the name of this individual being announced immediately, accompanied by bells and cymbals, right across the media: Nicolai Berge.

Why had no-one worked it out earlier? The accusations rained down. 'Berge had kept under the radar,' was the excuse, and the phrase was repeated *ad infinitum*.

I was at home, and was about to sit down in my chair and skate around my writing desk on the hunt for items for *A Life for a Life* (and perhaps take a look at what I had noted about the Hindu legal system), but on a whim – you might almost say an unlucky whim – I turned on the evening news instead, and there it was; the programme was of course extended, with reports and interviews and commentaries from all and sundry. Did the country come to a halt, as the saying goes? Perhaps it did. I don't know whether I was surprised. Yes. No. I had kept a bit of an eye on what Nicolai Berge got up to, perhaps because of my scepticism about the inbreeding, the nepotism, which you could sometimes see a tendency to in the Labour Party. Right from the first time I saw his picture in the paper – it must have been in connection with a leadership battle in Oslo Young Labour – I got the impression of a haughty appearance, of a frankly arrogant and unsympathetic personality. In the picture he had struck a theatrical pose, with a hammer and all (or was it a roll of adhesive tape?), and was posting some 'theses against the Labour Party' on a door down on Youngstorget. How childish, I thought at the time. What outrageous megalomania, dragging the august Luther and his heroic deed into a minuscule and no doubt sectarian Norwegian power battle. A single glance. That was enough. People have written books about that, haven't they? More often than is comfortable it takes only a couple of seconds to form an opinion about another person. It must derive from instincts we have developed in the course of tens of thousands of years, instincts which are vital to our survival. (Though I would make very certain that I didn't say anything like that out loud in a discussion in the staff canteen at the courthouse.)

What was my first thought? I remember it well. I thought: we will never see a greater scoundrel in the dock in a Norwegian court of law.

Or rather, my first reaction was not a thought, it was anger. I was simply furious that one man – one single individual – was the cause of this enormous uproar, which had once more knocked me completely off balance, and which had indeed ruined, *poisoned*, my existence for over a month.

For a second – no, two – I thought of the death penalty. That it was the only acceptable solution.

I had completely forgotten my writing desk and *A Life for a Life*. I sat in the smallest room, the one where I would otherwise sit with a cocktail and watch Sir Kenneth Clark wandering around Europe and enlightening me, but now the pictures were all about Nicolai Berge and his monstrous act. From what was said I gathered that he had been in a relationship with Gry Storefjeld, and I must say that surprised me greatly. How could she, clearly a talented young woman, a connoisseur of the complex poet Samuel Taylor Coleridge, fall for a repulsive nonentity like Nicolai Berge? The fact that Berge was supposed to have published a couple of short story collections in recent years was something which in all honesty I found hard to believe; if that was the case, it had to be an obscure publisher and stories of a contemptible nature. (I followed the literary scene with half an eye, and the fact that his books had escaped my attention entirely – in a country where even mediocre achievements are trumpeted from the rooftops – I took as a sure sign that they must be devoid of all quality.)

Berge: a verb in Norwegian which means to rescue, to keep safe. A positive word distorted into its opposite. A name transformed into a stream of spit cast in the face of a whole nation.

I felt a strong desire for a Negroni, but I managed to resist. I would have been tempted to put too much gin in it. This was not an evening for drinking. It would have ended really badly.

The next few days brought a bombardment of pictures and reports. Every morning before work I sat at my kitchen table with the newspapers around me, including the ones I had bought from the shop the day before but not managed to read. There were so many newspapers that I could hardly locate my small, exclusive jars of marmalade under the heap. Wherever I turned I saw Nicolai Berge's name or Nicolai Berge's face, a face which seemed to take on an ever more demonic gleam. The papers really went to town. 'Deposed Young Labour prince.' 'A family tragedy.' Nicolai Berge's life right from his earliest childhood was detailed for the nation. And then there were the pictures. Where did they get them from? Friends ('friends')? There was an avalanche of pictures in the tabloids. 'How can a boy from a cultivated home on Bygdøy allé finish up as a barbarian, a savage with a knife in the forest?' There was Nicolai Berge at his confirmation, there was Nicolai Berge in the class picture from Nissen secondary school, from a Young Labour camp on Utøya, with a glass of wine at a publisher's party. 'Looking like a normal Norwegian youngster,' was the caption. 'How did things go so wrong?'

Once more my days were spoilt. I could not find the peace of mind necessary to do anything at all, whether it was filling my Sætre tin with more notes or listening to music. Only my work in court was unproblematic, because there I could carry out my duties faultlessly whilst half asleep.

Despite all this I remembered Lev's advice, and in the midst of the turbulence I bought shares in precisely the companies he had suggested. In fact I regarded it almost as my duty, since I considered myself a citizen of one of the most unassuming and best administered colonies of the world empire of economic liberalism – at least, that had been the case until now. Of course I ought to have dabbled in such matters before, since I was a man with plenty of money in his account and who furthermore lived in the old banking quarter, with the Stock Exchange just around the corner. I was amazed when I discovered how much share prices had fallen in the last few weeks. It was only a question of time before everything would go up again. Even I, an amateur, could see that it was an unusually favourable time to buy, at the same time as I thought that this all confirmed my impression of Norway and Norway's place in the world. We pretend that we are a free country, that we decide our circumstances

Jan Kjærstad

ourselves, but in reality we are a colony subservient to an invisible world-wide empire; we are completely dependent on the caprices of the global economy, together with the latest shenanigans of the technology industry.

But Berge continued to disturb me. Soon it leaked out that the accused had nothing to say, that he refused to explain his actions. Until now he had given no information, either to the police or when he was remanded in custody. That gave rise to even more theories, if that was possible. Psychologists and other experts from every possible field of knowledge competed to get their ideas in print or be interviewed in the papers or on TV.

Of course they went after his father, Olaf Berge, as well. I can imagine how that must have been. The whole pack of them outside the house on Bygdøy allé. As I understood it, he did talk to the police, but he refused to say anything to the press. Several newspapers printed photos of Olaf Berge as he came out of his front door (it looks as if we have an army of paparazzi in Norway too). The photos showed a drawn, battle-weary face. A broken man.

It didn't take too long for a well-known columnist to write a long article about Nicolai Berge (I had half expected Ine Wang to have something to say, but if she did, then I missed it). The person in question put forward a theory – though in my eyes it more resembled an accusation – about what lay behind the crime. Again I was sitting at my kitchen table, and again my breakfast was spoilt as I read the article, half reluctantly and half greedily; this time the picture of the journalist was larger than the picture of Berge. He was a failed author, a damaged mind which craved attention, the journalist maintained, the attention he had not been able to attract with his fiction. He needed a work written in blood. And now the unhinged author was revelling in the press coverage, which could be seen as a kind of delayed debut. As I read this conclusion, two golden slices of toast popped up out of my shiny toaster like an audible full stop. I spread my orange marmalade (with a touch of rum) over the slices, and despite the fact that I had hitherto felt not a jot of pity for Berge, I could feel my lips forming the phrase 'poor chap!'

And at the same time, from the deeper layers of my consciousness: that really is going too far.

The most sympathetic people (if you can use such a word in this context) – and paradoxically enough they were acquaintances of Gry Storefjeld – claimed that he must have been momentarily insane. They had long regarded him as mentally unstable. In the newspaper *Morgenbladet* there was a critic who compared Berge to another author, the German poet Paul Celan, who in a moment of madness had attempted to kill his wife (and even his son, according to some reports) with a knife. I just shook my head about all this. If I remembered correctly, Celan stuck a knife in himself as well later on, and Berge had at least not tried to do that. Yet.

My daily routine was so out of kilter that I summoned Lev to an extraordinary meeting at our club, that is Limelight, and at the entrance to the Grand Hotel I stopped by the Narvesen kiosk to look at the rack of newspapers. 'No mercy for Berge' it said in huge letters on one of the front pages. It was a quote from Ståle Storefjeld, the son and brother. No-one could avoid registering the hatred which was now directed at Berge, and with that I am thinking not just about what the bereaved might be feeling, but about a kind of collective anger; it was as if people were in the mood for a lynching (in a way I was seeing my own first reaction on an exaggerated scale). No doubt it was also due to the surprise. People had been expecting terrorism, a complex plot. Something foreign and fanatical. Something religious and incomprehensible. A spider's web of apocalyptic dimensions. And then it transpired that the murderer, the *demon,* was a white man, an Oslo lad from a respected family, one of their own. The Labour Party killed by the Labour Party.

'Is this man evil?' asked another headline.

Normally I was never late, but Lev would have to wait a bit. I was rooted to the spot. I stood there staring at this headline. When I had been sitting at my writing desk earlier that autumn, thinking through the problem of evil, I had concluded that I had never believed there was such a thing as *evil people*. I looked at the people I passed sentence on, often for dreadful acts, and I could see that they were damaged individuals, that circumstances had not been in their favour. But the arrest of Berge made me wobble in my belief. What if Berge *was* evil? Was there a dark force within him? A lust for power which went beyond what was normal? A sick desire to rule over life and death? Was it possible that some people could actually be monsters?

Had I been too naïve all this time? I had no illusions otherwise about human beings as a species. I don't believe in progress. Oh yes, we are constantly devising new gadgets, but people behave just as bestially as ever. They have always derived greater pleasure from tearing down than from building up. Every technological advance provides the opportunity for a more barbarous war. More tyranny. There is no doubt that my days spent reading Jens Bjørneboe's books about the history of bestiality have left their mark on me; a thorough study of the dark chapters in human history might easily make you a pessimist. The road from Weimar to Buchenwald is short. Our civilisation is a thin veneer over barbarity. Just look at August 1914, a lesson we have already brushed under the carpet.

If there is anything my years in court have taught me, it is that human beings today are whoring and deceiving and betraying and killing as never before. From my judge's chair, not least in criminal cases, I have seen and heard people scheming and lying, and behaving with frightening brutality. You hug someone one day and knock them down the next. But is that evil?

In any case, there's little I can do about it. Apart from letting justice take its course, to express it formally. *Fiat Justitia*. All I can do is to listen, as if with an inner Geiger counter, to whether there might be any doubt about the guilt of the accused. And to feel pity for these unfortunate people.

Nevertheless, something told me I would have had serious problems if I'd had to be the judge in the Berge case.

I let my eyes wander over the headlines in the newspaper rack in front of me. It was like hearing the baying of a mob. On the very first day when Berge was driven to the prison hearing, several people had gathered along the last stretch of the police car's route before it drove down into the garage under the courthouse, and on the evening news you could see how people were pouring their loathing over Berge. 'Bloody coward!' one shouted. 'Child killer!' came from another. 'Son of Satan! You don't deserve to live!'

Behind all the noise there was also a demand that someone should be held responsible. Why were the killings not prevented? Where were the security forces? Why had they not picked up on the threat? You could read it from his blog, all those extreme posts, wrote one commentator. 'Berge is a black swan,' wrote a retired investigator, as if to excuse the security services. 'Nothing is more difficult to predict than something absolutely simple.'

That last statement sounded like a wise saying.

I really needed a diversion, I needed Lev's perspective, and I needed a very special cocktail. I needed Edgar. On my way into the Grand Hotel – even the name raised my spirits – I started to think about my year in London. I have never been religious. Visiting a good bar is about the nearest I get to an experience of the sacred. Could I say that there is a hint of communion about it? I thought about my visits to the American Bar in the Savoy Hotel, which I discovered on my first visit to London. After that I had been to the bar many times, and I never took a taxi there, I *walked*, as if it were a pilgrim route leading to a sacred site. Just as Catholics have their Santiago de Compostela, I have the Savoy on the Strand. I always thought: I'm not in London to go to the theatre or the museums, I'm here to go to the world's best bar. It was here I was served some of the drinks I remember best: Bronze Guardian, Eternal Whisper, Napoleon's Wish. When I sipped those cocktails, it was like opening a surprise package of taste. I don't know whether I ought to admit this, but my visits to the Savoy's American Bar are high points in my life. More than sensual experiences I remember those cocktails as incomparable stories. (A propos religion: it may be a slight exaggeration, but if I have a Bible, it must be *The Savoy Cocktail Book*.)

As I entered Limelight and inhaled the very faint aroma of the cigars of yesteryear, I could see that Lev had found his favourite place, just next to the signed photo of Charlie Chaplin hanging on the wall; the picture had been taken when Chaplin visited Oslo in 1964, and Chaplin and Limelight belonged together. Lev had several things spread out on the table in front of him. It looked as if he was clearing out some of the numerous pockets in the photo vest he was now wearing over a thin sweater. On the table lay a fan of membership cards, receipts from Bjerke trotting track, two mysterious keys, a Fisher Space Pen, an antiquarian mobile phone and several things I couldn't make out (a small pink plastic lobster?). And a mouth-organ. 'Can you play?' I asked, pointing. Lev took a handkerchief from his pocket and polished the instrument – for a moment I imagined it resembled the much-analysed tartan handkerchief and had to laugh silently to myself. 'It's a blues mouth-organ,' he said, 'It's something I get out now and then and use to get my pupils' attention.'

Lev had told me several times that it was getting more and more difficult to keep order in the classroom. We talked a little about the school, whilst Edgar took our order, two Mint Juleps – despite the fact that it was autumn, I said apologetically, as if I was half expecting an 'Objection, Your Honour' – before I turned the conversation to Berge, because this was of course the topic which was weighing on my mind; I think I was subconsciously hoping that Lev would confirm my aversion. As I gave vent to a vigorous condemnation of Berge (as a judge I would otherwise never do that, but I was in Limelight after all), I could feel how good it was to give free rein to the gnawing distaste I felt at the thought of that man. Then I paused and expected a salvo from Lev, that notorious critic of the Labour Party, but Lev surprised me by looking doubtful; he said not a word whilst Edgar supplied us with a glass each, in which mint leaves and bourbon were combined in perfect harmony, and it was not until he had tasted the drink, as if he was unsure of Edgar's skill, that he reminded me of a story I had forgotten – 'almost a modern fairytale', in his words – which might explain a thing or two about Nicolai Berge. 'Don't you remember all the excitement when Olaf Berge and Maj Runesen got married?' said Lev. I too sipped at my glass and enjoyed the effects of the first mouthful, the stimulation of my tastebuds. 'I do have a vague recollection,' I said, nodding gratefully to Edgar as he stood there expressionless in his white shirt and black waistcoat behind the bar. 'Each of them came from a powerful wing of the Labour Party,' I said. When I thought about it, Olaf Berge was perhaps one of the Labour politicians I had always approved of most; he had been a minister twice, in departments which were seldom in the news – he served in those ministries which people could never remember the names of, not even with a gun to their heads. As I saw it, Olaf Berge was an ornament to the administration of our small protectorate. 'When Olaf and Maj got married, it was almost like a royal wedding,' Lev went on; 'and when Maj became pregnant, expectations were sky-high, internally in the party as well. They were awaiting an heir to the throne, something absolutely exceptional.' Lev raised his glass, and for once it looked as if he had discovered that there was a difference between a cocktail and Edgar's cocktail. 'They were waiting eagerly for the boy's talents to reveal themselves,' said Lev. 'They were hoping for a kind of saviour, a Messiah, but Nicolai Berge was a disappointment – two eagles had produced a sparrow. I say, shouldn't a Mint Julep be served in a silver goblet, strictly speaking?'

I had to disguise my reaction (and not to the fact that Lev actually did know something about drinks) by taking two mouthfuls, one straight after the other. Unless I was very much mistaken, Lev was sitting there *defending* Nicolai. Suggesting that being a son of Olaf Berge and Maj Runesen might in fact have been a *handicap*. At the same time I could not avoid thinking of my own youth, of the piano and my parents' expectations.

'In all honesty, Lev ... are we not both sceptical of such a deterministic philosophy, of the belief that harmonious and intelligent parents are going to have harmonious and intelligent children?' I looked at Lev, at his large ears, as I did my best to conceal how exasperated I was. 'History surely shows us that the children of "geniuses" finish up in the best of cases as anonymous, conventional, self-satisfied people, or – and this is not uncommon – that they finish up as fiascos, as drug addicts or psychiatric patients. Unhappy and self-destructive.' Lev nodded and muttered something about the Kennedy children, before saying something which I interpreted nevertheless as a criticism of my spontaneous disapproval: 'Nicolai Berge has perhaps not lived up to many people's expectations of him, but he can definitely not be called a fiasco.'

My antipathy was kindled once more, perhaps provoked by Lev's statement. 'I can remember the first time I saw him on TV,' I said. 'It was a debate between young politicians, and it struck me immediately: he gave the impression of being completely *clueless*. He was fumbling for words. It sounded as if he hadn't even understood the questions he was trying to answer.'

Only the little mouth-organ was left on the table. Lev picked it up and played a snatch of blues. It sounded great, and Edgar smiled behind his palisade of teak. 'Chekhov,' said Lev. 'Once a gun appears in a story, it has to be fired.' He let the shiny object slide down into one of his many pockets. 'I was thinking more about the fact that Berge has published two collections of short stories, after all. And speaking of that ...' Lev had to stop and laugh. 'Did you hear that something has leaked from the investigation? In his flat in Nordberg there was a safe. You know, one of those solid old-fashioned safes. Comical, isn't it? They probably thought he was hiding machine guns or explosives, but when they got it open after a great struggle, all they found was an external hard disk and the manuscript of a new collection of short stories, with the title *Imperfect Tales,* or something like that.'

Even I had to laugh at that, at the same time as Lev signalled with a glance to Edgar. 'I think we are ready for another Mint Julep,' he said. 'We must have something to cool our anger at Wall Street.'

It transpired that Lev was still indignant about the economic chaos which was now being called a financial crisis and seemed to get more serious by the day. People were fooled, said Lev, they still believed that the banks were like my next-door building in the old town, the ancient and honourable Norges Bank, built of solid stone and with secure vaults in the cellar. But it wasn't like that any longer, now the financial institutions consisted of invisible networks, a web like that of the Hindu Maya, and when it began to unravel, everything unravelled. And not just unravelled, the fictions vanished into thin air.

I wasn't entirely happy to hear this; it was as if Lev was also puncturing my idea of a well-functioning global empire. 'Just try to relax,' I said, and I tried to get him a drink a toast – and include Chaplin in the toast – when Edgar arrived with a new Mint Julep; but Lev didn't want a toast, not even with Chaplin, he wanted to find an outlet for his fury that the Norwegian state had just come running with a rescue package for the banks. An inconceivable sum, several hundred billion kroner, had suddenly been made available for a long-term loan. Where did this money come from? When they couldn't even afford to give old people in care homes an extra bread roll for breakfast? I must be aware of the fact that we now had a social democratic government. So why was it policy to take from the poor and give to the rich? It was the same disgraceful story. Once more we saw how the biggest villains got away with it. Lev held up a finger as if to make sure I was following: 'First of all they, that is the banks, swindle you out of your money. Then in their greed they rake together so much that they undermine their own security and suddenly they're caught in their own trap. And what happens? Well, then you come along, little you, via your tax bill, and bail them out, all those millionaires. They rob you twice! And you stand there with your hat in your hand, bowing. There is no justice. It's just like during the war. The white-collar criminals get away scot-free.'

I don't believe Lev knew that he had touched a nerve in me by referring to the post-war trials. 'You need to watch your blood pressure,' I said. It was not only his large ears, his face too had turned a dangerous red. 'Stop worrying about me,' said Lev. 'This is what we have to do something about, an economic system which will destroy us in the long run. All this about Berge is a distraction. It absorbs all our mental energy, even though it's a little bagatelle. In the grand scheme of things.'

This was Lev, I thought, this was Lev as I liked to hear him. 'Well, I've bought some shares anyway, as you advised,' I said, to cheer him up.

'But not in Den norske Bank, I hope?' he said. I shook my head. 'Good, because when it comes to Den norske Bank, you need ice in your veins, as the financial whizz kids say. Wait till … let's say January, and then buy as many bank shares as you can afford.' He raised his glass, in which the mint leaves protruded like miniature palm trees on a desert island of ice. 'Skål for William Faulkner,' he said, 'the Lord Protector of Mint Juleps.'

It was no longer possible to find that precious peace in the evenings which I required in order to make progress with my book on just punishments ('Find out more about whipping the soles of the feet as a punishment during the Tang dynasty', I had just written on one of the half music sheets I placed in my Sætre tin). Seen from a broader perspective it may be that Berge was a bagatelle, but in Norway he was everywhere, a phenomenon which blocked a clear view wherever you looked.

From time to time I tried to vary my working rhythm, or ritual. I would get up from my office chair at the spacious T-shaped desk and go into the next room, where I lay down on the divan (I've always liked that word, with its aura of Persia). It's not just any old divan. I found it early on in my working life when I discovered it during a visit to the High Court in a storeroom to which the door was open. My escort explained that it was going to be thrown out; it was a shabby old piece of furniture which dated from Paal Berg's time as Chief Justice, when the divan had stood in his office. I asked if I could have it, and I have 'restored' it, though without changing the cover, because I like to lie on the same material on which Paal Berg – a lawyer with a colourful and inspiring career – had once lain when he was hatching out ideas and formulations. Occasionally I can imagine that I *am* Paal Berg, cabinet minister, judge, resistance leader, a man of consequence (in contrast to me), that I am Chief Justice (it's a good thing Dobermann has no inkling of this). It happens that different thoughts occur to me then, that the illusion bears fruit.

I have also kept hold of the old stereo system from Kjelsås, and I like to listen to certain pieces of music while I'm working, particularly because I'm writing on music paper. I am not a fan of symphonies and operas, and all that noise which is inescapably a part of them, I must have it pared down, reduced to a minimum, and that's why I have a weakness for quartets, but most of all for piano pieces. It might be something by Bach, or Beethoven. I find inspiration especially in Beethoven's late piano pieces. They sound different. As if suddenly, right at the end, he found a new freedom, fresh courage to compose something which was outside his time; to my ears it sounds as if – in the last five piano sonatas, for example – he surpassed everything in his own time and anticipated a music of the future. What if I could do something like that, on a lesser scale, I think. Of course it would be on a more modest level. Liberate myself. Could I not then perhaps conceive an original thought? Precisely because I would no longer care about what people (Dobermann!) thought, I would not give a damn about approval and success. Yes, it was a possibility I liked to play with. To step out of the stream of time. Become a true outsider, freed from the conventions of the day.

Would I dare to do it?

Or was my whole project, *A Life for a Life,* the result of hubris? Getting yourself noticed always carries a risk. Suddenly you meet resistance. Qualified criticism. Suddenly you are unmasked. It was tempting just to steer a steady course, not to upset the applecart, to protect the excessive respect I already enjoyed.

Make sure to keep under the radar.

Most of my records come from the two well-stocked music shops which used to be at the top of Karl Johans gate, both of them of course now gone, thanks to internet sales and new media formats. It gives me a special pleasure (and not merely for nostalgic reasons) to take out an LP and look at the large disc, with grooves like a kind of tree-rings, as if music is something organic. I put the records on carefully, savouring the crackling as the needle touches the vinyl (sometimes I wait to switch on the loudspeaker so that all I can hear is the whispering from the grooves), before that slightly fragile sound, which can never be reproduced on a CD or in the new digital formats, fills the room. It is of course just a habit, but it works; I can write more easily, perhaps also more musically, with this accompaniment in the background. It even happens that I can write the draft of a judgement here on the divan, on a sheet of music paper, with Beethoven's last six Bagatelles for piano in the background. I used to enjoy writing judgements. Not infrequently I would take my work home, and when the divan draft was done I would polish the language at my desk, perhaps as I rolled to and fro a little on my chair, looking out now and then at Akershus Fortress, where traitors were shot after the war. I tried to write simply and clearly. A judgement must be soundly argued (the summing up of the evidence must be watertight), but it must be able to be read by all. Thanks to windbags like my father, the lay preacher, and Arve Storefjeld, I make an effort not to use more legal terminology than absolutely necessary. (In court I always speak to witnesses in an easily comprehensible way and avoid making use of professional jargon.) Sometimes music helps me to find the rhythm of the language as well. I wouldn't maintain that a good judgement is a work of art, but there is considerably more work behind it than most people suspect.

Now and then I put my notes away and turn off the music. I just lie there. Savour the stillness. One of the best things about living on Bankplassen is the stillness, particularly in the winter. Even the fountain is silent then. It may be that I live in a luxurious apartment, but its greatest advantage is the silence. Other people travel far out into the wilderness, but I can just sit here and experience the same calm, the same peace of mind. I believe that the ancient Greeks understood that: the goal of life is not action, but contemplation. Thinking. Descartes was right. I never feel better than when I'm lying here on my divan, letting the stillness fill me. I have never understood this urge for distraction which takes up so much of our existence nowadays. Nothing, not even Sir Kenneth Clark, can compare with stillness; and that was why I felt such antipathy towards Berge, towards the whole Blankvann incident. All the *racket* it involved.

On this particular evening I did something unusual, I listened to a violin piece. Early on I had noticed what the media wrote about Sylvie, that poor little nine-year-old who had been swallowed up by the bestial chasm in Nordmarka, that she had played Paganini's Sonata in E minor with a sensitivity which had moved the audience. (Apparently she had also played Caprice No. 24, which I found hard to believe, because parts of it are really demanding.)

I owned that piece on an LP I once bought in one of the shops at the top of Karl Johans gate, where I had conferred with one of the enthusiastic and knowledgeable assistants – I really miss those conversations – in order to find the best recording, and now I put it on, Paganini's Sonata in E minor for violin and guitar, and I lay down on Paal Berg's divan and listened. I could not help the tears welling up in my eyes, or to be honest: I cried. I cried both because it is an entrancing piece and because the thought of little Sylvie's fate stirred me to the depths of my heart.

When I got up I recognised another feeling mixed with that, and I was not proud to register it: *hatred* towards Nicolai Berge.

Eventually, after several weeks, the worst of the uproar around Berge's arrest had fortunately died down, and even though I could still feel the shock in my body (which emitted the occasional tremor), I managed to resume my normal routine. I worked, I thought, I walked – it was time for my Barbour jacket or my Burberry trench coat. The cashmere scarf. Once more I could observe people with pleasure; I smiled at a young couple kissing on some steps, I gave a friendly nod to an old lady talking to the pigeons, and from time to time I stopped on a corner which presented a surprising view and made notes with a thin mauve felt-tip pen on a music sheet I had in my pocket (perhaps about the links between Roman law and the Code Napoléon). I also kept up my literary interests during this period; I was nearing the end of my rereading of Albert Camus, and I sat in the evenings reading *The Plague*, as if to find support for the attitude which formed the basis of my activities as a judge, and which fortified me every time I believed that my efforts were in vain. For as Dr Rieux said: 'You have to fight in one way or another, and not give in.'

Nothing could compare with my quiet days in my apartment on Bankplassen. Just me, Sir Kenneth Clark and Beethoven's late piano pieces. Plus a Sætre tin filled with nuggets of gold. I could often go over to the window and just stand there, letting my eyes move in an arch from the avenue of chestnut trees by the idyllic Grev Wedels plass to the

Museum of Architecture, or what was once the Norwegian Bank's first building in Christiania, designed by no less than Christian Heinrich Grosch, our master of classicism. I have barricaded myself in here, I thought, as my glance finally came to rest on Akershus Fortress, and I did not consider that to be a dubious action; on the contrary, I had barricaded myself against all the din which went on outside my walls (and at this time, incidentally, the media were devoting a great deal of attention – understandably, for once – to the fact that a black man had been elected president of the US).

The more days that passed, the more relieved I was that Berge and the Blankvann incident had disappeared from the attention of the media. As I saw it, all the scrutiny of this crime had almost destroyed Norway and Norwegians' phenomenal advantage: our unremarkable presence in the world. Our status as a parenthesis – a peripheral, well-ordered colony which never put itself forward. The hysteria around the Blankvann incident could easily have drawn the spotlights of the empire towards us, with the consequence that we might suddenly have faced awkward questions, in the worst case of an ethical nature, about what we were doing behind our closed doors.

Yes, we had had a close shave. One straw can break the camel's back, as the saying goes. Now we had to make sure that Norway remained a half-forgotten province, the model colony which for several decades had given its citizens the most advantageous living conditions in the world. I would be just as upset if someone began to examine my country with a critical eye as I would if they interfered with my private and painstakingly composed circles.

Time passed, the names of the months changed, it was Christmas and then New Year. In January, a day when snowflakes fell the size of feathers, I did as Lev had told me and bought a shamelessly large number of shares in Den norske Bank, when the price had fallen to 20 kroner. From here it can only go up, I thought, but despite this surge of optimism I still felt restless, and I knew what the reason was, because even though the Blankvann killings were only occasionally mentioned on the news, I could never quite forget the face of Nicolai Berge. It was as if I scented danger, anticipated that everything could unravel at any moment. Even the capital briefly appeared dangerous. At the beginning of January there were demonstrations against Israel's attacks on Gaza. There was fighting in the streets both in Slottsparken and along Karl Johans gate. Windows were broken and rockets fired, there were fires in waste bins and the police went around with batons and shields.

In addition to that, my oasis in Dronningparken was closed; but even when I was walking under the lime trees along Karl Johan I often thought of Sofie Nagel, 'the lass from Nordmarka' as I called her. Was not everything a matter of chance? If I had asked for her phone number, if I had been more persistent, my life might have been quite different. I might have had a family, been a solicitor, lived in Adamstuen. And she would have been alive.

I tried to behave as normal. Spring arrived. Then summer. I carried out my work at the courthouse conscientiously. I think few people will understand what satisfaction it gives a person – not least a person with such ordinary gifts as me – to stride into a room when everyone else has got to their feet, and then sit down, bang the gavel on the table and say: 'The court is in session'. I sit there in my black gown with velvet bands and pretend it's the most natural thing in the world that it is me sitting there.

There were also a number of rather boring and quite straightforward cases during this time (even if some people maintained that they were complex); and in order not to drift off completely as I sat behind my table, I had to resort to a few tricks to keep awake. Despite the fact that I normally make notes on the computer which is supplied for us judges, I like to click my ballpoint pen, a Ballograf I once got from Lev, and scribble down a word or a sentence on my notepad now and then. Often it is just doodles (which actually resemble writing), and I make them so that people believe I'm concentrating intensely and noting down a significant point. Sometimes I depress the top and make a doodle when it seems that nothing important has been said. People jump as if I've cocked a gun. I want them to be startled, to think that I've noticed something no-one else has noticed, which again strengthens their confidence in my competence. Amongst lawyers it is interpreted as a warning sign: 'Lord Malm clicked his pen!' If it's a long time since I've asked a question, I might imitate a psychoanalyst and suddenly say to a witness 'Could you expand on what you just said?' Again everyone in court sits up, as if they realise I have heard something they have not heard and which they ought to have heard.

So far no-one has exposed me. Despite my inner unease. My reputation as an intelligent and independent judge is intact. (I have not been accused of bias, either in favour of the prosecution or in favour of the defence.) Outside the court room I nodded to my colleagues and joked with the office staff, with whom I have always been on good terms. I exchanged strained conversation with Dobermann on the occasions when I bumped into him on the stairs or in the corridor. One day recently he invited me with overly friendly gestures into his office for a chat – where he at once took his place in his commander's chair and motioned me towards the small sofa. I thought he wanted to ask me something, but he just chatted about things generally, in a jovial way, as if we were friends and wanted to catch up on the events of the last few weeks. Even though I gave nothing away and played my part in this bizarre conversation, I was puzzled; I got the impression that whilst we were conversing Dobermann was assessing me, or *examining* me. It was, I thought on the way out, as if he was *plotting* something.

I asked one of the office staff what Dobermann's little dog was called. I should have guessed: Caesar.

I frequented Limelight. I talked and laughed with Lev under the picture of Charlie Chaplin. I consumed my dinners at Engebret Café or one of the other restaurants in the old town or the centre. I promenaded in the streets and observed life. I strolled around in Slottsparken, then later in Dronningparken, so luxuriantly fertile that it reminded me of Kew Gardens itself, and by the pavilion I could occasionally fish out the old compass from my inner pocket and enjoy watching how, after considerable efforts, it eventually pointed north. The weather got so warm that I could wear my linen suit again. I observed, I enjoyed life, I smiled to myself, I was a sight for sore eyes, I registered that my elegant figure attracted a certain attention (in a good way), I was an administrator, a civil servant – a butler, I thought in a moment of sardonic humour – on my way through the colony, a northern Gold Coast right on the outer edge of consciousness for the rest of the world, but where everything functioned impeccably because of the empire's successful overarching system (if you discounted a few little stutters in the economy). I raised my panama hat cheerfully to everyone who nodded at me; I was one of those who contributed to preserving civilisation and good manners under these peripheral skies. Here goes Peter Malm, I thought. Or for that matter, why not Lord Malm. I hardly know my times table, I thought. I have no idea who is the prime minister of Spain or Italy, I don't know how to spell Azerbaijan, I can't explain Keynes's economic theories or the difference between Herder and Hegel, I have an extremely limited intelligence, but look at me as I walk along in my light linen suit, swinging my walking stick courteously; I'm a respected judge in the kingdom of Norway, a blessedly insignificant province which exports raw materials and half-finished products and to which the world otherwise pays little attention. That's how it should be, I thought. May it continue like that.

September came. There was a general election, and Labour had a good result, they were still riding high on the wave of sympathy after the Blankvann incident – not even Nicolai Berge's past in Young Labour could damage them – and there was still a red-green alliance in government.

There were plans for a memorial in Nordmarka, near Blankvann. People quarrelled in the papers, there was no shortage of aggressive comments about where it should stand and what it should look like.

My days continued as before.

It was autumn and soon it would be Christmas, and without knowing it I was approaching the winter of my discontent.

III

The change happened in the middle of December, on a day which at first had seemed particularly promising. Even though I didn't need to be at the courthouse until after twelve, I had got up early and taken the time to make a proper breakfast, including two fried eggs – something I otherwise only do on Sundays. Outside, on Bankplassen, the silver maple trees were decorated with small lightbulbs. I had just finished eating, and was enjoying the last piece of bacon and toast, whilst I listened to the BBC World Service, an impartial voice which reported no news of any significance.

My mobile rang.

It was a shock. To be nominated as the judge in the case against Nicolai Berge. It was the last thing I had expected. Or wanted. It was Odd Bergmann, Dobermann himself, who rang. I recognised his voice even before he finished saying his surname, and saw him in my mind's eye in his office, where he had no doubt moved over to his Roman commander's chair and was sitting admiring the 'bold' colour of the socks he had chosen that day.

Normally judges in particular cases were allocated in rotation. But this was a special case, said Bergmann. They needed a judge who was above reproach. And where there was no doubt about competence. I could imagine Dobermann in his commander's chair. 'I want you to take this case, Peter,' he said, as if I was counsel for the defence and not a judge. 'The rule of law must apply to Berge as well,' he said. 'It is important that this swine – excuse me – gets a fair trial.'

A life for a life, I thought.

For a moment I regretted having become a judge. It was not difficult to acquire a reputation for being a good judge. But it was difficult to be a *really* good judge. Now – at long last! – you will be stripped naked, I said to myself. Now everyone will see that you are not a good judge, even if you are known as a good judge.

It felt like a cold shower, to put it mildly, getting a phone call like that as I was sitting in my kitchen that morning, hearing Dobermann's deep voice, hearing him talking about Nicolai Berge. I looked down at the remains of the eggs on my plate and immediately felt a burning desire to shout: 'I refuse!' *Non serviam.* I didn't want this case. On the other hand, if I said no or found some excuse it might make Dobermann suspicious, it could sow the seeds of doubt which might make my entire impressive façade crumble. I couldn't be sure, but I suspected that Dobermann was giving me the case – at the same time as he would say in public that I was an obvious choice – in order to expose me, so that I might make a scandalous *faux pas*, display a complete lack of professional judgement. In other words, it was a trap. He knew that I didn't want this case, not for anything in the world, he knew that I disliked sensation. That was exactly why he had given me it.

I hung up, and at the same moment a bewildering thought occurred to me. Was I wrong? Had I been wrong for many years? Was Dobermann perhaps less sceptical of me than I believed? He would hardly risk his own reputation by selecting an unfit judge.

I sat there pushing crumbs to and fro on my plate with my fork. Wasn't I also a little bit proud? Not to say flattered? Wasn't something whispering to me that I ought to show myself worthy of such confidence? There was no doubt that I enjoyed respect (completely undeserved); there were even people at the courthouse who thought I ought to be aiming at the High Court. I merely smiled at this; I could see at once that it would be an even greater hubris than writing a book, and I didn't want to tempt fate. The only thing I envied the

High Court judges was their magnificent surroundings, to be able to stroll every day down the splendid corridors of that old, richly-decorated building opposite the Ministry of Finance. Those green lampshades! I had considered procuring a lamp like that with a green glass shade for myself, I could imagine how good it would look on my desk at home.

I stared at my mobile. Again that feeling of being distracted. That someone wanted to disturb my precious circles. In my existence the two greatest boons are time and silence. Now both of these were threatened. I would have more to do. And there would be more noise. I had no wish to get involved with that monster Berge and this dreadful bloody business. Above all, I didn't want the probing eyes of a nation upon me. I just wanted to sit here, raised high above Bankplassen; I wished for nothing more than to potter about doing my own thing, writing little notes which I placed in my Sætre tin, notes I imagined I would be able to combine into a pamphlet, a flaming torch about the fragility of justice, and in which I planned to use the post-war trials as a shining example, since it was a reckoning we often had the audacity to brag about. At the same time I detected an even greater danger: I would not cope with judging this affair. I would disgrace myself. Perhaps Dobermann and everyone else would also sense that my sorrow at the death of Storefjeld and the others, even at that of poor little Sylvie, was not profound enough; in short they would realise that I was not of sufficient calibre to sit in judgement on this crucial case, or indeed to be a judge at all. My daring bluff would finally be exposed, on prime-time TV, as it were.

Again it felt as if everything was swaying. Even though I was sitting down. My coffee was suddenly tasteless. I felt as if I was eating my last meal.

I went through and lay down on Paal Berg's old divan. I had to find an excuse. I could tell Dobermann that I was debarred from taking the case, I could try to ingratiate myself, accompany him on a walk with his little Pomeranian, and as I was patting Caesar I could tell him about Sofie

Nagel. But even before I had finished that thought, I knew that I could never tell anyone about that episode in the forest. I could say I was ill. I could actually ask for some time off, pleading exhaustion, or depression, like Kjell Magne Bondevik did whilst he was Prime Minister. He gained nothing but sympathy and respect for doing that. In fact the very thought of having to concern myself with Berge made me feel exhausted. All sorts of mental health issues were accepted now. I could even risk being valued more highly if I admitted struggling with such a weakness. It was almost a recommendation to have been through a dark patch. People construed me as dark, I believed. (At a pinch I could tell Dobermann about that episode with the saw and the piano in my youth.) Yes, that might work.

Since I was now lying on the divan, I put on an LP with Beethoven's eleven Bagatelles, Opus 119, as if I wanted to help my thoughts to get over a barrier, and as I lay there listening and trying to follow the innovative sequence, my thoughts returned willy-nilly to my conversation with Dobermann, and I realised that there was something else, that my aversion to Berge and all he stood for was perhaps an even greater reason for me to refuse than my fear that my defects as an authority might be discovered. I could hardly be said to be impartial. My scepticism about the Labour Party made me also sceptical about some of the victims. Even Sofie Nagel. When I thought about it, I had always hated her a little for not getting in touch after our walk out of Nordmarka, out of our shared darkness. It would have been easier for her to find me than the other way round, I had told her where I worked. The whole affair was a nasty mess which I had not the slightest desire to get involved in. I wanted to remain in my idyll, and take my normal cases; they could be difficult at times, but nevertheless they were cases I handled brilliantly. I wanted to sit in Limelight and enjoy my Vodka Martini in peace, I wanted to remain a *flâneur*, and not to have to think about the legal complications of this case, not to mention the whole emotional inferno it would involve. Just listening to a repeat of the glorification of Storefjeld and the Labour Party would bring me to the verge of sleeplessness. My only talent was to conceal my lack of talent. With all the attention I would automatically attract because of this case, my whole cunning undercover operation could be blown sky-high. My whole existence.

I said yes.

They wanted to conduct a dignified trial, and they had approached me, Peter Malm. Yes, I'm the right man, I thought. The chosen one. In the newspapers there were bombastic articles about purging the country of evil. But my job was to preside over a trial, not to carry out an exorcism. My professional pride had been awoken.

When it became public that I had been nominated as the judge, a journalist from one of the newspaper magazines rang. At first I thought it was Ine Wang, but it was someone else. She asked me if she could interview me. I said no. It surprised me that a journalist could believe that a judge would appear in a magazine like any other celebrity (although afterwards I remembered that Dobermann had once let himself be portrayed, and I felt a certain pride that I had not allowed myself to sink to the same depths as him). She even suggested taking a photo of me holding some scales. What stupidity, what a cliché. What were they thinking?

The next months were different. Due to the extensive criminal case which was in prospect, I had less to do at the courthouse, even though I still had some civil cases which needed preparation. In my free time I tried to make some progress with my book, but my concentration had been ruined. Every time I rolled over to my desk I just sat there staring out of the window. I got nowhere.

However, one evening I managed to pull myself together; I decided it was important to maintain my routine and not give up the search for inspiration. I stood in front of the little walnut bookcase which houses my library, and since I had finished with Camus, I pulled out a book almost at random. It was *Bleak House* by Charles Dickens, a novel I had read in the course of my *annus mirabilis* in London. As I have explained, I lived in Tavistock Square, and I soon discovered that Dickens had also lived there for a few years, and that it was there he had written *Bleak House* amongst other things, and that was why I bought the book. And what a story it was. Never mind that it was in London that I found a historical context for the term 'just punishment', never mind the fact that it was there I was sexually satisfied for life by Miss Huxley; what I remember best from my stay is the delight with which I read *Bleak House* by Charles Dickens. Sometimes I think that was what I did during that year in London: I read *Bleak House*. It was a novel which took a year. I can safely say that Dickens' novel meant more for my legal work than *Norway's Laws*. Although I have read stacks of professional literature, it is *Bleak House* which has had the most influence on me.

Now I sat myself down in Wegner's uncomfortable (but now, thanks to my cushions, comfortable) wing chair and leafed through it, studying the underlinings I had made and the comments I had written in the margin as I sat in my room in Tavistock Square, reading it for the first time. I believe I liked that novel so much because in it Dickens describes the tangled universe of the law in a way that no-one else has done before or since; but as I glanced at those descriptions now and read some of the passages where Dickens explains the case of Jarndyce versus Jarndyce, I thought that they reminded me of the Blankvann case, because that too was beginning to take on encyclopaedic dimensions, and would soon embrace everything. Now that the case was due to come to court there was no person and no sphere of interest which did not have an opinion about the differing aspects, and they all broadcast bombastic pronouncements the moment they got the chance.

I have always read a lot of fiction. To be honest, I read as much fiction as I did law when I was studying. I have often maintained that all study programmes, including law, ought to have an obligatory reading list of at least twenty works from world literature, and *Bleak House* should be one of them. For my own part – and it was also significant for my choice of justice as a topic – I feel I have never finished with a novel like *Crime and Punishment* by Dostoevsky. Or *The Brothers Karamazov*, with its focus on killing; whichever way you look at it, revenge is the other face of just punishment. In the Young Lawyers' Reading Club we tried to seek out works which contained legal conundrums. Like Shakespeare's *Merchant of Venice*. Oh, how well I remember that – not least the discussion of the court scene there, for how should one interpret 'a pound of flesh'? The conversations around *The Trial* or 'In the Penal Colony' by Kafka were of course also a high point. We spent a whole night in June talking about Atticus Finch, the lawyer in *To Kill a Mockingbird* by Harper Lee. As I said, Dobermann looked in as well. Strangely enough. Looking back, I can hardly imagine a person who seems to be at a greater remove from the most significant merit of fiction: to be able to show ambivalence, uncertainty, doubt. It can be difficult to interpret a law, but it was more difficult to interpret a statement from Camus' *The Outsider*: 'How had I not realised that nothing is more important than an execution, and that it is in fact the only really significant thing for a human being! If I ever got out of this prison, I would go and see all the executions.'

Our little club was dissolved. One of us changed universities. One dropped out. One stopped reading fiction. I was the only one left in the Young Lawyers' Reading Club. In my mind I am still a member. My successful career as a lawyer (I almost said: the fact that I've got away with it) is due to my having read a great deal of fiction, and having acquired through these books a kind of fundamental understanding of the human condition.

On this occasion, however, I made no progress, despite the fact that I'd been sitting in my wing chair with *Bleak House* on my lap, and perhaps because I was extra disillusioned this evening and needed an extraordinary remedy, I resorted to one of my favourite programmes in the *Civilisation* series. The one about Romanticism. I mixed myself a Cosmopolitan and settled down. And it did help, I felt lighter. It was an edifying session, if I can put it like that. I also drank one Cosmopolitan too many. There was something about the combination of a Cosmopolitan and Sir Kenneth Clark's voice, his wise words about Beethoven's music and Byron's poetry and Rodin's sculptures (Balzac!), which made some thoughts react with other thoughts and provoke thoughts I had never thought before. I had an idea for *A Life for a Life* as well, and I scribbled it down on the half sheet of paper I have the sense to have always lying ready by my chair, before I went in and placed it in the Sætre tin on my desk. I felt almost ecstatic, though I can't explain why.

I sat there for far too long that evening. The next day in court I had to deploy all my skills as an actor in order to cover up a troublesome hangover.

*

One day something distressing happened, and afterwards I have had to ask myself whether it had anything to do with the fact that the public now knew that I was going to be the judge in the Berge case. Or was the drama just another sign that the world was out of joint? Whatever the reason: I was knocked down, and not just anywhere, I was knocked down in front of the Storting, almost as if it was a deliberate insult to our country's legislature. Even into my blessedly uneventful existence brutality was now seeping.

It was late, and I was on my way home from the Grand Hotel, feeling uplifted (after an audience with King Edgar), when I suddenly witnessed a scene. Right beside the statue of C.J. Hambro, that admirable character, there was a man harassing another man; he began to push him, and then to hit out so that the other man fell down. That wasn't enough for him, he then started to kick the man on the ground in the chest. It was late enough for me to be the only one observing the incident. Of course I should have turned back or gone round them in a wide semi-circle, but I stopped.

As I stood there watching that poor chap get maltreated, or you might rather say thrashed, there was something in me, a voice, which said that I couldn't just stand still and watch. In other words, there is some place hidden away inside me which refutes my facile claim (which I could flirt with in social gatherings) that existence is devoid of meaning. For the meaning of life, I thought as I stood there, or rather felt it as a tension in my whole body – the meaning of life is to save other lives. Or make things easier for other people, and soothe their pain. (It seemed to me that I had noted something about this in connection with natural law on one of my half manuscript pages.) Nevertheless, I hesitated. I was in the middle of a force field, with the National Theatre at my back and the Storting right in front of me. Did that affect me? Did I see myself as an actor in a classical drama? Did I intend to pay tribute to our elected representatives? I have never really believed in civil courage, in wanting to save someone when it is not strictly speaking necessary, but I must admit that I have been unsure about this ever since, when we were students, we read Finn Alnæs' *Koloss* in the Young Lawyers' Reading Club, and of course also Johs. Andenæs' provocative doctoral thesis on 'criminal negligence'. That made an impression. You could be legally responsible even if you refrained from getting involved. And now it was as if my body rather than my head insisted I should act. You must intervene! I can't express it, all I can say is that for a brief moment I experienced the truth of Kant's categorical imperative, which in its turn must be seen as the lowest common denominator of humanity's numerous attempts at systems of morality. I imagined that it was me lying there on the ground, and thought about what I would have wished a passer-by to do.

'Stop,' I said. 'Wait,' I said, and reached out a hand, an arm, as if by that gesture alone I could get the thug to stop kicking the prostrate man, and in essence I couldn't say or do any more than that before I was struck by an almighty blow, and when I came round I was lying on the ground.

My assailant didn't take my money, he took something more valuable than that: he stole my old compass from the inner pocket of my tweed jacket, the one I had got from Herr Haug. Without it I felt naked. I took it as a bad sign, a really unlucky omen.

Afterwards I had a nagging feeling that the whole thing was staged, that it was a kind of test. As I thought about it I felt increasingly suspicious that those two who were fighting were just pretending, that it was a diversionary tactic in order to rob me – I am almost certain that one of them winked at the other just before I intervened. Or was I mistaken?

Of course I did not report it to the police. I wasn't stupid. But as a result of that harsh meeting with the gravel in front of the Storting I kept myself to myself even more; I was afraid that if it was notified, it might attract attention, which might in its turn lead to a chain of investigations which would have the ultimate result that my hard-won camouflage would be stripped away and everyone would see that I was unfit to be the judge in the country's most important case since the turn of the millennium. I cursed my moral impulse, that idiotic inspiration which had pitched me head-first to the ground.

It is not always the case that it's a good idea to help others, despite what people say.

On the evening I got beaten up I lay on my divan with an ice-pack against my cheek, thinking. I regretted my decision. I reproached myself for not having refused and found a watertight excuse when Dobermann rang.

The opening day of the trial was approaching, and the discussion of Berge and the whole Blankvann incident was of course blown up enormously in all the media; it was as if the nation had forgotten the whole trauma, and all the horror had to be revived. Much of what had been said earlier was said again, and everyone who was involved was interviewed once more. It was like a re-enactment, partly in slow motion.

As for me, I had more than enough to do. I was sent the notice of indictment and the list of evidence early on, and in the following months I had a number of preparatory meetings with the legal representatives. Now, just before the case opened, things got even busier. At the same time I prepared myself *mentally*. For Berge.

One evening I met Lev, and it was he who said I ought to take a look at Berge's blog. 'For a long time I regarded him as a fellow partisan,' he added cryptically.

I remembered that I had read something about that, presumably from the time just after his arrest. There was an article, possibly written by a sociologist, in which Berge was described as one of those dangerous new elements in contemporary society: the hate-filled male loser, of the sort who finds an arena, a place to avenge himself, in the blogosphere. All of that was Greek to me, I knew hardly anything about the new social media. But I thought about Berge, and about the fact that it could be true: here was a man rejected by his party, rejected by Gry Storefjeld, rejected by the literary public. Could that give rise to a dangerous desperation?

'Isn't his blog shut down?' I said. 'Hasn't someone removed it? The police?' Lev looked at me indulgently over his Whiskey Sour, one of his favourite drinks. 'The first thing is that there's nothing there which is forbidden by law,' he said, 'and the second is that it's not so easy to remove things from the net. Fortunately.' Lev is a stout defender of freedom of expression, and he knows a great deal about the 'world-wide web'; there's an old hippie in Lev. He scribbled down a web address on one of my half pieces of paper.

The following evening, at home in my apartment, I took out the paper. I was doubtful. I was going to preside in the case against Berge. A judge should ideally not know more than others, a judge should only consider the evidence from witnesses and the proof which is presented in court. On the other hand I had already read a great deal before I took on the Berge case – against my will, I might add. And who would know if I glanced at my screen now for a few minutes?

I weighed up whether I should watch a Kenneth Clark programme instead, but my curiosity won. I sat down at my desk and switched on my computer. Berge's blog turned out to be called Pens, and as that word means 'points' in Norwegian, it immediately triggered positive associations with my father, who spent his whole life working on the railways. What can I say about it? From what I had read about Berge's hatred of the Labour Party, I had expected to find some fanatical views. But as with the law, everything depends on interpretation. It is possible that you could, with considerable effort, find traces of a dangerous ideology in Berge's blog, but to do that you'd have to contribute a good portion of fantasy, as well as over-interpret. I read several of his posts from the years before his arrest, and they were not fanatical at all, and certainly not right-wing extremism, as some had claimed. Some could be called provocative, but I could see that there was some justification for what he wrote. 'The Old Boys' Club has its home on Youngstorget and not on Holmenkollen,' I read at one point. The post was about those previous Young Labour members who now occupied influential and well-paid positions in banks, brokers, consultancies and the Foreign Office. To be honest, I started to find it quite amusing, and I suddenly fancied a Gimlet (was it the taste of lime I craved, or was it rather the thought of Philip Marlowe, Raymond Chandler's detective and connoisseur of Gimlets?) – but I managed to push the thought away; it was important to keep a clear head during this private little, what shall I call it, *preliminary examination*. As far as I could judge, most of the critical blog posts were written by someone to the left of the Labour Party, especially the posts which attacked Labour's restrictive immigration policy, and several of them could be used as starting points for fruitful, not to say important debates about the ideological foundation of the Labour Party. That was also the obvious intention of the blog, as far as I could see. 'Those features of "friendly" totalitarianism and top-down utilitarianism which characterised the Labour Party in its heyday have lost their appeal at a time when individualism rules the roost,' I read in one post. Nicolai Berge underlined the need for a fundamental review of strategy, and several times used the expression 'to navigate a new course', which awoke an echo in me; I thought at once and with sorrow about that precious compass which had been stolen from me. 'The Labour Party's lack of fervour, its irresolution, comes from the fact that everything has already been achieved,' Berge wrote. 'The reason that the Labour Party today faces an ideological crisis is that the affluent society, which was a utopia at the end of the 1940s, has now been realised.'

Was this Berge the murderer?

I read a post where he wrote about our longing for a politician who had a wider vocabulary and a better mastery of language than our present politicians, a politician who was not so damned media savvy and so careful not to say too much, a politician with fire in the belly who could actually *inspire* citizens.

I could not agree more.

Was I sitting there nodding in agreement with the opinions of a man I despised, or believed I despised? I was. I was sitting there nodding. I thought that a Gimlet would be a good idea now. I dismissed the thought.

I wanted to switch off the computer, but I sat there scrolling downwards, and even though I was just skimming it, my impression grew steadily stronger that this was quite an intelligent criticism of the Labour Party. But Berge wrote on more general matters as well, he wrote that politicians today were more concerned with opinion polls than with taking courageous and unpopular decisions in order to solve the climate problem, for example – they were more frightened of saying something wrong on TV than of letting the pollution of the atmosphere continue. He called for responsibility, innovation, action. Where was the person who could say something sensible about how the power of capitalism had freed itself from political control? What were we doing with an economic system which was getting further and further away from democracy?

I thought that this reminded me of something. Then I realised. It resembled the readers' letters Lev wrote. Even though many of these blogs were quite outspoken, they were all written with the thought that they could lead to something good. Did I feel a faint stirring of sympathy for Berge, or at least for his blog?

I wondered whether Berge could perhaps be regarded as a Michael Kohlhaas – in my student days I had been gripped by Heinrich von Kleist's novel – a man who becomes the victim of his sense of justice and for that reason does evil?

I got up to make myself a Gimlet, but then discovered that I had run out of Rose's Lime Cordial. For lack of a better idea I mixed a Black Russian, but for some reason it turned out wrong, there was too strong a taste of vodka and too little of Kahlua. Or the other way round. All this made me pause. How would I cope with this case if I couldn't even do something as simple as make a Black Russian?

*

I awoke to invigorating spring air on the Monday the case against Nicolai Berge was scheduled to start. A paradox, I thought. It had rained for a long time and now it was sunny in the colony. I dressed in one of my best suits from Savile Row and was filled with something resembling optimism as I strode through the streets on my way to the most important assignment of my career. It seemed also that a more solemn nimbus rested on Oslo Courthouse this morning; I noticed it from the top of Rosenkrantz' gate as the building appeared before me. I have always been sceptical about so-called postmodernist architecture, the way it plays with classical forms and elements, but for some reason the courthouse quickly found favour in my eyes – I can't help it, but on sunny days the façade in granite and Nordland marble makes me think of the impressive Viceroy's House in New Delhi, the British Empire's most imposing building.

I have always liked main hearings. I enjoy entering the sober, light-filled rooms, ready to follow the rituals which are still adhered to – just the fact that everyone stands up when I enter, as if I were a priest in church about to read from the Gospels. I don't just like it, I revel in sitting there with the lion rampant of the Norwegian coat of arms behind me, as I steeple my fingers, signalling that I am attentive and concentrated. Yes, I like it. To be an administrator. An admiral. Steering the ship between the Scylla and Charybdis of legal arguments, if I may be permitted to express myself slightly bombastically about the competing interests of the prosecution and the defence. I enjoy it more than I dare admit – perhaps because, behind the mask of seriousness and self-assurance, I feel humbled, I know that I am not worthy of all the deference everyone shows me.

There was of course something particularly special about this case. I registered that very clearly as soon as I reached C.J. Hambros plass and saw the TV vans parked in front of the courthouse (like small parasites around a large lump of sugar, I thought). The case had attracted the kind of attention I had never experienced before – and which I knew I would never experience again – and I could feel a kind of *pressure*, in the same way as you can occasionally feel a physical reaction to a fall in barometric pressure. What were all these people doing here? Wasn't it a bit like the old days, when people flocked to see a public execution?

By dint of walking along quietly, at the same time as I refrained from swinging my walking stick, I made it to the staff entrance without the journalists discovering me. (It could also just as well have been that I was still anonymous, even though my picture – a younger version of me, it's true – had been printed in the papers several times in recent weeks.) On the way in I thought about the Second World War traitors. For most people Berge was just as guilty as Quisling.

226

For that very reason this had to be a *just* trial, a kind of miniature treason trial which our society could be proud of.

And it is I, Lord Malm, who must ensure that Berge is treated in accordance with the general principles of law and order and democracy, I thought that same morning as I entered Room 227, the largest courtroom available, and settled down on the comfortable high-backed chair behind the judge's table. 'The court is in session,' I declared in a steady voice, and banged my gavel on the table. Not hard. But decisively. Many judges have stopped using the gavel. However, I appreciate this little tap which is like a starting pistol, signalling that the trial is under way. It reminds me of school, when the teacher came into the noisy classroom and clapped his hands, and we fell silent at once, ready for the voyage of education to continue. But as soon as I put down the gavel and looked round the room – I don't know whether it was because of all the excitement – I had the feeling that I was not in control, despite the fact that there was nothing indicating that I was not. It was as if Dobermann had persuaded me up onto a large stage under false pretences, to play a piano piece he knew I wasn't good enough to play. I put my fingertips together and swore to myself that no-one – no-one in the whole of Norway – would suspect that I felt like that.

For the whole of that first week I remained in my office after I had hung up my gown in the cupboard. I needed to rest before I walked home, and I didn't want to have recourse to Limelight during the case, for fear that someone might observe me and gossip to the press. On several evenings I went up to the roof terrace at the courthouse, since there was no-one there at that time. The view did me good. I sat on a chair, looking towards the Palace and Holmenkollen ridge behind. It was Berge who was bothering me. What was I to make of Berge?

When I entered the courtroom that first day and finally saw him face to face, my antipathy was awoken once more. I had the feeling of confronting an evil force. A kind of satanic presence. I can't put it any other way. (Or was I prejudiced in advance?) What would be a just punishment for such a person? I examined him, thinking: this is the man who killed Sofie Nagel, the woman who once stepped into a clearing in the wood, as if from nowhere, and saved my life. 'You poncy bastard!' someone shouted, and even though I immediately announced authoritatively that the person involved must hold his tongue if he wanted to remain in the public gallery, I could understand the outburst. Berge had appeared in one of those suits which were clearly his signature outfits and which were of a strangely old-fashioned cut, and his clothes naturally provoked the many people who wanted to see him, metaphorically speaking, in sackcloth and ashes.

Berge, such a strong, proud name. Ruined for ever. Even for the other poor innocents who happened to share it. If you hear someone say 'Berge', you are invaded by a feeling of nausea.

Otherwise everything proceeded as normal, apart from the fact that Berge remained silent; I had to accept an affirmative nod to the formal questions about name, profession, all that sort of thing, and I had to turn to the defence counsel with my question as to whether Berge was pleading guilty to the charge. ('His silence must be construed as meaning not guilty,' he said.) But the trial continued, and it was only that everything took a little longer, everything was more detailed, perhaps because everything was more weighty, the crime so exceptionally brutal, so difficult to comprehend. There was the opening speech for the prosecution, with its deeply serious content, there were the remarks from the defence, a couple of feeble attempts to correct the prosecution's presentation of the facts on a few points, and I directed it all with a tight rein; I had in the back of my mind the whole time that the case should be conducted in a way worthy of a society based on the rule of law. It was as if I wanted single-handedly to restore the impression of Norway (my Gold Coast) as a well-ordered, and not least meticulously administered, colony.

Justice. Democracy. Dignity.

The day Berge was given the opportunity to explain himself, he merely shook his head. I tried my hardest to get him to understand that it would be best for him if he talked, both to present his story and to answer questions from the court. 'If you choose to remain silent, it is my duty to inform you that it *may* count against you,' I said, looking at him as if I hoped that by the power of my glance I could conquer the antisocial impulse I suspected in him. Even though I concealed it, I was more engaged than I had been for a long time; I believe that a detector would have revealed that my pulse rate was abnormally high. But he still shook his head, seemingly uninterested.

I sat there alone in my office or on the roof terrace, pondering about Berge. His silence. The fact that he managed to remain silent accorded with the steadfastness which was necessary in order to carry out such a cruel deed.

I started to think about an article which had been printed just before Berge was arrested. It was written by a criminologist, who argued that the use of a knife and the slitting of throats could suggest that it was some kind of ritual murder. What if a religious sect was behind it? In their clinical precision the killings almost had something sacred about them, the author wrote. It could be that the perpetrators regarded the killings as necessary – in order to meet a criterion, to start a process, or so that they could be 'taken up'.

I had smiled, shaking my head, when I read that article. Now I remembered that Berge was a historian of religion, and sat there brooding.

These were thoughts I did not want to share with my two fellow judges. Even though we talked and discussed matters the whole time during breaks, there was much which I kept to myself, for the time being at least.

On several of these evenings in the office I discovered that I was sitting in the dark. It had got late, and I had forgotten to switch on the light.

The days passed, and I sat behind the judge's table with my fingertips steepled in front of my chest, so that those in court would believe that I was listening with particular interest. I have the reputation of being imperturbable, and I take that as a compliment. A judge should be imperturbable. Nevertheless it has happened, I must admit, in the course of long criminal trials, perhaps in the middle of a forensic psychiatrist's detailed and unfortunately also soporific report, that I have zoned out – zoned out to the extent that I can't remember what has been said – and then this listening posture can be a good camouflage.

During the Berge case I had a different kind of problem, and I'm not thinking about the greedy media spotlight, but that all the pieces had as it were shifted slightly out of their normal positions. That troubled me. The prosecutor's recurring hyena smile and her studied aggression. The stuttering voice of the counsel for the defence, as if he were apologising in every sentence for the fact that he had had to take on this thankless task. Not to mention the contradictory evidence of witnesses. Especially at the start I had a thumping headache, despite the fact that I refrained from visiting Limelight in the evenings. I felt ill because of this spectacular show which Dobermann had so craftily given me the task of directing. I was a circus director more than a judge; the prosecution, the defence and police witnesses of various kinds were artistes, and all around sat the whole of Norway as an audience, enjoying the spectacle. I was forced to take more painkillers than I liked to, and for the first time in a long time I had to take sleeping pills at night.

I was already looking forward to the end of these turbulent weeks, so that I could again enjoy uneventful normality, what I thought of as a colonial atmosphere, with the sounds of palm trees and waves crashing on the beach, a kind of eternal vacation (though well paid, of course). More than anything else I longed to return to my T-shaped writing desk with the old biscuit tin like a Kaaba in the middle; I missed being able to skate around on my office chair, placing pages of notes side by side in different formations in order to see if I could compose my fragments about justice and just punishment in such a way that the final structure afforded a glimpse of a new and undreamt-of coherence. (The latest note I had placed in my Sætre tin was about the tension between legalism and Confucianism in Ancient China.) I longed to be able to sit there in the evening again, watching Sir Kenneth Clark walking around in ruins and cathedrals, I wanted to read novels without easy answers, I wanted to listen to Beethoven's last piano sonatas (the second movement of No. 28, an almost jazz-like improvisation which expanded inwards, or outwards); but for now I had to put up with my days being filled with people who talked and talked, prosecutor, counsel for the victims, counsel for the defence, witness after witness. There was a 'factual summary', a ring-binder full of such thick documents that it could itself be used as a lethal weapon, there were pictures, dreadful pictures from the cabin at Blankvann, there were post-mortem reports and forensic scientists with their detailed explanations and horrifying close-ups, the whole thing almost unbearable (even though I was inured after many years in court), there was the inspection of the scene of the crime, with police tapes to keep the media wolfpack at a distance – there was witness after witness after witness, talk, talk and more talk, except from Nicolai Berge, for Nicolai Berge sat silent, he was present and yet not present, he poured himself a glass of water now and then as if to demonstrate that he was not asleep with his eyes open.

I had everything under control, but I had a feeling the whole time that something unexpected could happen at any moment.

One evening when I was going home early for once I decided to eat dinner at Engebret Café. It may be that it is not the town's best restaurant, although the kitchen does have its specialities (during the last few months, for example, I had eaten cod on several occasions), but this evening I ordered their lamb curry with mustard gratin, a dish I knew they mastered to perfection.

I had a book in my briefcase; I always carry a book, even when I go to a restaurant, both in order to have something to do whilst I'm waiting for my food and so that I'm not disturbed. I have a particular weakness for English literature, and today it was William Golding who had the honour of keeping me company. I never get tired of reading, and I know that makes me a better – or at least a less poor – judge; if there is anything fiction has taught me, it is that there is no such thing as truth. Or Truth. All we have is stories, fabulations. That's what I'm doing in court as well, weighing one story against another, looking for the story which carries most weight (and as I see it, this is what makes a discerning judge). In addition I try to enter imaginatively into what other people are thinking and feeling – whether it is the aggrieved, the victims, or indeed the accused.

It was precisely for that reason that it was so upsetting that Berge remained silent and refused to tell *his* story.

I have always been attached to Engebret Café, which had its heyday when Christiania Theatre lay where the Museum of Contemporary Art now lies, and the restaurant teemed with artists and actors. The café's patina is the best thing about Engebret (along with the generous open sandwiches); there are not many places left in the capital which still look as they looked at the time that the colony's three greats, Ibsen, Grieg and Munch, took their places there. But not even the warm surroundings and Engebret's antiquated atmosphere could brighten my mood this evening. The food arrived, and I had ordered an akvavit; that is something I rarely drink, and a sign that something was out of joint.

Even though the case was proceeding as it should and everyone, even the newspapers, were praising me for the way I was conducting it, I was still anxious. It was as if I was staging a great tragedy and was now eager to see whether the nation would experience the expected, the *necessary* catharsis. During this time I often caught myself trying to prove my distinction, and kept shunting perfectly innocent comments over into legal debate, after which I began to throw around aphorisms (like Storen! I thought) and short exegeses into which I tried to insert as much legal jargon as possible, and from time to time I managed to mention some legal nicety or other, even if it was completely irrelevant for the person I was talking to – like the head waiter at Engebret Café when I arrived – at the same time as I realised in the next breath that I had no idea what I was babbling about, and I didn't really understand it myself. The thought of my strained behaviour almost made me blush as I sat there. One thing was certain: when it came to the case against Berge, I had to put aside my prejudices, as they could be fatal. I impressed on myself that I must say as little as possible (although I did have to intervene once to ask a witness to tone down the panegyrics and remind them that the case was not about whether Arve Storefjeld was a significant politician or not).

What's more, I was uneasy about Lev. I had asked him if he would like to come and eat at Engebret's, but he said no. Something was wrong. I knew he was spending too much time at Bjerke trotting track. One on occasion I uttered a cautious criticism of him for frequenting that milieu. Then he looked at me strangely and said it was a reproach he could not understand. What did I know about it? About all the originals you could meet there, all the lively stories you could hear? The love of those beautiful animals? Betting on the horses was just an alibi. It was the atmosphere which attracted Lev, a world that most people were entirely ignorant of.

But he did bet. And he always wagered too much.

I thought about myself: was it better to bet on the Stock Exchange than to bet on the horses?

And behind that again: doesn't this too, my prejudice against it, show that I am a bad judge?

I sat leafing through William Golding's novel *The Spire* (I don't know whether I had picked it out by chance, it was a complex novel about ambitions and their fragile foundations), without being able to concentrate; and Golding demands a reader's full attention, he demands to be taken slowly, that's why I think so highly of him. I considered whether I should have dessert – cloudberries or blueberry cake or plum compôte – but I couldn't make up my mind. Why was Berge silent? I couldn't understand it. Because things looked bad. They really did look bad. There was that necklace, Gry Storefjeld's necklace, which was found in Berge's flat. It also transpired that he had taken a course in close combat in the army. It was unusual in the section where Berge was doing his National Service; there was a keen officer involved and it was a one-off, but it meant that Berge had experience of how to use a knife (the techniques of so-called 'silent killing'). In other words, he possessed the ability to kill someone in the professional way that had been demonstrated in the cabin at Blankvann.

One of the witnesses for the prosecution, a friend of Gry Storefjeld, told the court about this close combat training; he had once seen Berge demonstrate it. They were at a nightspot, Blå by the river Akerselva, and Berge was threatened by a larger man. Berge had quickly moved away, out of reach of blows and kicks, and when the man came towards him he stood half turned to the side, to make himself a smaller target, with his arms raised, his elbows close to his sides and his hands open – as if to signal that he didn't want to fight. When the other man kept coming anyway, Berge stepped quickly towards him and gave him an unexpected blow with his elbow in the solar plexus. The man crumpled to the ground. It all happened so quickly that hardly anyone noticed, but Gry's friend knew something about martial arts, that's why he remembered it. 'It's not often you see someone act like that, or use their elbow in that way,' he said. Afterwards Berge claimed that he had just acted instinctively.

When I heard that witness, I thought – of all things – that I would like to have mastered that art on the occasion when I thought I could stop a thug, but was instead knocked down right by the Storting.

Berge's temperament was also pointed out, the fact that he had a short fuse. Gry's brother spoke about a weekend trip to the cabin under Raudberget in Dovre. During a quarrel with Arve Storefjeld, Berge had become so angry that he had left the company late in the evening. But he had turned in the doorway and made a threatening gesture with the side of his hand, like a knife-blade across his throat. (You could hear a gasp in the courtroom as Gry's brother demonstrated the gesture – in slightly too theatrical a way, if you ask me.)

I dropped the idea of dessert. I closed the novel. I needed to go home and take a sleeping pill.

The weeks passed. Every day I sat in Courtroom 227 examining Berge. At the start he looked quite lost, as if he didn't understand what was happening. After some time it just looked as if his mind was elsewhere. Society's rules of due process were followed precisely, but at the same time Berge was in the stocks in front of a whole nation. Some commentators wrote that he would break down under pressure, but he didn't break down. Did he feel remorse? Impossible to say. I admit that I was preoccupied by Berge. I could not reconcile the stories I heard with that resigned but less and less demonic figure sitting unresponsively beside the defence counsel. Berge seemed unreadable. Was he, this young man in an old-fashioned double-breasted suit, a mass murderer? Was he concealing a fury, a *rage,* of greater dimensions than anyone knew? I have always believed that I am so fascinated by Mr Kurtz in *The Heart of Darkness* because Joseph Conrad lets him say so little. It was as if I half expected that Berge was suddenly going to stand up and shout

'Exterminate the bastards!' I could not penetrate him, get to the bottom of his thinking (I almost said: of the evil in him) – or find out who he was.

The horror! The horror!

Theories about a motive were of course the main focus. The deed could be a sign of psychosis; soon the forensic psychiatrists would take the stage, or rather enter the witness box. Their report was presented, and from what they had been able to discover (the foundation was somewhat shaky, given that he would not talk to them), there were no indications that he was not responsible for his actions. His behaviour in prison was also normal. But if there was no sign of psychosis, why did he do it? Were the killings politically motivated? Did Berge kill those five people because he was fighting for a greater cause, a cause which was unclear to everyone else (some totalitarian movement or other)? Was he under the influence of a theory known to only a few people in the world?

In the middle of the prosecution's efforts to show that Berge wanted to avenge himself on the Labour Party, to damage it, I found myself thinking that the other main theory appeared simpler: Berge had killed Gry Storefjeld and the Frenchman out of jealousy, and the others were just unfortunate to be in the same place. I had seen enough cases where jealousy lay behind the most aggressive crimes. Literature too – just take Tolstoy's *Kreutzer Sonata* – demonstrated how crazed jealousy could make you.

I did my best to spar with my fellow judges, a man and a woman, in the breaks; they also clearly had a need to air their ideas and discuss the evidence so far. They were both intelligent and conscientious people, but I had to remind them several times not to settle on one opinion too soon.

It was exhausting. Instead of enjoying the bright spring, or possibly taking leave to work near a lake in Northern Italy, I had to sit here in the courthouse listening to an endless stream of words attempting to pinpoint the motivation of the accused. 'Berge is the incarnation of evil,' wrote one paper, practically giving up on the whole affair. It was as if his silence and blank face provoked the commentators. 'Now we have our own Hannibal Lecter,' wrote another.

But what if Berge transcended all labels? What if the motive he might have had was impenetrable? I could accept that, but could other people, could the Norwegian people accept it? That was precisely the problem of judging in this case. The public's expectations. Their fear of complexity. And this was complex. But despite that, people wanted to *understand*. They wanted answers, they wanted conclusions, clear as glass, like in a syllogism. We all wanted to believe that we lived in a logical universe. But I suspected more and more strongly that it was not possible to get to the bottom of this case. To understand Berge. Sometimes the incomprehensible remains just as incomprehensible after all the explanations are finished. How many people can live with that?

In the evening I lay on my divan without listening to music. I wondered what Paal Berg would have done, how he would have approached this. For a few seconds I was tempted to ring Dobermann and have a chat. As far as I could see he was satisfied with me – although it's always difficult to know what a person like Dobermann actually thinks.

I dismissed the idea.

If the evidence was strong enough, Berge would be found guilty, even if his motives remained unclear.

The court had a day off, and I decided to approach the case from a different angle. After breakfast I strolled along to Universitetsplassen, but instead of going into the Law Library I went up the stairs to the second floor and knocked on the door on the left. I waited for only a moment before I was admitted. Not many people can do that, but I can. People know me. I was shown into one of the most prestigious rooms in the capital, or rather the whole colony: the History of Law Special Collection. A secret to practically everyone who hurries past outside the windows. For me – since I am not religious – this room is the closest I can get to a church.

It was too long since I had visited the collection (the last time was when I was searching for an entry in *The Legal History of India*), but now I took refuge here – and refuge is the right word. It is one of the most stylish locations I know, and has a librarian of the old school in terms of knowledge and experience, a woman who has more in common with Sir Kenneth Clark than with Miss Huxley, if I may put it like that. I looked around, registering the dark panels and the shelves of books (many of them extremely old) which covered all the walls, together with the narrow staircase which led up to the gallery and even more books. There are few rooms which provide a better opportunity to immerse oneself, to concentrate fully on a text. I nodded to the librarian as if to a friend (I think she was pleased at my appearance) and sat down at the large table, in such a way that I had a view through the Persian blinds up towards the Foreign Office and King Haakon, standing on 7. Juni-plassen and surveying the harbour. My alibi was of course that I was searching for sources for my *magnum opus* on punishment and justice, on power and justice, but my real errand was quite different. I wanted to read a work of fiction, and I wanted to read it in precisely this special room rather than at home. I took out of my briefcase one of the two books I had purchased discreetly, and even though the librarian had gone into her office, I didn't want to awaken her suspicion if she put her head in, so I placed it inside *Law and Colonial Cultures* (which I took from one of the shelves), as if I were a teenager and wanted to hide what I was reading.

Since I found Berge so enigmatic, despite the seriousness of the accusations against him, I had decided to take a look at his two collections of short stories, *Incomprehensible Stories* and *Dangerous Tales*, which had actually been published by a respected publisher. Bearing in mind that in a court case you often have to weigh one story against another, it was not an unreasonable decision. Yet it was nevertheless with misgivings that I opened the first one, at the same time as I felt myself transported back to my student days, where I often studied literature rather than reading law.

I don't know whether I would say that my misgivings were justified, but even if I am not a literary expert, I understood at once that these short stories were of an unusual quality. (The debut anthology contained over thirty stories, all comparatively short.) Most of all I was confused. And I mean that in a positive sense. Because what is a good book? A book which confuses the reader. One of literature's tasks is to make the reader question basic assumptions which have previously been taken for granted; and I am not ashamed to say that it was a solemn moment, sitting there in the History of Law collection and feeling how those stories made my thoughts form associations and divert onto unknown tracks. From time to time I felt *shaken*. I positively had to hold on to the arm of the chair. When was I last shaken by a book?

I was going to read the second collection at home, but I had already concluded that the reviewers could not possibly have done these books justice – and I use that word advisedly. For me, Berge's stories conveyed more than anything else a *sense of life,* they showed me something of how you could see possibilities and associations which belonged to the future, but which were denied by most people. There was a *tone* in these stories which I found exceptionally intense; it sounded so different from – what shall I call it – accepted parlance. It was years since I had immersed myself in tales such as 'From the Outposts of Empire' or 'The Book from the El Harta Well in Sahara'. The story 'Ramanujan' (why was it called that?) which I read at a table in the History of Law collection, with *Law and Colonial Cultures* like a shield in front of it in case anyone should pop their head in, was about five mothers, each sitting with a child in five different places on the earth, at the same moment, and telling five stories which were all self-contained stories, but nevertheless were continuations of one another and together made up one larger story. I almost had to laugh at the perception, at the *joy* this aroused in me. As I understood it, Berge's tales were an invitation to readers to reach out for other ways of using their imagination. It may be that they were a little exclusive, since they demanded a special sort of creativity. Was this what gave offence? To me it seemed obvious that the tales were linked, and that they were linked in quite a different way than tales which advertised the fact by flagging up the links clearly; it seemed that many of the tales had hidden passages to one another, which made deeper, wordless connections open up. It amazed me that no-one had remarked on that. I sat by the window looking up at King Haakon as he stood there with his back majestically arched, and I believe, or rather I *know*, that I was smiling slightly. I was – I was impressed. Gripped. Some of the tales gave me such sensual pleasure that they made me think of my childhood's pop-up books, those stories in which three-dimensional images rise up from the pages.

And as I read, a question persisted in the back of my mind the whole time: was this Berge the killer?

The long trial continued and my spirits remained heavy. The town was once again perfect for taking walks, even if the gates to Dronningparken had not yet been opened. On the way home from the courthouse I often chose a diversion round by the harbour, and when I do that I prefer a route which takes me down Rosenkrantz' gate, rather than going via Studenterlunden and Fridtjof Nansens plass. I remembered that the Heritage Director Harry Fett and the architect Arnstein Arneberg had put forward a proposal early last century as to how to make a better connection between the town and the fjord. They wanted to make Rosenkrantz' gate into a broad avenue, or more precisely, the stretch from Karl Johans gate down to the harbour, so as to bring the scent of a sea breeze up into the town. From the corner of the Grand Hotel you would be able to see down to the water, and at the same time catch a glimpse of Akershus Fortress. And behind that again, Hovedøya with its monastery ruins. They also suggested placing the Academy of Fine Arts on a part of the green below the fortress. I always tried to visualise it, and to my mind it was a bold vision. Yet another plan which came to nothing. It was always like that. Most things, even brilliant ideas, come to nothing.

Sofie Nagel. Something splendid could have some of that, and it came to nothing. Or was I the one who had thrown away the chance?

On one of my walks I passed the journalist Ine Wang. It occurred to me that I had seen her on that Saturday evening when I heard the first news of the Blankvann incident, or rather had just registered it as the swish of a poisonous arrow past my ear. I hadn't seen any news stories from her in the paper or the magazine for a long time, actually not for over a year, and when I met her I understood why. She was pushing a pram. She looked well. I didn't get round to saying anything to her on that day either.

Finally one Friday evening I allowed myself a visit to Limelight; I was beginning not to care.

Actually it was Lev who had suggested a meeting. 'It's time to partake of an El Diablo again,' he said. At one time we had had a merry hour over this rather unusual drink, which – in Edgar's hands, at least – could have a fluorescent effect. I understood that he had something to report, but as we sat opposite each other on our Chesterfield chairs, Lev maintained a poker face for a long time, whilst he fished for something in one of the many pockets of his photo vest. Finally he found it, a Polynesian navigation tool – threads running up and down inside a small frame made of thin twigs. 'You need help,' he said. 'Here, take this, it's something I make at school with the kids when they're learning about the Pacific.' Then, after a short pause, he told me – without batting an eye – that he was bankrupt. Or broke. He had gambled it all away on the trotting track. It emerged that he owed a great deal of money to a person he simply called The Musk Ox (from what I understood, he was a guy who was definitely not to be trifled with). Of course I could lend Lev the money, or give it to him, but it irritated me that he could be so casual and thoughtless when it came to money.

When I told him off and asked how on earth anyone could gamble everything away like that – we had not yet got our drinks, and I don't think I would have spoken so sharply if the sparks from an El Diablo had been filling my throat – he looked at me with an amused glance: 'You make such determined efforts to create a safe existence, Peter, but answer me honestly: would you rather have a phenomenal, gigantic piece of luck just once in your life, or would you prefer to have an insignificant little bit of good fortune every now and then?'

Edgar arrived, apologising for the delay; he nodded at a couple of Japanese tourists sitting at the bar. Lev took a gulp of his El Diablo, a larger gulp than is advisable with a cocktail like that. I took just a sip of my drink, and registered how it sank tenderly into my chest, as if a woman – not a devil at all – was embracing me, if that doesn't sound too sentimental.

It transpired that Lev had lost his job as well (or rather, that he had never had a proper job at Tonsenhagen). He had smashed a couple of mobile phones. 'It is too much,' he said, 'when eleven-year-olds are sitting playing on their phones instead of listening to the teacher.'

It was the popcorn tubs all over again, I thought.

I don't think the thought would have occurred to me a year ago, but a great deal had happened in a year, so now I said: 'You can come and live with me.' I myself was surprised at the suggestion. But one of the rooms in my apartment was empty, or rather it was full of boxes, things I had packed up before I sold my parents' house at Kjelsås, including things from my room as a boy. Perhaps Lev could help me to unpack it, and find a Matchbox car to put in one of his pockets.

'You could be my – what's it called – personal assistant,' I laughed. I laughed because I found the idea amusing. And possible. 'You could be my sparring partner,' I said. 'Perhaps I'll finally get that damned book written. I'm sure I'll never get it done otherwise.' Yes, I liked the thought. We could create a kind of colony within the colony, a little bulwark against the threatening disintegration associated with the Blankvann incident. I was already looking forward to our conversations about the treason trials, and it occurred to me that I needed to get hold of another chair, perhaps even a Wegner wing chair, supplied with good cushions so that it was possible to sit in it. I imagined Lev and me sitting there, floating, as we listened to Beethoven's late piano pieces (the variations at the end of the final sonata!), listening to notes which seemed to be searching for something hidden, something vital, or watching Sir Kenneth Clark as he wandered around Europe and made us gasp at his insights. I was already looking forward to showing Lev the programme in which Sir Kenneth Clark is talking about Dürer's 'Melancholia I' in Nuremberg, and then reading the quotations written on the beams in Montaigne's tower, before he moves to England and listens to Hamlet's monologue by the graveside with Yorick's skull in his hand. Whilst we each sipped our Vodka Martini.

'What book?' said Lev. 'Perhaps I haven't told you about it,' I said, 'but don't worry. You'll get to hear plenty about it.' I smiled. I could imagine how, with Lev's help, it could turn into something completely different, *Lev and Peter's ABC* or something like that; perhaps it would become a distinguished textbook, with the Sætre tin lid as a cover picture.

'I've drunk up all my miniature bottles of whisky as well,' said Lev. 'There were a few evenings when I felt … pretty dark. But it's over now.' (A picture came into my head: Lev lying on the floor, surrounded by miniature bottles, like a dead drunk Gulliver in Lilliput.) Lev signalled to Edgar, who took out two new tall drinking glasses from the fridge and began to juggle with tequila, crème de cassis, lime and ginger beer. 'Thanks,' said Lev, leaning forward and placing a hand on mine, 'that's a generous offer.'

I didn't know whether he was saying yes or no.

During those weeks it was as if everything got twisted round; I don't know how else to explain it. I don't know when it happened either, but one day I noticed that the courtroom had an aura of fiction. Presumably because it was going on for so long and was followed with Argus eyes by so many, people started – or rather the media did – to create stories. The various principals were given characteristics, epithets, as if we were part of an epic, or the germ of something which would grow into a myth, if I can put it like that. The press was particularly preoccupied with the female prosecutor; she had already been featured in several newspapers, and could boast of adjectives like 'heroic' and 'merciless'. In addition the reports were accompanied by pictures where she appeared to particular advantage. The mild-mannered counsel for the defence, who in the public's eyes had an impossible task (he must have been tired of being called 'devil's advocate') had also been accorded many column yards of description. (It would not surprise me if this tragic affair – with all the prestige it brought with it – became a springboard for the careers of both.)

I had no reason to be dissatisfied with the depictions of myself. As it said in one paper: 'Behind the judges' table sits the quietly-spoken but authoritative judge – by colleagues simply called Lord Malm – like an Olympian god, presiding over all.'

I wondered whether Dobermann had read that. Whether he liked it or not.

As a judge, I have often been astonished at how subjective memory is. Like now. In the case against Berge witnesses had taken the stand and related incidents from their childhood and youth in which the accused was involved, and we had heard several of the stories in completely different versions, without anyone reacting to the contradictions. Someone from his class at sixth-form college explained that when they had discussed their forthcoming military service, Berge had said that he would prefer to join the Foreign Legion; it wasn't only the gruelling training programme which appealed to him, it was also the perfect place for a lone wolf like him. Someone else from the same class claimed that Berge had considered being a conscientious objector, and undertaking civilian service instead. I had the continual feeling that the witnesses were making things up – that even the expert witnesses were making things up. The police as well, and the researchers.

I sat there behind my judges' table with my fingers making their usual tent shape, and thought about the facts, the incontrovertible facts from the scene of the crime: how many stories could be fashioned out of those? Even a story about alien invaders would not seem improbable.

But it did not look good for Berge. It really did not look good.

It tormented me.

Why would he not speak?

On one of those mornings when I was sitting thinking at the breakfast table – I wasn't even leafing through the paper or listening to the BBC World Service – my toaster played up. Something went wrong. My toast was completely burnt. I sat there for a long time, staring at the shiny masterpiece and the two slices which had not popped up cheerfully, as they normally did.

I had to open the windows. I began to be worried about myself, about my own powers of judgement.

I should haved liked to hear him speak. I had become convinced that simply hearing his voice would have made many things clear.

We were getting to the end of the trial, and my doubts grew. From time to time I covertly examined my two fellow judges sitting there straight-backed beside me. It was as if I hoped to discover what they were really thinking. What they were thinking but not saying in the breaks.

At the same time it irritated me that the defence could not manage to be more ... I'm not sure what the word is. Inventive? Creative? It was as if the defence counsel drew attention only to those matters which according to instructions he ought to draw attention to. I would have liked a more energetic attempt to leave no stone unturned, to find unexpected angles which might undermine the arguments for the prosecution.

When did I seriously begin to have doubts? It might have been even before the start of the trial, when I secretly studied Berge's blog. The last entry, written just before his arrest, took as its starting point some statements which 'a well-known Labour politician' had made in a wide-ranging interview from the beginning of June 2008. In answer to a question about the prospects for the world economy, the interviewee had reeled off something bombastic about there not being any underwater reefs as far as the eye could see ('and I am speaking here as the grandson of a pilot'); the economy would just grow and grow – not least in Norway. The latter fact was due to the Labour Party having created such good conditions for a healthy economic policy ('in the same way as experienced fishermen know how to find their bearings when they're setting out nets'). Berge showed in his blog entry, which was written a few months later, how wrong this Labour politician had been. He pointed out that the stock market – including the heavyweight Norwegian firms – was in freefall because of what looked like an international financial crisis. Berge believed that the politician's stupid statement mirrored the dilettante understanding many party members shared of the world economy, something which was again based on a lack of understanding of the more far-reaching consequences of globalisation, circumstances which made Norwegian politicians powerless – and which basically made us all into slaves of the market.

It was not difficult to deduce that Berge was writing here about Arve Storefjeld, and in the commentary field, which showed responses from before his arrest, people wrote that Berge was attacking, indeed dishonouring, the name of a dead person (there was no-one who addressed his arguments). From the angry comments I got the impression that it was taboo to say anything critical about the Labour Party in the difficult time after the Blankvann incident. The Labour Party was a sacred cow.

I sat in front of the screen, troubled; was it really possible that Berge had written that *after* having murdered Arve Storefjeld?

As the court case entered its final phase, my thoughts returned constantly to his two books. I remembered the last short story I had read in the History of Law reading room. It was a kind of monologue, or a ramble, and I gradually realised that the words were placed in the mouth of a man who must be in a dungeon, or some place where he was guarded, and by reading more and recalling fragments which were hidden away in my memory, I worked out that the man talking must be a Dalai Lama, perhaps one between the sixth and the seventh; we were given the story of how he had been discovered, at the age of two, as a reincarnation of the previous Dalai Lama. It was a strange and detailed history of how and why he had been plucked from all the millions of possible candidates, something about how, as a little child, he had recognised things they placed in front of him; but then something went wrong, or rather, they went wrong when as a teenager in the relatively new Potala Palace he revealed immoral tendencies, and showed himself in fact to be a wicked person. In order to conceal their mistake the priests had to imprison him and make sure that the story never came out, or was forgotten, at the same time as they found a new and better Dalai Lama.

I pondered this story for a long time, as I sat there surrounded by thousands of books which demonstrated how the law was conditioned by geography and history. What was it about? The possibility of something good being perverted into something evil, or at least something disappointing? Without my being able to see any direct connection, a thought emerged from my subconscious: Berge's secret, which prevented me from getting a grip on his nature, was that he was a man out of time.

That made me jump, because at the same moment I thought that, it occurred to me that I could have said the same thing about myself.

The proceedings were now in their last phase. The forensic psychiatrists had finished their performance. For the press at least it was a performance. For my part, their declaration had not been of the slightest help, despite their impressive terminology and exhaustive analyses, and I must admit that several times I sat there clicking my Ballograf pen, almost in protest. What eventually emerged from their report was that they found Berge fit to plead; he was not suffering from any serious personality disorder. (But outside the courthouse the debate raged; many thought he *was* sick, that he *had to* be sick, no sane person would slit the throat of a child.)

The declaration from the two psychiatrists was quoted far and wide. Around the country, and I believe also around the dinner tables of ordinary families, people discussed Berge's possible defects. It was as if the whole nation had gone back to school to study modern psychology (suddenly every Tom, Dick and Harry could explain the details of American diagnostic manuals); I almost expected to see the two psychiatrists as guests on Fredrik Skavlan's talk show, being greeted by laughter as they reeled off the symptoms of Asperger's syndrome. In my eyes the conclusion of their report was the result of blinkered vision. (This was of course something which I took care not to say out loud.) Berge could not be categorised as fit to plead or unfit to plead. The more I studied him, heard about him, read about him, the more convinced I was that he exploded all categories. The man in the anachronistic suit, the man I saw sitting there day after day with an introverted expression beside his defence counsel, defeated all analytical models. He was a person words could not reach. (But perhaps that was true of *all* people?)

You think automatically that either the prosecution or the defence must be right. But what if neither of them is right? Can that be the case?

It was good that it would soon be over, because the case repelled me more and more. At times I felt positively ill. It was no comfort that my shares had long ago doubled in value – or rather, they had trebled in value (the bank ones). I had an increasingly strong feeling that I was a Pontius Pilate. In my opinion it had not been shown beyond reasonable doubt that Berge was guilty. It may be that Berge had been in Nordmarka on the day the killings occurred, but the prosecution had not been able to prove that he had been at the scene of the crime. Nevertheless: could I be sure of his innocence? There was a lot of testimony against him, and a long trail of circumstantial evidence. All the self-appointed experts – and there were more and more of them – said and wrote that Berge would be found guilty. 'The weight of evidence' and so on. I understood that this was what 'the people' wanted. Should I be such a coward? I thought about my childhood Kjelsås, I thought about Herr Haug. Once more I was confronted by what I hated most in the world: the masses. I wished to write a wise judgement, a just judgement, but my hands were tied. Oh Lord. Oh Lord. What was I to do? Would it be possible to administer justice in this affair?

You must intervene! I heard the same inexplicable call that I had heard when I saw a man being beaten up near the Storting. At the same time I thought about the hue and cry, the uncertainty and unrest, which would be unleashed if Berge were found innocent. (And if that happened, where was the criminal? The criminals? Was it terrorists after all, a group of killers who were so professional that they had left no trace? Why did no-one mention that man with a black beard any longer – 'the jihadi', who had been seen by a hiker? It was supposed to be a man who looked fit and well-trained. One newspaper had given him the nickname The Vanished Man. I thought again about the expression 'ritual killing', about the article which suggested that an unknown religious sect might be behind the crime. What if there was something in that?)

I couldn't contemplate it.

If I had been a king in ancient times, I could have pardoned him. Shown mercy. With no discussion. But I was only a miserable judge, and I had to conduct myself according to the evidence and the law; I had to write a judgement, I had to furnish the people with a catharsis.

I could imagine the nightmare: 'Norwegian court scandal. Judge severely criticised.'

My kingdom for a compass.

To crown it all, Dobermann had begun to exhibit a friendlier side. He spoke to me with a new respect. He seemed satisfied, and I mean genuinely satisfied. One day he suggested that we should go out for a meal when it was all over; he wanted to talk to me about a couple of novels he had read recently. 'This is going really well, Peter,' he said. 'The rest is plain sailing.'

I didn't understand what he meant. But there it was. Had I been wrong about him all along?

Several times recently I had sought out the welcoming atmosphere of Limelight in the evenings, and I didn't even try to do it surreptitiously. After all, no-one would react if I drank a glass of beer. So who would hold it against me if I drank a well-mixed cocktail, one of the foremost indications of a highly developed civilisation? Despite that, however, I couldn't really get in the right mood. It was on one of those evenings that it hit me, as I was sitting waiting for a Vodka Martini, that this classic bar could disappear one day, that that was actually a possibility in a country which was so sadly lacking in appreciation of sites of significant historical interest. What would happen to the city, my colonial capital, without a bar like Limelight?

Edgar arrived with my drink. I felt like confiding in him, asking for this decent man's opinion about the trial, but I managed to restrain myself. I leaned back in my chair with the cold glass in my hand. I had begun to doubt that Berge was guilty. I sipped my drink, but it didn't taste right, and when a Vodka Martini doesn't taste right, something is seriously wrong.

We were about to begin the summing-up, and even before the prosecutor started on her speech – and she would no doubt produce a convincing and seamless account – I felt sure that she would only strengthen my doubt. Because if there was one thing I was sure of, it was that life did not operate according to such simple logic and such traditional chains of cause and effect as many stories do. Nevertheless the prosecutor in a murder case often thinks in the same way as an author of crime fiction; they are tempted to project events backwards in order that the fragments of the story might add up to the conclusion, the resolution, provided by the end of the story.

Nicolai Berge with a knife, slitting the throats of five sleeping people.

From early that morning I felt that this day would be special, and when I entered the courtroom I could almost feel the heavy responsibility weighing on my shoulders; it was as if the eyes of the whole world were directed at me. I was an administrator in this small country, and it was my task to make sure that this case reached an end, a verdict, so that the eyes of the world could be directed at something else. So that everyone could forget. It was time the population had something else to think about, it was time they understood that this was an exceptional case (five killings carried out in cold blood by one and the same person), and that something so extreme would probably not happen again in their lifetimes; in short, it was time to return to the uneventful daily routine and the comfort of living in a protected colony, enjoying the good things which were supplied to us via the invisible empire's extremely favourable distribution of global wealth.

Despite that, I chose this day to do something un-usual, something which no doubt would be perceived as controversial: before the prosecution's summing-up, I turned to Berge as he sat there in his three-piece suit, staring out of the window, and reminded him that he was allowed to speak right at the end, after the two counsels. Not only that, I appealed to him once more. I could see that the prosecutor was startled. I was known as a judge who rarely raised my voice or showed any emotion. Even though I used neutral words, what I did was in my eyes as good as pleading with Berge to say something, to explain himself. 'This is an extremely serious matter,' I said, trying to catch his eye. 'I would most earnestly advise you to think again!' I don't know why I should care about Berge, but I did. Where did this sudden sensitivity come from? Why so conscientious? I only knew that it would pain me to have to pass judgement without hearing what he had to say.

It was not possible to see whether Berge took my exhortation *ad notam*. He turned his head and met my eyes, but his expressionless face revealed nothing. I gave the floor to the prosecutor for the summing-up.

I needed a story to put on the other side of the scales. But it was Berge who would have to tell it.

NICOLAI BERGE

I

If I were to choose *one* memory? I close my eyes and see in my mind's eye Gry pirouetting before she stabs the spikes on one skate down into the black surface so that the ice spurts up, and then stands still, meeting my gaze. I am laughing, my breath emerging in a frosty cloud. It is night, cold as Siberia, a full moon. We are on Blankvann in Nordmarka, it's just before Christmas and the snow has not yet come. The ice is thick and glistening, a wide, inviting ice rink in the middle of the forest. We're staying at a cabin, Valen, just nearby. We are alone. It is dark in the windows at Blankvann farmstead. Even though there is a full moon, the sky is so full of stars that the whole universe seems closer. Yes, that is the memory. Everything brought together in a few long minutes. Gry and I holding each other's hands and moving backwards, me in the battered hockey boots I found in the cabin, Gry in her old figure-skating boots; we even manage a backwards turn, a little feat in itself. But mainly we run after each other, whooping and laughing, skating over as much of the lake as we can, as if we want to conquer the whole expanse, marvelling at the tracks we're making, drawings on the ice, writing something no-one but we can understand, our whole bodies exulting in the speed we achieve, in the fine hissing under the blades and how the ice core every now and then seems to sing. Later I'm standing some way off, watching Gry skating in a circle in the middle of the lake, before she makes a large figure-of-eight, gliding round it several times; that's how she kisses too, I think, with the tip of her tongue circling around my tongue, around my balls; nothing can separate us now, I think, we're together for all eternity, Gry & Nicolai, I look up into the starry sky, and I look around, at the bare spruce trees in a ring around the pool, silent trolls admiring the girl in the middle of the lake. The steel blades flash dully, two knives carving into the ice. She attempts a trick she has forgotten, a little jump, but falls over. Lies on her back, laughing.

Have I ever been happier?

The next day she took a photo of us sitting outside the front of the cabin. Dry frost and warm bodies. She used the self-timer on the camera, and nearly fell over as she ran back and threw herself down beside me; that's why she looks so gleeful. That's the picture of the two of us I like best. She told me later that she had stuck a copy of it in the visitors' book.

I never went there again. It was as if it was the Storefjeld clan's secret place. That was where her father took his cronies to discuss party politics and – like a male Lady Macbeth – to inflame even honourable people to instigate contemptible smear campaigns against their rivals.

And now Gry was dead. For several years we had made love so that the windows misted over. Now she was ashes, earth.

How could it happen? And how have I finished up here, in this ... mess, in what only eighteen months ago I would have thought of as a completely ... improbable situation? Is this my ... Karakoram? Why am I sitting here in this barren chamber in front of a judge who examines me day after day with an expressionless face? Or rather, I'm not just before a judge and his fellow judges ... For several weeks I have been exhibit number one when it comes to entertaining the Norwegian people, I have the eyes of a whole nation focused on me. *Idea: one day a judge arrives at Oslo Courthouse. Everything looks normal until he enters the courtroom and discovers that the interior is changed, the room is suddenly made of stone and there are hieroglyphs carved on the walls. His fellow judge, a man with a jackal's head, introduces himself as Anubis and explains the new situation. The judge's task is now to weigh souls.*

At times I feel that it's the fault of the party, that I should ... that I never should have joined it, have got involved with this mastodon.

Sometimes I *hate* the party.

I remember worryingly little. I must have been in shock, something must have wiped out parts of my memory. Now and then distorted scenes and pictures – they look almost cubist – float up in my memory, but I can't piece it together. I have chosen to say nothing. If I spoke, it would just be nonsense.

From before and after this ... these ... this incomprehensible ... I can remember more. Some things I can remember precisely. But I have only a vague notion of the days that followed after it became known that Gry was ... that Gry and four others had been ... had lost their lives.

One week passed. Perhaps two. Or three. I don't remember. A journalist rang. I knew who she was, occasionally I used to read what she wrote in the paper and the magazine. Something about her byline picture had always piqued my curiosity. She wanted to do an interview, or to be precise, she wanted to write a feature about me. She spoke quietly, respectfully. She could understand if I thought it would be difficult, she said. Even though she dressed it up, I knew what she was after. The portrait of me would be a portrait of Gry at the same time. There was no doubt a lot which had not been said about her, said Ine Wang carefully. That's for sure, I thought. Not to mention all the devilry which had not come out about her father, Arve Storefjeld.

Don't do it, screamed a voice inside me.

I asked for time to think, as if I were taking part in a quiz show. Something inside me told me not to play about with this. But the thought was tempting. I had read the obituaries with increasing incredulity. I don't know when I read them, but at some point I must have done. Much of it was simply untrue. Not least what they wrote about Storefjeld. Forgotten were all the Machiavellian plots. For someone who had heard

Storen slandering the party chairman when he was drunk, calling him an arse-licker and even worse, these solemn tributes tipped over into unbearable hypocrisy. And those writers who sang the praises of his daughter had never seen her peel off her clothes on a rock by the sea and dive into the water naked in front of a flock of bashful Young Labour lads, just to show how bloody liberated she was; she made it even clearer by floating on her back with her demonstratively unshaved pubic hair like a wet tangle of seaweed between her legs. (Even back at Nissen school I had heard the coarse talk among the lads, the joke that she could screw a light bulb, the business end, into her vagina, and make it light up.)

Or do I remember it wrongly ... was I perhaps still too groggy to register the detail of the articles?

I know I had thought about going to the funerals, but I decided that it would probably be seen by some as a provocation, since they knew that Gry and I, not to mention Storen and I, were not on speaking terms, to put it politely. But from the many reports and TV clips I registered that there was a service and a lot of Christianity. Petter Dass's psalm about God being God even if all men were dead. Not bloody likely, Storen would have bellowed. Both he and Gry were outspoken atheists.

The first, what should I call it ... lost time after 23 August was succeeded by days characterised by a deep ... I found myself in a state I'm not able to define, a kind of ... it sounds offensive, but it resembled a rush of creativity. Almost against my will I followed the affair in the papers and on TV and the net. I saw how several previously anonymous people had been picked up by the media spotlight, and I ought to have realised – or perhaps I did – that someone would get in touch with me sooner or later. *'I woke up one morning and was famous.' The beginning of a story about a man whose wife has an affair with a popular and charismatic politician, a Kennedy type. No-one knows about the relationship. During one rendezvous, one night at a hotel, there is a fire and both are killed, choked by the smoke. With that the husband is suddenly in the media spotlight. He wakes up one morning and his house is besieged by the press. After having lived as a normal person all his life, he is now a celebrity. His status has been upgraded. (Not sure, but keep the first sentence.)*

The next day Ine Wang rang at exactly the same time.

I said yes.

Why did I give in? Was it the thought of being ... that it might be a final ... declaration of love? That I might pay tribute to Gry by saying something nice about her? Or – I could not avoid the thought – was I doing it so as not to arouse suspicion?

Of course I should have said no, and found a watertight alibi. But then there was my vanity. And the knowledge that many of her old suitors from Young Labour would choke with irritation. I can't deny that that last point carried a great deal of weight.

On the phone Ine Wang asked whether there was anything Gry and I used to do together when we were living in 'the fortress' in Westye Egebergs gate. Perhaps we could do the same thing now, use it as a frame? That would have been a fine thing indeed. I thought about that euphoric time. I could have told Ine Wang that Gry and I often went down to Café Blå and got drunk on beer and vodka, then staggered home, played the blues and screwed until one of us had to beg for mercy. I could, just to see how she reacted, have told her about that time Gry had woken me up in the middle of the night and dragged me over to Vår Frelsers cemetery, which was close by, because she desperately wanted to make love on the large, flat granite slab which marks Bjørnstjerne Bjørnson's grave. I never understood her reasons for that; perhaps it was a form of blasphemy. 'Yes, we're fucking,' she whispered in my ear as we lay there, in parody of Bjørnson's words from the national anthem.

I rejected Ine Wang's suggestion, and could hear that my voice was more aggressive than I had intended. She apologised, and said we could meet anywhere. On the spur of the moment I suggested a little restaurant on Olaf Ryes plass; I had just walked past the place and remembered the name.

On the agreed day I took the metro down from Nordberg, thinking that there was a lot, a great deal, which I could never reveal to Ine Wang. Or ought I actually to try to adjust the impression people had of Gry? I had still not decided which ... strategy (which version? which filter?) to choose as I hurried up after the long-drawn-out photo session down by Akerselva to meet Ine Wang, who was waiting in the restaurant in Grünerløkka. I liked her at once. I think it was her black eye make-up. It was too much, and she knew it was too much. She must be quite a bit older than me, but for some reason I took her for someone my age; she seemed alert, eager, curious. A recent convert, I thought, without knowing exactly why I thought that. The introductory small talk flowed easily; I don't remember the whole thing, but I believe I talked about the music I was listening to, Shostakovich, and the first questions were less intrusive than I had expected. I struggled to find the right words, but answered as well ... as conscientiously as I could; I took out my fountain pen as if it was a stick, something I could lean on, and after a while – or was it quite soon, I don't remember – she managed to turn the conversation to the relationship between Gry and me. She asked how it was we had got together, and I could see that Ine Wang was not comfortable with the situation either; perhaps she was still unsure as to whether the feature would work out or not. Or whether she would find the 'missing link' she was searching for, whatever that might be. *A small girl is searching for shells on the beach when she finds a heavy, oval metal object, the size of her palm. It turns out to be a link which must have come from a thick chain. When the girl polishes it at home, she sees that the surface is covered with tiny characters in a language she doesn't understand. The following day an unknown person contacts her. (Which language? Dead? Alien?)*

I answered, and I believe I gave a long answer to Ine Wang's question, as if I wanted to make a good impression. I must have talked about Nissen, about the theatre, about

Gry's interest in Coleridge – yes, I'm fairly certain I said something about that – I drank from my beer glass and talked about us, Gry and me, I told her that we could lie on the floor over the map of Australia and find places we wanted to travel to, Wagga Wagga, Oodnadatta, Woolloomooloo; I had a suspicion about the kind of stories Ine Wang was digging for, and most of what I told her was half-truths. Even though I didn't want to disappoint her, I didn't want to tell her everything either; at the same time I kept cursing my own cowardice.

The truth was that Gry Storefjeld had made me light up. I don't know whether she had got wind of that vulgar joke from the group of boys at Nissen, but it happened regularly that she rolled me over onto my back and said, 'Lie still, I'll make you light up.'

From where I'm sitting in Room 227, the largest courtroom in Oslo Courthouse, I have no other decoration to rest my eyes on than a lion with an axe. It's strange to think of. For a large part of Norway's population I am the personification of evil. A gigantic ... threat.

I know that I ought to be paying full attention to every word that is said, but my thoughts are wandering in all directions, mostly of course to Gry and her ... to the relationship (the word is too weak) which is the reason that I am sitting here in a situation which is so serious that a whole battalion is writing long reports in the papers after each new day in court. Strangely enough I am not thinking so much about the verdict I'll receive. I have already condemned myself: I am an idiot. I have been blind. I spend most of the hours of the day on self-criticism. For the whole of my adult life I have had one great idea, and that is to do with the importance of foresight – which also involves being prepared for the improbable, the ... *unforeseen*. I would even maintain that this is humanity's noblest feature: our ability to ... see into the future ... to imagine what might happen. I based the whole of my political career on this idea – in fact my short stories too are based on our unique capacity to think beyond the here and now.

And yet here I sit. I never saw this coming. Not even if I had stretched my imagination to breaking point would I have foreseen that I would end up here, in Room 227, accused of ... murder. And that Gry Storefjeld would be among my victims.

Truth to tell, I had been entranced by Gry Storefjeld ever since I started in the first class at Nissen secondary school and saw her parading through the playground with her hips swinging gently and her hair – what I called in my thoughts Black Panther hair, without really understanding why; perhaps it was something to do with it being thick and black, so that it could make me think of a picture I had seen (in one of my father's books?) of Angela Davis, the rebellious civil rights activist, or that it gave me a feeling of being in the presence of something dangerous (a black leopard). Whatever it was, it was the first thing you noticed about her, hair that was always wildly disordered, or loosely put up, so that it encircled her head in a way which attracted everyone's attention. Gry Storefjeld seemed otherwise so scarily self-assured, and at the same time so slyly unpredictable, that I immediately gave her the nickname The Untouchable. Stay away, I said to myself. That was unnecessary. My crippling shyness would have prevented me talking to her in any case. Despite that, I was tormented by Gry's disturbing power of attraction when I saw her during breaks. The Untouchable – perhaps my great idea was launched, practically without my realising it, way back then. I couldn't help stealing glances at her, and I could see she was stealing glances at me. The Untouchable – and at the same time a challenge. She knew who I was, that I was Olaf Berge's son, and I knew that she was the daughter of none other than Storen. We came from different wings of a party in which arguments could lead to something resembling enmity. What I mean is, I believe Father and Storen regarded each other with mutual respect, but the kind of respect which maybe deep down was founded on mutual aversion. With the general public's fondness for simplification, Father was seen as the aristocrat in the Labour Party, whilst Storen was the proletarian. I don't know how far that was correct, but in a confidential moment, as we sat by an open fire, Father once said to me that democracy had to accept the idea of an informed elite if it was not to become redundant. I know that Father was disillusioned by seeing democracy sliding into populism, into something resembling what de Tocqueville called the tyranny of the majority; but I also know that he would never think of saying so in public. Nevertheless the two of them were poles apart, Storen's bluster compared to Father's courteous demeanour. *Chivalrous* was a word I often heard women use about Father. Storen's dream was to build as many roads, tunnels and bridges in Norway as possible, whilst Father's secret dream was to be Foreign Minister, to get to grips with global perspectives; he always read a lot about international politics. Father wanted to make Norway into a 'moral superpower', into the world's conscience. 'Why not?' I heard him say to a sceptical party colleague at a dinner party at home. 'Why should we be ashamed of such a label? We must never be afraid of criticising a regime which represses or prevents freedom of expression, even if it damages our exports.' I think that many in the party distrusted Father's eloquence. In their eyes, eloquence made voters suspicious. His opponents in the party never missed an opportunity to make snide remarks about his wealth, and about his home, the whole of the top floor of a villa on Bygdøy allé, an unusually light apartment with high ceilings, filled with Scandinavian designer furniture (most of it Grandfather's) – including a bar which was a miniature hall of mirrors. As a joke – but also, I think, to provoke people – Father called the luxurious apartment Camelot; he often gathered like-minded people for a conference around a huge oak table (which, however, was not round).

It was not until the last spring, while we were celebrating passing our final school exams, that I defied both my shyness and my resolution to stay away from Gry. She was standing on her own in the playground, looking through a newspaper. She looked ravaged, and her wild hair was even messier than usual; perhaps she had been carousing all night. Of all things, I thought about the rumour which was going round about her. That she had been to bed with Liam Gallagher himself, from the rock group Oasis. At the Roskilde festival. I refused to believe it. I didn't even believe she had been there, and I had never heard her talk about music. There were a lot of nice things you could say about Gry Storefjeld, but musical she was not. Once she sang in a play her class had produced. It did not sound good; it sounded just as bad as when her father sang 'My Way' – I had heard him in a clip on TV.

Despite that, her voice when she spoke was spellbinding. One of those slightly hoarse, throaty, morning-after voices; and when I heard her arguing with other pupils at break time, I could often hear a dangerous undertone, like a Hardanger fiddle tuned by a troll. And her gaze was in the same category – as she lifted it from the newspaper and fixed me with it when I was finally, after three years, standing in front of her – it was a kind of split-level gaze, full at the same time of scorn and curiosity.

We stood there, close to each other, for several seconds. I tried to hold her gaze, but in the end I had to lower my eyes, overwhelmed by her Black Panther hair, by her very presence. She waited. I searched for the words I had forgotten. Then she couldn't be bothered to wait any longer and went.

'Are you going to the Labour Youth meeting at St. Hanshaugen tomorrow?' I called after her back when I had finally recovered the power of speech. I knew she was a member of that group.

It was doubtless not by chance that the first thing I said to her was something about Young Labour, which was to be so fateful for me.

She swung round. 'If you join Young Labour, I'll leave,' she said.

At the same time there was something in her eyes which made me believe that she didn't mean it.

The next year I spent on National Service, but from the autumn when I began to study the history of religion, I made determined efforts to get to know her. She was at Blindern as well, studying English, studying literature, and we were both in St. Hanshaugen Young Labour; she had not left, and that spring we began to talk to each other, and not just that; on evenings which grew steadily lighter we wandered along the avenues in the area around Blindern, in the stupefying scent of hedges and then later lilacs, mostly talking about politics, but that then led to her telling me about Coleridge and me telling her about religion, about my interest in transcendence, about humanity's longing to penetrate beyond reality, to get *behind*, step through to the other side. 'Like cutting through a veil with a knife,' I said as I saw that she didn't understand what I was talking about. Or did I say that? I think I said that. Just then I was studying a topic for my BA, struggling with Hinduism; I wanted to write about *dharma*, about the conversation between Krishna and Arjuna before the great battle in *Mahabharata*, and I told her that I wanted to dig deeper into all this when I took my MA, perhaps even study a little Sanskrit. She just laughed at all that, and nothing came of it anyway; I got involved in something else instead, a dissertation I never finished. *Idea: give well-known battles a mysterious twist. Story from Tahiti in the Pacific, end of the 1950s. A seventy-year-old European, who has lived on the island for fifteen years, makes a living by painting colourful landscapes and writing science fiction. A mixture of Paul Gauguin and Robert Louis Stevenson. The natives explain that he is probably a Jew. His books are extremely popular. The man, who is bald and without a moustache, turns out to be Adolf Hitler, who writes under the pseudonym of Hieronymus Adolphe, and the stories, which take place in different galaxies, are modelled on the most important battles of the Second World War. (Too difficult? Needs a lot of research.)*

In the summer of 2000, that year of mythical portent, we were both going to the Young Labour camp on Utøya in Tyrifjorden, and I was looking forward to that camp with an anticipation which is difficult to describe. I had conceived a plan, and I got the idea on one bewitching summer evening in Eventyrveien, when Gry had explained her enthusiasm for Coleridge's poem 'What if you slept'; a poem about someone dreaming of a rose, and when the poem's 'I' wakes up, the rose is there in a vase by the bed.

I can hardly remember going on board the little ferry, 'Thorbjørn', or arriving on Utøya; everything was a chaos of practical activity that first day, but I saw where Gry put up her tent on the campsite, and that was important because I had smuggled a rose in with me, and I was so tense that I had difficulty putting up my own tunnel tent, christened The Tunnel of Love. In addition I was struggling with a problem; I was afraid I would have to use a knife to cut through her tent canvas that first night, but fortunately I got help from the friend she was sharing the tent with. After Gry had gone to sleep the friend placed the rose in a bottle and put it beside her sleeping bag.

The next morning Gry came over to me. With her hair fastened up in a deliberately careless way. It had rained a little during the night, and she was wearing shorts and rubber boots. Stood before me looking into my eyes with that split-level but nevertheless warm gaze, before she leaned forward and kissed me lightly on the mouth. It was as if something I had dreamt was becoming reality.

I had a two-person tent with me, and the next night I woke up to hear someone opening the zip. I shall never forget that sound. It was like an omen of ... light ... or a revelation. It was Gry who crept in to me, crept into the tunnel. We tried to be quiet, which just increased the thrill. I could hardly believe it, that I was lying there being embraced by a girl I had fantasised about for four years and who was desired not only by me, but by many others, not least a crowd of Young Labour lads. She chose my tent. And perhaps because I was so tense, so ... *ready*, it was so ... different from what I had imagined. I had been together with a couple of girls before, very short affairs, almost a kind of substitute, and that's why I was taken by surprise when the ecstasy which I had previously experienced for only a few seconds at the end of intercourse, if that, now started the instant she lay down beside me, the instant I touched her body, and I shall never forget the moment when she climaxed and whispered 'Oh God, oh God, oh God'; and the fact that it was she, The Untouchable, who was whispering that, gave me a feeling of possessing a power which had hitherto been concealed from me, and even though I knew on later reflection that it was an illusion, the feeling stayed with me.

It was the camp to end all camps. I can just about remember that I listened to lectures, took part in discussions and debates, joined a seminar in the School Room, grilled in Bolsjevika, played football, sang Nordahl Grieg's 'To the Young' – it was Gry, Gry, Gry, everywhere, all the time.

I had actually been sceptical about Young Labour from the very first time I showed my face at a meeting. Some of the members seemed so certain and insistent that you might think they were Jehovah's Witnesses. But now I couldn't care less about all that. I can't remember, but I believe I lost in all the debates, without being bothered about it, because I was a conqueror regardless, I had won Gry; I remember that I was proud, and that Gry's eyes shone with encouragement when I made a long and muddled intervention from the famous speaker's podium on the small covered stage, an entire little lecture to all the youngsters who were sitting or half-lying up on the slope in front of me. I gave my view, or tried to give my view, about what was the original cause of the insoluble conflicts in the Middle East; and the root of the whole calamity, I said, even though I knew deep down that it was an embarrassingly simple explanation of a convoluted problem, was the Sykes-Picot agreement from 1916, Great Britain and France's arbitrary division of the territory, and I can't deny that in my excitement I might have added something heated about the Balfour declaration; as far as I can remember there was applause, at least scattered applause, and whilst I was talking it seemed to me that I was talking only to Gry.

Presumably there were several outstanding politicians *in spe* sitting on the grass in front of me listening; many political issues, including significant ones, had emerged for the first time as ideas at the summer camps. And now I was standing here, on what was regarded as one of Norway's most important platforms, elaborating on the greatest and most difficult of all foreign policy problems, something I had discussed with Father as well, and despite that it meant nothing that I was standing there, nor that I forgot several of my points, because the only thing that mattered was to be able to kiss Gry afterwards, and to carry on doing it during and between all the other activities. And later the newly-elected Prime Minister came to visit. We sat on the same slope with our arms around each other, and I heard only half of what he said from the podium, though that did not stop me – intoxicated as I was – from asking a question about how far we were willing to reduce welfare in order to save the welfare state in the long run. I believe the Prime Minister was confused by the question, but I'm not certain, and I wasn't really bothered either, not even about what the Prime Minister thought. It was politics which had brought us there, but it was Lover's Lane I remember from that week, my walks with Gry in the evenings, she and I with our arms around each other along the steep cliffs; all the fine words about global suffering and urgent causes went over my head. As far as I was concerned, immanence was irrelevant, I was concerned with transcendence, and I had stepped through, I had crossed the frontier, I had walked through the canvas and into the arms of Gry Storefjeld, a girl I had thought was unattainable for someone like me.

She had made me light up.

I thought: I've got something none of the others have. The power of imagination. That was what she had fallen for.

In between the meetings we swam in Tyrifjorden, and we went swimming in secret too, swimming to places where no others could see us. Once we found something which looked like a little grotto, and as our bodies were burning even when they were under water, I pressed her so hard against the cliff wall as we kissed that she scraped the skin off the nape of her neck. I was upset and concerned, and put a plaster on it when we got back to camp. That was when she showed me a special scar, shaped like a crescent moon, just beneath the hollow of her throat, from a bad fall from her bike. I was even more filled with tenderness, and said she had to be careful; it was after that summer that I gave Gry the necklace which had belonged to Mother and which I knew had meant a great deal to her. I put it around Gry's neck, so that the heart and the anchor lay over the scar beneath her throat, and I told her that it would always protect her; I said that she was safe now, that we were an invulnerable double phalanx. We had cut through a membrane, we were *behind* it, we were beyond all danger.

Every time since then that I have driven down from Sollihøgda, on the way to Hønefoss or Hallingdal, I have slowed down so that I can catch a glimpse of that island, lying there gleaming down in Tyrifjorden, peaceful and idyllic. For me it has always had an aura of something paradisiacal. A beating heart.

I can't remember whether I told Ine Wang any of this; it may be that I did so, because I do have a memory of her sitting there in the restaurant on Olaf Ryes plass with a crooked smile, listening, as she jotted a few things down now and then, and kept half an eye on her recorder to make sure it was working. I tried to see what was on her pad, but her handwriting was more like stenography, signs which only she could interpret. The food arrived, and it tasted surprisingly good; I believe as well that I was relieved that the conversation was going so well, or better than I had feared. I had been dreading it,

because I've never been good at explaining myself, orally at least.

However, I would never have been able to make Ine Wang understand how much ... in love I was during those years.

How Gry Storefjeld ... bewitched me. Yes, *bewitched* me, because it was like witchcraft. I can visualise how her pupils vanished in ecstasy, seeming to turn upwards 180 degrees – as if she were a shaman setting out on an inner journey – or how she would lie there on her back after making love, breathless and with glowing skin and her Black Panther hair spread out over the sheet like a fan, just to throw herself over me again the next moment, in order to carry me away, take me with her to the other side. During these years I was more often in Gry's flat than in my own. It was in one of the four functionalist blocks which form an octagonal square in Westye Egebergs gate, on the hill above Fredensborgsveien; it must be among the finest things built in Oslo, and Gry lived on the seventh floor – in seventh heaven – with a view of Sirius and the Cape of Good Hope. The furniture in the rooms was spartan, there were film posters on the walls and tealights in empty jam jars, chairs made out of crates with cushions on and books standing on the floor against the wall. In the bedroom there were just two mattresses side by side beneath a poster with the Declaration of the Rights of Man. We needed nothing. We had everything. It was Gry and Nicolai. It was Gry & Nicolai, we were linked together, nothing could separate us. *An atomic physicist loses his job at a respected institute when he proposes an idea about eroto-energy, based on the theory of nonlocality. As he sees it, the world is kept in motion by the sexual acts which are occurring everywhere on earth at all times. He ends up as a guru in the foothills of the Himalayas, and over the years people come to him – including heads of state and former colleagues from the institute – to ask for advice. (Too eccentric. File in the B-folder.)*

I couldn't tell Ine Wang about all that, about my titanic infatuation. Or that Gry slept in a T-shirt with a picture of Snoopy on the roof of his kennel. That she could get dressed in twenty seconds, even get ready for a party in twenty seconds. That she wrote messages and memos in capital letters, as if she'd just learnt to write. That she insisted on referring to the constellation Orion as The Hour Glass. That she could survive for a whole day on Toblerone, her favourite chocolate. That she always wanted to make love during a thunderstorm, and that she would then lie almost motionless, in a position she called 'Listening Lotus'. That she ... I discovered that she didn't just have a scar under the hollow of her throat – her whole body was full of lesser and greater scars, as if she had lived recklessly, cutting and scratching herself constantly, climbing, slipping, falling. I lay and stroked her skin as we talked. We didn't sleep, we talked and talked, we couldn't get enough of talking, telling each other things, and when we had no words left, she rolled over and made me light up.

Of course, being together with Gry gave my status in the Young Labour milieu an enormous hike. But it also resulted in a higher temperature in our discussions. Some of the lads especially attacked my opinions with a fervour which made me suspect that it was not just a matter of disagreement, but more to do with envy and jealousy.

One day in January of the second year we were together Gry and I threw a party for friends and acquaintances; or rather, it was Gry who was in charge of the invitations, and her network was wide-ranging. The party was held in Maridalsveien, in Storen's house – he was at Dovre that weekend – one of those old wooden houses which lie along the river Akerselva like pearls on a string, houses which have been refurbished and turned into attractive residences, with a price-tag which no 'workers' would be able to afford, not even those who work in Oslo Highway Department, or what was now called Oslo Road. So for that matter Arve Storefjeld was a good illustration of how large parts of the working class had long ago been transformed into a prosperous middle class – or if you saw it in a global context: a class that was rolling in money.

It was a brilliantly successful party, a party people talked about for a long time, and there were many celebrities there. Not long before midnight I went out into the little garden; I was hot and needed some air. When I turned round I could see the old house almost vibrating with festivity; how it was framed by the snow which was glittering and twinkling, and through the windows I could observe the lit-up rooms where people were dancing or talking together, drinking and eating canapés, delicate little titbits which Gry and I had spent the whole day preparing. And in one of the windows, the one nearest to me, I noticed Gry standing talking to a cultural bigwig; I could see that she was positively shining, and I saw her abundant hair, her eager gestures, the black silk dress which was *floating* around her. I could hardly grasp that we were together, but we were, and I could not get it into my head that this lively, noisy party was for us, in our honour, as it were to celebrate our relationship, but it was; and I was standing there in the garden outside the house of Storen himself, with Myren industrial area on the other side of Akerselva, looking at the crowded rooms and the warm light streaming from the windows and down onto the snow. I was in a kind of existential Mecca. I was the centre. Gry and I, Gry & I and our love were the centre of this teeming, festive occasion; all these bright people, including the cultural bigwigs, were gathered here because of us, were standing there talking, eating, arguing, laughing, dancing because of us. But for all that there was nothing which counted more than Gry's face, which shone radiantly at me, really radiant, radiant with something I took for happiness, as she caught sight of me in the garden and blew me a kiss, as if she was touched, moved by the fact that I was out there watching it all from outside, that I, for all I know, was standing there in the snow radiant with happiness, or perhaps even more: with gratitude. And although it was so marvellous – like living in the royal palace with the fairy princess – I never thought that it would stop there, I took it for granted that we would carry on, that everything was on the way up, I didn't understand that this was the high point of my life. Seen from a distance it seems incomprehensible that only a couple of years later I would be sitting alone in a small flat, looking down on the town. That I would be exiled to a satellite in orbit around a marvellous world which I once owned, but had now lost.

When it came to it, my powers of imagination were not worth much.

I might have mentioned something of this to Ine Wang – not the party, but some of the rest – because she made more notes; this was clearly the kind of story she was hungry for, and it made me think of a ... psychoanalyst who suddenly hears a patient saying something she can follow up on later, and for that reason has to jot down some keywords. Or perhaps it was just a trick, I thought, because the sight of Ine Wang writing encouraged me to talk more; something harmless about films occurred to me, and I told her that Gry liked films, she was keen on Tarkovsky and Kieślowski and Sokurov. Ine Wang didn't know who the last one was. As I mentioned Gry's passion for films, I thought that it was a warning that she would one day fall for a filmmaker. It had irritated me as well that she liked Tarkovsky and Kieślowski, half the world shared her enthusiasm for those two, but I applauded the fact that she appreciated Alexander Sokurov, that was proof of independent thinking. *Moloch* about Hitler, *Taurus* about Lenin – disturbing and original films. And we saw *Russian Ark* together. The Winter Palace, three centuries, one unbroken take. Unforgettable. And that was why it was incomprehensible that she could fall for that charlatan Lefebvre, a filmmaker who with all the resources in the world would never have managed to make anything with an ounce of artistic value.

How could she give herself to him? It was a mystery. Unless it was a manifestation of her self-destructive tendencies.

I remember oddly little from that afternoon, that evening, in the restaurant on Olaf Ryes plass, but I have a vague notion that Ine Wang had a little smile around her mouth the whole time, as if the story of our love, Gry & Nicolai, was infectious, and made her think of something, perhaps from her own life. I followed the movements of her pencil as she filled the pages of her journalist's notepad with scrawls; I began to suspect that she was also writing something critical, perhaps a remark about my appearance or about my muddled and incoherent answers.

Then she changed the topic – it was as if she had pulled the points lever on a railway track – and asked where I had been that Saturday, that ... she had to stop as if to steel herself ... that Saturday when I heard the news about the killings at Blankvann.

I seem to remember that the question floored me for a moment. In my recollection I took out my fountain pen again, as if for help in balancing on a line over a bottomless abyss. 'I was in town,' I finally managed to say. I think she took my hesitation as a sign of emotion. 'I was in Oslo,' I said. In a way my answer was true. Over half of the Oslo area is forest.

Now, in the middle of the trial, I realise how absent I was at the start. The first days in Room 227 appear to me as a hallucination ... as fragments of a dream. I said nothing. I had had much more than a year to think, but the vital minutes, which were the whole reason I was sitting there, were still unclear to me. And everything got worse when I entered the courtroom. The whole thing was so unreal. The ... solemnity of it. The stiffness. I remember vaguely that I stood up, or was helped to stand up, for the questions about my identity, and that I nodded affirmatively instead of answering. The charges? I remember nothing of them. Not a word. Is that possible? It is possible. Did I answer yes or no as to whether I was pleading guilty? I – or rather my defence counsel – must have answered no.

I am aware of the fact that I ought to have listened with concentration to the prosecutor's introductory statement, but my thoughts were elsewhere. Or absent. The remarks of the defence counsel too made no impression. People talk about being momentarily deranged when committing a crime. I think about the future: is it possible to be momentarily deranged when hearing a verdict? *A man is sentenced to death and smiles with relief, as if he's been sentenced to pay a minimal fine. His defence counsel tries to get him to understand the seriousness of the situation. The man simply shakes his hand and says: 'Thank you, thank you. I owe you my life.'*

In any case, I did not make a, what's it called ... a deposition when the opportunity arose after the introductory statements, but I do remember the judge at that point fixing me with his eyes and saying ... *exhorting* me strongly to speak, to explain in my own words what had happened ... that morning in the forest. Yet his argument made no impression on me. I was more preoccupied with the way he spoke, his ... courtesy. The whole of his being exuded ... I don't want to say authority ... *impartiality*. Who was this man? I thought immediately that he must be a dry ... a boring character, one of those grey lawyers who spoke in an educated way but had never opened a work of literature. Hyper-traditional. It occurred to me that he would have looked good in a wig of the sort used by English judges. Nevertheless ... for some reason I felt that I was ... in good hands.

I sat up as the police witnesses took the stand one after the other, but I only became really curious – can I put it like that? – on the day when the other witnesses began to be called. It was as if that made me more attentive. No, attentive is not the word ... awake, perhaps. Nervous? And there was something about ... a kind of change of mood. Antipathy lay over the room like a mist. Even though I rarely met the eyes of the witnesses, I could feel how strongly they despised me, especially those who knew me from Young Labour.

'It was terrible,' said a girl I had been together with once at a political workshop on Utøya, 'it was a shock to discover that it was one of us.' Those last words became a chorus. I would bet that it's become a headline in the papers (I can't bear to read the papers whilst this is going on, even though I am allowed to do so).

Now and then I turn cautiously towards the public gallery, so that I don't attract too much attention. I would rather have been spared these ... voyeurs. These ... parasites. On the one occasion when I took part in a major public event as an author, I was supposed to talk about short-story writing with two other authors, both of them well-known names. It was a fiasco, I hardly got to say a word. The only consolation was that I could not see the audience because of the harsh spotlights directed at us.

But here I can see them clearly. Who are all these people who have come here to be present at my trial? I study their faces covertly. I can see disgust, I can see condemnation, I can see ... hatred, pure hatred. What are they doing here, why are they sitting here day in, day out, listening to these long-drawn-out testimonies? Why aren't they enjoying the fine spring days outside in ... I can hear how enticing the word sounds: freedom? Why wouldn't they rather be in the forest?

Of all things, I am longing for a track, a camp fire, a lake.

That was the worst thing about my time in custody. Otherwise there's not a great deal to say about life in prison. You get used to everything. And I did read a great deal as well, I wrote a great deal. I can't complain.

But I miss the forest.

Is it my love of forests which is the reason for my sitting here between a prosecutor who who is trying to have me locked up for life and a defence counsel who is doggedly ... who is doing his best to sow doubt about my guilt, or at least find mitigating circumstances?

On Friday 22 August – a few weeks before I met Ine Wang on Olaf Ryes plass – I made a trip into the forest. In retrospect I regard it as one of fate's many caprices; I had planned to travel to Copenhagen that weekend, as I wanted to see an exhibition at Louisiana Museum of Modern Art. But because of the weather I changed my mind and walked into Nordmarka instead. What would have happened if I had made the trip to Copenhagen?

On Friday afternoon I packed my rucksack; I packed almost impatiently, for I was in a good mood, without stopping to wonder about the reason for my good mood, and I was travelling light, though I had enough with me to camp out for a couple of nights. The weather, the excuse for my trip, was warm and settled; not even the overpaid and incompetent meteorologists could announce, or forecast, the weather wrong for the coming days, so I packed just a fleece and a thin shell jacket, and made do with a smaller rucksack than normal. I didn't even take my tarpaulin – the canvas square I normally rig up over where I'm sleeping – as I wanted to sleep under the stars, and my light 3-season sleeping bag would be more than adequate at this time of year. And then I have a pair of Gore-Tex boots that I can walk to the North Pole in without getting blisters. On an impulse I put a copy of Graham Greene's *The End of the Affair* in one of the side pockets; it was a book which had belonged to Mother.

I soon found myself in the area between Sognsvann and Svartkulp lakes, and shortly after that on the path which led onwards to Øvre Blanksjø. The plan was to walk via the Skjærsjø dam and up to Fagervann, the lake which is so finely placed between the hills of Stutehaugen and Lyberga. I stepped over roots, and balanced on a temporary log bridge over a swamp. I relished each step. Or rather my lungs, my whole body relished each step. The softness underfoot. The tiresome heat between the blocks in Nordberg was transformed into a comfortable warmth in the shade beneath the trees. *A woman looks back in the autumn of her life and realises that all her relationships have been with men whose surnames were the names of trees. Fredrik Spruce, Henning Birch, Steinar Elm, Thor Greenwood, Martin Hazel, and so on. She wonders why it turned out like that. I wonder whether I was a druid in a former life, she thinks. ('Druid' comes from an Indo-European word for oak – dru. In Celtic mythology the oak tree was regarded as the portal between the worlds. They also had the same word for oak as for wisdom.) Plot: she's never been with anyone called Oak or Oakley, and she decides that before she dies she will find someone with that surname. (Not sure. Could be too one-dimensional. File in the C-folder.)* After just a few minutes in the forest I felt an alertness I rarely feel in town. Or was it more that everything was put into perspective? During my studies I had read about Hindus who divided life into four stages, and I thought that I must already, as a young man, have reached the last, where you wander into the forest and live ascetically.

Where does this – I almost said fateful – love of the forest come from? It started when I lived in Romsås, when we messed around in the forest just as much as we visited one another's houses or played between the blocks. As children we knew every inch of the forest nearby, we knew which trees, rocks and hillocks were the best bases for our Star Wars figures. The whole of Røverkollen hill was transformed into the forest moon of Endor. During these years I was more in Lillomarka than I was down in Grorud or in town. When I was older I expanded my radius and hiked as far as Nordmarka itself, over Movatn and Tømte. I still have my well-used map from that time, full of small crosses and dotted lines marking out the routes, and notes in tiny handwriting (as if they were secret messages). In the same way as I could at one time lose myself in Tolkien's map in *The Lord of the Rings*, I can sit today over my map of Nordmarka, feeling the names like a caress; Norskeperskallen, Trehørningen, Mago – all evoke warm memories, small private stories. When I was older I appreciated particularly the way the forest let you get away from the endless noise, not just the traffic but the ceaseless background noise of the media, all the babble created by information, news, gossip, comment sections. The forest was a zone which set my thoughts free. I could feel it on that Friday as well, as I walked on a carpet of pine needles along Nedre Blanksjø – my thoughts were unfolding in a different way from normal, wandering along paths which had not been marked out by a thousand others. Rocky mounds, pine barrens, ravines covered in thick moss. Could there be anything more uplifting than coming upon a clearing; walking through thick forest, and then, unexpectedly, finding an opening, suddenly standing there bathed in sunlight? At such moments I could now and then have ideas which would never have occurred to me anywhere else – at least, that's what I imagined – or sudden insights, which I jotted down at once. Often they were never used, but it gave me pleasure to be standing there with the stump of a pencil and a tattered notebook in my fingers, writing, whilst I absorbed the smell of heather and undergrowth and watched the fine beams of light falling diagonally down through the fir trees.

On the eastern side of Øvre Blanksjø I sat down on my regular rock. I always sit here. Sometimes I get out my notebook and leaf through it to see whether there is any difference between the ideas I had in town and those which come to me in the forest. *A woman. Perhaps a doctor. A person who does not speculate as to what will happen to her after she is dead, but rather what happened to her before she was born – prompted by dark visions and dreams.*

It was the sight and sound of a jay which had made me scribble down those sentences.

As I sat there on the rock, my glance rested on the barren tree which had been hanging over the surface of the water for many years, creating a special atmosphere by the pool. Hardly anyone ever came here. Even on Sundays I could sit here alone, although it was not far to Sognsvann. On the way up I had picked blueberries, and filled a small bag. I rummaged in my backpack. If I was going to be out for several nights I would pack light food, like crispbread, rolled oats, a freeze-dried ready meal; but this time, for a shorter trip, I had allowed myself something extra: a pint of milk in a flask. I filled a plastic bowl with blueberries and poured the milk over them. Sugar from two of those paper tubes that you get in cafés. Heavenly. Also because it took me back to my childhood, my youth, that unproblematic existence in Romsås.

The time before Gry Storefjeld.

Eating blueberries was part of a game we played in my family; we were working out how best to survive in an emergency. In our fantasy we imagined how we might be surprised in the depths of the thick forest by hurricanes and earthquakes, or in the winter by a heavy snowfall which prevented us getting back to town. So we made lists of everything nature could offer by way of food, from fish and insects to edible plants and roots, but we also invented survival packs, things we should always carry in our backpacks. An anorak, a folding spade, a box of raisins, that kind of thing. Early on Father gave me something he himself had used in his youth, a small cooking pot with a lid that was tightly secured by three steel clips. Inside were unlined wind mittens, nylon rope, thin wire, a box of matches, a whistle, a wound dressing, stock cubes, three large safety pins, a penknife, a tiny pair of pincers, plus several other things I've forgotten; and everything had to be in the right place in order to fasten the lid on again. As time went on, and even up to today, I have been aware of this constant challenge: what is the optimal survival kit, packed into the smallest possible box? I have sketched out many suggestions, some of them quite fun – with and without condoms (for collecting water). I think to myself: if I have this in my pack, and a catastrophe occurs, then I can as it were start civilisation all over again. I have to have room for everything in something which is no bigger than a small sandwich box. I often take it with me on walks, as if to test the equipment. In the evenings, over my campfire, I can get it out and examine the objects, think about possible improvements. Was there anything I could get rid of? How much do you need in order to save your life?

Towards the end of the interview, as I was looking through the window towards the parking place on Olaf Ryes plass, towards the fountain which lies where the paths meet in the middle, Ine Wang asked me what she called a difficult question. At least, I'm not sure whether that was how she put it, and I'm not sure either whether it was at the end of the interview; I have a vague feeling that Ine Wang had not finished her omelette – although I don't believe that she ate more than half of it anyway. Were there perhaps less positive sides to

Gry? she asked. Something along those lines. Or did she put it even more pointedly, did she say 'unpleasant'? (Did she use the word 'nasty'?)

What I do remember is that I was on the point of blurting out several little anecdotes which would have shown Gry in an ... unflattering light. I almost told her about that time when Gry was a drama student at Nissen and appeared on Karl Johan as a mimic; she was made up in whiteface and copied the movements of passers-by. I witnessed this performance by chance, and I remember that it seemed to me to be a little unkind, that she was inadvertently revealing something of her character. In my eyes it was too cheap, attracting attention by making fools of other people. I felt sorry for the passers-by who first of all laughed as she imitated their way of walking, and then became upset and embarrassed and tried to get away as quickly as possible, all of which which Gry of course also mimicked, to general applause. She was making money (or was it perhaps in aid of International Youth Day?) by making people look like idiots, and that disappointed me, at the same time as I had to admit that she was a fantastically good mimic.

I was also tempted to talk about her devil-may-care attitude. Her insouciance. She didn't bother about contraception. 'Don't worry about it,' she whispered in the tent on Utøya. 'It's the safe time of the month.' The following week we got undressed by the mattress in her flat. I assumed that the risk would be greater now, and got out a condom. It was a carefully chosen condom, I had bought the pack before the camp on Utøya with Gry in mind, even though I didn't dare to believe there was a chance; I kept one in my little wallet as if it was a banknote of unusual value, something which could be exchanged for services which were out of this world. When she saw it, she grabbed the condom from me and stretched it out like a rubber band, aiming it at the wall so that it smacked against a picture – or rather a front page which her father had torn out of *Verdens Gang* and had framed, and which he later solemnly presented to his daughter. It was the front page which announced that Einar Gerhardsen was dead; the whole page was given over to a photo of the old statesman's hands resting on his stick, and Gry called it her altarpiece. I thought that was sacrilege, a condom pinging against the picture of the father of the nation; it must be about as bad as if a Muslim were to draw a picture of Mohammed. She laughed and sat astride me, abandoning herself to a ride which soon sucked every millimetre of sperms I owned up into her. It was as if she wanted everything to be hazard, everything to be fate.

Should I have said that to Ine Wang? Just to see her face?

Of course I kept my mouth shut. Instead I recounted a harmless anecdote about playing chess. I think it must have been then that I asked for another glass of beer. It began to dawn on me that I should never have said yes to this interview, and the realisation grew stronger when she asked me just after that whether I could say anything about why Gry and I broke up.

No, a voice inside me screamed. I can say nothing at all about that.

Because she was a cunt. The words almost came out of my mouth. I was on the verge of suffering from Tourette's. I wondered whether I should just get up and leave, without any explanation.

Instead, I mentioned something – I think I said it half-jokingly – about Gry's 'quarter-life-crisis', about Gry actually saying that 'our relationship was not sustainable'. I've forgotten how Ine Wang reacted. I seem to remember that she laughed, and it wasn't just on account of the wine; in fact I felt much more like sitting there looking at Ine Wang's rather over-made-up face than talking about Gry and me.

As if I had a bad conscience about that somewhat flippant answer, I tried to explain our break-up in a different way. I had to start again several times, but eventually I managed to say that it was more that politics had come between us. Different views of what was important. I reckoned the Labour Party was facing a crisis. She pointed out that they had good prospects. They had just been in government, even though only briefly, and could easily do so again in 2005. The red-and-greens. How could I call that a crisis? I believed that the crisis was so fundamental that it was not yet fully apparent, but that was why it was so much more important to start the debate now, to put our heads together to plot a better direction, informed by a completely new vision.

I managed to explain this last point quite well, and Ine Wang took it up eagerly. She wanted to know more about the clashes around the leadership contest in Oslo Young Labour. Her gaze challenged me to answer honestly. She had clearly done her research. All of this both flattered and irritated me. I hesitated ... I thought I might dismiss the whole affair as a bagatelle, but then, I don't remember why, I changed my mind and gave Ine Wang my version of that idiotic power struggle between myself and a self-assured girl from the upper-class area of town, a sworn adherent of mild indoctrination when it came to upholding party discipline. It surprised me that Gry supported the other girl, even if she was a friend, and it surprised me even more that when it came to smear campaigns, this election in no way fell short of the older members' strategy of 'crushing you like a louse'. Basically our little battle was just mirroring the incredibly ugly power struggle in the wider party at this time, a poisonous fight for the leadership which led to splits, secret meetings, negative briefing and bitter personal enmities.

Did I eat all of my burger or was half of it left? I don't remember. But I do remember that I squirmed as I recounted the episode about the election, and that I could read a certain surprise in Ine Wang's eyes. It seems to me as well that in an attack of honesty I repeated their accusations that I lacked the common touch, and no doubt that was true – in that way I resembled my father, the Aristocrat. They said I gave the impression of being arrogant, but that was because they misinterpreted my shyness. However, I did admit to Ine Wang that I had problems with certain things, amongst other things anything which smacked of rituals, anything which smacked of mass mobilisation and the shouting of slogans in unison, anything which made me think of those shoals of fish which make precisely the same turns at precisely the same time. Like the Mayday celebrations. Gry and her mates always began this day with a long and extravagant breakfast, lots of pickled herring, lots of schnapps. After that it was a group march to Youngstorget with its cliché-filled speeches and hearty applause. Then followed the procession in which those well-heeled youngsters behaved as if they were back in the hard 1930s, marching behind the proud, anachronistic banners and brass bands of the trades unions together with the small number of older men and women who had a reason to be there. 'Arise, ye wretched of the earth.' Never had a procession consisted of fewer wretches. I was also fed up with the endless whining from Storen and the others about trades unions, trades unions, trades unions. A stuck record. Not to mention the national conferences where solid middle-class people stood singing old workers' songs as if they were in a karaoke bar. Oh, what a masquerade! My project was to modernise the workers' movement. Fight for a new set of values. Re-invent democracy. Look ahead. Arm ourselves for the unexpected.

I said nothing about these last thoughts to Ine Wang. I don't think so anyway. Nor did I mention that I couldn't stomach electioneering, having to go round and spread the message. I felt like a second-hand car dealer when I knocked on people's doors or stood by the metro trying to convince people with Labour Party slogans, or handing out leaflets as if they were adverts for a new restaurant in the area. Gry had already learnt the trick of holding someone's upper arm at the same time as shaking their hand; it was as if it conferred a special intimacy on the contact and on the ensuing conversation, all with the aim of persuading – fooling, I thought – the other person into voting for the right party. Giving out roses seemed to me to be a cliché as well – like a pathetic attempt to pick someone up, or ask them out on a date. After all, the Centre Party didn't go round handing out four-leaved clovers.

Gry was otherwise good as a speaker, but I could soon hear that it was too simple; it was just excerpts from the party programme, the same set expressions, or a variant of her father's rhetorical phrases, which together with her burning conviction gave her opinions the illusion of being important, of being true. I thought we would become a team, that I would be able to give her *substance*. But she didn't want that, she wanted to be banal. 'Only banalities hit home,' she said. 'And you have to appeal to people's emotions. What you say goes over their heads,' she said. 'You underestimate people,' I said.

'Dessert?' asked Ine Wang. Or perhaps that was later, I don't remember, I just remember that I had disappeared worryingly deep into my own thoughts, because from the first moment there had been a large group within Young Labour which had regarded me with suspicion. They were the most single-minded ones, the ones with no sense of humour, with whom you could only talk politics, strategies, the next election, those who lost interest and glazed over if you started to talk about football or art or travel – or worse, they had parrotted a few phases, such as 'I like Lars Saabye Christensen', but you could see that they didn't mean it and had never opened a work of fiction. They always called me The Foggy Prince, and that annoyed me, because I could see clearly, and they were the ones who were wandering in a fog without a light. *A Chinese man returns home after a long journey to the West in the 8th century. He tells about a people who sail in long narrow ships and worship gods with one eye who make thunder by throwing a hammer as they ride across the sky. Their writing consists of straight lines which can easily be carved into wood or scratched on stone. The man is thrown into a dungeon because no-one believes him. Eastern version of Marco Polo. (Usable, needs developing further.)*

But I had prepared myself for that meeting about the leadership of Young Labour; I made a kind of campaign speech, and although it is possible that my delivery wasn't too good, my opinions should have been clear enough. I mentioned specific causes we ought to fight for, like improved public transport, more focus on the opportunities in Groruddalen – I had grown up in Romsås, after all – and not least, that we must oppose the proposed amalgamation of Oslo hospitals, which the Labour Party had supported – a catastrophic misjudgement in my opinion. But my main priority was to talk about basic principles, about our world view and our ideology. I asked the classic question about what needed to be done, and I said that we must reform root and branch, we had to rebuild the party in order to make it ready for twenty-first-century challenges, like competition from manufacturing in Asia, and migration, especially from Africa, where populations were growing fastest. Did I mention the danger of ecological catastrophe? I don't remember. But I did point out that we lacked the tools to deal with these matters, and I said that the work that awaited us could be called 'the labours of Hercules' – but I could see from the eyes in front of me that the labours of Hercules meant nothing to them, and that the general knowledge which you'd been able to take for granted was fast disappearing; and perhaps that was the reason, I thought, why neither these youngsters nor the party leaders took my appeal seriously. From as far back as 11 September 2001 I had argued that we needed a reorientation. We were *exposed* like never before, we were vulnerable in a whole new way. In an article in *Dagsavisen* I wrote that we were citizens of the world, and that thinking about national politics without an international perspective was impossible. But in the debate after my speech at this election meeting, everything degenerated into an internal power struggle. From the podium I was called a Judas, and worse, because I had written about internal party conflicts in the press, even though all I had done was to criticise 'vote-grabbing policies', and say that the Labour Party must not agree to a dumbing-down process, where we compromised our ideals because we were terrified of a drop in the opinion polls.

The Labour Party needed a survival pack as well.

I didn't say that. I ought to have said it.

There was something about that election meeting which made me think of the Labour Party – and no doubt other parties as well – as a religion. In the Young Labour battle I had a strong feeling of being 'sacrificed' on the altar of that famous solidarity. Many people thought I was the best candidate, but in order to keep the peace they chose the girl, Gry's friend, a person with no qualifications other than the gift of the gab, who no doubt – at some point in the future – might become a good Minister of Culture, that consolation prize among the ministerial posts.

Did I say anything about this to Ine Wang as we sat there on Olaf Ryes plass? Probably not. Presumably I made do with repeating that Gry and I had not always seen eye to eye when we came to a political crossroads. Or rather, I would not have used the word crossroads, it would have stuck in my throat, since it was one of Arve Storefjeld's favourite expressions.

Something was happening. I looked across at Ine Wang as she sat there opposite me with her black-lined eyes and a pencil with teethmarks on it in her hand. The whole situation was changing. What had been meant to be an interview was beginning to tip over into something else (like in one of my short stories, I thought). Especially towards the end of our conversation, even though I tried to resist, I was feeling a stronger and stronger attraction to Ine Wang; there was something about the gleam in her eyes ... it looked as if her whole body was filled by something or other ... a special ... spark. It may also have something to do with the fact that it was raining outside and the place seemed more and more welcoming – there was even a small open fire burning in the corner of the restaurant. At some point I must have had a coffee; I have a clear memory of drinking an espresso, and feeling revived. I remember too that Ine Wang started to ask about my writing, and that I answered as well as I could, in fact that I became eager, perhaps inspired by the sparks which, as it were, leapt from her, even though she had probably never read anything by me, but it was easier to talk about things like that than about Gry, and all that ... trauma. As far as I remember we even talked a bit about music, about David Bowie of all things; I could see that Ine Wang was an attractive woman, and I was surprised when I gathered she was single. The rain poured down outside, and appetising smells came from the kitchen; people were laughing at a nearby table, and I didn't want to go, as she asked me the routine questions which were covered in all the features, and I answered first of all flippantly, then properly, and found myself wishing that she would drop the article. That she might make a suggestion instead. Something exciting. Like asking me to go on somewhere. Inviting me for a drink in one of the many pulsating bars in the neighbourhood.

She paid, packed her things together and we left the restaurant. Out in the rain, surrounded by all the enticing lights reflected in the asphalt around Olaf Rye's plass, it seemed as if Ine Wang didn't want to go home either, but in the end she shook my hand politely and thanked me for the interview. She hurried towards the tram stop and just caught a tram which was arriving. I stood there for a few minutes, staring up into the air. The drops of rain looked shiny, like glass. I felt like listening to David Bowie, but I didn't have any Bowie on my iPod.

I've looked for Ine Wang in the courtroom. Searched for her, actually. I would have thought ... She hasn't been there at all, on any day. I thought perhaps she would be a witness. I hoped she would be a witness. Just so that I could see her. Hear what she had to say. Perhaps she would have explained what we actually said that evening in Grünerløkka. On the other hand they couldn't call everyone I had talked to as a witness. For all I know they might have investigated her, perhaps even interviewed her, and decided that she had nothing significant to contribute.

On recent days I have noticed that the judge, that inscrutable figure, has begun to throw ... what should I call it ... searching glances at me when witnesses say something, as if he wants to study my reactions, or provoke me to ... Now and then he takes out a biro and makes notes. I would like to see what he's writing. Was he already convinced of my guilt? *A judge is sitting with his fellow judges, discussing the case: 'We have the answers, but we will never find the questions.'*

What will be said in this room tomorrow? In a week's time? I try to imagine what might happen towards the end of the trial. I can't even manage to do that, even though I have so often got up on my high horse and pronounced that humanity's noblest feature is our ability to see into the future and imagine what might happen. How embarrassing. Is all ... Have I lost ... I notice how I'm trying the whole time, almost in a panic, to be receptive to the new ideas which occur to me, the harbingers of new stories. As if to convince myself that ... my powers of imagination are intact, or at least not dead. That in the end they can perhaps save me. Save us all.

II

As I was sitting there on that rock by Øvre Blanksjø, on Friday 22 August, on my way towards a place to camp out by Fagervann, I could feel something pulling at me, and it was pulling me from a different direction. Oh, these chance occurrences – although we are rarely aware of them, aware of how they direct us here and there. For why was I sitting here studying two dragonflies flying low over the water? Why was I not on my way to Copenhagen and an exhibition at Louisiana which could perhaps have given me much-needed inspiration? Was it because I suddenly felt the urge to sit in the lotus position and meditate next to the peaceful Øvre Blanksjø? As I looked at the dry tree leaning out over the water, I understood that there was something quite different pulling at me. Earlier that week I had bumped into one of Gry's friends – actually the one who had been sharing a tent with Gry on Utøya that first summer – and as if it was the most natural thing in the world she told me that Gry was going to Valen that weekend together with her father. I pretended I knew already, or I didn't react at all. Nodded cheerio and good-to-see-you.

Is it right to call them chance occurrences? Do we lack a word for those small events which can lead us to make the most fateful decisions?

Our meeting took place in Operapassasjen. Was it just by accident – again I wonder about that word – that we bumped into each other just there? Whatever it was, I was suddenly standing rooted to the spot in that passage between Storgata and Youngstorget, without a thought for the offices of the Norwegian Labour Party which were on the floors above me. In a few days Gry would be at Valen, sitting on the grass looking out over Blankvann. Impossible to dismiss the information, it hooked itself into my consciousness. *A couple in love are out strolling in modern Paris. They are in Rue Dalayrac, and on impulse they walk through Passage Choiseul. When they emerge at the other end they don't know where they are. People's clothes are strangely different, the cars have gone. They are suddenly in London in the year 1830. They wander around until they come to Piccadilly, where they soon discover Burlington Arcade. They walk into the passage in the hope that they will find their way back to Paris and their own time, but when they come out on the other side they are in Avenida de Mayo in Buenos Aires. The year is 1911. And so on. A tour of the world and of history via well-known passages. (NB: usable.)*

Gry Storefjeld. The knowledge that she was, or soon would be, at Valen, was a magnet to my thoughts. It was not because of the weather that I had dropped the trip to Copenhagen.

I tried to resist. When I sat down on that rock by Øvre Blanksjø, as I sat there enjoying my blueberries with milk and sugar whilst being entertained by two dragonflies, I had perhaps still believed that I would be unrolling my sleeping bag at Fagervann; but now I was overcome by an irresistible impulse, which of course was not an impulse, but a plan which had been fully formed for several days at a deeper level of consciousness. I was not heading northwards, over the Skjærsjø dam to Fagervann. It dawned on me that I was on my way in a circle, anti-clockwise; I wanted to turn back time, I was heading north-west, in the direction of the Kobberhaug hostel, towards Blankvann, I was on my way to Gry. In my subconscious I had been on the way there all the time. I had to make one last effort. I had been struggling with the thought of Gry for four years. Of course I ought to leave her to her own devices, but I would have no peace until I had confronted her one final time. I didn't believe in her relationship with this Frenchman, it was just a game for her. In many ways I saw my hike through the forest as a rescue

292

mission. *Operation Gry*. One last attempt, and if it failed I would let her go. Cross my heart and hope to die. Was that really what I thought? Yes, the expression 'Cross my heart and hope to die' passed through my thoughts, even though I had not used it since my boyhood in Romsås. There was something else as well, a detail, which justified my decision to make one last attempt: I saw a picture of her recently in the paper, taken at some political conference or other. Around her neck she was still wearing the necklace I gave her. A heart and an anchor. Mother's necklace. The fact that Gry was still wearing that necklace must mean something. Was it perhaps a secret signal? I remembered what I had said when I placed the charms just below the scar at the base of her throat: 'The anchor is there so that love will hold fast'.

I had stared at the picture of Gry in the paper, almost hypnotised by the necklace around her neck. It may be that it didn't say anything certain about love, but it did say something about hope. And hope was the greatest of all. I had thought the same thing when I was studying different religions: at bottom they were all an expression of hope. That there was something more. That there was a meaning behind the meaninglessness. Just as there was behind meaningless break-ups.

It was hope which made me change direction, rinse out my bowl and pack my backpack, before I set out on the barely visible path up the steep grass slope, so that I met the track which led down to Store Åklungen lake. Possibly there was an irrational element to my actions as well: I believe that Blankvann exerted such an attraction because it was a forbidden area. Gry had said that we should not meet any more. The place was taboo. In other words an irresistible temptation.

Yes, that's how it was. Of course. I could see that now. This was not a normal camping trip into the forest, it was a romantic quest, and like all such quests it was not without its dangers. Storen would be in that cabin as well, and I could not be sure that I wouldn't be met by a furious greeting:

'Come one step closer and I'll break your neck, you milksop!' For all I knew he might have a shotgun there, perhaps even a rifle. It wasn't the hunting season yet, but God knows what he might be capable of. 'It was an unfortunate accident, I thought it was a badger, they've been pests round here for a long time.'

I crossed the forest road at the southern end of Store Åklungen and followed the path which took me over the marsh, past Lynhytta and along the western side of the lake. I had changed direction, I was on my way north-west. Autumn was already approaching, the undergrowth looked drier and the colours were fading – quite different from in May, when you were walking through fifty shades of green. There were also fewer flowers, and fewer butterflies fluttering over the ground. I stopped in a couple of places to pull off some birch bark which was peeling off the trunks, and put it in my pack.

Instead of going into Ullevålseter café I circled round it to the north, it just happened like that, it was as if I didn't want to meet anyone, or was half embarrassed about my change of direction; but up there on the hill I suddenly registered that something was different. I stopped. Listened. I looked around cautiously, and not far away I discovered an elk; it looked almost camouflaged, a huge male with impressive antlers, standing in the shade browsing on some young leafy branches. To start with I felt the situation was dangerous and became afraid. Some instinct or other. My thoughts went to the combat knife I had in a side pocket, a Cold Steel knife with a sharp blade. Then I relaxed, and almost pulled a face at myself. It was a long time since I had seen an elk, even though I regularly came across elk droppings, those little balls we got up to such pranks with as kids. I was close enough to be able to see how the animal was gnawing with its large upper lip. The long thin legs always made me think that the elk was standing on stilts. I carefully pulled out my mobile phone and took a picture. The elk disappeared northwards at the same time as I sent the picture to Ask Diesen.

Ask was a friend, or an acquaintance, from student days. Three or four years ago I had taken him to camp out just near Fagervann. Ask had been fascinated by elks ever since he read Mikkjel Fønhus's novel *The Troll Elk* as a boy; in one of his dissertations in religious history he had written about deer, from the four stags at Yggdrasil to the figure with antlers on its head in Sami mythology. He was so desperate to see an elk that I took him on a safari. I knew of several elk tracks in Nordmarka and I promised him that we would see elks; but we saw none, and he teased me mercilessly about that. But now I had actually seen an elk, the first one for a long time, and that was why I got excited and sent him the picture. 'Finally found The King, just by Ullevålseter,' I wrote triumphantly. I laughed at myself, at my excitement, as I trudged onwards. I took the sight of that splendid animal as a good omen.

Straight after I heard a ping and up popped a smiley; a colon and bracket, from Ask Diesen. Strange. You don't see someone for many years, and then suddenly you get a smiley. Another good sign.

I turned my mobile off completely and put it in my pack. I walked across and down the steep overgrown slope south of the Aurtjern lakes. Sometimes I have what you might call a transcendent experience in the forest. At certain points, perhaps as I am walking between two trees, I can have a feeling that I'm walking *through* something, that I've reached a kind of secret area. That I so to speak *vanish* from the world. Disappear. Perhaps it was not so strange that the thought occurred to me as I worked my way down this slope, because once, in one of the darkest parts of the wood, I had come across a 'secret shelter' just here. I doubted that I would be able to find it again. Strange. There were a number of illegal shelters like that in inaccessible places. Most of them were just for holiday use, but you could also find huts where people lived, where they survived. Could I have done that myself, left everything behind, taken refuge in a primitive hut somewhere in Nordmarka? I believe I could have. Sometimes the thought was enticing. Rousseau, Thoreau. Burn all my bridges, live from hand to mouth, be a hunter-gatherer. Perhaps that would inspire my writing, give me a new perspective. *A shipowner lives like a hermit. Has never been with a woman. In his seventies he suddenly discovers the need to pass on his genes. He puts an advert in the paper, and in the course of the next ten years he has twenty maids in the house, one after the other, each girl employed for about six months. He makes them all pregnant. Each of them gets a small fortune and gives birth to the child.*

However, the improvised retreat I found last year was of a different kind. I had stumbled on it as I navigated at random down the steep hillside. Not many people can have known about that hut, as there were no paths in this rugged landscape.

Outside the shelter sat the figure of a man with a ravaged face. To begin with he behaved threateningly, growling and rocking his massive body to and fro. Then, after appraising me with a vigilant glance, he relaxed, as if he recognised me. We got talking. The man had long hair and a thick black beard, and his clothes were hanging off him in rags. Several minutes passed before I realised who he was. He was Panther Hansen. I had known him on National Service. I remembered that I had seen a missing persons notice several years ago; he had been living in Nittedal, or I think it was Nittedal, and had been admitted to a mental hospital. Perhaps it was the hospital which had issued the notice. Every year there were many people who disappeared without trace.

Well, I thought as I stood there on that steep slope, here was one of them. The thought occurred to me: Christ, here sits The Vanished Man.

Enok, he was called. Enok Hansen must have seen what I was thinking. 'No-one in my family is alive any longer,' he said. 'So hold your peace. I'm doing fine.'

I felt curious and wanted to ask how he managed, but I kept quiet. From what I could see he had no problems surviving here. I thought that he perhaps broke into other cabins, or into houses in Maridalen or Vettakollen.

On the hut wall hung some elk antlers. A hunting trophy? All around there were small white skulls like ornaments in different sizes, they could be deer, fox, hare, squirrel, I'm not sure. Several adder skins hung down from a stick fixed horizontally over the entrance. It was so peculiar that it looked almost sinister. In an alcove inside I could see a ham and parts of animal carcasses strung up on ropes from the roof. In another 'room' I could glimpse shelves full of tins. In the middle of the hut stood a small stove of the type we used in twelve-man tents in the army, with a pipe going up through the turf roof. And what was that? I'm sure I could just make out a little collection of toys, a clockwork figure, a matryoshka doll, a snow globe which you could shake to make snow whirl over the scene inside.

Was he mad? Impossible to know. He spoke in a calm voice. He looked like something between a madman and an Eastern sage.

Between the adder skins hung strings of dried fungi. It would not surprise me if they were magic mushrooms.

So it was in the army I had met Enok, a giant well over six foot tall. I didn't know him, and it was seldom we exchanged words, but we were in the same troop. I understood that he was more than normally preoccupied with something he called the tao of physics, with holism and loads of such mumbo jumbo, and also with Syd Barrett from Pink Floyd; he gave the impression of being a mystic, and kept himself very much to himself. He had seen the Star Wars films hundreds of times, and said that we ought to have laser swords in the army as well. Once in the canteen he held forth about Erich von Däniken and about how the earth, long ago, had been visited by intelligent aliens. They would soon return, he claimed, but evil beings from the planet Barsoom would try to prevent them. 'We'll be ready, Enok, you can rely on us,' we said, as we patted him on the back in a comradely way in order to hide our laughter. On exercises we discovered that he was an expert in stealth, so good and noiseless that we called him Panther Hansen. Altogether he was much more eager than the rest of us. I can remember that on the hand-to-hand fighting course he did all the exercises with a zeal which was almost frightening. Our instructor praised him as well: 'Watch Hansen, he's a natural.'

His eyes looked different now. They burned; it was the sort of gaze you saw in fanatical believers. There was an old, battered Bible by the entrance, the sort with thin paper and gold edges. Enok tore a page out to roll himself a cigarette. For a moment he sat there staring at the writing. 'The prophet Isaiah is better than Rizla,' he said appreciatively, and lit up. As I understand it, he came from a deeply religious home. In the army he had occasionally quoted from the Book of Ezekiel, that treasure chest for confused souls.

'Important to camouflage the camp,' he said, pointing. 'They can see it from the air when they arrive in their ships.' I could smell something other than tobacco from his smoke. 'Who?' I asked. 'The Barsoomians,' he said.

How unreal it felt, sitting outside that hidden hut in Nordmarka, on a steep hillside where hardly anyone ever set foot; it was like being in a kind of Middle Ages, cheek by jowl with the city. Here he lived like a hermit, and if you didn't know better you might regard him as a holy man. As if he had read my thoughts, he showed me a notebook with incomprehensible symbols in it; it looked like Mayan script or something like that, and he maintained it was a message he had received, after he had heard a voice in his heart. Did he know that I had studied the history of religion? 'We must conceal ourselves from the Barsoomians,' he said. 'And only iron can protect us. Only chains can set us free.' Enok, Panther Hansen, was playing with some lengths of chain – as if he wanted to chain himself fast, or give the impression of being a kind of Prometheus; that he wanted to perform a heroic deed, but was chained up by the gods. He must have filched the chains from cabins, where they hung down from the gutterings. 'We must follow the chain of reasoning,' he said, 'link by link.'

I understood little or nothing of what he was talking about. It was like having stumbled upon a Mr Kurtz, sitting muttering to himself in the heart of a dark forest. 'Everyone who has allied themselves with the Barsoomians...' Enok said then, 'there's only one way to finish them off.' He looked at me as if I knew the answer. 'While they're asleep,' he said. 'The only chance.' He ran his index finger across his throat, at the same time sending me a meaningful glance. 'But watch out for your hands,' he said, pointing at a pair of thin gloves lying on a tree stump near the entrance to the hut. 'Their skin is poisonous.'

He spoke slowly, normally, not like a madman, but he was mad, he was utterly and completely mad.

I glanced over at the elk antlers. Perhaps he sometimes fastened them to his head to perform a ritual dance?

I almost felt like laughing at him, but I stopped myself. I felt sorry for Enok Hansen. Or – I had to stop myself again – perhaps you shouldn't feel sorry for him. Perhaps Enok was fine. So long as the Barsoomians left him in peace.

Peculiar, I thought as I left his hut. Almost like a scene from a folk tale. Or a dream. I thought the same thing again now, as I crossed the slope. I peered in all directions, but I couldn't catch a glimpse of Panther Hansen or of the dwelling I had come upon the summer before. *You can't escape your fate, people say. The story of one person who did just that.*

Just before Vestre Aurtjern I came upon a logging track. I followed it for a short distance before I turned off through the trees, and again it was as if I stepped over something, a kind of threshold, and into a different reality; now I found myself in an ancient forest where I was wading through high bracken and clambering over dead trees which were lying rotting, then I made my way along the edge of a swamp before I reached higher ground and the pine barren on the east side of Magnusputten pool. It was getting towards evening, and I passed through zones with different temperatures, warm air which was suddenly replaced by cooler air; it was an experience which reminded me of my childhood in Romsås, when I came home from the football pitch with my shin guards in my hand and my socks turned down to my ankles, feeling warm and cold air alternately wafting against my legs. Now it made my thoughts zigzag between 'shall', 'shall not', 'shall', 'shall not'. I found my regular camping place on a point out by the water. I let my pack slide down into the heather between two small pines to which I used to fasten my tarpaulin in bad weather. The pool was quite still. On the surface there floated water-lily leaves. And two ducks. People never came here. Never. In winter a ski track cut a blue line across the ice. In summer you never saw a soul.

But in a cabin not far away sat Gry Storefjeld. Around her neck still hung the necklace I had given her.

One last attempt.

I'm not sitting in a courtroom, I'm sitting in my Karakoram, and I can't see the road which has brought me here … to the end of the world. I try to follow what's happening, but I can't; instead of listening to what the prosecutor and the defence counsel and the junior lawyers are asking the witnesses, my thoughts leave Oslo Courthouse and move to the square outside. I try to recall C.J. Hambros plass in my mind's eye, to visualise the four … no, five roads which meet here, to walk along them and conjure up building after building, with as many details as possible, to think of all the times I have eaten and been happy in places around here. Together with Gry as well. We went shopping here too, bought bed linen at Fru Lyng's and trainers at Løplabbet. We went to – what's that café called – Herr Nilsen, and we were more absorbed in each other than in listening to a second-rate jazz trio. And now I was sitting here listening, or trying not to listen, to witnesses explaining how much I hated her.

With all my problems remembering things, I am impressed at the memory these people have. It seems they remember everything I have done and said. When the break-up occurred, I am supposed to have said to Gry: 'You'll soon meet your Nemesis!' It was a friend of Gry's who stated that on the witness stand, and in her view I was planning my revenge already back then.

I have no memory of that, and I was glad when the judge asked the witness if she had been present when I said it. It turned out that the friend had only heard about it at second-hand. From Gry.

It's as if the judge ... I wish he had asked the witness whether she knew anything about Nemesis and Greek mythology.

There is a chasm between ... I must let that thought go.

Again that acknowledgement ... or that fear: my powers of imagination are weakened. They aren't adequate any longer.

'An incomprehensible act,' said one witness. I registered that precise sentence. The word 'incomprehensible' has been used by many. No doubt by commentators as well. I agree. All this is incomprehensible. Words are inadequate. Words for this ... that ... don't exist.

As the days pass, it strikes me how self-satisfied all the participants seem. Or proud. They think they're involved in conducting an exemplary trial. Presumably the newspapers are writing a lot about that as well. All of them ought to be more ... humble. It's as if, by using so many resources and so many column inches on this case, they are lulling themselves into a belief that events like this (I'm deliberately choosing such a neutral word) will never happen again. But it will happen again. No-one can protect themselves from terrible events. The unthinkable. We think we are prepared, but we are taken by surprise every time. Whatever we do – we will never be prepared.

Self-deception. Endless self-deception.

Ought I to stand up and say that? I sit still. I can feel the judge looking at me. As if he ... it's almost as if ...

For all I know he's just looking forward to getting home to his wife. Eating dinner. Doing the crossword. Having a glass of liqueur. Watching a rubbish soap on TV.

Ine Wang got in touch again. I had half expected it – though no, that's not true, it was a surprise. She rang. She would like to talk to me again, she said cautiously ... *considerately* is perhaps the right word. I don't remember exactly what she said. Something about needing a couple of extra pieces of information for the portrait to be as good as she wanted it to be. Did she add 'for Gry's sake'? I don't remember.

Once more the thought 'just say no' hit me. A new chance to ward off this defamatory project, this ... desecration. It was certain to inspire general condemnation.

I said yes. We made an arrangement. 'I can provide a late lunch,' I said.

I baked. Why did I do that? Did I want to impress her?

Before she arrived I was sitting in my study writing my blog, Pens. My logo is a set of train points which I remember from the old Märklin train set Father had kept from when he was a child. A left-handed switch. I've always liked that idea, of being able to switch something onto a new track. A Y, a fork in the road. To my mind it was also a little related to Grandfather's inventions – hinges, mounts, handles, things which could open windows and doors in a better way. It was two years since I had started the blog. I regarded it as time off when I was writing those posts, and I tried to compose a new one every week or every fortnight.

While I was waiting for Ine Wang I worked on the draft of a typical Pens post. About Norway and oil. About the fact that it would not last. About the refusal to face up to reality. About the necessity of revising your operations when circumstances changed, circumstances which lay outside your control. I found an example, perhaps not the best one, but I wanted to use it anyway; it was only a blog, and not many people would read it. Suddenly there will be no demand for oil, I wrote, and Norway will become a backwater. Like certain ports in South America, just think of Valparaíso in Chile, I wrote. Valparaíso had based its prosperity on ships seeking harbour there on the voyage around Cape Horn, but lost all its traffic when the Panama Canal was built.

It was too far-fetched, I deleted it. I was beginning to be less sharp.

I was nervous. Why was I nervous?

Then she was there, a ring at the door and a voice over the intercom. I remembered that I had just seen her on TV. It was several weeks since I had been able to bear watching TV, but the night before I had switched on just in time to catch the end of a programme where Ine Wang was talking about Arve Storefjeld. It struck me that she looked good on TV; her heavy make-up looked almost natural. I stood there for a long time admiring her before I became aware that she was praising Storen's 'ambitious transport policies'. It upset me so much that I switched off.

But now I opened the door to Ine Wang, and soon after she was standing in my study looking inquisitively at my three screens, as if she believed that I was a stockbroker, at the same time as she was admiring the view. She was also fascinated by my desk, where large pieces of tracing paper were sellotaped to the surface. One glance was enough to make me explain: 'For me a new book is a *terra incognita*, and I am slowly exploring it, filling it with names, words, sentences, lines, links, networks.' She laughed. I could hear that it sounded pretentious and exaggerated. I carried on regardless: 'When it gets full I stick a new piece over the top, start over as it were, although now I can make out words and sentences and lines underneath, in a way I can write and think and sketch on top of it, use it as a ramp.' She lifted up the top piece of paper as if to examine the effect. 'So you write on the cloth as well?' She still had a smile around her mouth. 'Is that what's called a palimpsest?' she said. 'Yes, perhaps you can see it like that.' I liked the fact that she knew the word palimpsest. It was a long time since I had talked to anyone who knew the word palimpsest. *'The Splinter.' After Shostakovich. (Keywords on the corner of a paper cloth.) As the result of an accident a man gets a crystal chip in his eye, and after that he is able to assist the security services. Thanks to this man, several terrorist actions are averted. When faced with the sea of seemingly irrelevant information from investigations, he is one of the few who can filter out the vital pieces of knowledge and then put them together. The man with a splinter in his eye has a unique ability to see how facts which seem to have nothing to do with one another can in fact be connected.*

She moved around slowly, leaving a faint trace of almost undetectable perfume. A scent of something ... complex. She wore less make-up than last time. She had hung up a leather jacket in the hall and was wearing a classic white blouse and black jeans. Tight-fitting. She looked good in tight-fitting jeans.

She said something about how it must be fine to live here, that you could walk straight into Nordmarka. And on the way into the living room – at least I think that's when it was – she asked whether Gry and I were active outdoor people.

'We rarely went walking in the forest,' I said.

'Do you go walking now?'

'Sometimes,' I said, or I think I said. 'It's been a while since,' I added.

By Magnusputten I cut some spruce branches and laid them on the heather so that the curved side was on top – that was something we learnt watching black grouse lekking when we were boys, how to make a sort of springy mattress which smelt of resin and pine needles. I found some wood, took the birch bark out of my pack and lit a fire down by the water's edge. It wasn't allowed at this time of year, but I had made a secure firepit here many years ago, with slabs of rock as a base and stones in a circle around it. I wanted the smell of it, that's what I like most about fires, more than the flames, even though I can sometimes see dream-like pictures in the fire (in my student days I read with interest about Zoroastrianism). Everyone has a theory about how to build a fire, about the shape it should have – it's a small step from fire-building to architecture – and I had my preferences too, though I wouldn't want to impose them on anyone else.

I looked for the two ducks which had been floating on the pool, but I couldn't see them. It was a male and a female. A pair. A good omen, I thought.

After a while I got out my fire kettle and frying pan, the only things I had left from the aluminium cooking kit Father had given me one Christmas in Romsås, and which had been in constant use in Nordmarka throughout my youth, for everything from porridge to most of Toro's packet soups and casseroles. I remember what a pleasure it was to unpack it and see how perfectly all the parts fitted together – it became an inspiration for the survival packs I played around with later.

I had with me a small cool bag, just large enough for two eggs and some thick slices of bacon. I fastened the handle to the frying pan and placed it on the stones where the heat was greatest. The bacon began to sizzle as soon as I laid it in the pan. I turned the slices a couple of times before I cracked the eggs into it. I was hungry. Or I *became* hungry at the sight and the smell. I habitually made this simple meal in the forest in the evenings; I had done so for many years, ever since I read the Hemingway short story 'The Battler', in which Nick Adams, who has been thrown off the train one evening, sits by a fire together with two strangers. More than the story I remember the meal they shared. It was only a couple of sentences, but I remembered it for the rest of my life, and it always made me feel hungry thinking of those sentences; there was something about the way one man put the ham slices – I always thought of them as thick slices of bacon – into the frying pan and how the fat began to sizzle, how the hot fat later bubbled around the eggs, and there was something about how the bacon slices and the eggs were laid on slices of bread and how the men finally dipped the crusts of the bread into the warm bacon fat, especially the last part. Remarkable. A masterful short story, and all you remember is the bacon slices sizzling in the fat.

I put a couple of slices of bread on my plate and tipped the bacon and egg onto them. I waited for a moment, and then I ate. Was I thinking about Gry? Gry who was only a couple of kilometres away? Right then I wasn't thinking about Gry. I filled the soot-blackened kettle with water and put it on the fire. When the water had boiled I tipped some coffee in and let it stand.

It is difficult to describe the feeling of well-being which always comes over me by a campfire (though no doubt it has something to do with primeval instincts). Every time I'm sitting by a fire, watching the flames dance, breathing in the scent of smoke, memories of former camping trips pop up, ones I've been on together with other people as well. Fragments of conversations, anecdotes, discussions. At home too I had the best moments with my father when we were sitting by the open fire in that large apartment on Bygdøy allé. He said things to me then, whilst he was keeping the fire burning steadily, which he could never bring himself to say otherwise.

I looked into the bluest flame. Then she appeared and filled my whole consciousness. Gry. I could turn around and walk back, go home or go to Fagervann tomorrow morning, I said to myself. I stared into the flames as if in a trance. Suddenly it was like standing in front of a burning bush. Feeling a call. I had to go on, I had to go to that cabin, I had to show myself to Gry. Stand there. I had no message, I just needed to twist something into place.

The unthinkable. Why should the unthinkable not happen again?

No dithering now, I said to myself, or to the flames. Just by standing there by the steps I would give her, give us, one last chance. The rest was up to Gry. Regardless of the outcome, something would be healed. *A man is searching for a former lover who has moved to Australia. Searching at random, he doesn't know where she lives. Searches in Wagga Wagga, in Oodnadatta, in Woolloomooloo. After ten years he finds her in Wandering on the west coast. 'What took you so long?' she says.*

At a party six months after the end of our relationship I heard that Gry had made a fiery speech about how she didn't believe in love. I heard it through one of her malicious friends. Gry had jumped up onto the table in bare feet, raised her glass of wine and proclaimed that marriage belonged to the Stone Age. Free us from love! It must be an echo of something she had read. But then she got together with a new man, to top it all one of an extremely doubtful character, and told everyone that it was serious.

I had to save her. If nothing else, I had to stop her marrying that Frenchman. He was simply not good enough for her. It wasn't the fact that he spoke Norwegian with an idiotic accent (I always thought of him as an Inspector Clouseau), it was that his films were so utterly without value. I had forced myself to watch a couple of them, and it was practically torture. The thought of her sitting astride him was unbearable. I didn't even want him to get to know her more vulgar sides. I threw the last piece of wood on the fire and remembered things I had almost forgotten and tried not to think about, but nevertheless found myself thinking about. Like the fact that Gry was not one to bother about a bikini line or about trimming hair generally. One winter whilst we were at Nissen she turned up in the playground wearing a fur hat and with an old-fashioned muff, the sort you put both hands in – I heard her say it belonged to her great-grandmother. They were dramatising a scene from one of Tolstoy's novels. A couple of years later she was lying naked beside me, and she pushed her thick bush against my prick and whispered: 'Come into my muff.' That's how she was. And now I hated the idea that she might perhaps be saying the same thing to that revolting Frenchman.

I looked up from the fire and gazed out over the water. I can still turn back, I thought. 'Tomorrow morning I'll turn back and go to Fagervann,' I said out loud.

Magnusputten lay there like a black, bottomless crater.

I know that the media are following my slightest movement; no doubt they are even commenting on the way I pick up the carafe and pour myself a glass of water. If I were to whisper something to the defence counsel, it would create headlines: 'Berge talks!' No-one likes the fact that I've chosen silence. Or perhaps they do like it – it gives more room for ... speculation. Psychologists and psychiatrists are having a field day, I bet the rivalry between them is being seen as an entertainment in itself, as a kind of ... sideshow to the main attraction. But how can they sit here day after day, a whole flock of them, all with odd-looking glasses? Haven't they got a job, a practice?

Now and then I look around covertly for Father, as if I believe I might see him amongst the public. I think about the survival kit he gave me. It can't help me now. As far as I can understand, Father didn't say anything of interest when he was interviewed by the police, so neither the prosecution nor the defence wanted to call him as a witness. I can understand that he doesn't want to sit in the courtroom. To be gawped at. I remember how affected he was by Mother's death, but it suited him to be the widower of Maj Runesen, killed in an accident; he had even won more votes on the back of it, partly because Mother had met a – what would you call it – a heroic end. People said she had saved the lives of three young people. And then this comes along and destroys everything. His son. Hated by a whole nation. I heard that someone spat at him when he was on the way home. In his face. How he must be suffering. The father of a mass murderer. What an indescribable disappointment I must be for him. He asked to talk to me whilst I was in custody. I couldn't face it. I think ... I know I ought to talk to him, but I would never be able to find the words, and he would just be even more miserable.

I am in Karakoram. I'm at the end of the world.

Even though it is hellish sitting here, and I try to pass the time by thinking of other things, I did wake up, as I said, when the procession of witnesses started. It happens that I find myself listening with what might be called interest ... or in disbelief, to what I hear about myself, especially from the witnesses for the prosecution. Much of it astonishes me. For example what certain Young Labour members can bring themselves to say. I wouldn't have thought that they had any particular opinion of me, but now they were sitting there and had clearly thought a great deal about me; they had lots to say, which was ... peculiar. Like ... one previous Young Labour leader said without blinking that I had always suffered from a Messiah complex. I admit that I had to grab hold of the carafe after that assertion, even though my glass wasn't empty. A girl I had never spoken to, who was studying psychology, stated that I was a typical narcissist. I don't remember what examples she gave – I must have been struggling to remain sitting calmly in my chair – but I do remember that there was some sniggering from the public gallery. And that the judge asked for quiet. And that he looked across at me, as if to watch ... to see what effect it had on me. Several people claimed that I was a young man who had lost his way, that the weight of expectation had destroyed me. I glanced at them now and then, remembering conversations we had had on Utøya or in meeting rooms in town, even in cafés, and now they were talking about my violent jealousy, my aggressiveness, my insensitivity, my ... lack of empathy. The last expression became a refrain, even though I had never heard any of them use the word empathy before.

I'm thinking the whole time: maybe they're right.

At times I almost feel like bursting into tears. Especially every time someone mentions Sylvie, that gifted little girl. Just the thought of ... It's impossible not to be ... I force myself to keep a straight face; I can just imagine the comments: 'He's crying! It's too late to shed tears now!'

Ine Wang is still not to be seen. Did I expect to see her here? I don't know. Is she perhaps ... ashamed of what happened?

I'm exaggerating. It's not hellish to sit here. It's just meaningless. I try again and again to find an explanation of why I'm sitting in Courtroom 227 and not outside, on a bench in Studenterlunden, or at my desk at home, studying the layers of writing on my tracing paper. I can't find any explanation.

It's as if my powers of imagination have been left at Valen, as if ... I don't know.

When Ine Wang interviewed me at Nordberg, she was interested in the fact that the flat had been Mother's; she kept looking round, as if she was searching for a key. She asked me, at the same time more or less excusing the fact that she was asking, if I could tell her more about when I was growing up, and I had no objections to talking about that; I had a perfectly normal and happy childhood in Romsås. I wasn't aware of the fact that we were rich, or at least had more than enough money, until we moved down to Bygdøy allé.

I don't remember clearly what I said, but there were several major things I left out. Like the fact that everything, or a great deal, was destroyed when I was twelve.

I've often thought about the idea of freedom, and I have not thought less about it while I've been in custody. In political circles as well there is a lot of talk about freedom. That it is a central aim to give people increasing amounts of freedom. That every person must have the freedom to become what they want to become. But is that not a grandiose illusion? People are unfree from the start. At least in the sense that they have not chosen their parents, sex, appearance, country or historical moment. What you can struggle to obtain on top of this is really insignificant.

Nevertheless: I had the most favourable starting point.

It was when I was twelve that I discovered what high expectations people had of me. And that I was disappointing them. It was also around this time that I realised I had problems standing in front of an audience; even having to read aloud in class was an ordeal. It's one thing to be shy, but what was worse was that I was practically unable to speak; for a long time my teacher thought I was struggling with a stammer. It made me think of a man I often saw in our neighbourhood in Romsås, a well-dressed man who looked like a film star. I admired him. One day when I was shopping for food I happened to stand behind him in the queue at the checkout, and that was when I heard him speak for the first time. The man had a comical piping voice. What a let-down. That's how it was with me, except that it wasn't the pitch of my voice that was the problem. I expressed myself like a clumsy oaf. I had heard several times how good Father was at making speeches, and I knew I would make a fool of myself if I was forced to open my mouth on a platform.

It wasn't until I became a teenager that it occurred to me that I ought in theory to be something unique. I was a product of the union of two Labour Party dynasties: Olaf Berge with all his ballast from Groruddal, and Maj Runesen, who belonged to the Labour aristocracy in Odda, with a father who before he became a politician had worked in the foundry – the very word 'foundry' made many older Labour Party members go weak at the knees – and a mother who at times had worked in the kitchens in the old Hardanger hotel. Mother's father was no longer alive when I was born, and I have only a vague memory of her mother from a visit to Odda when I was four, just before she died. As a boy I heard about Mother's childhood in Folgefonngata and her adolescence in the so-called Sande blocks; Mother was almost unstoppable when she began talking about the workers' flats in Murboligen and the Youth Centre and the Labour Party meeting rooms. She told me once that both her own and Father's parents had been more than normally keen for her and Olaf to get married – it was not far from an arranged marriage, she told me with a laugh. Mother felt almost as if she was part of a Jane Austen novel, in a universe where marriage was the most important thing of all. 'You know, we were the Social Democrats' golden couple,' she said, laughing, as she gave me a playful nudge. It was on the same occasion that she let slip (and I'm not sure whether I really wanted to hear it) that I had been conceived on a trip to Denmark. Father and Mother were amongst the Labour Party representatives who went down to attend Jens Otto Krag's funeral in the summer of 1978. Father admired the Danish politician, and I believe he saw himself as a Norwegian version of the former Danish Prime Minister. Mother didn't spell it out, but I understood that all this had heightened expectations; not only was I, as it were, the offspring of two champion breeders, but to crown it all my conception was so to speak achieved in almost sacred social-democratic circumstances.

He'll become something great. At the start I thought it was a joke, something that's said about all children. But eventually I understood that people really meant it. They thought about Father, who was known for his almost threatening eloquence, and Mother, lauded for her cleverness and her administrative abilities. A boy with two such talented parents was destined for something ... a leading position in Norwegian society.

So to that extent the Young Labour witness in the trial had not plucked the words 'Messiah complex' out of thin air. But I was not the one who suffered from it.

They gave me the names of both of my grandfathers, those two Labour Party giants from Odda and Furuset respectively, Daniel Nicolai, but I only used the second one; the first one was too weighty, too Biblical and too loaded with prophetic connotations – or perhaps it was simply the whole socialist inheritance I was unwilling to be a part of. *Who am I? A young man wrestling with this idea thinks about the fact that he has sixteen great-great-grandparents, and that he knows nothing about them. He begins to study them, one at a time, and feels that he is slowly being chopped into pieces. Ends by becoming schizophrenic. (Keep this one. Might be developed into something.)*

However, there was a lot people didn't know about Mother. Even though she was clever and respected, for most people she was just a figure in the background. Mother didn't put herself forward. That might also have been a protest against Father, who she thought put himself forward too much.

Mother had a secret. She drank.

I don't know whether she drank in Romsås. It was not until I was a teenager that it occurred to me that she rarely made dinner and that she seemed completely uninterested in household tasks; it was Father who took care of those. After work she spent most of her time lying on the sofa reading Graham Greene, with a small glass of Armagnac beside her. Graham Greene and Armagnac belonged together, she claimed. (Since I've begun to read Graham Greene myself I have thought that it ought rather to have been whisky. Or gin.)

According to what I've been told it was Mother who insisted that we should live in Romsås, at the top of Groruddalen, where Father's family also had its roots; it was in this valley that Grandfather had built up his metal works. Mother regarded Romsås as a social democratic showcase of a successful residential area, with roads in a ring around groups of white blocks, six housing co-operatives next to open countryside with large airy apartments, with an impressive view and easy access to all facilities: kindergartens, schools, food shops, shopping centres, library – 'Romsås is for the Labour Party what Holmenkollen ridge is for the Conservatives,' she said. But it was clear that Father longed to be in town; every evening in the summer I could see him on the verandah with a cigarette, staring unhappily down at the town centre. And I don't think he understood what was happening to Romsås, how the milieu was more and more being influenced by immigrant families. I don't know what Mother and Father said to each other, or whether Father issued an ultimatum, but when I was about to start secondary school we moved into town, to Grandfather's old flat on Bygdøy allé. And now it was Mother's turn to be unhappy. After two years they separated – according to Father it was the model of a civilised divorce – and Mother moved up to Nordberg. She regarded it as a sanatorium, she told me. She wanted to get away from the noise and the exhaust fumes. Father stayed in Bygdøy allé, alongside the decaying chestnut trees.

I had of course been blind, because it was only now I discovered that she drank. That little glass of Armagnac which accompanied the reading of Graham Greene had just been to deflect our attention. I thought that was all she drank, as she gave the impression of almost having a bad conscience because she allowed herself a few centilitres every evening after dinner. I thought that someone who lay there on the sofa with a wry smile and a book, whilst Frank Sinatra sang 'You Make Me Feel So Young' in the background, had to be a person with no problems at all.

Mother worked as an administrator in the Ministry of Social Affairs, which in the 1990s became the Ministry of Health and Social Affairs; and it was here, in the government quarter, in a department which was supposed to take care of people's health, that Mother sat and drank herself to death. Perhaps someone noticed, but said nothing. The press didn't write a word about it either – if they knew anything. I don't know why Mother drank, I just know that the reasons why people do things are often less clear than we would like them to be. Perhaps Mother drank because she was inhibited and needed alcohol to loosen up. Or because Father spent all his time on politics and she was unhappy in her marriage. Or – who knows – because she missed Western Norway. Perhaps she just liked being drunk? Before the Wall fell it might even have created a bit of excitement in her daily life if someone had suspected her of spying – because it was an undeniable fact that Mother had contacts with Eastern Europeans, with names like Tovaritch and Smirnoff, Wyborowa and Zubrówka. But during all these years there was no-one who mentioned the fact that Mother drank, and perhaps that says a lot about conditions in the workplace, about the blindness which can develop in the grey multitude which in more official language is called the civil service. On the other hand she carried out her work punctiliously and was one of the department's greatest assets, especially in Labour Party circles, where she was praised for her work as the driving force behind important health initiatives; she can take the credit for a milestone of a parliamentary report.

I blamed myself afterwards for not having done enough. But I did try on one occasion. I talked to her about her drinking and explained that I was worried. 'You don't understand,' was all she said. 'Thank you,' she said, giving me a hug. 'I'm absolutely fine.' I didn't know what to do.

It happens, when I'm lying awake at night, that I ask myself whether Mother might have been drinking because I was such a big disappointment.

Ever since I have been very young I have wanted to protect people. At Tiurleiken School there was a nasty gang, the worst kind of bullies. There was one little chap in particular who was picked on, and one day they were going to 'christen' him by pushing his head down the toilet. I could see that he wouldn't be able to cope with it, and that this would be the event which would destroy him for the rest of his life. 'Take me instead,' I said, although I don't know how I plucked up the courage. I didn't think they would do it either, but they did. First several of them pissed in the toilet bowl, then one of the hooligans added a large turd, and then they pressed my head right down into the stinking hole before they pulled the chain, so that I was in a whirlpool of urine and shit. One thing consoled me as I stood under the shower at home after having missed the rest of the day's lessons: I thought that this would make a difference to the weakling, that it would give him the strength to choose the right path. I thought as well that it would give meaning to the rest of my life. I had saved someone, I had not lived in vain. But that's not what happened. The little chap chose to side with the bullies. Everything went wrong. I moved away and lost touch with him. A few years ago I heard that he had become a pimp and had already spent some time in prison. Some people just don't want to be protected.

As I said: this idea of freedom, that everything would be all right if people just had the chance to choose, is an illusion.

One summer holiday Mother drove home to Odda. She liked driving, and she had bought a little Audi; she thought it was appropriate that the word could mean 'Listen!' in Latin, because that was what she did while she was driving. She often drove a long way, and fast, and whilst she was driving she nearly always listened to Frank Sinatra. It was curious, she once told me, because first of all she had been keen on Nancy Sinatra, and it was Nancy Sinatra's hit 'These Boots Are Made For Walkin'' which made her leave Odda and move to Oslo to study. One of Mother and Father's friends told me that Mother had sung 'Somethin' Stupid' at their wedding, and that everyone stood there thunderstruck, because she had a warm and distinctive voice, and no-one could understand why she didn't use it more. But with that song 'Somethin' Stupid', where Nancy sings a duet with her father, Mother discovered Frank Sinatra and fell head over heels for him – that is, it was the 1950s edition she fell for, Frank Sinatra from the time when he made his first comeback. So the background music of my childhood was LPs like *Songs for Young Lovers*, *In the Wee Small Hours* and *Songs for Swingin' Lovers!*. Mother reckoned that Frank Sinatra was an inspiration for her political work, because everything, she said, depended on timing, on knowing when an important but controversial reform could be pushed through.

Late one Saturday evening, whilst visiting a cousin in Odda, Mother had suddenly decided to drive home to Oslo. 'I love being behind the wheel at night,' she said, 'especially when it's light like it is now.' She said nothing about the fact that she liked to drive fast and that it was even easier to drive fast when there were few cars on the road. 'But you've been drinking,' said the cousin. 'It's a long time since I had the last one,' said Mother, as if insulted. What the cousin didn't know was that Mother always had some 'emergency supplies' in the glove box, half a bottle with a spy's name on the label. My guess is that it was empty and discarded in a rubbish bin before she swung out of the centre and over the bridge. And it was on the way along the lake to the south of the town that she met a car, in the middle of one of the few left-hand bends, and the other car was going so fast that it had crossed over onto the wrong side of the road. I have always thought that Mother could perhaps have taken avoiding action by swerving over to the left, but I believe she deliberately chose to pull the steering wheel to the right, thereby driving off the road, over the stone barrier, which was partly broken just here – or had been made into a slope so that it could be used as a ramp – and out into the water; on top of everything else this happened in one of the few places where it was quite deep. It turned out that the three youngsters, including the driver, had been drinking. But they didn't do any tests on Mother; it took quite a long time before the car with her in it was hoisted up out of the water. So that's how she became a kind of heroine. Two of the youngsters in the other car even became members of Young Labour in Odda.

I have tried to visualise the situation. The Audi flying through the air and then sinking into the water with Mother inside. As far as I know she made no attempt to get out. As far as I know she might have been extremely satisfied with the situation. Was Frank Sinatra playing on the sound system? 'Too Marvelous for Words'? (Frank Sinatra would no doubt have got out, because Mother told me that before his comeback in the 1950s he had expanded his lung capacity by swimming as far as possible under water.)

When Mother died and I moved in to Nordberg, there was surprisingly little in the apartment that I had to get rid of; it was mostly clothes and empty bottles. The whole safe, which for some incomprehensible reason she had acquired and to which I found the combination on a piece of paper in her bedside table with the department's heading, was full of empty bottles. I have no idea why, except perhaps that Mother wanted to preserve the illusion. She was a spy, who consorted with Poles and Russians, Wyborowa and Smirnoff.

Mother was a reader, but apart from Graham Greene's collected works there were not many books in her small bookcase, and only one of them did I read myself: *Bleak House* by Charles Dickens. From the numerous underlinings I could see that it must have meant something to Mother. *An unmarried woman, a keen reader, finds a novel someone has left on the train. She has read the novel herself, and becomes fascinated by the original and amusing comments in the margin, which she is sure must have been written by a man. She puts a notice in the newspaper. 'Where is the person who has written "How can anyone be so blind?" on page 225 in* Portrait of a Lady?' *A man answers her. They start a relationship.* Mother read Dickens' *Bleak House* and found a whole world, a hundred fates woven together, which she recognised, and by the time I closed the novel I had found a new explanation for Mother's alcoholism: bureaucracy. Mother didn't drink because of her marriage or because of me, she drank because she was a pawn in an enormous public sector. Drinking was a virtue of necessity in order to survive the power play and the intrigues in one of the kingdom's largest and least effective departments, a warren of offices where responsibility was dissipated. Perhaps her drinking was actually a kind of rebellion, I thought. A protest against the endless battle for promotion in the civil service hierarchy. A protest against the pedantry and the deluge of forms, all those who insisted on following protocol and demanding that the most insignificant little detail had to be properly documented. I remember her saying to me once: 'It's like being in the stomach of a monster.' By drinking, she managed to endure the meaninglessness of the innumerable meetings, reports, travel receipts – being a part of what Dickens in another novel called the Circumlocution Office, a department whose function was to do nothing.

No-one saw it. That she drank. None of her many friends in the party either.

Was that why I became so sceptical of the Labour Party? Because they let her sink?

I seem to remember that I was jerked out of my own thoughts and digressions by Ine Wang talking to me. It seemed almost as if she had had to snap her fingers to get me to react; and I reacted by going over to the music centre and switching off the music, the Frank Sinatra album which was playing – because I had of course kept Mother's LPs and

CDs. Ine Wang had got out her notepad, placed her recorder on the table and pressed the button. She wanted to go back to Gry, she said, to our relationship. She glanced at me to see whether that was OK. Then she asked if I had been to Dovre.

Oh yes, I had been to Dovre; I told a few harmless stories about the place and the fine walks you could take from there. I had a bit of a bad conscience for not giving her the uncensored version; as early as the autumn after the Utøya miracle Gry and I went up to Dovre, where we had the cabin under Raudberget to ourselves. I went on about walking up Brattbakken to the plateau from where you could see Snøhetta mountain, but Gry said 'Fuck Snøhetta, fuck the mountains', and instead she pulled out a Toblerone, a bar she reckoned she had been addicted to ever since they had played with the triangles at primary school. 'It'll be enough if we reach these summits,' she said, breaking off a Matterhorn for me; she wanted to stay in the cabin and make love, not go for walks, she wanted to screw, we were going to set a record, she said, we would screw until we made Dovrefjell tremble. She didn't use the word screw, she invented a code-word, called it hard labour. 'Now we've got to get down to some hard labour,' she said. 'We've set a new record for hard labour,' she wrote in the guest book. As an author I know that the word 'record' comes from *recordari*, to remember, to recall, and that autumn week at Dovre really was unforgettable; I wouldn't be surprised if Dovre had listed slightly now and then after our joint efforts. At the same time it occurs to me that the Latin word has in a literal sense something to do with the heart, and that is right, because it wasn't my groin that was affected, it was my heart. The ancient Romans were right: the site of memory is the heart.

Did I say anything about all this to Ine Wang? I hope not.

From what I recall she changed the subject and started to talk about my provocative political views. Or did she say 'inflammatory'? She mentioned something I had posted on my blog, Pens. I said she had misunderstood, and I said it rather heatedly; I said I was tired of people interpreting everything on that blog in the worst possible sense.

She wasn't stupid, she realised that I was starting to resist her questioning. 'You promised me something to eat,' she said lightly, as if she wouldn't mind if I had forgotten. Now that I think about it, I'm not sure whether it was then that she said something about the food; it might have been earlier, or it might have been later – it worries me how muddled my recollections of that evening are. I got up, apologised, and said something about being a poor host. It took a while before I got the table set and put out the spreads and the croissants I had baked. Whilst I was pouring out tea from the teapot, I mentioned something about my weakness. The fact that I was not a good speaker. I must have confided this to her because I wanted to help her get started again. I explained that I could see clearly in retrospect that I would never have been a good politician, that I would never have been able to lead the local group, Oslo Young Labour. 'It was a good thing I lost,' I laughed. 'I can express myself in writing, like in my blog, but not orally.'

'That doesn't tally with my impression,' said Ine Wang, as she split a croissant lengthways. 'I heard that you were a talented young politician.'

I think she threw out that lie in order to encourage me to open up some more. Or perhaps she didn't understand the problem. She didn't understand what great hopes my parents, and indeed several of the party bigwigs, had had of me. I was to be a leader. I had one grandfather who was an entrepreneur, another who was a manufacturer. 'There's something special about you,' Mother would say to me, almost cryptically, as I was growing up, and I almost believed it myself, until I understood when I was twelve years old how the land lay. I remember especially presenting a project in school. My work was excellent, but I was hopeless at talking about it. Seldom has a classroom been more full of giggling. I was distraught, and told Father about it. He didn't get upset; he told me that there were many ways of working for something like politics, and you didn't need to be an orator, you could *write* speeches instead. He pulled out a book from the shelf about John F. Kennedy and pointed at the author's name: Arthur Schlesinger jr. 'You can read that when you're older,' he said. I told Mother as well about my experience in the classroom. I think she was tempted to give me a glass of Armagnac, but she just stroked my hair and said it would all change with time.

I hoped that Mother would be right, and that's why I became a member of Young Labour.

It didn't change with time.

Right after my defeat at the Annual General meeting of Oslo Young Labour I was due to take part in a TV debate; it had been arranged long before the election, and I had worked hard to get on it. Of course I ought to have withdrawn, but I refused to see sense; I wanted to show those idiots that they'd chosen the wrong leader. I had made thorough preparations; it was to be a debate between representatives of the various parties' youth organisations, and had attracted a lot of attention in advance, so there were masses of people watching the broadcast. Dear God, what a catastrophe. I was supposed to be getting my revenge and impressing everyone, but every time I was given the word I just muffed it; I messed up as no Young Labour representative has ever messed up on a TV screen. I had so many good arguments that I thought that would be enough on its own, but I couldn't utter a coherent sentence. It wasn't lack of knowledge which felled me, it was my fumbling for words. Plus my shyness. That almost paralysed me. In addition to that I was distracted by something. Perhaps it was one of my fellow debaters, a voluble girl from the Liberals. Or something in the studio. The mobile cameras, which trained their sights on you like threatening weapons. The harsh light. A sardonic smile from the chairman of the debate, who introduced me in an offhand way. Afterwards leading Labour Party activists called me talentless, and said I ought to forget any idea of being a politician; I was simply a drain on the party. I imagined that my TV appearance must have been a colossal disappointment for Father – Mother was dead – but he said nothing, just behaved as if he had not seen my pathetic inadequacy. My doubts resurfaced with added weight. In order to be a good politician today you had to be a good talker. To be a politician involved hundreds of TV appearances like that one, nerves of steel, being ready to compete in eloquence with cheap points and false smiles. I thought of all the stress I would be confronted with. It was not worth it. No matter what the rewards were.

I don't remember how much of this I told Ine Wang, but I must have told her some of it, because I remember that she put down her piece of croissant with cheese and a little fig jam and noted down something on her pad, after which she looked at me and smiled, almost sympathetically.

But I definitely did not tell her that it was during this time, when everything was tense, that Gry and I did something we should never have done: we went up to Dovre again, and we were stupid enough to go there at the same time that Storen and Sofie Nagel drove up to the cabin under Raudberget in their dinosaur of a Chevrolet, and even worse, with Ståle, Gry's detestable older brother, in the back. It was miserable wet weather all weekend, with fog. I had always felt uneasy in Arve Storefjeld's company, particularly because he never missed a chance to say something poisonous about being an intellectual – he knew that I wrote – but never more than now; it was like sitting under a hailstorm of vituperative comments. He's an idiot, I said to myself. He can't see that every politician is an intellectual, that politics means producing ideas, and that the vital thing is to change the way people think. It was agony being shut up in a cabin where I had to listen to a potential father-in-law's tirades of oversimplified – and what's more, outdated – opinions, which he furthermore peppered with his banal and frequently repeated metaphors from fishing and road-building, even occasionally mixed with a reference to the fact that his father had worked at Christiania Steel Company. You had to 'bloody well be able to straighten a nail', you had to 'hit the nail on the head, for fuck's sake'. It was unbearable.

My misery reached its nadir during Saturday dinner, even though Storen had made an exception and served rare steaks with fried onions instead of his favourite meal, the eternal fry-up ('that's proletarian food, Nicolai, real proletarian food'). The rest of us had been reduced to an audience for Storen's embarrassing monologues, in which he made sure every now and then to mock all those bloody arse-lickers in the party who didn't support the same causes as he did. Surrounded by the log walls, I felt as if I had been transported back to Viking times, and it wouldn't have surprised me if Storen had begun to eat meat with his hands. I think even Sofie Nagel was embarrassed. Gry's brother just sat there with a scornful smile, as if none of it had anything to do with him.

After a completely paralysing session, in which everything I said, every subject I brought up, was met by sneers and hostile laughter, the situation became more and more tense. Of course Storen was informed about the battle in Oslo Young Labour, and unfortunately he had seen that deplorable TV debate. Devouring his steak, he left no-one in any doubt that he saw no future for me. He sat there in his ostentatious white shirt, speaking with exaggerated emphasis, and at the same time gesticulating wildly, like you see actors do in the TV dramas from the 1960s. He is an ignorant and overbearing tyrant, I thought. And since Gry was still in my eyes a multi-facetted rarity, it seemed to me extremely doubtful that she could be the daughter of such a breathtakingly simple and primitive person as Arve Storefjeld.

If nothing else, I was looking forward to a night of 'good hard labour'.

The last pieces of steak were swimming in blood. Storen was in his element, sitting there in his chair carved from a single piece of tree trunk, throwing out one cliché after the other, no doubt also to show a greenhorn how a politician ought to talk. He poured more whisky into what looked like an old preserves jar, and for me it was as if the fog had descended thickly inside the cabin as well. For one reason or another I started to talk about music, even though I knew that Storen was tone deaf; it was torture to hear him howling along to the party song, 'east of the river, east of the bridge, there is courage, there is faith' (despite the fact that he lived on the wrong side of the river). I warmed to my subject, and I was pleased with my own performance – just for once I managed to speak in coherent sentences, which was no doubt due to the fact that in a genial moment Storen had also poured me a generous measure of whisky – and I carried on until I got round to Mahler (how did I finish up there?). I ended by pronouncing that in my opinion the first bars of the fourth movement of the ninth symphony were the loveliest moment in musical history. Or rather, the whole thing started with the pause after the third movement, I maintained, in the silence after that glimpse of hell, all those violent and chaotic passages. 'You think: what now? What the hell's going to happen now? And then those unbelievably moving harmonies start to flow towards you, and almost bring you to your knees.' Even though I could see that Storen was getting more and more red in the face, I continued: 'Perhaps what happens after death is like that – a short pause, and then those indescribable harmonies and quietness. All the horror transformed into beauty. Those are seconds which must bring tears to the eyes of even the most hardened soul.'

Storen's expression said plainly that such garbage had never before been dished up within these walls.

Everything might have been all right if I had not finished off by saying that the ruling committee of the Labour Party ought to listen to more Mahler. Learn from his radicalism. His originality and vision. His willingness to incorporate new ideas into the old. I knew I was pushing it – and the whisky must take its share of the blame – but deep inside I felt that the idea was worth considering.

Storen sat looking down into his glass. The silence was ominous. Then he exploded. 'You don't belong in the party, you're just a pretentious little prick!' he roared. He didn't shout, he roared. 'You need to get your fingers dirty with some asphalt, you bloody theoretician! We need policies, not drivel!' It was like hearing an ox bellowing. I stood up, I'd had enough. 'If I see you again I'll steamroller you!' Storen yelled as I left the room. That last expression was one of his favourites, a kind of allusion to the glorious days of the Highways Department.

I dashed to my room, grabbed my backpack and left the cabin. Gry didn't follow me, or call me back. I walked the considerable distance down to Dovre and sat outside the station. The whole time I expected Gry to follow me. Show solidarity. Apologise for the way her father had insulted me. I hoped. She didn't come. I slept on a bench and took the morning train to Oslo. *Three of the world's worst villains meet in secret. Cory Neba, Giardia Lamblia and My Xo. Their villainy has terrified people on every continent, but now they have a wager about who can break down a living being first. In front of them sits a young man tied to a chair. They begin a kind of torture. Slowly it becomes clear that it is a bacterium, a parasite and a virus which are competing. (For the C-folder. Or reject.)*

It was during the time after that that I was strengthened in my belief that Young Labour, or rather the whole Labour Party, bore a dangerous resemblance to a self-satisfied and overfed Church congregation; there was something about the intermezzo at Dovre and Storen's denunciation, the physical aggression it provoked in me, which made me nail up – or rather glue up – 'Ninety-Five Theses for a Reform of the Labour Party' at the entrance to the offices down in Operapassasjen. Strictly speaking it was only ten theses, with subsections.

I was inspired by Martin Luther, and thought the party needed a Reformation. For me the Labour Party was what the Catholic Church had been for Luther. The present-day Labour Party had for too long been like a papal enclave with its cardinals, bishops and priests. A hierarchy with an incomprehensible language. A power structure which had lost its meaning.

My action certainly got publicity. Several newspapers printed pictures with more or less ironic comments. The whole affair finished with me – and it was the first time in many years this had happened – being excluded from Young Labour. I responded naturally by burning my membership card, just as Luther had thrown his notice of excommunication into the fire.

I am unsure what I think about this action today.

It was shortly after my exclusion that I called at Father's flat and picked up a bundle of Grandfather's suits and indestructible well-made shoes to take to Nordberg. I packed them in two old suitcases which had also been left there, suitcases covered in stickers from hotels in Europe which did not exist any more. It was now that I began to dress like 'a bourgeois', elegantly, almost in protest at Young Labour's boring hippie outfits. The suits were still hanging in the wardrobe in Bygdøy allé, in one of the rooms Father never went into, as if out of respect for the deceased. Grandfather and I were the same size, and the suits fitted me as if they had been tailor-made for me, even though the cut was different from modern ones. I liked that, wearing the suits of an entrepreneur, an innovator; I believe I can say that I wore the suits with pride, and that they made me carry myself differently, with a straighter back. I was shouldering the inheritance of a Labour Party man who had not only been able to sing the Internationale, but also created and improved things, and made daily life easier for many people with new mounts, hinges and handles.

All the time I was waiting for Gry to take my side. So that from our fortress, the heights over Fredensborgveien, we could together take up the fight for a new Labour Party. No-one could be better equipped than us two, the children of two factions. But she did not take my side. Nevertheless, to all appearances our relationship continued as before, or at least we made ample use of the opportunities to carry out 'a good bit of hard labour'. A whole year passed before the catastrophe occurred.

Ine Wang would have had plenty to digest if I had told her all this. Or did I tell her something of it? I don't think so. As far as I remember she was still preoccupied with Pens, my blog, and we talked for a while about the discontent which no party can suppress, this eternal whining from the population after 'more!' 'more!', like a spoilt child; and as I suddenly felt how sick I was of all politics, I asked if she would like a glass of Armagnac, and when I had served it she asked me a startling question. I think it must have been then, anyway. At any rate it was so sudden that I pretended I hadn't heard it; my thoughts were wandering as well, and I was looking out of the window searching for some place down in the depths of Oslo – possibly Youngstorget. She raised her voice and repeated the question: 'Did Gry smoke marijuana?' I turned towards her. Perhaps Ine Wang regretted the question, or feared she had gone too far, because she busied herself with her glass and raised it to her mouth. If I remember correctly, she pulled a face, as if the contents were too strong or she was caught off guard by the taste.

I showed no reaction, leaned over the table and took a slice of salami with fennel. 'No, she didn't,' I said, or I think I did. 'That's just a rumour, there's no truth in it.'

Once more: a half-truth. A half-lie. Or a big lie.

I could have said she was getting warm, but I kept quiet; I didn't want to tell her about the opium. I didn't want to say anything about how self-destructive and vulnerable Gry was behind the tough, sexy façade.

Towards the end of our relationship I understood that my love for Gry was also based on a desire to save her. I saw early on that the self-assured mask was a cover for a lot of insecurity. I could help stabilise her. Once again it was that idiotic protective instinct which was switched on.

When we got together she was rolling her own cigarettes (like her father) and smoking with a greediness which made it look as if she wanted to burn through the whole cigarette with her first puff. Then she suddenly stopped smoking with no problem at all; everyone said she would start again, but she didn't. 'People don't know the first thing about willpower,' said Gry. But then the opium problem arose. The excuse was her study of Coleridge. Actually I could understand the idea. That was perhaps something of what I found most genuine about her, her interest in Coleridge, interest in the iconoclastic poetry of that period. She said it was his imagination which fascinated her. And since Coleridge had taken opium in the form of laudanum, a tincture, she wanted to try that, which meant smoking it; she managed to get hold of some, together with the right sort of long-stemmed pipe, apparently of top quality – she had been amazed at how easy it was nowadays to get hold of whatever you wanted. I was not to be frightened, it was just an experiment, she emphasised several times. I treated it as a joke. But she carried on with it, saying it did her good. She maintained that it fertilised her consciousness with synthetic intelligence. 'Relax, I can stop at any time,' she said. 'Don't you remember how easy it was for me to cut smoking?'

For me, opium was as anachronistic as absinthe. I couldn't take it seriously, but I noticed that it had become a habit, and it was beginning to get dangerous. She also managed to get hold of a variant of laudanum from one of her many admirers, a dubious pharmacist who had a talent for falsifying opium records. I tried to get her to stop. She defended herself, telling me she wanted to expand her consciousness, like I did. 'Yes, but I'm trying to do it with words,' I said, 'not with opium.' I also wanted to stop her because I was afraid she would short-circuit something, like Axel Jensen, an author I prized highly, who was never the same again after being given LSD by R.D. Laing in London. You take something you think is an innocent substance, a harmless smoke, a few drops in a glass of water, and you're followed by diamond-encrusted toads and luminous Martians for the rest of your life.

She didn't stop; I don't know if she was an addict, but I heard that she carried on with opium after we split up as well. I felt just as helpless and powerless as I had done when it came to Mother and alcohol. I had visions of Gry one day throwing herself into the depths and letting herself sink with a smile on her lips. *Too Marvelous for Words.*

I said nothing about this. I pressed Ine Wang to eat more. 'Try the blueberry jam,' I said. 'I picked the berries myself.'

She raised her eyebrows. 'Amazing,' she said, not without a hint of irony. 'I've never had the patience. Don't you think it's boring in the forest? Nothing but fir trees.' She laughed.

If she only knew, I thought.

The days in Karakoram, or Courtroom 227, pass at a snail's pace. I try to follow the proceedings, but I keep losing track. There's something about the judge as well; I keep thinking about his solemn ... his compelling words at the start, after the prosecutor's opening statement, how he almost folded his hands in prayer as he said that I ought to explain myself. There's no doubt that during the course of the trial he has become more ... interested in me. At the beginning he never looked in my direction. Now he often sends me ... penetrating glances. Or is it more an expression of curiosity? He asks the witnesses more questions too, and makes more notes. He makes me nervous. Or ... shy.

I try not to look at him. Or at his two fellow judges. Instead I fix my gaze on the national coat of arms on the wall above them, the lion with the axe, one of the few things in the room which is ... which can stimulate my imagination, and give me some hope that it hasn't gone completely into hibernation. (Or perhaps it's not called an axe, but a *halberd*? And why is the creature standing on one leg?) *A judge pronounces an unjust sentence and is decapitated when the axe falls from the coat of arms and hits his neck.*

Now and then, when I glance towards the public gallery, I can see that there are several celebrities there. I even know the names of some of them, even if I don't know what it is they do, or why they are celebrities. What are they doing here? Am I so ... thrilling? Do they regard the trial as a kind of *event*? Watch how he behaves! A sensation. *The silent man.* Or is it in order to be able to say something when they are interviewed outside? So that their celebrity status can be enhanced?

When I come to think about it, I'm a celebrity myself now.

Was I a bit startled one day when I recognised some colleagues sitting in the places right at the back? Reputable authors. Presumably they're here to gather material, to be able to write a book about me. The thought makes me dizzy. I can positively see their mouths watering when they look at me, as if I'm a tasty morsel they're about to bite into. Is it possible? A best-seller based on my life? Of course, that's what's going to happen, people will write novels about this. *The tragic fall.* There'll be a competition to see who gets there first. I'll become a whole industry. *Berge.* A word. Impressed on the national memory. I swing between feeling elated and being angry.

My ears prick up every time there is talk of what might have happened in those few hours before the five people were done to death in Nordmarka. I dare say that I am every bit as ... curious as all the others breathing in the heavy air of Room 227.

Nothing is so bad that it's not ... All those witness statements, some of the information I have more or less unwillingly picked up, have opened a door in my memory, activated nerve circuits which must have been switched off. I am beginning to remember more. Even more.

All those things we don't understand. Black swans. Black leopards. Panther Hansen.

It is simpler ... it is more complicated than anyone present believes.

How many times have I been back in that camp by Magnusputten on the night of 22 August? I had decided, or at least I thought I had decided, to turn back the next morning. At the same time I knew that Gry was quite close, and it was almost as if I could catch the scent of her when I breathed in.

It was an unusually fine evening, warm and still with few mosquitoes. I tried to envisage Gry in the cabin, at the place they called Valen. I wondered what she was doing, whether she had already gone to bed or whether she was perhaps sitting on the steps with a glass of wine, talking to her father. Slandering other Labour Party politicians or opponents in other parties. Was the Frenchman there as well? The very thought of Gry and that repulsive Lefebvre in the same cabin made me grind my teeth in despair.

The sun would soon set. I got out my notebook; I had a few thoughts in my head, micro-epiphanies, and wanted to pin them down on paper before they disappeared. I was in the middle of working on a third collection of short stories. It would be an extensive volume again, consisting of many short pieces. *Ten people are sitting round a fire telling stories. The surroundings look idyllic and the mood is almost pastoral; the reader's thoughts are led to the framework structure of Boccaccio's* Decameron. *The stories surpass one another in their inventiveness, and the narrators appear extremely wise and cultured. Towards the end it is revealed that the setting is a refugee camp, plagued by hunger and sickness. The people around the fire are emaciated and clad in rags; they are all fleeing from a barbaric catastrophe.*

There were only embers left amongst the stones. I fetched some water and extinguished them. When I dried the kettle and put it in my backpack I discovered that I had brought my survival pack along without really being aware of it. As I stared out over the surface of the water, which was growing darker and darker, I tried to remember what it now consisted of (apart from the kettle, which was part of it). A thumb compass, three matches and a striker, two fish hooks and a line, a needle and thread ... what else ... a small whistle, a bandage with compress, the smallest Swiss Army knife, a pocket mirror for signalling ... a coil of thin steel wire, a miniature torch. Once more I sat and pondered. Was there anything missing?

A hand to hold on to?

Before I settled down I filled the cap of my hip flask with Armagnac. The first sip especially seemed to me like a fiery caress. Otherwise I drank little. But this was a ritual on my forest trips, a capful of Armagnac before bedtime.

I wriggled down into my sleeping bag. The smell of resin and smoke mingled with the scent of pine needles. Everything was still. Or everything was a soughing which you couldn't hear unless you listened for it, and the soughing came not just from the forest, but from something behind it, something over, under, beyond. A kind of base note of existence. That was perhaps what I treasured most in the forest, lying in my sleeping bag letting that soughing lull me to sleep. I know of no finer lullaby.

Despite that I couldn't fall asleep. I considered getting out my head torch and reading some pages of Graham Greene, but I dismissed it. Out here in Nordmarka I could see how dark the evenings had become. A half-moon was hanging low in the sky. A bracket. The word *hilal*, from Islam, occurred to me. Was I thinking of a sickle? It was actually Gry's scar under the hollow of her throat which rose up in my memory. It's only later that I thought about a sickle.

As the darkness intensified, more and more stars and constellations appeared. It annoyed me that Orion was not visible at that time of year. The hour glass.

Just before I fell asleep, I realised that I had changed my mind. I was no longer on the way home.

May she be there. May she welcome me warmly. May she regret everything. May she take me back.

I liked having Ine Wang in my flat. There was something about her face, a mixture of eager concentration and ... Even though she had cut down on the black eye make-up, she was still wearing that dark lipstick which gave her mouth, particularly her upper lip, a noticeable voluptuousness. The questions she asked were serious ones, but at the same time I could hear a kind of exploratory undertone in her voice, as if she was inviting me to, or was open to, something other than what we were talking about. Something was happening between us. Ine Wang must have registered that shift as well. Whilst I was telling her about Gry Storefjeld, I suddenly had a vision of Ine Wang naked. Did the macabre reason for our meeting also have a titillating effect? Whatever it was, I had no objection to it; I enjoyed sitting there feeling attracted by her. More than attracted.

I asked if she would like another little drop of Armagnac. At least I think it was at that moment that I suggested it. Anyway, she said yes; it may be that she hesitated for a moment, but she said yes. 'This is a good Armagnac,' she said. I don't think she knew whether it was good or not.

There must have been a brief pause whilst we sipped the brandy. For a while we just sat there chatting. It was pleasant, and I should have liked to have her there visiting even without the journalist's pad. I had the impression that she felt the same way. She kept running her hand through her hair, which was cut in a youthful but becoming style, as she threw enquiring glances at me, glances which had nothing to do with the interview situation. That's why I was disappointed when she abruptly returned to Gry, even though Gry was the reason we were there, because there would be no point writing a feature about me if it didn't at the same time tell readers something they didn't know about Gry Storefjeld.

I found myself admiring Ine Wang's dedication. If it was dedication.

'There are always two sides to a case,' she said. 'Can you really not see anything negative about Gry, looking back? I know you don't want to speak ill of someone who's dead, but surely I'm allowed to ask ...'

In other words, she wasn't satisfied with that innocent story about the chess game. But saying something negative about Gry ... Wouldn't that be close to ... blasphemy? I could always say that Gry had dirt under her fingernails. But was that negative? I could say she made lots of spelling mistakes when she wrote, as if she'd never bothered to learn to spell properly. Or that she was a tad too liberated.

After the break-up I had made a collection of Gry's undesirable features, as if to comfort myself. Like the fact that she lacked a sense of humour. (But why then did we so often laugh together?) Her ignorance about many things – including things she ought to know about – was enormous. (When I said that the Goldberg variations was a book about sex techniques, she believed me.) She was a notoriously bad time-keeper and always arrived late for meetings. Sometimes she stole things from shops, including things she had absolutely no use for. 'Why do you do that?' I asked. 'It gives me a kick,' she said, as if that was a good enough reason for stealing.

Now and then it struck me that her looks were all she had. Her hair. Towards the end of our relationship it began to be clear to me that the reason she seemed so deep, so mysterious – and men remarked on it constantly, their eyes shining – was because she was just remarkably simple. She wasn't especially smart. She understood little of Coleridge; she was blind to his theological speculations, and even though she read the poetry of that period she had little knowledge of literature beyond that. She never finished her dissertation either; the whole Coleridge enthusiasm was just a schoolgirl infatuation which evaporated when she encountered serious research. The only thing she retained was the opium. What I had long taken to be originality was just caprice. I have always hated any talk of inheritance, of genes, but as time went on I must admit that Storen's naivety became more and more visible in his daughter. Not just that – behind her charm, she possessed something of the same craftiness as her father.

After some time the list was quite long. It made no difference, I just loved her even more.

'The worst thing I can say about Gry,' I said to Ine Wang, 'is that she didn't like my short stories.' I said that as if it was a flippant remark, but I meant it. Gry didn't understand that someone could spend their life writing fiction, when reality presented so many urgent challenges. 'You talk like a fantasist,' she told me. 'Just take your hopelessly impractical talk of "supranational perspectives".' 'What do you mean?' I asked. 'Well, take for example what you say about how it's not us, Norwegians, who need to integrate immigrants, but that it's us, Norwegians, who need to be integrated into the world.' She had to stop to utter a false laugh. 'It's because you're a writer,' she said, 'it's your passion for literature which has destroyed your grasp of practical politics. You're turning into a crazy Don Quixote!'

She might not have read *Don Quixote*, but she had at least heard of him.

We argued a lot about that. She got annoyed every time I got out my notebook and wrote something in it. She accused me of living more in my thoughts than in the real world. I defending myself by saying that thoughts were part of the real world, and attacked her for having a narrow view of reality; I said that was not good for a future politician. I made that last comment because she confided in me one evening that she was setting her sights on becoming a cabinet minister. In that case, I said, she had to open her eyes to the fact that our ability to make things up – to imagine things that did not exist, but might do so – was a massive political resource.

She just scoffed at that. Threw cushions at me. Called me a dreamer.

In the end that was what made our relationship untenable. I had fallen in love with a girl who praised Coleridge's imagination, but who herself had an imagination you would need a microscope to find. She was not able to transfer the imaginative force she found in Coleridge – 'that synthetic and magical power' according to his *Biographia Literaria* – to other fields. Like politics. She had already become a conformist, who spoke like all the other politicians; she was an echo of the newly-elected Prime Minister.

I believe I stopped myself in time, and that Ine Wang only heard my complaint that Gry didn't like my short stories. If I remember correctly she made a note on her pad, perhaps about my frown, about how I was struggling to find words. I saw that her hand was shaking slightly as she raised her glass of Armagnac. She had lovely fingers, with an elegant nail varnish which matched her lips.

Can I write about this … about the trial? Can I use it some time? A variation on Kafka's *The Trial*? I ought to take notes. Write about feeling as if my head is once more being pushed down into a toilet full of piss and shit. But that would only create an uproar. He's *writing*! The devil is sitting there indifferent, writing. Isn't that proof enough of his guilt? Such a derisory lack of interest. Such a glaring absence of … *remorse*. Pity. He ought to be sitting with his head bowed, but to his shame he's sitting there writing, as if nothing has happened.

Better to memorise my thoughts. Write them down in the evenings. Gather together as many as possible of these notions, the seeds of new stories, try to convince myself that there is still … hope, that I still retain a small portion of imagination. Story-telling as … survival tactic.

I can feel all the glances directed at me. How I am being examined. Measured. Weighed. I hear that there's a great demand for places. People want to see this. Have something to tell their grandchildren. I can understand them. They will never get to see a monster like me again. I'm a freak show.

As for me, I focus on the national coat of arms on the wall above the judges' bench. *In the Middle Ages a man is about to be executed, but as he kneels on the scaffold with his head on the block, the crowd yells in terror and flees. The man glances up and sees a lion coming towards him on two legs, with an axe in its hands.*

Occasionally I glance towards the reserved public area, where the families are sitting. It's difficult to look at them. They are the only ones I feel … a deep sympathy for. There are no words for their sorrow. The court can condemn me to a hundred years in the darkest cell, and it would not soothe their pain. I can see the woman I think must be the mother of Sylvie, the little girl. Was she a film director? She must want to kill me. For one second I meet her eyes. I can see only wonder.

Do I regret asking Ine Wang home to my flat? I do remember that I was more and more taken with her, that it struck me how attractive she was with her tight black trousers and her white blouse, made of a material which looked thick, and yet so soft that I felt like touching it. And at the same time I had misgivings, and felt that I definitely ought to end the interview, or even cancel the whole feature, though I didn't know how to do that. Then the next second, because she asked a new question about my relationship with Gry, a sharper question, I thought that I ought to tell Ine Wang more about my writing; I actually decided to do that, even to talk about it in detail, but I stopped even before I got started, because I must have realised that she wouldn't have understood anything about it either. Understood that it was probably all those sentences, often failed sentences, which made my relationship with Gry so difficult. But writing was what I wanted to do. It was the key to understanding who I was.

It was an experience in the Utøya camp in 2002 which awoke my desire to write. It was two years since Gry and I had got together, and now I was once more standing on the island's famed podium, more composed this time, less distracted by my crazy infatuation, and I talked about the Conservative government's asylum policies, about the restrictions, about the danger of Norway appearing as a cold and cynical country; I referred to something the High Commissioner for Refugees had said, and spoke about the whole migration problem, our fear of people with different religions. I believe I spoke intelligently, in the kind of complex sentences the subject demanded; but I saw that I was not managing to carry people with me, and more and more of them started chatting to one another instead. Some were lying back in the grass half asleep, others just walked off, and even Gry's eyes were closing. People wanted rhetoric. They wanted phrases. They wanted feelings. Slogans. If you shouted 'Solidarity!' you would be rewarded with instant applause. That's too cheap, I thought, as I carried on speaking doggedly about my subject; I said that everything was in transformation, everything was in movement, not just in the Balkans, in the Middle East, in Africa, and we had to be open to it and learn to exploit it. Immigration could lead to a welcome mutation. I said that we had to fight against our xenophobia, we had to realise that we were an extremely small number of people and we had a colossal unused land mass; I said that we ought to be a democracy which could see beyond the nation state, and that we ought to transform Norway into a land for settlers, with a pioneering mentality and culture. It seemed as if my words were evaporating into thin air before they reached the ears of the youngsters on the ground. I could see that people were fiddling with their mobile phones or lying back on the grass as if they were fainting with boredom.

I don't know where it came from, perhaps it was an unconscious experiment, but instead of ending with my conclusions – and possibly a banal oversimplification which might stir them into life – I began to sing. I have heard that it's a trick which people who stutter sometimes resort to. And in a way I was a stammerer, I hadn't mastered the art of speaking. I was just as surprised by it as my audience was. Suddenly everyone was looking at me. I sang. It was completely misplaced, but I sang. I knew I had a good singing voice, my teacher told me that in primary school. I must have inherited it from Mother, but I never used it; I didn't like singing, although every now and then I hummed something, or sang a verse, and if other people were around, they always stopped and listened as if they had heard something unusual. When I was standing on the podium on Utøya it occurred to me to sing 'God Save this Land of Ours', I don't know why, possibly I meant it ironically, and I sang it to the same tune as 'God Save the Queen'. I sang the first, second and last verses, and I sang it in the way you can hear performers singing the American national anthem *a cappella* for the Super Bowl final, I gave it all I had, using the full force of my lungs; I could hear that it sounded fabulous, I was a master-singer, with just the right amount of vibrato, just the right amount of air, and the choice of 'God Save this Land of Ours' was a fortunate one, as it suited my voice range perfectly. Suddenly I had my listeners in the palm of my hand; they were almost drooling on the grassy slope, and would have followed me over a precipice – like a Jim Jones in the jungle, I could have made them drink from the cask of poison. It was the first time I had experienced what a kick it was, standing on a podium and making a whole congregation rock in unison. How peculiar, I thought. To have a father and a mother, two masterminds, who thought they were going to give birth to an Einstein, or at least a new leader of the Labour Party, and they bring forth a miserable anthem singer – yet who knows, maybe Mother would have applauded it and said there was nothing the world needed more than good singers.

The whole seance, my performance or whatever you'd call it, had of course been completely unexpected, and I think that's why it had such a powerful effect. Gry stood up, clapped her hands and shouted 'Bravo!' In enthusiasm. In amazement.

So I did have a talent after all, an exceptional gift. I just hadn't realised it before. Yet in the midst of the spontaneous applause, the heartfelt applause, an ovation the like of which I have never received before or since, I was sure of one thing: I would not use this for anything. I didn't want to be yet another musical seducer who makes the public sway together in a crowded hall. Yet another flash in the pan.

I have still not reached my point, because the discovery of my latent ability was not the most important result of that performance. In retrospect I can see that something radically transforming happened to me on that podium when I resorted to singing. It wasn't the audience reaction – I almost said the adulation of the masses – which changed me, it was a sense of the whole event: me, there, on a podium on a small island in Tyrifjorden, all the youngsters on the green hill and 'God Save this Land of Ours' ringing out over the grounds; it had something to do with seeing all the many layers of meaning, this song's history woven together with my own situation, woven together with the situation of those youngsters, woven together with the long traditions of the place, woven together with the demanding realities of migration. It was precisely this multi-facetted insight, which at the same time made me see everything with almost supernatural clarity, the blades of grass, the expressions on people's faces, the metal fibres in the microphone, which revealed how important it was to practise foresight, to keep your eyes open for the unexpected, things that sneak up on you, as it were in your blind spot.

In other words, it was imagination which awoke in me, and in a different way from before – my breaking into song was basically a manifestation of imagination. It was here, on the podium on Utøya, that I discovered I owned a creative talent, just that it lay in a completely different field from the one in which my parents, and for that matter I too, had expected it to lie. A voice. But I wanted to try to transfer this voice, which also involved a special *vision,* to writing. For a long time, ever since I stood in the crowd on Youngstorget for the first time, I had been sceptical about oral appeals, about demagogy. I didn't want to use speeches or songs, I wanted to use writing, because when I thought about that strange performance I discovered that there were stories latent in me, stories which I would never be able to use in politics because they were too complicated and contained too many chains of cause and effect. That's why I wanted to descend to the level of myth, I wanted to get *behind*, to cross a frontier; and I felt that I had already crossed over something when I came down from the podium, that the Daniel Nicolai Berge who had climbed up onto the stage was a different one from the one who came down to be embraced by Gry Storefjeld. For a long time I had been a bird placed in an aquarium, I was simply not in my right element. Something had happened. I breathed differently. Everything suddenly had a meaning, even what I had long thought were mistakes and fiascos. That was it. I was going to write. I had always read, and always felt a special pleasure when I registered that the turbines of my imagination started up as my eyes fell on the first pages of a novel, but I had a permanent bad conscience at this activity because I felt I ought to be reading factual material, I ought to be studying; I was going to be a politician, after all. *A series of novels in French becomes an international success. The author uses a pseudonym. Inventive, improbable, sometimes daring stories. Everyone tries to discover who is hiding behind the pseudonym. After many years it is revealed that the author is a Catholic priest. It turns out that the books are constructed around admissions he has heard during confession, but the stories have been changed just enough to prevent anyone getting suspicious. What people thought was pure invention is real-life accounts.*

Now I was going to write. Fiction. And even though I was far from convinced that I had a great gift, I was certain that it was here I should apply myself – use that voice, that vision, whose existence I had glimpsed on the hill at Utøya. I began to write whilst I was studying. Carrying on with the history of religion was mostly a camouflage, or in order to have a base (and at the same time it gave me access to an arsenal of unique stories). I didn't write in order to become famous, or because it was my last chance to avoid disappointing Father, now that Mother was no more. I wrote because it was my only chance to make a contribution. I, a tongue-tied man with no gift for speaking, decided to become an author. I wrote and wrote, I wrote just as persistently as I had once courted Gry, sent it in to publishers and was refused time after time. Of course I was disappointed, but at the same time I was content. The truth is that I had never felt so content. I was writing, I was using the only talent I had.

I made a friend, Anders Wiik, who was studying literature ('You need to find out what's been written so that you don't write the same thing over again'). He was good at tennis, and had lived in the US as an exchange student. I saw him play, and he wasn't just good, he could have been a star. But he wanted to write, and he wanted to drink; he should definitely have drunk less. I know it is a prejudice, but it amazed me to meet a guy who knew more about literature than I did and who came from Sand, at the northern tip of Storsjøen lake in Odalen. But that's how it is today, you can easily sit in the middle of the forest and still follow all the ins and outs of world literature, keep up with all the developments, all the journals and magazines. Nord-Odal library had had the internet from 1997, Anders told me, and before that they had provided everything that a young whippersnapper who was fascinated by literature could desire. Anders took a particular interest in the town's famous son, Sigurd Hoel, especially in what Anders thought was Hoel's best novel, *The Road to the End of the World*, perhaps because he shared a name with the central character; he wanted more than anything else to disprove Embret's abominable statement, uttered as Anders is about to go out into the world: 'Many strange things will happen to you. (...) And afterwards – you will realise that everything had already happened before you were ten. (...) After that it's just repetitions.'

'To hell with Freud,' said Anders.

'Freud was a mummy's boy,' I said.

'Freud founded a religion,' said Anders.

Anders insisted that we should mix blood; he had found an old-fashioned steel pen nib which we could use to make holes in our skin. Now we were 'Pen brothers', he said afterwards. We could just as well have called ourselves the 'Salon des refusés', because we constantly received rejections; despite that we weren't bitter, because we wanted to write differently, and we understood that being rejected was part of that, it showed we were on the right track, we were in our element, we were not far from being invincible, so we just wrote on, and Anders said it was the attempts that counted, not the success. We wrote and wrote, read what we had written to each other, made suggestions for improvements or said it wasn't different enough, that it was too similar to everything else, when we were supposed to be renewing the language of the tribe, for fuck's sake. Our stories were going to be a counterbalance to all the sentimentality. We gave each other encouraging thumps on the back and laughed. We often sat in the cheap Asian restaurants in the area around Torggata, exchanging rejection letters between the dim sum and noodle soup with grilled pork. It was Anders too who taught me to listen to Mahler, 'a key figure in the whole of twentieth-century music'. 'Listen to this,' he said, as we sat there in front of a poor quality stereo set in his student room at Kringsjå. 'The first movement of Mahler's Ninth Symphony is in D major, and you expect Mahler to return us there safely in the last movement. But what does he do?' Of course I couldn't answer that, and just waited for Anders to go on: 'He drops the whole thing down a semitone, to D flat major! It almost makes you fall off your chair!' It was because of Anders that I rated this symphony – and the fourth movement – so highly; it was Anders who explained to me what modulations are, and without thinking about it I tried to insert something similar, a kind of sliding scale, into my stories. We carried on writing. Submitting books. Receiving polite rejection letters. Then, almost as an anticlimax, we were accepted. By two different publishers. Mine was a collection of stories, Anders' a short novel. The publishers who accepted my book had appointed a new editor, and it was this person who saw something in my stories. Is it really so random? I thought. A new reader, an *open* reader – and everything turns around? My acquaintances were amazed – they had never seen me writing – and even Father was surprised. Gry frowned. I should have seen what was coming.

All the things you can't foresee.

Unfortunately, neither Anders nor I received any attention when our books came out, although a few tabloids printed a postage-stamp note about Olaf Berge's son having written a book. No-one came to listen when we did a reading either, not even when we read 'in stereo' at Mono, the premises in Pløens gate which looked like a rock club, where we stood side by side and took it in turns to read excerpts from our books.

As I worked on my second collection of stories (this was after Gry and I had broken up) Anders sent in a manuscript of two thousand pages to his publishers; his aim was to write so many brilliant passages that they would eventually cause a short circuit in the reader's head. You would be able to see who had read the novel, he claimed, because they would be walking around like a kind of zombie. 'Or perhaps they'll be deprogrammed so that they can be reformatted?' I suggested. The manuscript was refused. Everywhere. 'Bloody cowards,' said Anders. 'Damned mainstream junkies.' But he didn't give up; the mistake was that the manuscript was too short and he needed to make it twice as long, he said, to insert more voices and more digressions, and as he was expanding the masterpiece and creating a kind of Mahler's Eighth Symphony in novel form, he intended to launch a Plan B at the same time. It must have been the Chinese restaurants in Torggata which gave him the idea. He often asked them for fortune cookies, but they weren't on the menu, and you didn't even get one when you ate there and were about to pay the bill. Anders wanted to start a business which made Chinese fortune cookies. 'Norway needs fortune cookies now that the oil age is coming to an end,' he said. 'And then the two of us can write the texts for the strips of paper inside. You're familiar with Taoism and Confucius.' 'And you can dig up quotes from world literature,' I said. 'Think about it while I go back home and sort out the finances,' he said.

His authorial ambitions had shrunk to writing texts for fortune cookies.

I heard no more from Anders. I tried to ring. I sent several emails, which were never answered. I wrote a long letter and posted it to Sand in Nord-Odal, but heard nothing back. I imagined that his texts for fortune cookies had been rejected as well.

Or that he'd started playing tennis again.

Or that he'd drunk himself to death.

I had another collection of short stories accepted. The least negative criticism was printed in a student paper, where the stories were called 'meditations in narrative form'. This time there were also some reviews in the bigger papers. All of them of the discouraging kind. The most irritating thing was that they all placed the stories in the Kafka tradition. It's as if people automatically seized on Kafka when they wanted to signal that these were not traditional stories. But if anything had inspired me, it was rather the stories of the Argentinian Julio Cortázar (and the modulations of Mahler, I might add). I too was seeking that point in a story where the content turned around and became something other than the reader had expected, and everything went in a new direction, as if there was a set of points in the middle of the story. My central thought was to compose alternative chains of cause and effect, to push things out of their normal positions and show that what seemed logical could conceal something frightening or absurd. Optimally, I thought – and I'm not sure whether this was in my strongest or my weakest moments – the reader would glimpse a new way of thinking in these stories, or in the stories as a whole, and my hope was that this way of thinking might in the long run also have political consequences. Because what politics needed more than anything else was imagination. I still regarded myself as an outsider member of Young Labour.

When I recapitulate these thoughts, I look down at the ground and shake my head. You poor romantic, I think.

Should I have said something about all this to Ine Wang, after all?

I kept my mouth shut. That was probably the wisest thing.

'Were you upset when you broke up?' asked Ine Wang. I don't remember exactly when she asked that, just that it was towards the end of the interview.

'Yes, of course,' I said, 'but that soon passed.'

Is that what we said? Did I answer so categorically?

By this point it was becoming more and more clear to me that this whole undertaking, the feature, was a massive misjudgement on my part; it could go badly wrong. I had said yes because the request took me by surprise. And because

I liked the journalist. How am I going to get out of this, I thought as I looked at the woman who was sitting on the sofa opposite me. There was something about the material in her white blouse which emphasized the contours of her breasts. And had she opened another button, or had it been open at the neck like that the whole time? I had to bring this to an end and get her to go. Yet at the same time I wanted her to stay – at least until I found a way out. Could I use the tension which had arisen between us? Or was that only something I imagined? I asked, or at least I think I asked, whether she would like a few more drops of Armagnac.

'Just a small glass,' she said, 'to anchor things. I have what I need now.'

Did the word 'anchor' make me jump? I don't remember.

I had put the bottle away and had to get up to fetch it, and whilst I was doing that I thought again about her earlier question as to why we had broken up; I've thought more about it since too, in fact to be honest there are few things I've thought about more. Why did we break up? Because of everything, I could have answered. Wear and tear on all joints. Or I could have said that it had been over for a long time. That it was that trip to Dovre which had inflicted the fatal wound.

Yet the break did not come straight after that. Our relationship returned to its normal course. Apart from the fact that we argued more. In restaurants I wanted to tip heavily, whereas she didn't want to tip at all. I said it showed a lack of respect for workers. When we travelled to a town abroad I wanted to visit bookshops, she wanted to find cheap hash. And so on.

The truth was that the break-up was a bolt from the blue for me. We disagreed about many things, but in my opinion we were fine. At least better than most other people. After four years I was just as bewitched by Gry as I was when she crept into my tent on Utøya and made me light up.

She finished with me one day in late July. It was the summer holidays, and there were few people in town. I was waiting for her between the columns on the steps outside the Deichman library on Hammersborg. The place had been a meeting point for many years. She would usually come from the Labour Party offices on Youngstorget and I from the library's loans desk. That was in itself an indication of the fact that we were drifting apart; for her it was ever more politics, for me ever more books. She wanted to find simplifications, and I was searching for nuances, contradictions. Despite that we normally kissed each other here on the steps, perhaps because the impressive columns made you think of a temple and we saw it as a kind of ritual.

As usual she was late, but it didn't matter, because I was in a good mood; I was going to make my debut as an author in a month or so, and I had visited the library in order to borrow Alain Robbe-Grillet's *La Maison de rendez-vous*, a novel which had been published in Norwegian in the famous Yellow Series, and in which the French author had apparently created a Hong Kong which both resembled and didn't resemble the real Hong Kong. As I stood there, partly waiting for Gry and partly regarding the warm yellow cover with its nimbus of quality, I was thinking that this very novel could become a decisive inspiration for new stories, and I was looking forward to reading it when we got home to Gry's flat in the fortress. Or rather, after we had made love. *Possible story titles: 'The Manuscript in Walter Benjamin's Suitcase', 'Sebastian and the Art of Dovetailing', 'Lynx & Lynx'.*

It was a warm summer's day, and thick clouds came sailing like black pirate ships over the sky above the Ekeberg ridge. I have always appreciated the area around Deichman, with the main fire station and the old police station as neighbours. As a child I thought it must be the safest place in town. I liked admiring Gry as well, with the characteristic swing of her hips, as she rounded the corner of the Y-block and came walking towards me, as if on a catwalk, over the raised platform which covered Arne Garborgs plass; but on this day, when she finally came into view, I could see at once that something was wrong, or different. At first I thought it was her black clothes, the slight air of the military or the police about her figure.

Then I realised: she had cut her hair. And not just a little; she had cut it really short. One centimetre over her whole head. Sinéad O'Connor. I understood immediately what that meant. She had cut away her lovely hair in order to make herself strong – she had done the opposite of Samson. I stood there on the steps, knowing what was coming. It was as if she had cut her hair so that she could avoid saying it.

But she said it anyway. Breathlessly. As if she'd been running. Or as if she was nervous after all, and dreaded passing on the message. We had to finish, she said, and I could see at once that her decision was final. We had quite simply grown apart, she said. We had reached a point where our relationship was a drain on us rather than a bonus. She kissed my cheek. The whole thing seemed rehearsed. I could hardly utter a word; as usual I stood there struggling with sentences which got tangled up in my head. I didn't react at all, but I felt as if my face was cracking. She didn't say any more. We stood there for ... I don't know how long. It was as if she just wanted to make sure that the message – *the sentence,* I thought – had sunk in. 'I've got a meeting in Youngstorget in five minutes,' she said then. She kissed my cheek again and walked rapidly back the same way she had come. 'Next year there'll be a Prime Minister from the Labour Party up at the top there,' she shouted back, pointing at the government buildings.

As if that were a plaster on the wound.

She was a member of some committee or other. In a year there would be an election. She spent a lot of time with the party big-wigs. She was already aiming at a government post. That was another reason for her dropping me. She could see that I was, or at least would be, a hindrance. I watched her go. She was literally walking away from me. Her swinging hips disappeared around the Y-block. It was not just sorrow and despair I felt, it was just as much *hatred.* May you fall over, I thought. May all the misfortunes in the world strike you. I registered that my hatred encompassed the whole of that damned government block. A bloody Tower of

Babel of bureaucratic Norwegian quasi-social democracy! Fucking concrete shitpile! Yes, the Y-block too, with those damned Picasso decorations and everything. As far as I was concerned, those buildings could quite happily disappear from the face of the earth. The curses I hurled over there in my thoughts were so strong that I could hear the echo of them in a clear room in my consciousness.

I stood there between the columns, gasping for air. I couldn't breathe. *La Maison de rendez-vous* slipped out of my hand. I sank down on one of the steps and sat there until I could get my breathing under control.

Ine Wang had asked if I was upset. I could never have told her just how upset. It was only with difficulty that I managed to stagger to Egertorget and find the right metro. Once home, I suddenly felt so sick that I had to go to the bathroom and throw up, even though my stomach was empty. My nose began to bleed for no reason. No-one had punched me, but I was bleeding. I threw up again, even though I only had mucus to bring up; I vomited sour bile whilst drops of blood fell from my nose and down into the toilet bowl. The only thing I didn't do was shit myself. Once I thought the worst was over, I began to cry. Blubber is perhaps a more accurate word for it.

After the break-up I stayed in bed for a week, incapable of doing anything and with a brain which felt inflamed and swamped by feverish thoughts. When I got up I tried to write. It was no good, it was just lines which ended in ellipses, dot dot dot, and I thought that all these full stops were tears. Then the next moment I was annoyed that I was giving in to depression, intoxicated by my own self-pity.

She didn't answer the phone, but she did send me a text to tell me when I could come and pick up my few things from her flat. 'Don't say anything,' said Gry as she opened the door to the fortress. 'Don't destroy those four years, all the good times.' Of course she understood that I was weighed down by accusations of epic proportions. When she caught sight of my miserable face and my drooping shoulders she couldn't resist it, she imitated my posture. It reminded me of the time she put on a show as a mimic on Karl Johans gate, when she copied the poor people who tried to sneak past. 'You must have inherited your bad heart from your mother,' was all I could get out. 'Don't be melodramatic, this is completely trivial,' she said. 'You've broken my heart,' I said, at the same time as I despised myself for uttering such a cliché. I could not express myself verbally. 'Hearts aren't made of glass,' she said, 'the heart is a muscle, and it's a robust devil.' I stood there with my few things in my hands, two pitiful plastic bags. She kissed my cheek and let me out.

It was torture. Pure torture.

Gry & Nicolai. I tried to write a love story with the title '&', but couldn't. & was a knot, and had invaded my body, threatening to stop all vital functions.

In the midst of it all I became uncertain. As I lay there tossing and turning, rewinding those years with Gry in my head again and again, as if in remembrance of things past, I perceived clearly something I had long suspected, but had refused to admit, which was that Gry, that person whom half of Norway reckoned possessed a remarkable political talent, and in addition called 'charming' and 'intelligent', was in actual fact an extremely limited individual who was distinguished only by a strong lust for power and an exaggerated opinion of herself. She concealed her mediocre talents behind self-assurance and boldness. Did it not say everything about Norway that no-one uncovered that? But instead of letting it all go and leaving her in relief and gratitude, I just loved her more than ever. I was unable to let Gry go, even though I understood that I had to let her go.

Some weeks passed. Several times I went over to Westye Egebergs gate and sat down on the mat in front of the door to her flat, even though I knew she was not at home. It was as if I wanted to absorb a last remnant of her by osmosis. I sat on Bjørnstjerne Bjørnson's grave for a whole afternoon. Yes, we love. Not just that, in superstitious faith I spent a night walking around those four blocks on the hill above

Fredensborgveien. *Twelve* times I walked around that circle, anti-clockwise, muttering ceaselessly 'take me back, take me back, take me back'. The whole thing was of course utterly pathetic. I wasn't myself, I was afraid I would lose my mind. It was only in short glimpses that I managed to see the funny side, the glaring stupidity of the situation. I was crazy with love for a woman who didn't deserve my love, and what's more, didn't want me.

I waited for another text, an email, I waited for an old-fashioned letter. Every day I opened my letterbox with a pounding heart, because I hoped to find a letter, a long letter, a short letter, in which she would write something with her childish capital letters and many spelling mistakes which made it easier to comprehend the incomprehensible.

I phoned and phoned, but she never picked up. In the end I put my mobile in the fridge; I didn't want any more to do with it, and I forgot about it. One day it rang, and I could only just hear it, a signal from the inside of the fridge – from the North Pole, I thought. I opened the door and took it out. It was Father. 'How are things?' he asked.

One of the few things which could divert me during this time was to play about with my survival pack. I found at least one new thing which ought to be included: two paracetamol.

I ironed shirts, I had suits cleaned, I polished shoes every day. I liked the smell, it took my mind off things. In Bygdøy allé I had also found Grandfather's shoe-cleaning set; it was a complete little lifesaving kit for shoes, with tubes and tins and brushes and cloths – a kit worthy of an inventor and innovator. I was almost tempted to set up stall on Karl Johans gate and offer to shine people's shoes for free, so that I could both be distracted and do a good deed (a good bit of hard labour, as Gry would have said).

I spent a lot of time in Nordmarka in the months after the break-up. My thoughts were less unbearable when I was walking through the fir trees, standing on a hill and seeing a glimpse of a pool where I could bathe. It was as if the forest gave me comfort.

Should I have told Ine Wang about this? Would she have understood? I reproached myself for babbling on about unimportant matters, whilst I kept all the important things to myself.

I observed her surreptitiously as she sat there with her refilled glass of Armagnac, 'to anchor things', leafing through the pages of her journalist's pad as if she was searching for something, a question she had forgotten. It is possible that she changed the subject and began to talk about other things. Perhaps she had enough. My memory is not reliable. No doubt I pretended that I was listening attentively, but in all probability I was searching desperately for a credible excuse, some way of putting a stop to the whole feature. Or do I remember wrongly? It would not surprise me if I had disappeared into my own world again, and was thinking about that Saturday in August when I had taken refuge in the forest once more.

As soon as I awoke on that bed of spruce branches by Magnusputten, even before I had opened my eyes, I knew that the next few hours would be decisive for the rest of my life. But I – I who at meetings of Young Labour had insisted on the importance of taking into our calculations that something unforeseen, even improbable might happen – I had no idea of what awaited me just around the next bend.

I woke early. Woke to the sound of birdsong. But it was nevertheless not like in April, when you were surrounded by layer upon layer of birdsong – when not even Phil Spector could have created a better wall of sound.

I was nervous; I didn't bother with lighting a fire and making coffee, just ate a slice of bread with jam from a small plastic box. I didn't want to spoil my appetite; I imagined myself eating breakfast, pancakes with maple syrup, at Valen together with Gry and the others. I thought it not impossible that Storen himself, after four years, would forget about old disagreements and demonstrate that hospitality which was so legendary in the Storefjeld mythology. Perhaps he would finally acknowledge me. To be honest, I had often secretly admired him. His gifts as an orator. His myriad of amusing anecdotes. His social intelligence. His phenomenal memory – it seemed almost as if he knew the names of every single Labour Party member in the country. I was actually fairly certain they would ask me in, no matter how awkward it might be.

One last attempt.

My thoughts were interrupted by a sound which seemed to come from Lørenseter lake, not far away. I heard a shout. Several shouts. The sound carried clearly in the silence. It didn't sound like shouts for help, more like exultation. I crept out of my sleeping bag and walked quickly in the direction of the sounds. When I reached a small hill with a good view down to Lørenseter lake, I could see a strangely-dressed man standing on a kind of raft, or rather three or four thick logs which didn't look to be fastened together very securely. The man shouted: 'And I will persecute them with the sword!' At least I think that's what he said. And then: 'But they will put a rope around thee and bind thee fast!' Or something in that vein – I'm less sure of that last one. It sounded like something from the Bible. In any case, the man was not bound with rope; he had wound some chains around himself. They made him look like a suicide bomber, and the links looked like explosive charges.

Despite the distance I had recognised the figure. It was The Vanished Man. It was Enok. Panther Hansen.

'Hi!' I shouted, or I think I shouted. 'Hi!' he answered. 'Hi, hi, hi!' he shouted. Like a merry child, I thought. A child who has discovered that a place has an echo. Then he let himself slip down into the water and disappear, at the same time as the logs drifted apart. I was standing quite a distance from the lake. Nevertheless I began to run towards the shore. But because I was looking at the surface of the water I fell and banged my knee. I cursed, it was painful. I sat between the hillocks rubbing my knee as I watched the water. There was nothing I could do, it would take a long time for me to swim to the place where he went under, and I would almost certainly not find him; the lake could be deep and the chains would have dragged him to the bottom, and in any case I would never be able to untie them from his body.

It was dreadful. I started shaking, and buried my head in my hands, thinking feverishly through various alternatives. I sat there for a long time, until I calmed down. There was nothing I could do about it in any case. That was a man who *wanted* to die, I thought. A confused soul. Rest in peace, I thought.

The forest formed a thick wreath around the lake.

Panther Hansen, the master of stealth, had stolen into eternity.

I decided to wait until I returned home to decide whether I should report it to the police or not. I postponed the whole problem. Right then it didn't seem to me that Enok's death was a tragedy. On top of that I was impatient to continue my expedition. I had to get to Blankvann as quickly as possible. I was possessed by the thought of Gry Storefjeld.

I packed and cleared up, telling myself that time was short if I was going to make it. I found my way over the uneven terrain back to the loggers' track. Gry, I thought. A final chance. Gry, Gry, Gry. It was madness. It was as if I thought she would disappear if I didn't hurry. I tramped onwards towards Valen, but left the path and walked through the woods on the northern side as I passed the Blankvann farmstead. As if I was still ashamed of my expedition and didn't want to be seen. I knew I ought to stop. It was quite clear to me. I ought to turn round and walk to Fagervann, sit down under a tree and read Graham Greene's *The End of the Affair*.

Enough. I carried on. My legs moved automatically. Take me back, take me back, take me back. Why did I not stop this crazy expedition? I don't know. There is no answer. I don't know what I was doing there. I can never explain it. I could say that my body took me there, all my irrational tendencies, but that explains nothing. The truth is that it is a mystery.

I came onto the path which led up the hill to the north of the lake. Did I hear a helicopter? I don't know, the sound died away. I felt exhausted, though that might have been because of my doubts. It occurred to me that I should have taken some pills, steroids or something, which would have given me courage.

'What if the ice breaks?' she had said on that December evening when we were here many years ago. 'Blankvann is fifty metres deep.'

'The ice won't break,' I said. 'I know all about when the ice is safe.'

Again I vacillated. Was I too optimistic? What if my visit provoked a new scandal, something reminiscent of that fatal visit to Dovre.

But then: hope. Hope drove me on.

My plan was to get to the cabin early, so that they had to invite me to join them for breakfast. Unless they sent me packing. It was Gry who had introduced American pancakes for breakfast. It was strange: all that criticism of the US, but people gleefully took over unhealthy eating habits. I'd seen how Storen poured lots of maple syrup over his, before loosening his famous belt.

May she be there. May she be in a good mood. May she show me warmth. May she regret everything. May she take me back.

I knew it was a vain hope. I refused to believe it was a vain hope.

At the top of the slope the path entered a darker area. Sentences were jockeying around in my head: I happened to be nearby ... I didn't know there was anyone here, I just wanted ... I was looking for some rare orchids at the southern end of Blankvann and then I thought ... Is anyone looking for a good bit of hard labour ...?

Operation Gry.

Even though much of what happens during the trial makes no impression on me, and even though much of it is so unreal that I'm not able to make any sense of it, my days in Karakoram – Courtroom 227 – are so full of astounding information that I will have enough to think about for several years. I have a greater and greater desire to make notes as I'm sitting here. Perhaps I have finally found the perfect place to write. There's something about this ... absurd situation, all this meticulously choreographed ... ceremony, which gives me the strangest, but I believe also most *original*, ideas. Can it be compared to being thrown around by violent forces and then suddenly finding oneself in the eye of the cyclone? As I said, people would quite certainly misunderstand, or they would perhaps think I was noting down points for my defence. I wait to write notes until I get home ... I mean: back to my cell. Some evenings I scribble down these story sketches almost desperately ... as if they are the tail end of a creative ability which is slipping out of my hand. *An author writes good books, but can't make a name for himself. Then, in a major magazine interview, a celebrated pianist says that she reads his books. Six months later a famous biologist explains in a culture programme that the author's books have been an inspiration to him. Soon after that a top politician mentions one of his novels in a survey. That same summer, a photo is taken of a sporting legend as she lies on the beach with his latest book. And so on. Slowly, curiosity about the author is stirred. Title: 'Utopia'.*

I've found another thing you ought to have in a survival pack: a stump of pencil and some paper.

I did listen attentively, for once – this is several days ago now – when one witness, a girl from Young Labour, talked emotionally about collective guilt. That everyone had failed. 'We should have seen it,' she said. 'Berge was a man with serious problems. Someone should have sounded the alert. Persuaded him to seek help.' The prosecutor asked what she meant, and the witness explained about my furious rages. My limitless self-obsession. My scorn for other people's weaknesses. Where did she get that from? In addition she picked out my blog, which not just she, but many others, considered was full of depraved thoughts. 'We should have seen it,' the witness repeated, and she actually had tears in her eyes. 'We've failed, all of us.'

Other people too have expressed strong opinions about my personality in their testimonies. Several have insisted that I'm confused. They have repeated things I've said in varying contexts, even while we've been sitting round a café table drinking beer, and they claim that it always sounded to their ears like opinions verging on madness. As an example one person mentioned 'all that claptrap about transcendence, about getting to the other side'. Was anything said about 'delusions of grandeur'? I don't remember. Several – and I note that they are witnesses for the defence – are of the opinion that I am not of sound mind. From what I understand, the question of whether I was responsible for my actions is being debated heatedly in the media, and that's even before the forensic psychiatrists have had their say. My defence counsel is extremely interested in this, and says it is of central importance. That it can actually be a help, or work to my advantage.

All this makes me … thoughtful. Uncertain. As if I have never understood who I myself am.

Am I on the point of *becoming* disturbed? One day I saw the lion in the coat of arms above the judge's head moving. *Leo panthera.*

I ought to tell them about Panther Hansen, I thought.

One thing I am glad about, that Ine Wang's portrait of me was not among the documents. Or who knows, perhaps the defence counsel could have made use of some of my statements if the magazine had printed it; I did say a lot of nice things about Gry to Ine Wang. Yet the feature came to nothing. I did find a … way out, although I still wonder whether it was the right one. But as they say: it takes two to tango.

Day had turned into evening, and through the windows in the high block in Nordberg we could see the light retreating from the town beneath us. Ine Wang had switched off her recorder, taken a last mouthful of Armagnac and uttered a sigh of pleasure, or what I interpreted as a sigh of pleasure, before she put the glass down. Her glances became more and more bold, almost inviting. What had been an interview situation had morphed into something else. I was having thoughts which both excited and disturbed me. I tried to stop myself, but I had to keep looking at her lovely lips. I wouldn't mind feeling them against my neck.

She got up, packed her things, and was ready to go. She just stood there, as if she was waiting for me to make the next move. Her legs in those narrow black jeans were uncomfortably close to my eyes. I sat still. Nothing is inevitable, I thought. She carried the plates and teacups into the kitchen – I'm not sure whether she was being polite or wanted to see the kitchen. I felt a surge of desire, but I didn't say or do anything. But if she came back into the living room and put her arms around me … I could show her the bedroom. I left it to fate. (Fate? Is that anything other than the sum of random events?)

I weighed up for and against. The best thing would be if she left and nothing happened. I could ring her the next day instead, and say that I didn't want to be featured after all. That I had changed my mind. I could give Gry as the reason. All the horror. Say it felt wrong. And of course apologise profusely.

We stood in the hall. Her eyes were slightly unfocused – unless it was my eyes playing tricks on me. We stood there chatting about this and that, almost talking nonsense in order to prolong the moment. I had the impression she was flirting with me. Or more than flirting. She was an alluring woman. Special. She stood there looking at me oddly. Enquiringly.

A prickling in my body.

She put her jacket over her arm. I opened the front door for her. She could still take a step towards me, and touch me with her fingers, those fingers with the elegant nail varnish.

I hoped she would. Or was I hoping to avoid it?

Out in the corridor, as she was waiting for the lift, it seemed as if she tried to pull herself together and return the situation to its original setting: 'Did you never see Gry Storefjeld after you broke up?'

'No,' I said. And before Ine Wang disappeared into the lift, I added: 'Well, I did see her a few times in large gatherings. At a distance. I didn't talk to her. I was finished with her. She was out of my life.'

The door slid to and the lift descended in the shaft.

Five minutes later there was a ring at the door.

'I forgot my notepad,' she said.

One second later we were kissing.

When I think about Ine Wang, it is with a feeling of warmth.

Of course Gry wasn't out of my life. I was lying to Ine Wang. I could have amputated parts of my hippocampus and Gry would still dominate my memory. For four years I had been blinded by loss; I could hardly manage to think about anything else. I thought about her not least on that morning when I cleared up my camp by Magnusputten and set off for Valen, to launch a final rescue attempt.

But who was I trying to rescue?

Take me back, take me back, take me back.

The path I followed up the slope led to the Kobberhaug hostel, and I had to search for a while before I found the almost invisible track which turned off to the left and led to the ridge over Blankvann and the back of Valen, the Storefjeld family cabin. It sounds peculiar, but I felt as if I was crossing a threshold into another zone. That something was radically changed, even if I couldn't put my finger on what it was. Things glowed with a rare intensity. The fir cones, the pine needles, the moss. I stepped past a stone which seemed alive, as if it was breathing.

Taboo. The word quietly kept watch in my consciousness.

The entrance faced towards Blankvann, and I had to pass by the cabin to get round to the front. Everything seemed slightly distorted. Twisted. Wrong. The forest behind the cabin was vibrating. Shimmering. It looked black, even though it was a cloudless late summer morning. I almost felt like rubbing my eyes, as if something was wrong with my sight.

Relax, I said to myself. Lower your expectations, I said to myself. I was here for one simple reason: I wanted to get rid of a fever which had plagued me, which had weakened me for four years. The best-case scenario was that something joyful would happen. And even if nothing changed, I would not have made the trip in vain. I imagined that just to see her, to hear her say something, no matter what it was, would be liberating, and help me to get her out of my system once and for all.

Keep calm, I said to myself. Regardless of what happens, it's a win-win.

As I saw it, there were no unforeseen factors.

I was standing in the yard. All my senses reached a pitch of intensity I had known only a few times before, at decisive moments. Like when I placed a rose beside Gry's sleeping bag on Utøya.

Several memories tumbled into my head. Like the time she bought a skipping rope and we skipped with the kids in Westye Egebergs gate, shouting out all the old rhymes. When she played Mahjong and made a concentrated effort to learn the more complicated board game Go. When she bought whole pineapples and peeled them the way they did in the tropics, expertly, and we ate them with juice running down over our chins. When she danced with such individual moves that it looked as if she was dancing to a different tune than all the others. That she had dark blue eyes, but they changed to blue-green, luminous, when she cried. That she called my prick, in its two incarnations, David and Goliath.

Several crows were hopping around at the edge of the yard. Perhaps they were used to finding food there. Storen liked crows. He once said that he regarded them as relations of Hugin and Munin, the ravens in Old Norse mythology which brought news to Odin; and that was appropriate, because Arve Storefjeld was a sworn devotee of gossip. He saw gossip as capital, and wanted to know everything about everyone so that he could spin his intrigues. The cabin, I thought, was not a breeding ground for ideas, it was first and foremost a centre for gossip.

My heart was almost audible, and made me think of the throbbing of an old motor boat. I remembered our almost physical clash in Storen's cabin at Dovre. That time my heart had thumped so violently that I was frightened. I had been more afraid of my own heart's fragility than of Storen's fury and threats.

I looked at the entrance. I began to regret my expedition. I thought: this is a reckless undertaking. A pure gamble. Turn back! You and your stupid survival pack. You have no chance of rescuing yourself from this. The whole idea is crazy. *A 'humanist' decides to live in a way which will disprove, or transgress, Darwin's ideas. He manages to fall sincerely in love with and marry a woman everyone else finds ugly, even hideous, and in addition with what seem to be genetic deficiencies, and one who may perhaps not even be able to have children. At the same time he takes a job as an aid worker and travels with his wife to one of the most dangerous countries in the world. He wants to see how far love and idealism can carry him, and whether he will manage to survive despite everything. (Sounds a bit forced. File in C-folder? No, destroy.)*

The whole cabin seemed dead. Precisely that: dead. Gry at least was usually up by this time. The annexe too looked empty.

I don't know whether I remember correctly, but I had the feeling of being threatened, that there was danger ahead. A beast of prey. Something or other. I dropped my pack and fished out a Cold Steel knife from a side pocket, the extra knife I always carried in the forest. I bought it in a shop in Storgata straight after my military service, no doubt because our close combat instructor had shown us exactly this knife, and said that it was a first-class weapon. A San Mai III with a six-inch blade. Steel which felt charged. I never actually felt unsafe in Nordmarka, but I liked to have the knife ready in my pack, just in case. I liked to believe that I held my fate in my own hands. At the same time I knew that this was not the case. We never hold our fate in our own hands.

The front door was open. I peered in and saw no-one. They must be out, I said to myself. I turned round and put the knife in its place in my pack before I went in again, leaving the door open.

I had expected to smell pancakes or scrambled eggs, but I was met by an indefinable odour; it seemed to be of something sharp or sweet, like medicine. Almost like in a hospital. Or was it sulphurous?

I could hear a rushing sound. It took a while before I realised that it was my own blood, rushing in my ears. I went from the hallway through into the living room. I stopped. Took it in. Walls, floor, ceiling, furniture. The room looked remarkably familiar, but at the same time completely alien. Creepily alien. On the table stood a bottle of XO cognac, a circular Rémy Martin. I remember Storen deliberately pronouncing Rémy Martin as if it was a Norwegian name. The bottle was almost full, which struck me as a small miracle. That was not like Storen. And in the midst of all this, without being able to understand why it was happening right now, I had a sudden revelation, so strong that it made me think of passages in texts about religious figures: at that moment I understood – and in such a fundamental way that the enchantment left my body for good, quite literally, as if claws had released me – that my obsession with Gry was based on a delusion. In reality I had long ago realised that she was right; the link between us was not strong enough. As I stood there on the cabin floor it was as if '&' became ' – '. I was free. The whole expedition was a mistake, a misunderstanding. Or a success, since it had led to this redeeming insight.

Now at last, I thought, this relationship is over, for me too.

As I stood there on a worn rag rug in the living room, my eyes were drawn to the bookcase. I had glanced through the contents that time Gry and I stayed here overnight.

There was a signed edition of Gerhardsen's memoirs, full of underlinings. There were several volumes of Kåre Holt, Kjell Aukrust, Mikkjel Fønhus. Roy Jacobsen's *The Victors* was there too, unread.

The cabin seemed deserted. Not a sound. I thought: they've left. They've gone off in a great hurry. A threat, since the door was open? Did the last one to leave just forget to lock it?

Something told me I ought to back out and steal away.

A new Karakoram, I thought. Or did I think that? I don't think I thought that. Not then, at least.

I stayed there. I stood still without knowing what to do. At the same time I was filled with a sense of calm I had not felt for a long time. Perhaps because of the relief. I had understood that I could let Gry go. It was over. Finally over. I didn't really need to see her or talk to her. I could turn round now, I ought to turn round. I stood still. I stood in the middle of the living room floor and slowly turned round in a circle. I remembered that December evening Gry and I had been at Valen. Everything had looked different then. Much darker. But I remembered the visitors' book. I went over to the bookcase, pulled it out and began to leaf through it; I found the pages where we had written. Later she had also stuck in a photo of the two of us in front of the cabin, the same one I had at home. I put my fingers on it and pressed, as if to get closer to that moment.

I read what she had written under the picture; it just said: 'Hard labour x 4'. I had to smile. That was brazen. Even Storen must have been able to crack that code.

I looked through to the end of the visitors' book. On the last page someone, a child, had drawn a picture and coloured it. 'Friday: Gry and me baking waffles,' it said underneath. Had there been a child here too?

I felt uncertain again. A mobile began to vibrate on the living room table; the noise scared me so much I almost lost my balance. I understood less and less. I walked towards one of the bedrooms, where the door was ajar. I looked in.

Then everything went black.

I believed I could conceal it. I believed that no-one would ever know I'd been in that cabin. To be honest I was surprised the day I was arrested.

Then I thought that it was inevitable. That it almost seemed predestined. That love, and perhaps even more a misplaced love, would lead me here, into this courtroom, accused of murder.

I am Norway's most detested man.

III

Was it perhaps by chance that the police became interested in me? First of all I guessed that it must have been Ask Diesen who contacted them. He could have shown them the photo of the elk which was taken in the forest just by Ullevålseter the day before the killings. I don't remember, but it's quite possible that I also had the Cold Steel knife with me that time Ask and I were near Fagervann, and perhaps I even told him about my military service. Ask Diesen was a conscientious man. No doubt he had become suspicious and not hesitated to tip off the police.

During the court case I started to wonder. Ask Diesen was not called as a witness. Yet the police might have talked to him anyway. Perhaps Ask explained that he didn't know me, that he'd only had very superficial contact with me. A smiley. That was all.

According to reports, however, it was an 'anonymous tip-off' which had made the police knock on my door. Or rather practically besiege the whole block. At last they had a chance to show off all their equipment. The tip-off could have come from anyone. And of course the police found the picture of the elk when they impounded my mobile phone. It's included as evidence in the ring-binder of documents which the various parties leaf through as though it's an absorbing thriller. As I understand it, you can also confirm the position of the mobile by gathering data from base stations nearby.

It was strange to see that picture of the elk on the day they showed it on the large screen here in the courtroom.

It's a fine picture.
I long to return to the forest.

The first days after I somehow staggered home from Valen are just blackness. But when I came round – or however you would express it – I was calm. I was also calm in the weeks that followed, when I met Ine Wang amongst other things. At that time I had a clear idea – if there were any clear ideas in my mind – of who it was who was behind the crime. It could not have been anyone other than Panther Hansen.

One of the first things I remembered when I recovered my ability to think reasonably coherently was what happened that Saturday morning in the forest, the sight of Enok drowning himself in Lørenseter lake. It was only then that the full significance of that episode dawned on me.

What did I do with what I knew? I did nothing. It would be untrue to say that during those first weeks after the Blankvann incident I debated with myself as to whether I should notify the police about Enok Hansen. When the memory resurfaced I was in no doubt. I had to keep quiet. I must on no account get mixed up in the investigation. Just the thought of all the former Young Labour people, all of Gry's friends, finding out that I had visited the cabin – the thought of the mockery and the speculation that would arouse – tied my stomach in knots. I would have some explaining to do, as they say.

Oh yes, I have reproached myself afterwards. I am ashamed of myself. Such unworthy terror at having to account for what I was doing in that place. Such desperate irrationality.

I don't know whether this can be used in my defence, but during those weeks I was certain that the investigators would discover it. Find their way to Enok Hansen. By using bloodhounds or some such things. All their sophisticated equipment. I could not believe that he hadn't left some clear traces, something or other which would lead to a speedy resolution of the matter: that the killings were a result of madness, a sick man's fantasies. *An elderly person is found dead at the end of a jetty. There's no way to identify him, but there are many indications that he was a sailor. Five unusual tattoos are found on his body. The novella: five stories about the man on the basis of these tattoos. From five ports in different countries. Together they provide the basis for a hypothesis about the man's identity. (Is there any point collecting these ideas?)*

I have thought a great deal about the moment when I was arrested. It was a ... shock. I can't find the right word for it. 'Unreal' is too weak. The seconds when the police streamed into my flat, uniformed men looking threatening and shouting orders. As if I was mortally dangerous. What has puzzled me most is why I kept silent? How on earth I could do that? Why didn't I call out at once, why didn't I protest to the whole world? Why didn't I refuse to move from the spot, why didn't I let them carry me out screaming and protesting my innocence – that the arrest must be due to a colossal misunderstanding?

Once more: it must have been the shock. The assault on my nerves. A form of total paralysis of my speech organs and my ability to rationalize. But why did I not explain myself later? In retrospect I can see that the reason for my silence must have been different again. In the aftermath of my arrest I was struck by total confusion. Chaotic thoughts which gave me a headache. I wasn't just worried that I might have been wrong about Enok Hansen; there was also the shocking fact that there were minutes, possibly even hours, which seemed to have been wiped from my memory. All this made me think that ... at least open my eyes to the possibility that ... well, that it was me ... that it actually had to be me who had done it.

For a long time, several weeks, several months, I thought like that. That I must have repressed it. Somehow or other, I thought, I have managed to wipe out my dreadful acts at Blankvann.

But for the most part I didn't think at all. I was struck by an enormous lethargy. Apathy. As I see it, I must have slid into some form of depression. Everything was a fog. My mental life had practically gone into hibernation. When I look back, all those months in prison have almost vanished from my mind. And what I remember is not worth talking about. My time in custody appears to me to have been one endless grey day. I soon fell into a routine; I like routine, and I have no complaints.

My cell is eight metres square. It doesn't sound much, but it's enough.

It's as if I'm now trying, during these days in Courtroom 227, especially the last few weeks, to recover what was lost. In the evenings I lie in my cell thinking through what has happened in the courtroom up to now, as if I'm searching for arguments as to how … what I should do, whether I should perhaps ask to speak after all, to explain myself. Again and again I try to recapitulate … to reconstruct the course of events. As I said, I was present and yet not present during those first days. I hardly managed to follow what was being said by the prosecution and the defence and the judge and the police witnesses. I wouldn't say that it was surreal, and neither did it seem as if I was split, as people often say, that a part of me was watching it all from outside – it was more as if the whole of this enormous and carefully staged tableau was a … joke, something I didn't need to take seriously, despite how bloody serious it was. Yes, it *was* a play, with costumes and everything – a drama which was aimed at giving the nation catharsis, and I was struggling to understand whether I belonged to the players or the public – it was completely foreign to me to think that I might be playing the central role.

In the end it became impossible for me to close my eyes to the fact that it was me all this was about. Yet I still couldn't get it into my head, just as I had not been able to get it into my head while I was in custody, and there was soon one question which overshadowed all the rest: how could they think that I, Daniel Nicolai Berge, was a killer, a terrorist? What was there about me, about my life, which made people think that?

For the first time the thought of suicide struck me. For a couple of seconds. Then I dismissed it.

Gradually I understood, partly from what my defence counsel was saying, that they had important evidence. There was the necklace. There was the special knife. There was the fact that I had been trained in close combat in the military. And not least, there was the picture from Nordmarka, taken the day before the killings.

Added to that was what was identified as my *hatred* for the Labour Party. One of the witnesses for the prosecution, a historian who was apparently an expert on political ideologies, claimed that my blog could be read as a manifesto. That it was one long declaration of war on the Labour Party. The prosecutor quoted copiously from my blog as well – especially from posts where I was writing about betrayal. ('The Labour Party is the party which is best equipped to answer the pressing questions of the day, but they have betrayed their cause, they have sold themselves to the philosophy of growth, commercialisation and pop-ulism. In their powerlessness they have relinquished the efforts required to create a coherent ideology and instead abandoned themselves to the easiest way out of all: prag-matism.')

I felt like protesting. My blog was only an exercise book, my posts were thinking out loud, a one-man intellectual smithy. But in court everything was distorted.

I was silent. And the fact that I was silent was also due to a feeling of colossal indifference. Everything was meaningless, after all. For several evenings I lay in my cell examining all the gods, great and small, which I had come across during my studies of the history of religion. None of them could help. I was alone in a meaningless existence. All I had was bad, or slightly less bad, stories. Behind and above the immanence there was no transcendence, simply more immanence.

I was in doubt as to how I should dress for my first day in court. In the end I asked someone to collect one of Grandfather's favourite suits from the flat in Nordberg – a double-breasted suit with chalk-white stripes. When I had found it in Bygdøy allé, I discovered that the gold cross of the Royal Norwegian Order of Merit still hung on the left breast; Grandfather must have forgotten to take it off the last time he wore the suit. It was fine, a medal with the King's motto on the front: All for Norway. I kept it, but from that day on it lay hidden in the inside pocket. The defence counsel advised me to choose a different outfit, as he thought people might misunderstand. I ignored his well-meaning advice. I wanted to wear a suit which had belonged to an innovator. No doubt people would make fun of it, but I wanted to dress as I normally did. I was a man out of time.

Because of my paralysing indifference – does pathology have a term for that? – I stopped brooding over what people thought about me. Only one thing pained me: Father. What he might be thinking. I imagined him in his apartment on Bygdøy allé, sitting there every day, a straight-backed man with heavy jowls, following events on TV and in the papers. A man fatally wounded, thanks to me. On one occasion my defence counsel gave me a long article about Father. I felt I had to read it. Two journalists had written about Father and his career, and in the same article there was also a lot about Mother (but not a word about her drinking). They were digging around in Father's and Mother's lives as if to find an explanation of how two such gifted people could bring a monster into the world. I have dragged the whole family down into the dirt.

As far as I can remember I once said in a launch interview something about trying to shift the deeper levels of consciousness by using the literary text as a bulldozer. I would of course never have been able to achieve that. It was only now, by being accused of standing behind five cold-blooded killings, that I managed to create a small disturbance in the unconscious life of people's souls. I had, to put it bluntly, made an indelible impression. I would forever have a name which disturbed people. Berge. A thorn in the flesh of Norway.

I could understand their longing for revenge, even though no-one used the word revenge. People talked about 'a dignified trial'. The truth is that the majority of the population would prefer to have tortured me, would prefer to tear me apart, limb from limb. Five people have been done to death in a horrific way. I can understand people's rage. If they could have what they wanted, they would kill me five times over.

Hatred. The word is repeated constantly in court. I've been thinking about it. Did I hate Arve Storefjeld? Did I ever nurse hatred towards Gry? I don't know.

It's strange. During the course of these last few weeks it's as if all negative thoughts have let go. Now I can just see the good in them. Gry's unshakeable optimism. Her impulsive actions, like that Sunday she persuaded me to go with her down to the Ulvøy bridge to fish for mackerel because she wanted fresh fish for dinner. Even Storen has redeeming features in my recollection. His appeal to voters, his incomparable charm. His passion for old-fashioned wooden skis. His fry-ups were actually very tasty, and surprisingly enough he knew several Tor Jonsson poems by heart. It was a pity, I thought, that we never got together, just the two of us, to sit down and drink a glass of Armagnac in peace and quiet. Perhaps we might even have hatched a few ideas which would release the unused potential of social democracy. Despite what everyone believes, my heart is still with the Labour Party.

The prosecution strategy was clear from the first moment: they wanted to build up a picture of me as a heartless and brutal person. I caught myself almost admiring how witness after witness slowly transformed my portrait into something that resembled that increasingly revolting painting which Dorian Gray hid in a locked room. I don't remember when it was – everything has got jumbled up – but one day someone I just about recognised stood in the witness box and explained how I had once threatened Gry in the kitchen with a knife; she had seen it from the living room. But that wasn't how it was. By racking my brains I worked out that this episode happened after a Young Labour meeting when we invited people home to supper in Westye Egebergs gate; I had been standing chopping melon and putting the pieces on a serving dish together with Serrano ham, and this person must have seen me as I was gesticulating eagerly during a discussion, and quite by chance had the knife in my hand. Gry was just pretending to be frightened – it wasn't for nothing that she had studied drama at Nissen.

I ought to say something. About The Vanished Man. About Panther Hansen. I couldn't bring myself to. I don't believe the court would have wanted to hear it either. I don't believe the Norwegian people, if I can use that expression, would have been able to bear hearing that story. Because it's a story which reveals between the lines that terrible things can have such random and banal causes that they become incomprehensible.

Nothing is more complicated than simplicity.

Every time I wondered whether I should talk about Enok Hansen, I looked around in Courtroom 227; I turned discreetly towards the public gallery and studied the faces. What did I see? I still saw condemnation, revulsion, hatred, but I also saw … fragility. The sight made me think that these people would have problems if they came face to face with meaninglessness – with something that was so simple that it was impossible to grasp. They would not be able to live with having made such an error of judgement. That what they took to be the incarnation of evil was in reality madness pure and simple.

Enok Hansen would not be a story which satisfied them. It would be a bitter let-down. Enok Hansen and the Book of

Ezekiel would, to put it mildly, not bring anyone deliverance, not to mention the longed-for catharsis.

Nevertheless, every evening I lay in my cell considering the matter. I decided I would stand up the next day and tell them about Enok.

Then when I was sitting there in Courtroom 227, in the crossfire of probing eyes, I remained silent after all.

At some point a most inappropriate thought popped into my consciousness, perhaps also as a reaction to all the unfavourable references, because one day I discovered that I was feeling ... almost proud. To tell the truth I have always regarded myself as a limited person. The only remarkable thing about me is that I have chosen to write. That's why I was ... no, not proud ... I felt encouraged, I felt *stimulated* as I sat listening to these witnesses and heard about all the various aspects, I almost said dimensions, which they read into me.

There was one witness statement in particular which I could not get out of my head and which I lay thinking about in the evenings. A young woman who was completely unknown to me had taken the stand and said that she had once been a friend of mine. It was clear she was well-read, and she said that I had always made her think of Tom Ripley, the main character in five of Patricia Highsmith's books – that I was concealing something shameless and depraved ... or did she say 'monstrous', I'm unclear about that bit ... that behind my mask I was a truly evil, or no, she didn't say evil, she said an *amoral* person, without scruples, and if I was on the point of being discovered, I possessed the ability to wriggle out of it at the last moment. It was only now that justice had caught up with me. She added 'Thank God'. The judge gave a little sniff, which made me think that he didn't approve of that addition. He pulled a face. Or was it a smile?

I had never read Patricia Highsmith, but I decided to do that as soon as I got the chance.

I sat there half-paralysed, half-fascinated, following these witness statements and feeling as if I were being split into separate avatars. *A person with the same ability to change form and colour as certain octopuses. He or she is able to imitate any other person or creature. Could be a zoologist who specialises in molluscs. (Already used? Too similar to* Zelig*?)*

One of the aims of the court case was to reconstruct what had happened in that cabin on Saturday 23 August 2008. I believe I may say – I am tempted to add: on behalf of all of us – that no efforts were spared. As I remember it, it was particularly those who examined the area around the crime (are they called crime scene investigators?), together with the principal investigator, who at a fairly early point in the proceedings had contributed important pieces of the 'jigsaw' (as one of them referred to it). It was at that point that I had as it were woken up and began to follow, after the stupor of the first few days. Day after day I sat listening, not least when the forensic pathologist went through the post-mortem reports, and one macabre picture after the other was shown on the screen in the court. Nevertheless I was doubtful, and I am still doubtful. I don't know whether I would say that I am … disappointed, but what emerged was, to put it mildly, only a part of the truth.

It may be wishful thinking, but I do believe that for a few people in Norway, at least, it must appear fantastic that I, Daniel Nicolai Berge, could be the man behind that foul crime at Blankvann. But the truth is even more fantastic. It cannot be said too often: the problem with us humans is that our imagination does not stretch far enough.

I can remember more and more. During the last few weeks more pieces have emerged, pieces of the nightmare at Valen. It's as if all the words in Courtroom 227 have thrown a switch in my memory. I remember that I was standing in the cabin, and that I felt a strong desire to get out fast. Instead of that I went towards one of the bedrooms. The door was ajar and I pushed it open with my elbow. The scene which met me was one my eyes refused to take in. Or it was like when the director of a horror film lets the camera zoom in and dolly backwards at the same time. The whole room lurched and I almost fell over. Then everything went black.

I don't know how much time passed. I came round somewhere on the forest path to the north of Ullevålseter.

Everything had vanished. It was like waking from a coma, although I don't know what it's like waking from a coma. The next moment a picture floated into my mind. It's only now that I can hold on to that picture. I saw Arve Storefjeld and Sofie Nagel lying there in separate beds, with bloody gashes in their necks. Even at a distance of several metres I could see that they were dead.

I staggered onwards, half-stumbling, half-walking, through the forest above Ullevålseter.

A new piece emerged. Gry. Gry in the other bedroom. There too the door was ajar. I couldn't see the bed. I hoped. I hoped fervently that Gry wasn't in it. But when I pushed the door with my knee, terrified, and peeped in, she was lying there. With a dreadful wound in her neck. The pillow red with blood. Gry was dead. She who was the reason I was standing there, the one I had hoped to meet so that I might finally find peace, was lying murdered in her bed.

I can remember more of it now, the pictures don't vanish immediately. I was numb with horror, and at the same time I could feel my tears running down. I have a vague feeling that I stood there paralysed. That I told myself I must do something, I must call for help. My mobile was in my pack outside, but I didn't go out, I didn't get it out and switch it on. I couldn't bear the thought of getting mixed up in all of this. What should I answer when they asked why I was there? 'I was in love?' 'I thought I was in love?' 'I wanted to get her out of my mind?' 'It was an attempt to exorcise myself?' It would be better to detach myself from this, to get away and disappear. Not to leave any traces. Not even electronic ones.

It must already have occurred to me back then: this is meaningless. There is no logical explanation as to why Gry is lying here dead.

Jan Kjærstad

I don't know how I managed to get home, I just know that I didn't meet anyone. I must have followed the same route as on the way up the day before. Much of this has disappeared, but during the next few days, in which I spent most of the time lying in bed at home in Nordberg, I picked up somehow or other, through the TV and on-line news, what had been said about the incident at Blankvann. It must have been only then that I realised that two more people had been killed, Lefebvre and his daughter; they had been sleeping in the annexe. I asked myself if I might have gone out there too, but I didn't think I had. I don't know how I would have reacted if I'd seen that little girl.

More pieces emerged. I had stood in the bedroom where Gry was lying. I stood there for quite a while, it seemed to me. I thought about the *glow* which had always emanated from her. She shone. Now she was extinguished. Her skin looked like marble. Of all things I thought about her performance as a mime artist in whiteface, how she had made fools of people by imitating their way of walking. I looked at her hair. After the break-up she had let it grow again, but now her thick Black Panther hair lay like something wilted on the red-stained pillow. My eyes wandered to the scar beneath the hollow of her throat, the half-moon souvenir of her bike crash. Now she had crashed fatally.

Where are you now? I said, or I thought – or I whispered in a nightmare long after. In Wagga Wagga? Oodnadatta? Woolloomooloo?

I remembered what it felt like to hold her in my arms. I liked to let my fingers follow her spine upwards, one vertebra after another, as if I was playing an instrument. My fingertips had retained the feeling. I don't know how long I stood there by the bed staring at her, I just know that I have never felt so impotent, so denuded of hidden powers. Gry was dead. A girl who had once lain beneath me whispering 'Oh God, oh God, oh God'.

376

Then I noticed the necklace, the one I had fastened round her neck as a talisman. In the back of my mind I could hear, like a mocking echo, my assurances that it would protect her.

My mother had once been given that necklace by her mother. An anchor next to a heart. Hope and love. Both Gry's brother and the prosecutor described the necklace wrongly, they talked about an anchor of silver and a heart of gold. It was the other way round, because it was hope which was the most important. I believe Mother also placed hope highest of all, precisely because she lived a life of such resignation.

I couldn't bear the thought that the necklace should be left there, tarnished as it were, at that dreadful scene. I took it off her; the fastening was right round by the pendant so that I didn't have to lift her bloody neck, but I could get hold of it with my nails. I'm not sure that I would have been able to touch her skin.

Gry.

The Untouchable.

Ironically enough, the public has now become interested in my two short story collections. Not just that: the publishers have asked me if they can publish the manuscript which was found in my safe, with the working title *Imperfect Tales*. I said that the stories were not quite finished. So they suggested a new title, *Unfinished Tales*. They were impatient, almost tiresomely persistent. According to the publishers my stories would be read with great curiosity by many people.

Perhaps that's not so strange, I thought.

My first two collections have been republished in specially designed paperback editions, naturally with an appropriate foreword in which the head of the publishing house discusses their ethical misgivings about re-issuing the books. Nevertheless, 'after careful consideration', 'in the public interest', and so on. I was sent the books in prison. The covers had been given a purely graphic design, simple lettering, plain Roman capitals against a single-colour background, as if they were terrified that any illustration might provoke the wrong associations. I remembered how melancholy I had felt at going into bookshops and never seeing a glimpse of my books. How I would have liked to see those elegant editions on the shelves, or perhaps even exhibited in the window, those two covers with their colours carefully contrasting, in shades which made you think of a Rothko painting.

My publisher has been on the witness stand. I felt almost sorry for him. I have never really understood my defence counsel, but I realise that he is doing his best for me, despite the fact that I have been an uncooperative, what's the word … client. I think his strategy is to produce witnesses who can 'normalise' me, help to create a counterweight to the picture of me as one-dimensionally … evil. Or perhaps he wants to show that I have some positive qualities too. Despite everything. Anyway, my publisher sat there, without looking down, and said that he, the publishers, had believed in my talent. That they still believed in my talent. I felt like getting up and embracing that courageous man. I know there's no parallel, but it made me think of those literary aristocrats who defended Agnar Mykle during his trial in those bad old days. I also noticed that the judge exhibited something like eagerness towards this witness. 'Can a book which is panned by the critics nevertheless have literary value?' he asked. 'Yes,' said my editor. I know it sounds strange, but it almost seemed as if the judge wanted to disrupt the picture of me as a failed author. The expressions of the other participants in the trial betrayed the fact that they were taken aback at this sudden intervention on the part of the judge. (Have I misjudged him? Something tells me that he is a person who eludes straightforward characterisation.)

All this led to my stories now being interpreted by the country's sharpest literary critics. At last I was being *read*. It was remarked that many of my stories were about people who were operating on the very edge of known reality. By means of an unexpected twist (yes, finally that word was used) they were given the chance to cross over a border, to reach an insight which had previously been hidden. However, it did upset me when a professor wrote that some of these protagonists could be characterised as inhuman.

I have been thinking, often in the evenings, in my cell … about everything that has been said and read out during the trial, all these attempts to understand and explain me, all the interpretations and analyses which now include my books as well. It has become clear to me that I am now a … person of interest. Quite literally. My person has become a corpus, a text, and there is disagreement as to how it ought to be read.

The realisation takes me by surprise. Also because I am uncertain. I can see how easily I myself – if I wished to – could contribute to deciding what significance it should have.

The case is approaching its end. When I think back and try to summarise it, it seems as if all the days in court have blurred into one for me. Everything comes to me higgledy-piggledy, even though I know that the proceedings are following a carefully constructed schedule. But now and then I am calm enough to gather some of the threads together. One evening, as I was lying in my cell, I began to ponder about the defence counsel, this … conscientious lawyer who everyone agreed was carrying out his thankless task in an exemplary and irreproachable fashion. I saw how he was quietly attempting – in the face of the prosecutor's picture of me as a hate-filled and cold-blooded murderer – to win sympathy for what he called 'the enigma of Berge' (I liked that designation, it could be the title of a short story). Through his questions to witnesses and experts he constantly drew attention to 'Berge's lack of contact with reality'. 'He lives in a fantasy world' was one of the refrains. Everything which was said in court about my 'bizarre notions' was cited by the defence counsel in support of this view, which he then, without saying it directly, let appear as a corrective to the prosecutor's bombastic claims about a precisely planned revenge attack.

Oh yes, I have been tempted to … perhaps I ought to have assisted him. Several times I have had to restrain myself from signalling that I would like to speak. For example, in the circumstantial evidence the prosecutor had singled out something several people had mentioned, that I was for a while abnormally interested in internet gaming, including those extremely violent games where you get to shoot people; that I had sat up all night playing and not doing anything else – a clear sign both of social isolation and of fascination with violence, they maintained. I could have explained that many of the games came from the time when I was planning to write an MA thesis on the history of religion, in which the aim was to show how several of these games, since they were based on myths, seemed to point towards a new form of religion. In religious societies as well you could see how groups of people disappeared into a simulated reality. In the later period I played more because I was searching for new ways of writing, and I was especially concerned with how as a player you moved up from one level to the next, and how the new levels became increasingly difficult. I asked myself if it could be a model for the composition of a type of multi-level stories.

I could have told them all that. Why didn't I tell them?

Because – despite everything – I didn't want to appear as the confused person the defence counsel makes me out to be?

I don't just want to be dumb. I am dumb. I don't think I would have been able to speak even if I tried to. At best I would have mangled my words more than I had ever done on the podium in my Young Labour time, and they would just take it as proof that I was guilty.

Occasionally I sit there thinking about my survival pack. The optimal kit. How wonderful it would be if you could preserve love as a concentrate, in the same way as you preserve broth in a stock cube.

Next to the fishing hook and the striker: 2 grams of love.

*

It was not until late in the trial – and it may be because of his surprising question to my publisher – that I realised that the judge must be identical to a man I had once seen in town. One day in June four or five years ago I was strolling through Slottsparken with Father, on our way to the Artists' House, and after we had passed a man in a light linen suit with a walking stick, who had raised his panama hat when Father nodded to him, Father had turned to me and said in a low voice: 'There goes a just man'. I was surprised at the word *just*. Father must have realised that, because he explained that one of his friends had once had to be a witness in a court case where the man in the linen suit had been the judge. 'My friend was full of praise for the way this judge had led the proceedings, and even more for the sentence he had pronounced.'

I must talk to Father when this trial is over.

Father turned slightly to look after the man, who was disappearing in the direction of Dronningparken. 'I see him now and then,' said Father. 'I've always thought he resembles Lord Mountbatten.' Father glanced at me. 'The last viceroy of India,' he added, 'a figure from the dying days of the British Empire.' I nodded as if I understood. I just thought that the man – or the figure – was reminiscent of an English gentleman.

I didn't see his face that time, but I now understood that it was Peter Malm we had met in Slottsparken.

I have thought a lot about this judge and wondered about him. At the beginning of the trial he seemed absent, sitting with his fingers together and listening, at the same time as he was not listening, or at least I got the impression that he was not listening. *A counsellor, a soul-healer as they're sometimes called … a story which turns on this peculiar word … A soul-healer, someone who receives clients in an office. Helps them to get a soul. Theory: we're born without a soul. A soul is something we form in the course of our lives, and it's all that survives when we die … Something like that. (I've forgotten what I was thinking. It's as if my very imagination is failing.)* But during the next few weeks something lit up in the judge's eyes, as if he had had an idea – exactly that, an idea – and I could tell that he was examining me more and more closely. I suspect that he doesn't buy all these witness statements that I'm lacking in … empathy, that there's always been something demonic about me; I think he understands that it's not me behind this crime, and he might well declare that 'there is reasonable doubt as to whether the accused is guilty'.

Perhaps Father is right, and he is 'a just man'.

Will I be found innocent?

I almost said: is there a danger that I might be found innocent?

After a long day in the courtroom I often lie in my cell feeling ashamed of how little I know about people. How much did I know about Gry?

Of course she was not shallow. That was only something I thought in order to defend myself. The truth is that I didn't understand her. I was not even close to understanding her. She was unfathomable. She was unfathomable just as all people are unfathomable. I have always been sceptical about people – they often call themselves researchers – who think that by brandishing a theory they can pin down a person's identity or personality. There is no bottom in people. There is just mystery upon mystery upon mystery, all the way down. Why is it that we can't live with this?

I thought I was finished with her. I *was* finished with her. But I still loved her. That beauty. That witch. I loved the funny, crafty, intelligent, simple, unpredictable, strong-willed, vulgar, strange, wild, warm, reckless Gry Storefjeld. It is beyond comprehension. I love her still.

Something else occurs to me. It has been mentioned several times in court that I had few close friends. Of course in order to reinforce the picture of me as asocial, as a loner. But it was true, I did have few friends. And I was almost glad that no-one had discovered Anders Wiik, my companion and fellow writer from student days. One summer I became curious as to why I never had an answer from him after he had fled home to Hedmarken, or so I assumed. What had happened? Naturally I didn't believe all that about Chinese fortune cookies, that was just said as a joke. One weekend I went up to Sand in Nord-Odal, thinking that he would be sitting there on his own writing obsessively, perhaps in a cabin deep in the forest, and that the two-thousand-page novel manuscript would by now have expanded into a magnum opus of six thousand pages, a novel which would 'destabilise all accepted perspectives' (his avowed aim), a monumental work which would create a 'before' and an 'after' in Norwegian literature, and which not least would make everyone in the village forget everything about Sigurd Hoel and the belief that life was fixed after the first ten years. But now his parents told me that he had hardly been home before he disappeared again. That information astonished me. But did they know what he was doing now? I asked. I thought he might have taken up his tennis career again and returned to the US. 'He climbed,' said his father, who must have realised at that moment that I knew nothing of Anders' fate. 'He died in an accident in the Trango Towers.' It took several seconds for the significance of his words to sink in. 'Trango?' I said. 'In Karakoram, Pakistan,' said his father, thinking I didn't know where it was. And I didn't know either. Right at that moment I thought that I knew nothing at all. About people. About the world. About life. 'He was a climber?' I said. 'There was a report in the newspaper,' said his father, with a hint of accusation in his voice. Or did he say it in order to help me, to comfort me? They themselves seemed calm, as if they had reconciled themselves to the loss of their son. I understood nothing. Anders Wiik hated nature. Once when I wanted to climb the Kolsås ridge he said that he couldn't do it, even the slightest height made him dizzy. I couldn't even get him to come into the forest to pick chanterelles. I didn't understand it. How did the road lead from Nord-Odal to the Trango Towers? Or was it literally an attempt to take 'the road to the end of the world'? I tried to write a story about it, 'Karakoram', but couldn't manage it. I was ashamed. We had mixed blood, we were 'Pen brothers', and I knew nothing about him.

In a way I deserved to sit here, I thought. Accused. It was a crime to know so little about people as I did.

For the survival pack: one Chinese fortune cookie.

In the course of the last few weeks I have often caught myself longing for an unexpected modulation, for someone to say something, or some evidence to be brought, which would make this whole nightmare slide into ... what should I call it ... a different *key*, something more uplifting.

Several times I have been tempted to create this ... twist myself.

Because I could easily get free. I could break my silence – yes, I would be able to – and help my not inordinately competent defence counsel, even though he has made ceaseless attempts to demonstrate the loopholes in the evidence presented. Gry could have given me the necklace several days before she went to the cabin. Many people had the same knife, and also had close combat training. The fact that I had been at Ullevålseter on the Friday did not prove that I must have been at Blankvann on Saturday morning. The judge knew that, his fellow judges knew that, they had presumably long since noted the arguments for the defence. The judge was clever. He would ask himself whether there was an alternative way of interpreting the evidence. Through his long years on the bench he had no doubt seen how the prosecution sometimes fixated on a theory and interpreted the evidence in the light of it.

Above all I could tell them about The Vanished Man.

But would they have enough ... imagination to understand it? Could anyone stretch their powers of understanding far enough to see that that was a possibility?

What would they have said about Enok Hansen in court? For here ... *here* the defence counsel could really have resorted to the word 'mystery'.

The problem was that I had started to doubt it myself. That time I stumbled on his shelter, I thought I had seen a knife in his belt which was almost identical to my own. Now I was no longer sure. Could Enok, that improbable personage, really be capable of carrying out such an act? Was it not just wishful thinking on my part? Was it not perhaps pure chance that he had drowned himself in Lørenseter lake that morning when I was on my way to Valen?

What if I was wrong? I couldn't be one hundred percent sure that Enok Hansen was responsible for the crime.

And if I told them about it – would they not just take it as proof that I *was* mad?

I imagined myself saying it, standing up and saying that The Vanished Man had vanished for good, without trace. That the truth lay wound about with chains at the bottom of a lake.

It sounded … It didn't sound …

Now the forensic psychiatrists – the last couple to take the floor, as it were – have finished. They have presented their report and made their statements. In the process they have supplied a long, and – I believe – entertaining story about what they discovered at the bottom of my soul. It is tempting to make fun of this, but I shall let it lie. In any event, they concluded that I was responsible for my actions. Not that that made any difference, of course. These platitudes encased in quasi-scientific language simply made the debate outside the courtroom flare up again, reaching new heights. According to my defence counsel, sober-minded colleagues fell out about it in public. Once again people were arguing in all the media as to whether I was sane or not.

I can't say for certain, but it appeared as if the judge squirmed at several of the questions and answers in connection with the experts' report.

We're nearly at the end of the road, or whatever you'd call it. People seem relieved. It's as if the degree of complacency is increasing. I notice how the prosecutor and defence counsel are sending each other cautious smiles, as if to congratulate each other with … a job well done. Everyone is pleased. Everyone praises the system. I can imagine the commentators writing that the trial has been a model of its kind. But if they don't get to the truth – how impressive is it then?

Regardless of that, most people – indeed practically everyone – takes it for granted that I will be found guilty.

But if I am found innocent …? I daren't think about the uproar which would ensue.

It is the last day in court. The defence counsel is summing up.

I don't know when I got … I am convinced that … It is only now that I can see what I must do: I must protect the people around me, my fellow countrymen. I must protect them from their own ignorance, their … lack of imagination. I must provide these killings with a comprehensible logic, give everyone who is following the case a story which contains acceptable cause and effect. I think about Grandfather's Order of Merit in gold which is lying in my inside pocket. Perhaps I ought to hang it on my left breast. That would be appropriate. All for Norway.

I have to confess.

I have to give them simplicity, I have to give them what they want.

It is as if my decision becomes a ramp. I experience a lift-off in my thoughts which is reminiscent of the one I had when I was standing on the podium on Utøya, when instead of speaking I broke into song: 'God Save this Land of Ours'. Again it is as if I can see all the different layers in the situation: me, here, in the dock in Oslo Courthouse, the court's officials with their various agendas, the grief of the relatives, the curious audience in the public gallery, the media's zealous coverage of the case, a whole nation's opinions and expectations and needs; and once again all this weaves itself together and gives me a multi-dimensional insight which supports my decision. I can see things around me with almost supernatural clarity, the claws of the lion in the national coat of arms, the texture of the judge's robe, a smear on the reading glasses of one of the junior lawyers, the spring light streaming in through the window to C.J. Hambros plass. I can see what my role is, what I can contribute.

I must transform this vision into a story. I must speak. I must confess. Do the unforeseen.

Yes, I think, as I observe that the prosecutor has smudged the mascara on one of her eyes. Of course. It's as if I have rediscovered the red thread of my life. Because is this not what I have always been striving for? To tilt things, to push them out of line. *To switch the points.*

This is the moment in the trial when I can stand up and say something which makes the story twist and go in a different direction from what everyone had believed.

Suddenly it's all obvious. A consequence of my whole life. To go to prison. To cross a threshold. To disappear from the world, as it were. To be a person outside time.

Before the summing-up started, the judge reminded me that I could say something right at the end. He must have read my thoughts.

Yes, I must break my silence. I must stand up. No more writing. I must forget all these ... not useless, but ... these ideas for short stories. Now it's a matter of acting. Stand up. Speak. Don't stumble over words. I can't tell them the truth, what I believe to be the truth, but I can confess. Say what is necessary. And in a convincing enough way to be found guilty. I must think of ... the well-being of the nation. I must give them peace. Make the incomprehensible a little less incomprehensible for them. The decision fills me with ... I don't know what it fills me with. Or wait: it fills me with hope. I take it as a manifestation of ... yes, exactly ... *rediscovered imagination.*

If anyone still doubts whether I had been in the cabin, I could tell them about the circular Rémy Martin bottle which was standing on the living-room table that morning, and that it was almost full. I could tell them about the final pages in the visitors' book, about what little Sylvie had written and drawn there. With a bit of luck my prints would still be there on the photo I put my finger on, the picture of Gry & Nicolai.

Is this perhaps the aim of life: to prevent other people discovering life's meaninglessness?

I think about what will happen if I am found guilty. I will have to spend many years in prison. To atone. Can I cope with that? The monotony? I can cope with that. There's not much you need in order to survive. To pass the time in a cell seems to me to be one of the least meaningless things I can do.

I think about Father. We must talk together. Is there an open fireplace somewhere in the prison? When he comes, he can bring the survival pack.

One thing is missing: a little anchor of gold.

I'm on fire. I'm on the point of looking at the judge, as if to signal that I'm ready to talk.

Then my doubts surface again. Perhaps I ought to tell them about Enok Hansen after all. Perhaps that would be the best thing in spite of everything. They could search the lake. Perhaps they would find him. Or they could seek out his shelter and possibly find evidence there. There must have been several people who had come across Enok in all those years he was living in Nordmarka.

No, I must confess. Say that it was me.

Or no, I must remain silent. Leave everything to the judge.

The defence counsel has finished his summing-up. The prosecutor has no comments. Uncertainty overwhelms me. I still don't know which alternative I will choose. What would be the right thing to do. The best for everyone. I can tell them about Enok. I can confess. I can remain silent and surrender to the unpredictable.

It is completely quiet in the courtroom.

The judge looks at me. For a long time.

'Berge,' he says. 'You may speak now.'

Afterword

Something like that could never happen here. A terrorist attack like the one in Madrid in 2004, which killed nearly 200 people, or in London in 2005, with over 50 dead, could never happen in the quiet little backwater of Norway. These are the thoughts of the journalist Ine Wang, as she investigates a seemingly motiveless crime, a barbaric killing of five people in a remote cabin in the Norwegian countryside. They are also the thoughts of the judge Peter Malm, for whom the advantage of living in Norway is that it is an unregarded corner of the world, where nothing dramatic ever happens. The political cataclysms which provoke bombs and mass shootings in other parts of the world will never affect us here.

Yet that, of course, is precisely what happened. Three years after the summer in which the killings in this novel take place, on 22 July 2011, Anders Behring Breivik bombed the government offices in Oslo and then travelled to the island of Utøya in the Oslo fjord in order to shoot as many as he could of the youngsters who were attending the Young Labour summer camp. 77 dead in all. That was Norway's Twin Towers moment.

Berge is not about the Breivik case, but without it the novel would not have been written, as the author Jan Kjærstad has acknowledged. It is a story about a Norway sleepwalking into unforeseen catastrophe, relying on its lack of strategic significance to protect it from the horrors which happen elsewhere. Some of the background story is set on Utøya, at a Young Labour summer camp which is an idyll of comradeship and young love. Other events happen in and around the government offices, where anyone at all can come and go freely; Ine Wang often sits in the foyer working, watching cabinet ministers come and go and wondering why security is so lax. When five people are killed in a cabin in Nordmarka, the extensive forested area which for all Oslo-dwellers is the lungs of the city, a place for hiking, camping and communing with nature, it is a shock for which all are totally unprepared.

The events in the novel are narrated by three distinct characters, who give us three very different perspectives on the crime and its aftermath. First is Ine Wang, who has just completed a biography of Arve Storefjeld, the popular Labour politician who is one of the killer's victims. For her it appears at first to offer the scoop of a lifetime, which is then slowly transformed into something much more complicated as she gets closer to those involved in the affair. She is young and ambitious – though conscious that she is not so young any more, and worried that her career has stagnated, that all the important things in life lie behind her. The killings give her a renewed sense of purpose, of urgency; her voice is sometimes breathless, her sentences long and crowded as her thoughts pile up.

The second section is narrated by Peter Malm, the judge who is asked to preside over the trial of the suspected killer. He is a rather older and much more sober character, a man whose chief pleasures in life are solitary ones: eating his carefully composed breakfasts, drinking cocktails prepared by a dedicated bartender, reading peacefully in libraries and working on his planned book at home in his study. He regards his native land as a model colony, unruffled by global upheavals; for him the killings are initially an unwelcome intrusion into his peace, attracting the attention of the outside world in a disturbing way. As he becomes more personally involved, his view of the case also changes radically. His is a more learned voice, occasionally pedantic, always measured; yet despite his apparent gravitas, he suffers from imposter syndrome, and is always expecting to be 'found out' as incompetent, ignorant or inadequate.

Nicolai Berge, the third narrator, is the man in the dock, the person accused of the heinous crime, and the former lover of one of the victims. He chooses to be silent throughout his trial – to start with because he cannot remember what happened, and later on, because he feels unable to explain what he knows. He is a writer, an unsuccessful one, whose books have made no impression on the literary world; he lives more vividly in his imagination than in reality. He is thoughtful, often expressing himself hesitantly and tentatively, plagued by indecision – a nonentity in the eyes of a barnstorming politician like Arve Storefjeld.

Berge is a city novel, and a strong sense of place runs through the narrative. All of the central characters live in or near Oslo, and their attachments to different areas are important to their sense of identity; they can be followed around on a map. For Ine Wang the places where she works are associated with energy and challenge: the newspaper offices in Akersgata, or the government offices on Einar Gerhardsens plass. Home is the suburb of Ski, in a conventional town-house district, which was only ever meant to be temporary and from which she longs to escape to central Oslo where life will no longer pass her by. Peter Malm cherishes his quiet refuge in the city centre, an apartment above the old-established Engebret Café among the historic buildings of Bankplassen, with a view from his windows of the original Norges Bank, and beyond that to the reassuring bulk of Akershus Fortress. From here he can walk to his workplace at Oslo District Court or stroll around the city centre as a *flâneur*, and along Karl Johans gate to his favourite destination, the Queen's Park, Dronningparken. Nicolai Berge, from a wealthy family, used to live among the elite on Bygdøy allé, and in his happiest time, when he was the lover of Gry Storefjeld, his life revolved around her flat in Westye Egebergs gate – on the seventh floor, in seventh heaven. When they split up he was exiled, or so it seemed to him, to his nondescript flat in Nordberg, north-west Oslo. All three characters' paths cross and recross as they move around the city.

Above and behind the city stands Holmenkollen ridge, which looms over the narrative as it looms over Oslo. Behind it is Nordmarka, a place of recreation which has suddenly become a place of horror. Deep inside Nordmarka is Blankvann, a peaceful lake with a farmstead – again, easily found on a map – near which is Arve Storefjeld's family cabin. Storefjeld too is associated with geographical locations, with the archetypally Norwegian Dovre mountains (in the popular imagination he stands as firm as they) and with the working-class Myren district of Oslo – although he now lives on the wrong side of the river, having deserted his working-class origins and joined the middle class. Location in this novel is an indicator of personality and a measure of achievement.

Much of the action of the novel takes place in a courtroom, beneath the heraldic axe-wielding lion of the Norwegian coat of arms. It is Peter Malm's arena, where he presides with impressive dignity over the carefully choreographed proceedings, and Nicolai Berge's mountainous Karakoram, a remote and unfamiliar terrain in which he feels confused and isolated. It is not a coincidence that Charles Dickens' novel *Bleak House*, that depressing study of the convoluted machinations of the legal profession, is a common point of reference. For Ine Wang it means little; it is a book recommended to her by her boyfriend, and which she never managed to finish reading. For Judge Peter Malm, however, it is a seminal work, which he read in London when he discovered that he was living in the very house where it had been written: 'what I remember best from my stay is the delight with which I read *Bleak House* by Charles Dickens. Sometimes I think that was what I did during that year in London: I read *Bleak House*. It was a novel which took a year. I can safely say that Dickens' novel meant more for my legal work than *Norway's Laws*.' And for Nicolai Berge it was one of his mother's books, which finally gave him the answer as to why she became an alcoholic, the endless tedium of being a cog in a bureaucratic labyrinth: 'Mother didn't drink because of her marriage or because of me, she drank because she was a pawn in an enormous public sector. ... By drinking, she managed to endure the meaninglessness of the innumerable meetings, reports, travel receipts – being a part of what Dickens in another novel called the Circumlocution Office, a department whose function was to do nothing.' During the course of this novel Peter Malm is trying to write his own book, in which he wants to draw up some kind of universal template of justice – but his research has produced a mass of documentation which threatens to overwhelm him, and he is compelled to recognise the fragility of all legal systems: 'The fact was that power always triumphed over justice'. The question is, will that also happen in Courtroom 227, in the trial of Nicolai Berge?

In translating the novel I have attempted to be faithful to the different speech patterns of the three narrators – the near stream-of-consciousness of Ine Wang, the studied eloquence of Peter Malm, and the self-reflective hesitancy of Nicolai Berge. I have kept place-names as they are where they can easily be located on a map, whilst making it clear in geographical locations whether the reference is to a lake, a mountain or a park. Sometimes the literal meaning of a location is significant enough to need an explanation; for example, Peter Malm's suggestion that the main street of Oslo was so peaceful that it ought to be renamed Sorgenfrigate only makes sense if you know that the word means Carefree Street. The premises he passes on his perambulations around the city also require the addition of an occasional prompt; the foreign reader cannot be expected to know that Svaneapoteket is a chemist's shop, or Halvorsens Conditori a café. At times a fuller comment is necessary to explain specific cultural references. Ine Wang mentions Reodor Felgen without telling us that he is a fictional character invented by the writer

Kjell Aukrust, and Nicolai Berge refers to a psalm about 'God being God even if all men were dead', expecting the reader to know that it is by Petter Dass. And when Berge and Gry make love on Bjørnstjerne Bjørnson's grave and she whispers in his ear 'Yes, we're fucking', the reason for that is obscure unless you know that Bjørnson wrote Norway's national anthem and that Gry's words are a parody of the first line.

The names of the characters in the novel often have a resonance which is not immediately apparent to non-Norwegian speakers. Arve Storefjeld's name is as bombastic as its owner; Storefjeld means literally 'large mountain', and the man loves to be photographed standing four-square and practically naked in front of snow-covered peaks. His first name too resonates with status, as he is referred to as 'Arvingen', the inheritor of a proud Labour tradition. His daughter's first name Gry – similar to that of the other female Norwegian leader, Gro (Harlem Brundtland) – means 'dawn', which inspires a play on words, 'Morning-Gry', as she is photographed early one day on Utøya. Peter Malm's surname means cast iron or metal ore, appropriate for someone who incarnates the ideal of irreproachable impartiality in the public eye. And Berge (pronounced with a hard 'g' as in 'gate'), the man reviled by the whole country as a cold-blooded killer, bears a name which seems a cruel irony – 'a positive word distorted into its opposite', as Peter Malm observes. The reason for this, that it is a Norwegian verb which means to rescue, or to keep safe, needs to be supplied by the translator.

I am grateful to the author for answering my queries about his novel, and to my editors, Helen Mawby and Claire Thomson, for their careful reading of my translation and for the many helpful comments which have greatly improved its accuracy and consistency. Any mistakes or infelicities which remain are, of course, my responsibility.

Janet Garton
Norwich, August 2019

ERIK FOSNES HANSEN

Lobster Life

(translated by Janet Garton)

Life in a grand Norwegian mountain hotel is not what it used to be; Norwegians have deserted the traditions of their native land, with its invigorating ski trips and lake-fresh trout, for charter tours to 'the infernal south'. Sedd's grandparents are fighting a losing battle to maintain standards at Fåvnesheim hotel, which has been in the family for generations, whilst the young Sedd observes developments with a keen eye for the absurd and a growing sense of unease that all is not well. He has his own demons too, as he tries to unearth the truth about his father, an Indian doctor who died as Sedd was conceived, and his mother, who was 'taken by Time' when he was a toddler and whom he remembers only as a foxy-red sheen in the air.

Death stalks this peaceful place, as cracks in the polished surface begin to show. The first to die is the bank manager, who has kept the hotel going on credit, and whose demise has ominous consequences for the whole district. Then the new bank manager's daughter almost literally pesters the life out of Sedd; he has trained as a life-saver, but finds saving people more complicated than he had thought. He becomes obsessed with a locked room, which he imagines will reveal the truth about his mother – but it refuses to give up its secrets.

ISBN 9781909408524
UK £12.95
(Paperback, 394 pages)

VIGDIS HJORTH

A House in Norway

(translated by Charlotte Barslund)

A House in Norway tells the story of Alma, a divorced textile artist who makes a living from weaving standards for trade unions and marching bands. She lives alone in an old villa, and rents out an apartment in her house to supplement her income. She is overjoyed to be given a more creative assignment, to design a tapestry for an exhibition to celebrate the centenary of women's suffrage in Norway, but soon finds that it is a much more daunting task than she had anticipated. Meanwhile, a Polish family moves into her apartment, and their activities become a challenge to her unconscious assumptions and her self-image as a good feminist and an open-minded liberal. Is it possible to reconcile the desire to be tolerant and altruistic with the imperative need for creative and personal space?

ISBN 9781909408319
UK £11.95
(Paperback, 175 pages)

AMALIE SKRAM

Betrayed

(translated by Katherine Hanson and Judith Messick)

With high hopes, Captain Riber embarks with his young bride Aurora on a voyage to exotic destinations. But they are an ill-matched pair; her naive illusions are shattered by the realities of married life and the seediness of society in foreign ports, whilst his hopes of domestic bliss are frustrated by his wife's unhappiness. Life on board ship becomes a private hell, as Aurora's obsession with Riber's adventures as a carefree bachelor begins to undermine his sanity. Ultimately both are betrayed by a hypocritical society which imposes a warped view of sexuality on its most vulnerable members.

Amalie Skram was a contemporary of Henrik Ibsen, and like him a fierce critic of repressive social mores and hypocrisy. Many of her works make an impassioned statement on the way women of all classes are imprisoned in their social roles, contributing to the great debate about sexual morality which engaged so many Nordic writers in the late nineteenth century. Her female characters are independent, rebellious, even reckless; but their upbringing and their circumstances combine to deny them the fulfilment their creator so painfully won for herself.

ISBN 9781909408494
UK £11.95
(Paperback, 136 pages)

Lightning Source UK Ltd.
Milton Keynes UK
UKHW021236141119
353531UK00007B/335/P

9 781909 408531